ENEMY
IN THE
MIRROR

ENEMY IN THE MIRROR

ELI CANTOR

Crown Publishers, Inc.   New York

Inquiries should be addressed to Crown Publishers, Inc., One Park Avenue, New York, N.Y. 10016

Printed in the United States of America
Published simultaneously in Canada by General Publishing Company Limited

Library of Congress Cataloging in Publication Data

Cantor, Eli.
    Enemy in the mirror.

    I. Title.
PZ3.C16784En   [PS3505.A574]   813'.5'2   77-7897
ISBN 0-517-53112-7

To my wife, "Pat"

Part One

"Out of the dark past
A child is born
With joy and grief
My heart is torn . . ."
—James Joyce

1

On the dais in the grand ballroom of the Waldorf-Astoria, the typewritten card at the place of honor read: PHILIP M. REYNOLDS.

Philip Reynolds glanced at it again, with a touch of distaste. He would have prepared something more in keeping with the distinguished company at the head table—no charge to the sponsoring charity, of course. Hardly anyone understood the importance of quality graphics these days.

"A man who—"

Sitting straight and distinguished-looking above the crowd, Reynolds had resigned himself to the banquet's predictable protocol. He had doodled with crumbs on similar fern-decorated tablecloths—always forming alphabet shapes—through dozens of such salutes to an industry notable. It was gratifying that tonight he was "the man who—," but the clichés of the master of ceremonies seemed about someone else. He felt at a distance, almost physically absent, watching and listening through a recurring veil of indifference and detachment.

The obligatory joke was being told. "As you know, Phil Reynolds is in terrific demand as a speaker throughout the advertising industry, and he appears all around the country even though he tells me he hates making speeches. I asked why he accepts, and he said, 'I love the introductions!' "

It tickled the audience, and Reynolds laughed dutifully. They did not suspect it, but he would vastly prefer to be in some quiet bar. At the cocktail reception, he had been a banana-head to let Helena corner him and take the martini away. But it had hardly been the place for another fracas. In fairness, she had done it for his sake, and it hadn't been easy for her, he knew. Give credit where—

Reynolds glanced at his wife, seated at Table 1 just in front of the lectern. Although the table was round, she had made her place unmistakably the head of it—the professional hostess, her patrician face perfect for a Rolls-Royce brochure. Helena, seeming white-gloved even when naked, with the elegant lift of head, the Gentile nose, the smiling accent of Georgia, and the aristocratic lips that made her kisses more galvanizing when they permitted passion. Or had done so once.

And the same woman was the attentive mother, and good neighbor, tennis buff at the club, who loved nothing better than getting those delicate hands black with the loam of her garden. He could quote the plaque hanging in their greenhouse, which he had calligraphed for her himself (no typewritten place cards in their home!). It was an old Chinese saying: "If you wish to be happy for a few hours, drink some wine. If you wish to be happy for a few days, cook a fine feast. If pleasure for a week is your object, marry and go on a honeymoon. But if you wish lifelong happiness, become a gardener."

Helena Reynolds felt her husband's gaze and gave him an encouraging nod. She saw gratefully that his expression was clear; he hadn't sneaked any drinks behind her back. Although the dark rings under his eyes gave his face a gaunt cast, he plainly appeared a man who deserved the night's prestigious award. Helena wished her brother and sister had come up from Georgia. They would swallow the taunts that had estranged them following her elopement sixteen years before. Tonight, there was nothing Jewish-looking about Phil, and some of the most eminent men in New York were paying him tribute, including Rodney Graham of the Mayflower Grahams, seated at the end of the dais.

Helena had met Rodney Graham for the first time at the reception. Though he was short, his bearing gave him a commanding presence. Blond, green-eyed, all WASP, impeccably dressed, he was not a man to dissemble. Phil had applauded Graham for creating an outstanding young agency much like his own, and doing it on his talent, not the Graham money or power centers in Wall Street, Washington, Detroit, and Newport. Rod Graham had praised her husband to her generously and genuinely. She sensed a rapport between the two dissimilar men. If they ever got together, Madison Avenue would shake. But Phil was a loner.

Helena turned back to the center of the dais. Her husband was dark, black-haired, and aquiline. His eyes reached her, as always, with their contradictions. Beneath bony brows, Philip Reynolds owned the eyes of a dozen men—an artist's and a hunter's, a poet's and a golfer's, a wordsmith's and a manager's, a lover's and a drunk's. In the recent years of their marriage, Helena Reynolds was finding that the only coherence in her husband was his inconsistency.

She had been intrigued rather than disturbed by his complexity when his Yale roommate, Duncan Talbott, had brought him to Northampton. On that long-ago weekend Phil Reynolds had taken over every subject that came up, from Art to Zen. More disquieting, he turned out to know what he was saying; and at the same time Helena glimpsed an appealing shyness. She put his brashness down to insecurity. They had fallen in love like birds shot out of the sky, the way she remembered duck hunts down home.

That was what Helena wanted to dwell on tonight, not the ugliness of last Saturday when she and Duncan Talbott found Reynolds sprawled senseless in the club parking lot. He had had the grace to be ashamed on Sunday, and had apologized to Talbott, their oldest friend as well as family doctor.

Dr. Duncan Talbott at Table 1 had a countenance that people took in less as a generous nose, broad mouth, and rugged chin than as an archetype of what a physician's face should be. Talbott had grown from a skinny, earnest medical student into a sturdy, leathery-skinned family physician esteemed by everyone in the small Connecticut town he served.

Over the Sunday brunch, he had listened skeptically to his remorse-ridden friend saying, "It's the chicken-egg bit. The agency's growing too fast. Right now I'm pitching Acadia Motors. They have a new small car in the wings. It's big bucks and prestige, and we have the inside track. *But* I had to hire the best copy man in the auto business. He doesn't come cheap, and neither do his assorted buddies on the team. Then there's new space I had to rent." Reynolds' hand was shaking as he poured more coffee for Talbott. "It'll come out green after we land Acadia, but meantime we're hemorrhaging."

Talbott's shaggy eyebrows did not come down.

Reynolds badly wanted him to understand. "It's the classic growth story, how to finance success in an undercapitalized business." He smiled sourly. "We're suffering from *success!*" He poured Helena more coffee. "Obviously, my drinking that way was stupid, but the bank had turned me down again and—" Reynolds stopped, searched Helena's waiting face. "And I won't take another cent from Helena."

Talbott cleared his throat gruffly. "This is between the two of you."
Going to the door he said, "Phil, I advise you not to kid yourself. I
believe there's more than business pressure behind your drinking."

"What is that supposed to mean?" Reynolds asked.

"You're letting it all float by you." Talbott enjoyed using the
Madison Avenue phrases he picked up from his friend. "Come in for an
examination, and we'll talk."

With the doctor gone, Helena reached out a sympathetic hand to
Reynolds. "You didn't tell me about the bank."

"Your father left the trust for you and the girls."

"For family emergency!" With a sense of shadowed urgency, Helena
wanted her husband to know she was always on his side.

He shook his head, stubborn. "Suppose Acadia gets away?"

"Oh?"

"Rod Graham is pitching too. And others. You have to be out of your
mind to pretend anything is certain in this rat race."

"Phil, please let me help."

He kissed her smooth cheek, liking the faint perfume. "Thanks. I'll
manage."

"A man who has brought new distinction to our field by the example
of his innovative thinking and—"

Reynolds' smile was wry and self-deprecating. The tiresome man at
the microphone should have known what had happened just that morning when he had returned from a new bank's final rejection. With a stiff
drink in his hand, he stood looking out his window at the Christmas
shoppers thronging Madison Avenue. They were his customers, the
people he spoke to in every ad he created. A rabid impulse seized him.
His hand actually moved to open the window. He visualized loosening
the glass to watch it drop from the thirty-first floor, gathering speed—
what was it, x feet per second per second?—until it smithereened below,
a blind fate-bomb shredding some innocent skull to bloody strips.
Innovations indeed!

Reynolds shuddered. What kind of unbalanced lunacies slouched in
his secret gut?

He had shaken off his self-disgust by telling himself it was only a
fleeting aberration any person might have some time. He had not been
convinced.

"A man who—"

Reynolds eyed the basket that held the rolls. The food had been
unimaginative but not bad, considering there were at least a thousand

guests. It always struck him as remarkable that any kitchen could serve so many meals. It took a better manager than he was.

He scanned the great high-balconied ballroom. All these people to honor him. He remained unsure why. There were more high-powered names around ad alley that could have been used for bait. But he was "hot" because his young agency had walked away with so many Clios, Andys, Effies, and Gold Key awards, and he was personally known as a top guru in launching new products.

Why couldn't he feel elated, as others would? Why did he feel that it wasn't *him* on this dais? His daughter, sitting beside Helena, was grinning at him ecstatically, forgetting the braces on her teeth. It came to Reynolds that Selma did look grown up. It pleased him to see how smartly she wore her pink formal dress. Thirteen going on forty, of course, and holding her own, without the slightest embarrassment, talking to the man on her left, who was black. Beneath all their thumb-nosing, the kids today were okay, Reynolds observed silently—and gratefully added, especially kids like his: Selly there and the younger ones at home, Dorothy and Midge.

He was glad he had overruled Helena and insisted that Selma's dress be made by one of his client-designers. Helena thought it too old-looking but Selma adored it, and Reynolds' philosophy was to let his daughters make their own decisions, "as long as you don't hurt anyone, including yourselves." He regretted the argument with Helena. Something sand-papery had been coming between them increasingly.

To Reynolds' fond eyes, his daughter was an enchanting preview of the gracious woman she would be in a few years. She had something of Helena's reserve, but in Selma it was provocatively stirred with a seeking wit and an intensity she had probably inherited from him. She was going to be a heartbreaker, Reynolds was father-proud certain.

It was another of the times—occurring more frequently recently—when Reynolds wished his mother and father were still alive to witness his rise. He turned from the thought abruptly.

"A man who—"

Selma seemed honestly impressed. Her glances to the dais had been full of admiration. It was good for her to see him this way instead of— Tonight would help Selma put things in perspective, understand that people aren't one-dimensional. That thought was too painful too. He started to reach for another roll, then remembered his weight problem. Why did he want the roll? He wasn't really hungry. He supposed it went back to the days in Chicago when his mother had made him clean his dish. Yiddishe Momma shoving husky chunks of cornbread at him, "well-baked." He remembered the fragrance, texture, taste, gone forever in this synthetic age. Bread, staff of life. "How can anyone eat meat without bread?" In the warm ballroom, Reynolds plainly heard the querulous voice out of the drafty Chicago kitchen, although his mother had been dead since he was twelve years old. His father, though not Jewish, had given his mother no trouble on the bread score. He had devoured his loaf as he had devoured everything.

"A man who—"

Reynolds dropped the roll and looked back to the agency table where the black man, Ted Watson, had turned from Selma to the lively young lady on his other side. She was Penny O'Hara, Reynolds' new secretary. Her fresh-for-the-occasion gown was pale green. It set off her gypsy-black hair and her Irish cream face. Her look was what you would want in an ad for fresh spice, say, cinnamon. Reynolds had caught that special image the day he hired her six months ago. It was a bonus, for this Brooklyn nineteen-year-old had—wonder of wonders—grammar and spelling as well as unalibied typing and steno. Miracle! There was a joke going the rounds: A businessman says, "My new secretary can't spell, which makes her inability to type a positive blessing." Ha, ha, and another fart for the Age of the Second-Rate.

Reynolds was reminded of Spengler's *Decline of the West,* which he was rereading. "Most seminal prophecy of our time," he had scowled to Talbott. Doom, entropy, and death—the way he himself had begun to feel, burned out, on a wobbling axis. The problem—he had added his own jeremiad—was not just the bankruptcy of civilized values at the end of the twentieth century; the problem was a value vacuum. It made for a degenerate and marrow-sapped society.

One reason his ads worked so well, Reynolds speculated to Talbott, was that he cared about the integrity of both the product and the presentation. He did not hesitate to turn down clients. Start with quality, he enjoined his people, and tell the truth without puffery. The secret of his ads, he considered, was that they were, of all things, *comforting.* In a world of cynicism and suspicion, his copy struck a note of believability and reassurance. It was an appeal whose time had come.

Believability and reassurance. That seemed what he was searching for himself. _

Penny O'Hara had an air of her own middle-class integrity. Convent-trained, she kept a watchful distance from the agency's creative types who dressed in tired jeans, fringes, and garlands of buttons promoting every cause from Whales to Gay Liberation. The girl had made it clear she was engaged to an auto mechanic, saving with him for a house on Long Island. No babies now, she assured Mr. Reynolds earnestly. He needn't worry about breaking her in only to have her leave.

He had not been wrong to believe in her. The girl was all over the shop, helping wherever she could, and taking in everything she could learn. Reynolds was certain her conversation with Ted Watson was about the new computer typesetting they were using in much of their print production.

He had to admit it wasn't helping his acid stomach to see the bright eyes so intent on the mahogany face. In an oblique way he felt a twinge of jealousy. It was gone in an instant, but it was a surprise. There was nothing between him and Penny O'Hara. There had never been anything between him and any woman in the office, or elsewhere. People might find that hard to believe in this age, and he had wondered about it at times. Certainly there were opportunities, fully and visibly harvested by his colleagues all around him. Apparently he owned an uncommon streak of old-fashioned morality; or maybe, rather than any kind of austerity, it was his saturation with his work. It simply felt natural and right not to play around. He did not feel deprived or cheated, even though the years had cooled his marriage. Helena remained his wife, and he seriously accepted his commitment to their relationship.

Penny caught Reynolds' eye with a shy smile. He nodded back neutrally. Penny read his expression as stern—a reminder of her place. She dropped her head like a scolded child. Reynolds was sorry at once. The girl was sensitive, and certainly not responsible for the trajectory of his thoughts. From the head table he fashioned a smile, but Penny had turned quickly to Ted Watson.

Reynolds grew more irritated with himself. Why was he dwelling on Penny O'Hara? With all of his pressures, the last thing he needed in the world was an office affair, especially a December-May complication—though that did seem to be the trend these days, Reynolds mused sourly. Not for him, he silently avowed. In any case, Penny had never given the slightest sign of such interest, and would probably bound away like a deer if he did. He wished he had altered the table arrangements and placed Penny with the second agency group where she would not be under his nose, and where he would not fancy he was smelling faint, provocative cinnamon.

"A man who—"

Seated next to the black production manager, Penny O'Hara was both ill at ease and pleased. She had no prejudice, but it seemed to her that heads were turning at nearby tables. It didn't take much to start rumors on Madison Avenue, she had already learned. At the office, ladies' room hints about her and Philip Reynolds had astonished and infuriated her. To Mr. Reynolds she was just another piece of office equipment, like his typewriter and drawing board. As she *should* be, she strictly agreed.

At the same time, Penny was grateful for the opportunity to be with Watson. She was ignorant of print production, had never conceived how basic it was to the operation of an advertising agency. And, no one in advertising disagreed, Ted Watson was a superstar in his field. He was a scholarship whiz out of the Rochester Institute of Technology, an expert in word processing, phototypography, computers, printing plates, all strange and wonderful to Penny O'Hara's eager inquisitiveness. As everything was Wonderful in her job. Working with a man like Philip Reynolds made her realize that the people she had known before were "off the rack." Philip M. Reynolds, recipient of the advertising industry's highest honor tonight, was another world all by himself. It was a world she could never enter or share, of course, but she could happily learn from it every day.

"A man who —"

Ted Watson had to be invited, of course, Reynolds considered. It was positive for the firm's image that they had a black man high up on the team. Still, he made Reynolds a little uneasy. It wasn't Ted's color; he was too faultless in his job, too damned handsome. He looked like a twin brother to that glorious Nefertiti at the Metropolitan Museum. He could have just about any female in the office, and probably did. It would be deemed a mark of enlightenment these days, Reynolds glowered inwardly. He allowed himself a rueful smile. Who would believe the old Yale liberal would be harboring reactionary prejudice? Yet, it wasn't he who had changed so much as the world. The world was on its head these days, with its values and ideals spilling out of its pockets.

"A man who —"

Actually, Reynolds admired and respected Ted Watson. His mind went back to their first meeting, shortly after he had started the agency. His then production chief, a burly Archie Bunker type named Willie White by appropriate coincidence, had needed an assistant. The eager, uncertain, black neophyte was one of the applicants. Reynolds had liked it that, in addition to Watson's outstanding school record, the young man was soft-spoken, did not sport a thumb-nosing Afro, wore an Ivy League suit. But there had been a hard confrontation with Willie White.

"I don't work with any nigger," the man had announced.

Reynolds had said, "This fellow is head and shoulders over the other guys. He's the only one with a real handle on the new computer stuff—"

"Without me!" Willie White flung the gauntlet down confidently. Phil Reynolds knew television, but print production wasn't his field.

Reynolds thought it over, and had to concede. Especially in a newborn agency it would be foolhardy to bet on an unknown and lose a proven veteran. Although he was nettled by White's ultimatum, he was about to concede when the man added roughly, "These damn boogies only work long enough to rip off unemployment insurance anyway!"

The blatant bigotry outraged Reynolds. He stood up, eyes hard, voice soft. "Without you then, Willie. I'm hiring Ted Watson."

Willie White had not stayed even for a break-in period, and for months Reynolds secretly regretted his decision. Schedules crumbled, emergencies multiplied, clients complained. But he saw Ted Watson working to exhaustion, learning fast, silently pleading for the chance to prove himself. Reynolds remembered his own struggle to get a foothold. In a reasonable time, Watson won the respect of the agency's suppliers. A strong web of loyalties and support formed among them. The strand running from Ted Watson to Philip Reynolds was a bond of gratitude that grew every year. Watson knew what had transpired with Willie White. He knew the risk Reynolds had taken with him, and he felt in Reynolds' debt for opening a wide career when he could have hoped for only a crack in the door elsewhere.

"I owe you," Ted Watson had told Reynolds once when they were having a quiet drink after work.

"Forget it," Reynolds had said. "You pay me every day."

Remembering, Reynolds was pleased. His instinct had been right, and it had all worked out well. Decency often paid. Still, if he were to be totally honest with himself, he would have to ask whether he would take the same chance today.

Reynolds was irked with himself again. Turning, he saw a flutter of fingers from his head proofreader-librarian. Lillian Schuster was a tiny woman, nearly hidden by the extravagant floral piece on the table. She was a middle-aged widow with a timorous air and eyes that flicked away from any direct gaze, but she was a flaming Amazon against any trespass of language such as "... *like* a cigarette should!" Reynolds and Lillian

Schuster were of one mind that that vandal copywriter ought to be feathered in the tars of his cigarettes and ridden out of town.

With the woman, Reynolds shared an unusual hobby. They clipped typographical errors and printed malaprops for a collection that was both entertaining and a dire warning to the agency's own writers and proofreaders. Just that afternoon, Lillian had garnered two trophies. A newspaper's classified section advertised "Clean comfortable rooms, reasonable rats." A racing magazine wanted "A boy to take care of horses who can speak German." Reynolds himself had brought in a Schenectady paper from a visit to an upstate client; it reported that "the population of Sing Sing Prison has reached an ill-time high."

It amused Reynolds again as he considered the moral of all such bloopers. Nobody was perfect (despite the encomiums the MC was heaping on him). Who indeed was to throw the first stone? Yet, Lillian had to cool him down on the infrequent occasions when their own shop came a cropper. His personal span of tolerance for any slip was close to zero, and growing smaller, he knew. Somebody had to insist on standards.

Reynolds returned the woman's eager look, careful to keep his own smile impersonal. It was no secret around the agency that Lillian Schuster was in love with the boss, and also that she expected nothing from him but the job she did so well. In the improbable event that Reynolds might have responded, the woman would have panicked.

Reynolds returned to his crumbs. The last thing he wanted was to psychoanalyze Lillian Schuster. Her defenses were her own affair, and they seemed to work well for her. Despite Duncan Talbott's endorsement of psychoanalysis, he didn't believe in headshrinkers anyway. He had seen too many people boasting of successful therapies while figuratively swinging like antic monkeys from chandeliers.

Lillian Schuster pretended to need a drink of water. She did not want Phil Reynolds embarrassed by the mistiness in her eyes. Her mind went back to the night he had hurried to the hospital, unasked, when her husband had been critically burned in a car crash. He had pressed on her more money than she needed. Through his friend Dr. Talbott he had arranged for the best care. And his reward had been scurrilous, malicious, ignoble gossip about the two of them! She supposed she should have been flattered that some people thought her attractive enough. Phil Reynolds had helped simply because he was that kind of man. She did not love him, she revered him. He deserved every honor the industry gave him, and more. She was delighted she was here to cheer for him on this wonderful night.

"A man who—"

Between Lillian Schuster and Penny O'Hara sat the new, heavy-weight recruit to Philip Reynolds and Associates, Jock Rogers. As Reynolds took in the florid face and southern-type goatee, he thought again that the man spelled frightening red ink if they didn't land Acadia. But risk was the name of the game. If he had wanted to be just one of the tribe, he would never have left his comfortable $70,000-a-year spot as creative director of a major shop six years before.

But that was another matter Reynolds wasn't going to pursue this night. He forced his attention back to the master of ceremonies, who was now reciting his biography. It always amused Reynolds to hear the guest of honor spoken of like a political candidate. He was "a man who" had been born and raised in Chicago, but had spent his early summers on his grandfather's Ohio farm, and had never shaken that good earth from his feet (and who had never skinny-dipped with the other kids, Reynolds recalled, so they wouldn't see his giveaway pecker. Don't be psycho-Semitic, Reynolds admonished himself.). The speaker was convinced this background explained Phil Reynolds' magic ability to reach people everywhere, from Middle America to Metropolis.

"A man who" had a truly American family. His father, self-educated, had risen with American mobility from street cleaner to streetcar conductor to office supervisor. His mother, of immigrant parents—who, far from demanding that the schools teach in their Old World language, had flocked with their neighbors to learn English—this man's mother had become an English teacher herself. Traveling by trolley to her night-school class, she met the man she was to marry. "A story from which many of today's immigrants could take inspiration," the MC added with scolding emphasis.

Reynolds dropped his hands to his lap so no one would see his fists. He thought sadly that the speaker should have explained that his father was a Methodist, and that it was fantastic and still inexplicable that he should have married a Jewish girl in the Twenties no matter how appealing her photographs showed her to have been. Whatever had started on that fateful trolley had soon turned vicious. Well, both long dead and buried. His father headed the list of things decidedly to be unremembered right now, Reynolds told himself.

Reynolds shifted more uncomfortably as the recital went on. He could remember feeling proud of his biography once, even lofty. But that was before he had proved himself. Now the Who's Who facts seemed stale. People shouldn't need to present credentials to the world like an engraved card. Performance should speak for itself.

It was another person, in any case, who had won the scholarship to New Haven, who had taken the poetry prizes, who had been a teaching fellow in English for two years. It was even difficult to connect with the apprentice who had swept the floor of the small agency that had given him his start in advertising. All light-years from this dais.

Reynolds scrambled the crumbs he had formed into a question mark. Duncan Talbott would seize on it as a subconscious sign, but Reynolds knew it was impatience with the speaker's hyperbole.

To Duncan Talbott, seated on Helena Reynolds' right, the evening was a prickly affair. On the one hand, he was happily sharing the occasion; on the other, he had a disquieting notion that Reynolds was not. His old psychiatry professor had told him he had a useful instinct in this area, but at the same time one had to be cautious. Aside from the drinking bouts and some out-of-character shouting incidents at the club recently, Phil Reynolds didn't seem to present what might be called significant clinical symptoms. The successful, brilliant man on the Waldorf dais was the last person in the world whom anyone would ever suspect of needing psychological aid. And they might all be right, Talbott considered, but he wished he did not keep sensing a jagged nervousness in Reynolds, who was continuously fiddling with the crumbs on the tablecloth. His friend's eyes seemed to go blank and distant as Talbott watched.

What the doctor could not know was that Reynolds had slipped away from the ballroom again. He was back in the desolate landscape of a dream that had shaken him the night before. Into a gray cemetery under a seamless gray sky a weird gray psychopomp led a procession behind a floating gray coffin. The earth spread apart by itself, a lurid red gash like a huge cunt, and the coffin tilted into it, lifted and dropped, withdrew and plunged, while the procession keened. The earth gulped closed, engulfing the coffin. The psychopomp swelled to giant size and Reynolds, a cowering boy beneath it, saw in terror and confusion that it was both woman and man. It had no breasts on its chest, but large nipples protruded from heavy testicles. They dripped yellow milk as the figure began to masturbate. As its orgasm spurts steamingly, the psychopomp shrieks in Yiddish: *"Cheese for the mouse!"* The watching boy, Reynolds, is overcome by an indescribable stench. His daughter Selma, older than he, runs in to proffer a handkerchief dipped in perfume. He grabs it and suffocates her with it. He then slices off her nose and eats it, horrified but unable to stop.

The MC's hand brushed Reynolds' cheek as the speaker gestured dramatically. Reynolds, coughing with the still-real foulness of his dream, reached desperately for his handkerchief. What a time to go ape! What craziness to have a maniac dream like that! He had heard that in psychoanalysis you could discover the whole ball of wax in any single dream if you really peeled it, but he didn't have the foggiest clue in this crazy spook. He must really have tied one on before Helena got him to bed last night.

Ought to take Helena back to Hawaii. That had been an exciting trip. Standing on the live volcano on Mauna Loa had given him the shakes, no matter how much the broad-brimmed rangers reassured them. He could hear the threatening rumble below. It wiped out villages when it decided to, flung lava down to spawn new beaches, beaches of *black*. That had surprised them. Hawaii was supposed to be all candy colors of travel posters, ice-cream pink, flower-yellow, grass-skirt kootchie-kootchie green with Aloha rum, leis, and roast pig—and all the while Old Volcano is biding its time to broil a luau out of *you!* Black beaches in the Garden of Eden.

"A man who—"

Was that trip eight years ago? No wonder he was getting pickle-vinegar. Reynolds came perilously close to shouting out loud, "The hell with all this, I want a drink!" For the thousand mouths in his gut-nest were abruptly open, the distended beaks of baby birds caterwauling, showing disgusting red-lined craws, not baby-cute but savage shark-hungry wide, distended down the insatiable tunnels—alimentary, my dear Watson! He fought the impulse down, and showed the room a false smile that hid his inner turbulence.

Reynolds shaped crumbs into a long worm. We are all earthworms at that. From birth to death we are wiggling noodles in the universe, serrating God's earth mouthhole to asshole, to make a friable garden whose crops we never get to witness but which apparently nourish Him.

The crumbs curved around the cold coffee cup and wriggled on. Eat, digest, crap, screw, be honored = Life.

We are God's shit, Reynolds thought, seeing the words as a headline of philosophy, to be set in 144-point Cooper Black. The idea brought a shudder of revulsion. He felt as if a cold wind had entered his ears, freezing his brain. For a gasping moment he was sure he would be unable to speak.

The MC's hand touched Reynolds' shoulder deliberately this time, bringing him back to the event. The introduction was waxing to its climax: "And so I have the privilege and honor of saying to the family, friends, and colleagues gathered to honor this man tonight, that there are no words of fulsome praise to adequately do justice"—here the speaker turned to his right and started to applaud with a gesture calculated to bring the crowd to its feet—"Mr. Philip M. Reynolds, of Philip Reynolds and Associates!"

Reynolds saw Lillian Schuster break up at the same moment the unwitting jest hit him. The word "fulsome" was misused by every corny speaker in the land! It was a felicitous irony because "fulsome" was the precise opposite of laudatory. It meant foul, loathsome, sickening! "I give you stinking praise!" (And the turkey had gone on to split an infinitive as well!)

A thousand people on their feet, applauding with gusto that sounded sincere, appreciating him, his accomplishments, liking him personally. Ballroom resounding, spotlights playing dramatically from the distant balcony. Reynolds felt his shirt sticking to his back. A blip gigged through his head—"fulsome" might be only too appropriate a description in his case. Angrily he flashed the specter away. Of all problems, *that* secret putrescence must not intrude now! With a practiced smile, Reynolds bowed left, right, center, and around again, and then to the balcony.

Phil was a pro, Helena thought proudly. With renewed gratefulness, she observed Selma taking it all in.

Photographers' bulbs laced into Reynolds' eyes. The hand-clapping gave way to a buzzing and humming that faded into an expectant silence. Reynolds found that he had his voice, firm and urbane as always at a microphone:

"Mr. Toastmaster, honored guests—when I am introduced so generously, I'm reminded of a story said to be true about Justice Oliver Wendell Holmes at the unveiling of his portrait in the Harvard Law School. The painting showed Holmes in all his Brahmin impressiveness. When asked what he thought of it, he responded, 'It's not me, but it's a damned good thing if people think it is!' "

Reynolds spoke on "Computer Versus Creativity," an abiding controversy in advertising. You could get all your copy fixes with test paragraphs, recall checks, focus group work, and the rest of the adman's paraphernalia, he said, but the trouble was that the Devil could quote statistics as well as Scriptures—why else should the public be rejecting some six out of every ten new products which passed Go on the research boards? The gut truth to him, Reynolds said, was that the computer-oriented people—whether on the client or agency side—viewed people as ciphers more than as persons. Wit, insight—even, yes, poetry—might often be more effective.

Reynolds was careful not to hit too hard. It wasn't smart to overplay the pundit on a night like this. It was a time to remember that tact was the art of firing people up without making their blood boil. Reynolds was effective, knowledgeable, assured.

At the end, two prospective clients shook his hand enthusiastically. He gave Helena a quick nod and wink. Rod Graham came along the dais to grip Reynolds' shoulder. His congratulations were genuine. In his direct way, he added, "You and I ought to have lunch, Phil."

"Glad to."

The sweat running under Reynolds' shirt was not all from his speech. Graham clearly had something in mind. *Deo volente,* a possible merger. It was a prospect he had considered a distant chance, but one he was not in a position to advance.

Reynolds nodded agreeably to Graham. "Give me a buzz after the holidays." You call *me*—oneupsmanship. In business, the more eager you are, the cooler you play. A merger with Rod Graham would be reprieve *and* the wild blue yonder he never had enough capital to fly! They could go national, international. He'd always said you work just as hard thinking small as thinking big, maybe harder.

His people were waiting in a semicircle below the dais. Selma reached her father first. Her arms went around his neck for the first time in years in a confession of new affection and respect. It moved Reynolds nearly to tears when she sobbed, "Oh, Daddy, I'm so *proud* of you!"

2

Reaching home, Reynolds went directly to the bar. Tonight he had right, reason, excuse, but he kept his back to Helena and Selma so they wouldn't see the Scotch fill nearly the whole glass before he made a show of ice and soda. It was easy to wave off the nudge of guilt he felt. Helena even agreed to join him in a drink, and invited Selma to bring her hot chocolate to the crackling fire.

Selma said, "You look like the cat with the canary, Mother."

"I suppose I am," Helena smiled. She carried a package to Reynolds. "Surprise. I wanted you to have my own award, to let you know I agree with every word they said about you tonight."

Selma jumped up as Reynolds lifted out a beautiful leather portfolio of his most notable advertisements. She cried out, "Oh, that's merely neat and nifty!"

Reynolds took Helena in his arms.

Selma moved to hug them both. It was a special moment for her, to see her parents happy this way, and to be with them alone instead of sharing them with the girls asleep upstairs.

After Helena went up with Selma, Reynolds settled in his easy chair with a bottle beside him. The den was dim and pleasant, all leather books and brass lamps glowing on the mellow antique furniture Helena had collected over the years. The fire was low, and snapping soothingly. The first drinks were spreading their warmth through Reynolds' body. He yawned deeply with a satisfaction that went down to his toes. The medal sitting on the bar *was* real, the speech *had* gone well, it had been a record turnout, Rod Graham surely had an agenda. And Helena's thoughtfulness touched him deeply. Reynolds nodded with his drink. Helena did try to understand and to help. He truly ought to count his blessings, not his beefs. *That* was the whole secret of peace of mind, he repeated to himself as he poured another drink.

It was a blessing that alcohol worked so quickly. He badly needed this relaxation. That lunatic dream! No question he was under too much pressure, couldn't keep being Pooh-Bah in the agency. Trouble was, when he tried to delegate, nobody did anything right. Helena had chided him: "You're not looking for assistants, Phil, you're looking for replicas of yourself, and of course there aren't any." In his head, Reynolds knew his wife was right. But when he saw someone ineptly handling a job he himself could manage in a moment, there was a rasping inside, a bodily shuddering, like chalk on glass. He'd take the pressure, thank you.

Drinking did seem the only thing that took the monkeys off his back lately. It was easing him deliciously. The soft sounds of the fire were like strokes on his cheeks. His eyes half closed. It was like being in velvet sleep but awake enough to be conscious of the enfolding pleasure.

With the bottle held upright between his thighs, Reynolds fell asleep, his chin dropped to his chest. Selma came down the stairs on tiptoe.

"Dad?" she whispered.

Reynolds' eyes opened defensively, seeking focus through the whis-key haze.

Selma didn't seem to notice. She was filled with the night's adventure. She enthused, "I've been telling the kids about the affair. They want to see your medal."

The cowl began to dissolve. Of course Dorothy and Midge should see the medal! Reynolds got up, fighting his unsteadiness. He didn't want Selma to suspect what he knew—had again drunk too much, too fast. Not really squiffed, but Selly would think so if he wobbled. Reynolds took a deep breath and held it, swelling his chest. It helped clear the fumes sometimes. "I'll take it up, honey." Good. Speech was clear, not thick or pasty. Better not try to say too much, though. Lately he hadn't been able to control his voice too well after a couple of drinks. Another symptom of how bone-tired he was.

With great care, Reynolds stepped to the bar and lifted the medal. It gleamed golden and precious in the light, hypnotic. He blinked. Didn't need anything else unfocusing his eyes. He made his way to the stairs without weaving, though the floor tilted a little. He reached the banister, and was safe. "You coming along?" he ventured to Selma.

"In a minute. I'm thirsty first."

"Okay." He was up to the landing. "Where's mother?" Speak ordinarily as if the room were not rocking.

"Taking a bath."

Later, in his pajamas, coming down for a final drink to top off the great night, Reynolds was startled to discover Selma at the bar.

"Hey. I thought you were asleep, baby!" By now the quantities of liquor had dimmed his ears so that he didn't hear or care that his speech was slurred and plainly drunken. "You don't have to clean up here, baby. Maid'll do that in the morning." Then astonishment froze his tongue.

Flushing guilt-red, Selma lowered the glass from her mouth. "I was just tasting mother's wine—"

Anger exploded in Reynolds like the flaming of brandy at a lighted match. "Lemme see that!" He lurched to Selma as she started to pour the drink out. He grabbed the glass from her trembling hand. Scotch, not wine! "What'n hell you think you're doing?" His secret guilt about his own drinking added to the flame.

Suddenly his daughter was a stranger. Instead of cowering—a sinning child caught red-handed—she met his anger head on, her natural rebellion fueled by the whiskey she had taken. "Just what *you* do all the time!"

"Don't you talk to me like that!"

Selma challenged her father. "You're drunk right now!"

The truer it was, the more fiercely Reynolds needed to take umbrage at it. What he did as a grown man was no excuse for his daughter to be sneaking drinks. "If I ever catch you doing that again, I'll—"

Selma cut him off with hostility born of her panic. She had not meant to be swimming in these sudden currents. "Oh, don't make such a stink about nothing."

"Don't talk back to me!"

"This isn't the Middle Ages, you know!" The girl was defending herself blindly. She did not want to be insolent, but Reynolds found her conduct outrageous and intolerable. The last checkrein snapped and he careened out of control. A hand that was not his splashed the liquor in the glass at his daughter as he heard himself shouting hoarsely, "No back talk!"

Selma's terrible cry of pain sobered him. Had he blinded her in this crazy instant of drunken fury? Reynolds cried desperately, "Selly! Are you all right?"

The girl was cringing at the bar, weeping. "You ruined my dress!" There was a wail of disbelief. "I was going to wear it to the Christmas dance and now you've gone and ruined it!"

Reynolds stumbled to his daughter. "Baby! I'm sorry!" Silently he was giving fervent thanks that only the dress had been hurt by his wild lapse. "The glass *slipped*." He held Selma in an agony of remorse, silently begging her to believe his lie. He was doubly disgusted with himself, but he could not let Selma believe the truth. "It slipped, honey! I swear!"

The girl pulled away fiercely, her fists to her eyes. "Oh, Daddy! *Why* do you do things like that?"

The next morning in Duncan Talbott's examining room, Reynolds was saying, "Thanks for checking Selly out last night." He needed to confess to someone. "Dunc, the glass didn't slip. Selly knew it, but she let Helena think it was an accident. Christ, I could have blinded her!"

"Exactly!" When Talbott had arrived in response to Helena's frantic call, Selma had told "Unc Dunc" the truth. "Daddy went berserk. He didn't even look like himself. His face got all twisted up, like Dr. Jekyll and Mr. Hyde!"

Talbott went on solemnly, "Selly said you went into a 'shark frenzy.' " He didn't add that Helena had not been fooled.

Reynolds protested. "Come on. I'm sorry as hell, but I was just drunk, not demented!"

Duncan Talbott decided it was time to make a tentative move. "Phil, you ought to give some thought to getting help."

The answer came with an easy laugh. "I can stop drinking any time I want to."

"I'm not talking about AA—" Talbott began, when, without warning, Reynolds started pounding on the enamel table holding the doctor's electrocardiograph apparatus. His face blazing red, Reynolds was thundering, "I'm sick of all of you, goddammit! Helena bellyaching I need help in the office, you and your AA!" The table rocked under his blows. "All I need is for you do-gooders to mind your own damn business!"

Talbott barked angrily, "You break that machine and I'll break your goddamn neck!"

Reynolds rubbed his fist, glaring at Talbott. "Just be my damn doctor, then, not my father confessor!"

"Shark frenzy! Selly was exactly right!"

"Eh?" For a moment, Reynolds was puzzled. Then he was shouting and hammering the table as abruptly as before. "Not one of you knows what I go through or gives a fuck!"

"Get the hell away from that machine!" Talbott gave Reynolds a hard push unexpectedly. It stopped the violence, but Reynolds stood panting, glaring at Talbott with vexation.

"Now sit down and shut up and listen!" the doctor said.

Mechanically, Reynolds dropped to a small white stool. His head was turning with confusion; there were too many things he wanted to say at once and he could not get them out of the narrow bottle of his throat. He made a small sound he meant as acquiescence. Suddenly he was aware of a deep, inner fear of the violence that had catapulted him out of control.

Talbott spoke quietly now. "I think what you're doing is your way of asking for help, Phil. There's a doctor I'd like you to see. If I'm wrong, no harm's done. If—"

"A psychoanalyst?" Reynolds interrupted in an offended tone.

"Yes."

The word hung in the air along with the smell of lemon polish and quality leather in the bright winter sun beaming through the bottle-glass panes of Duncan Talbott's office, spotlighting the revulsion on Philip Reynolds' face. "You've got to be out of your stethoscopic mind!"

"You want a sugar tit, Phil? If I spotted cancer, you'd want to know. Why not this?" Talbott went on in a half-lecturing tone. "People think of analysis in dramatic terms—deep depression, sex deviation, suicidal thoughts, that kind of thing. Actually, your drinking, your outbursts, your compulsiveness about work are far more common symptoms."

"*Symptoms?*" It was a threatening word. "You're way off base. I'm out there every day running a business that's pretty damned creditable if I do say so myself—"

Talbott snapped, "I'm not talking Peyton Place, Phil! All of us live with powerful forces in the unconscious. At our age, real changes take place—chemical, physiological, psychological." The doctor smiled at his friend. "Even philosophical, like the campus radical turning conservative."

The words brought a curve to Reynolds' lips. How well he remembered the bull sessions in which the two of them had settled the nature of the Universe, God, good and evil, ontological and teleological purpose, communism versus capitalism, everything. It was funny, Reynolds thought palely, that he had felt the breath of eternity closer down his neck when he was young than he did now that he was nearer to it.

Talbott was pointing his thin gold pencil at him. "These changes can rock a man's boat hard. We seem to be sailing along fine, but a lot of heavy cargo can suddenly come unstuck and start shifting around very dangerously."

"Lost me," Reynolds said.

"Cargo—your inner feelings, doubts, worries. Just *because* you think you have everything safely stowed away, the confusion can raise hell when it jacks-out-of-the-box at this time of life."

Reynolds tried a small laugh. "You mean an old goat turning to *le sport?*"

Talbott did not accept the invitation to ease up. "Some men get a perpetual hard-on about now, yes. But I'm talking about what happened last night." He went on quickly, forestalling the disclaimer Reynolds was about to voice. "Not just the mess with Selma. The way you took the whole affair at the Waldorf."

"I don't follow you." Talbott saw that Reynolds was genuinely puzzled. He measured his words. "It all slid off you like water off a duck's back, didn't it? The speeches, the award, the applause, everything!"

"You really are out of your gourd!"

"You went through the motions, but you were miles away most of the evening."

Reynolds rose. "Dunc, I have a helluva hangover. I'm getting into bed with a bottle of aspirin. See you later at the club." He tried the grin again. "I promise I won't drink tonight."

The doctor dropped his pencil and waved his fingers in the air in a habitual gesture of impatience. "Somebody's got to lay it on the line with you, dammit. You have to make your own decision, of course, but I wouldn't be your friend if I didn't warn you that I think you're running out of time."

Reynolds refused to hear more. He ducked through the crowded waiting room, with his friend's last words echoing in his head disturbingly. "Running out of time." It wasn't like Duncan Talbott to say that casually.

When he turned the ignition key, Reynolds felt his brain start to chug along with the motor. Talbott had struck a live nerve. He had to admit, to himself at least, that it wasn't only the incident last night or the blowup with Talbott just now. Damned near everything seemed to set his teeth on edge. He had become the quickest gun on Madison Avenue, blazing away at his employees, suppliers, even clients, at the slightest provocation. He had thought of it as justified impatience with under-par work, but now Talbott had given him a pretty tough idea to chomp on. Maybe, as Talbott insisted, it *was* more than liquor and overwork.

And while he was leveling with himself, what about the execrable secret he harbored that *no* one guessed—the lurking shame he blocked out of his own consciousness most of the time? Duncan Talbott, damn him, was into a nastier can of worms than he ever suspected. It was nobody's damned concern but his own!

With rising irritation, Reynolds tried to shut off the disquieting thoughts. After all, he told himself defensively, he had never done that depraved thing except when he was drunk and not responsible. All he needed was to quit the liquor and everything would square away. Ace-doctor Duncan Talbott might be, and best friend, but this time his diagnosis was wrong!

Satisfied for the time being, Reynolds drove slowly down the snowy streets of the town, nodding with a fixed smile to neighbors who waved to him from the sidewalks.

With a frown he saw that the Italian grocery had been redone and sported a new shingle, "Emporium." To Reynolds it was more phony than the pink "Sweete Shoppe" opposite. Disneyland? Nostalgia si, fake, no! Reynolds' headache flared again.

Turning off Main Street, Reynolds passed the Episcopal church, spanking modern—"Ye Newe," by God! It impressed Reynolds that churches, guardians of tradition, seemed in the forefront of modern architecture. In hamlet and glen everywhere in the country, you saw exciting, fresh church designs. Well, he supposed Chartres and Notre Dame had seemed far-out in their day.

Too bad the peace of God wasn't for him. Because of his parents? Aside from having him circumcised, his mother had given him no exposure to Judaism, and his father had paid him no attention except to scold and beat him. Whatever the reason, it was too late to alter his agnosticism. Reynolds would like to have believed that churchgoers had true faith, but he was cynical. To him, organized religion was a hoax. All the prayers, ceremonies, sacraments, from Baal and Buddha to Voodoo and Zoroastrianism, seemed the abracadabra of a savage's fear of nature and children's wishes to believe in Santa Clauses. Drums and organ music for the impressionable. Cathedrals for Inquisitions and Aztec altars for cutting out human hearts. Paintings and sculptures to give form and reality to humbug. The greatest copywriters and public relations geniuses of all were the authors of the Bible, the Homer of Greece, Reynolds mused. They sold the product superbly. Well, if a placebo works, is it fraud?

Another turn brought Reynolds to the road that wound up a considerable hill to his house. The snowplow and sander had been through. High taxes but good service. Reynolds told himself again he ought to take more interest in town affairs, especially the new proposal to build low-rent apartment houses. He wasn't against decent housing for poor people, but just as obviously people like himself should have the right to enjoy the fruits of their own work. The trouble was that the U.S. was backing into Karl Marx without realizing it. What else was Welfare, for example, than redistributing wealth according to the Communist Manifesto: "From each according to his ability, to each according to his need." Great for those with the need, not so hot for those with the ability.

Yes, he had changed indeed. And need make no apology for it!

The large house came into view atop the hill. Alone and grand, its long, low expanse swept the crest. In summer it looked like a sleek ship sailing smooth green waves of lawn. Now the high glass clerestory of the two-story living room caught the sun and flared it back to Reynolds in the car like a welcoming beacon. The terra-cotta roof tiles showed red through the snow where the wind had blown patches away. Reynolds cherished this house. He had designed it and built it while at the old agency, and paid for it too, without touching Helena's money.

The biliousness returned. He might need help with the mortgage, at that, if Acadia didn't pan out and if all Rod Graham wanted was a friendly lunch chat.

As he signaled the garage door open, Reynolds thought how good a shot would taste after the disturbing session with Talbott, but in the house he walked past the bar without stopping. He had meant his vow to Helena and Selma last night and was definitely going to cut down the drinking from now on.

Leaving his office, Duncan Talbott rested his doctor's bag on the flagstone steps and locked the heavy red door. He was thinking of Phil Reynolds unhappily. He was convinced now that his friend was disturbed, but treatment was impossible unless help was freely sought. Reynolds would continue to delude himself and hide behind his incontrovertible success, as he had done that morning. It always amazed Talbott how much a flawed man like Reynolds could achieve. Such people nurtured a snake inside that sucked unendingly at their energy and force. At the same time, it was the fierceness of the neurotic's need to mask his illness, and, often, to present a glorious self to himself and the world, that fueled a Philip Reynolds. The compulsiveness frequently led to accomplishment beyond the capacity of less driven men.

But Duncan Talbott knew how much self-damage and agony can exist beneath a facade of growth. It was the measure of how sick his friend was, the doctor considered sadly, that he had so little awareness of his inner disruption. Tonight at the club, again, people would be crowding around Phil Reynolds' table to hear his Madison Avenue tales—at least until the drinking reduced him to the mumbling they whispered about later.

People don't understand that a man like Philip Reynolds is fleeing them all, friend as well as stranger, in the crooked, broken track of an animal that has been shot but does not know it is bleeding and wounded. He had been right the night of the award. On the dais, he had seen not the face of a man receiving a laurel wreath, but the mask of a lost tracker searching to restore a soul he did not even know he had forfeited. Talbott was convinced now that Reynolds' outbursts were the clinical symptoms of an inner strife wracking the man with a torment so fierce that he had to anesthetize himself with neurotic conduct.

Turning his car toward the hospital, the doctor told himself he had done all he could. Unfortunately, there was no pill he could give Helena and the girls against the siege they were probably in for.

Reynolds' dream that night:

A great pink boat named Kar II was sailing from New York to Hoan, China. All the passengers were monkeys, all males, all with huge, circumcised penises. The ship hit an iceberg and started to sink. The lifeboats were missing, everyone would die. The whole pack started masturbating, for one last taste of the good of life. They all shot at once, over the side. The freezing water congealed the mess to form a rubbery raft onto which all leaped to safety. They sang and pranced about, congratulating themselves on their "Operation Prickstrap," until, without notice, large canoes brought natives who cooked them with chicken fat and mice and breadfruit for a tasty stew. But it turned out that the monkeys were full of DDT, and the natives turned belly-up and died too. The only thing left alive in the dream was a single, white-whiskered mouse that had avoided the traps.

3

Gussied up for the office Christmas party, Lillian Schuster had supervised the decorations. Desks were moved aside for dancing. Red and green streamers, wreaths and holly, were festooned everywhere. Mistletoe hung conspicuously from sprinkler heads. "Merry Christmas" tablecloths held a generous food buffet—platters of roast beef, corned beef, turkey and tongue sandwiches, wrapped in glistening amber plastic tied with holiday rosettes. Cheese chunks and vegetable salads were on hand for the office health faddists. The hired accordionist, dressed in a tired tuxedo, wheezed trial chords through his battered amplifier and went brightly into "White Christmas" as Lillian gave her crew last-minute instructions.

Humming along happily, the small woman with the over-made-up face lowered the window blinds, and saw with pleasure that it was snowing briskly. Madison Avenue was a white haze, the traffic lights winking like tree decorations on a Christmas card scene. She moved to turn out the bright efficient fluorescents to make the large space more inviting, and stepped back with a glow to view her work. It was nearly one o'clock, party time. Come, Jesus Christ, have a Jewish corned beef sandwich on rye at your birthday party, courtesy Philip Reynolds and Associates.

Lillian Schuster tapped across the room in the high heels she had put on especially for the party, and poured her first drink of this year's revels. Anything could happen and probably would.

Penny O'Hara kept her surprise until twelve thirty. Then she went to the refrigerator in the lunchroom where she had hidden the split of vintage champagne. Back in her small, file-lined room next to Reynolds' office, she smoothed her white jersey dress over her hips, and patted her new hairdo in the mirror. The high-priced stylist had promised that the upsweep would make her look older, but the girl studied her oval face uncertainly. The only thing she was sure of was that her boss hadn't noticed her dress or hair today, as every other day.

When she opened Reynolds' door softly, he was bent intently over his desk—an expanse of heavy glass resting on two carpenter horses made of gleaming steel. It was piled high with files, portfolios, and legal-looking folders. She called, self-consciously, to the top of his head, "Coals to Newcastle, but Merry Christmas."

Reynolds dropped the ubiquitous red crayon with which he marked up copy, TV boards, memos, and the rest. He was wearing his usual outfit, Penny saw, with no special sprucing for the party. The suit was one of his charcoal flannels with soft, narrow stripes. His shirt was a blue button-down, open at the collar. His pulled-down tie was plain dark blue. Penny had heard some of the arty types joke about "Phil's uniform," but she thought it absurd for people making their money—from $50,000 to $80,000, it was widely known—to sport their mannered blue jeans, sandals, and, some of them, fancy ribbons around Portuguese pigtails. When you really had genius, Penny thought about Reynolds with a proprietary pride, you didn't need to flaunt outlandish costumes.

To her, Philip Reynolds looked exactly right. He projected an executive air in every motion, coupled with a vibrancy that illuminated every plane of his handsome face. Although he was obviously older than most of the staff, he seemed younger and more vigorous most of the time. She knew at first hand the multiple burdens he carried. It wasn't just the nerve-wracking pressure of turning out the famous ads without a letdown. Even in the six months she had been working for Phil Reynolds, Penny had come to understand "uneasy lies the head . . ." In the course of a day, she saw this man make decisions on which thousands and thousands of dollars rode, hiring and firing people, okaying this ad, dumping on that one, with hundreds of people and their families all depending on his being right!

Penny's thought continued: All that was to say nothing of the murderous calendar she set up for Reynolds regularly—the conferences, interviews, meetings with the staff, with the account executives, lawyers, accountants, real estate people, bankers, and, always and especially, with the agency's clients who would talk to no one but the head man, demanding, demanding, demanding. She hadn't realized it at first, but she soon saw that it wasn't enough for Philip Reynolds to be the best writer and the best creative director around, he also had to hold a hundred tugging reins as the agency forged ahead.

Penny recognized that her image was probably exaggerated, but it was more than enough to explain Reynolds' blowing his stack every now and then. The wonder was the patience, good humor, and animation he displayed most of the time. The entire staff felt the electricity that emanated from this office, and for Penny it made coming to work a special joy.

People like Mickey and her father could never begin to understand what "fat-ass bosses" do behind a desk all day. To them, only something like changing tires or unloading ships was "real" work! This beautiful office would baffle them utterly—the soft blue carpet, the eye-opening Calder lithographs, the steel and glass furniture, the "working wall," filled from floor to ceiling with tacked-up work in process.

Penny placed the champagne on the bar cabinet, saying with a nervous little laugh, "It would get warm in the grab bag. Anyway, it's just for us."

Reynolds looked at the label appreciatively. "What did you do that for, Penny?"

"To say how much I appreciate everything," Penny said sincerely.

Reynolds held the bottle for a moment. He was on the wagon. But Penny didn't know it, and she had gone to the trouble and expense of bringing him a gift. He couldn't hurt her, she was too loyal, too nice, too helpful. One glass wouldn't hurt. He had always said he could quit whenever he wanted to. He could prove it sensibly today.

Penny watched the glasses fill with the bubbling gold. Quality. Worth it. Phil Reynolds was lifting his glass to her, smiling. "To people who know how to spell." Gratefully she heard him go on, "That's a stunning dress, and I like your hair that way. I could sell you for a Vogue cover right now."

They laughed and drank together, a little stiffly, but it made a pleasant pre-party interlude of their own. They talked about Penny's growing interest in advertising, and Reynolds volunteered avuncularly, "Why don't you study at night?" He named some schools she might attend.

Penny turned away, pretending a cough. How could she tell this man, of all people, of the perplexed nights she had spent lately debating just that possibility? Before this, she had thought in terms of a job, but not a career. A job was just to mark time and save money for the real business of life, marriage, and children. A career meant—what? The girl glanced at the small diamond on her finger, and checked herself. This wasn't the time or place, and certainly Philip Reynolds had more important things on his mind than her sudden mental acne. With relief she heard music. Better get to the party.

Reynolds was finishing his drink, standing near the mistletoe Penny had tacked up in the morning. She moved to him and lifted her head primly, her hands straight at her sides. Reynolds smiled, still carefully avuncular, and said, "Merry Christmas, Penny."

The warmth of her young lips was more champagne. She smelled of cinnamon, yes.

Reynolds stopped his arms from going around her, and stepped back quickly, saying, "Personnel should have the bonus envelopes ready. Would you get them for me, please?"

At one thirty, Reynolds entered the party room. He congratulated Lillian, and she beamed. The noise was deafening. The bar was three deep, and the musician had his amplifier turned up so that it took shouting and two-fingered whistles from Reynolds to get the crowd silent when he climbed on a chair in the center of the room. Lillian and Penny, with Ted Watson between them, stood nearby, expectantly. Reynolds lifted a paper cup in a toast (the champagne had led to a Scotch and then several more): "All the merriest of Christmases and a great year ahead." There was cheering, clapping, and stomping. Reynolds held up a hand. "I'm afraid there isn't enough in these envelopes this year to cheer about. You all understand our situation. I hope I can make up for it next year. Meantime, these checks are a token of my appreciation for the great job you've been doing."

The applause was less enthusiastic.

"Now, just to be a little different, the way we try to be in our ads, let me start calling names from the back of the alphabet." There was some laughter and a scattering of hand-clapping led by Lillian. When Reynolds had distributed a dozen envelopes a rowdy voice shouted, "Half a week's pay! Big deal!"

Reynolds jumped off the chair in instant fury, exploding, "The son of a bitch who said that is fired! As of right now!" He rushed at the man—

one of the mailroom clerks—not seeing the frightened, gawking face, only Helena's concern when he had asked her for a separate loan to pay these bonuses. Reynolds held nothing but his hatred for this turkey who had dared to dump on the gift. His fists slammed murderously at the amazed fellow. He wanted to break the skinny, defending arms, see more blood spurt from the thin nose. He was deaf to the shouts of consternation around the room, Penny's cry, "Oh, my God, stop him!" and Lillian yelling to the accordionist, "Play, stupid!" Ted Watson, Jock Rogers, and other men sprang to pinion Reynolds. The clerk darted away, pressing a bloody handkerchief to his face. Reynolds, still struggling, nearly pulled loose to run after the man. Finally, back in his office, he was quieter. Lillian signaled everyone to leave but Penny. She fixed a drink, which Reynolds took dazedly. "Here, this will help you calm down," Lillian said. "Christ, you had us scared, Phil."

Reynolds sipped the drink. His eyes were vacant. "Okay. Okay," he said numbly. He tried to smile to Penny when he saw her concern, but only a grimace came. Penny felt out of her depth. Bewildered, she could only nod in response. She had never seen Philip Reynolds like this.

Lillian spoke gravely. "Phil, you'd have killed that jerk if Ted hadn't stopped you. I don't think you realize how you were clobbering him."

"Oh, come on. I shook him up. He deserved it." He wasn't going to explain further to Lillian or Penny. It was entirely justified. The man was insufferable.

"We've called a doctor. I think you broke his nose. He can sue you, you know. He can go to the police." Lillian spoke chokingly, trying to say what needed to be said.

Police? To Reynolds, the word came as a sudden splash of icy water.

"Assault and battery, Phil," Lillian went on angrily as a way of expressing her own dismay. "You can't go around beating up people because they don't like your bonus. There are consequences, you know."

Consequences.

The word rolled around in Reynolds' head, an oiled, ungraspable marble. Suddenly the fight was unreal to him. Obviously, it had happened, yet it had not involved *him*. Someone else had scuffled, but it was his own skinned knuckles his secretary, Penny, was tending with a wet towel. He felt dizzy, disjoined.

"I'll talk to the sausage-brain," Lillian said. "Can I offer to pay him something to forget it?"

Reynolds nodded. "Use your discretion, Lil." His thoughts knotted.

Christ, he *had* slugged that man. It wasn't a fantasy or an impulse like dropping a glass out the window. This time he had acted out his violence, though he didn't remember intending it. As he hadn't meant to throw whiskey at Selma? What would a lawyer plead—temporary insanity?

Temporary?

Duncan Talbott's voice echoed hollowly in Reynolds' ears: "Overreactive!" "Compulsive!" "Classical neurotic symptoms!"

Reynolds got up shakily. "Go back to the party," he told the two women. "I'm all right now." He went to his desk. "Some work I want to clean up anyway." As they went out, he said, "Thank you both—and tell Ted and Jock thanks for me."

When they were gone, Reynolds took a bottle to the cane rocker near the window and pulled the curtain back. He saw the snowy whiteness but it became a screen on which Duncan Talbott's face loomed. Was his friend right, then? A wry smile came to Reynolds' lips. He remembered something his mother had said after arguing with herself about spending money for a new coat. She had told his father, "Well, I finally made up my mind—I definitely might get a new coat this winter."

It seemed he, Philip Reynolds, definitely might need a psychoanalyst, no matter how fiercely he resisted the alien notion.

It might be getting to be time to admit to himself that what Talbott saw was only the tip of the iceberg.

He took a heavy slug from the bottle, and sat staring sightlessly at the driving snow.

The free-flowing liquor and whipped-up music had started the party going again. Some people were buzzing about the fight, but most were dancing as though there had been no interruption.

To Penny, the sound of people partying was like the operas she tuned in, over her mother's complaint, every Saturday afternoon. There was a counterpoint of the laughter and the voice babble and music that pulsed on until, sometimes, it all halted at once, as if on a conductor's signal. The momentary silence would bring quick embarrassed titters like piccolos and flutes, and the invisible baton would start the noise up again *forte*. One might hear a flash of a soprano solo from a woman's table, then a bass passage from men at the bar, or a full chorus of mixed voices. Sometimes laughter came like a cymbal. And you could always tell when a story had been off-color. There was an edge to the guffawing that Penny was hearing now. She was at the bar with Lillian for a fresh drink, and listened as Jock Rogers demanded loudly, "What do Martian women use for Kotex?" People snickered in anticipation of his punch line: "Brillo!" The man's soft belly heaved under his red-checked vest. Penny arranged her muscles into a smile but felt a little sick. His jokes were clever, and she'd heard he made them up himself, but this was one man she did not like. She was pleased when Lillian Schuster shouted, "That joke sucks!"

Lillian turned to an incident that had happened at their type shop. A new girl at the service desk was being harassed by an art director who insisted on a type face that the girl could not find in any of her books. Lillian heard the girl say finally, "I'm sorry, sir. That type face is not available anywhere in the world—you'll have to try someplace else!"

Giggling hard, Penny half started toward Reynolds' office to repeat the story, but turned back. He wouldn't be in the mood, would probably say the shop was supposed to have the damned typeface even if it hadn't been designed yet!

Penny took a long swallow from her cup, not caring that she was drinking much more than usual, and followed Lillian to a table where the proofreading team was eating. Lillian, whose eyes were beginning to shine with liquor, started to hold forth on why all publications ought to use Fowler for style. Penny listened with fascination. She had never heard of Fowler before, but gathered immediately that he was an English authority on copy editing. Lillian was explaining with religious ardor, "He says put *all* punctuation outside the quotes *except* where the punctuation is part of the material being quoted. Sensible? With other authorities, you put commas and periods inside the quotes, but colons, semicolons, question marks, and exclamation points go outside!" The woman lifted a bony finger. "What the hell is the sense in that? They're out of their squishes! Fowler gets all his shit together! But American publishing uses the *Times,* or *GPO,* or *U. of Chi.,* or nothing at all! We have got to get the industry to standardize!"

One of the women laughed, "We're on enough crusades as is, Lil."

A man chortled, "The sausage-brains out there don't know the difference and could care less!"

Another woman laughed, "Right on!"

"Right on!" Penny heard it with delight. So many things she had never heard before—people arguing over typographic style that she'd never even thought about—people in this room who were important artists, writers, opinionmakers. Right now she even liked the people she didn't like, including supreme egoist Jock Rogers. And Ted Watson, bringing her another drink—next to Phil Reynolds, her best teacher. She drank thirstily. She knew new decisions were forming inside. She was going to stay in advertising. She wasn't sure yet about Mickey, but this was her world—where they spoke a new language she loved, where clients were "crackers" and "bubbleheads" when they "pissed" on a campaign concept—where Phil Reynolds' ads were "merely great," and where Jock Rogers thought he was so giant that when he spit in the Hudson there was a high tide in Tobago. (Lillian had come up with that.) She would stay and work and learn, learn, learn, and maybe some day she too would write ads that would "knock the socks off clients!" Ah, sweet language never heard on Flatbush Avenue. It might be vulgar sometimes but it rang in her ears with an elegance that made her a member in new standing of this special family singing "Good King Wenceslaus" in resounding, drunken harmony.

Later Ted Watson was saying, "Looks to me like you could use some coffee." The music and the dancers and Ted Watson's handsome face kaleidoscoped in Penny's eyes. Drinking beer with Mickey wasn't like this at all. She was grateful for the strong hot drink Watson handed her.

"Want some cream?" he asked.

"I'll take it black," she mumbled.

He laughed aloud. "You're too sloshed to mean that as a pun." She gave him a blank look. "You sure are pickled and stewed if I ever saw one," he said.

" 'nupyerear!" Penny laughed mechanically. It was the Flatbush toast for "And a Happy New Year." Ted Watson didn't get it, and Penny O'Hara didn't try to explain.

By late afternoon, the room had thinned out. Black coffee by the quarts had been poured down scalded throats by helpful friends. Most of the couples who had disappeared into offices along the corridors had emerged by now, their annual adventure concluded after screwing, sucking, mutually masturbating, or whatever each of them had wanted and been permitted to do. An assortment of earrings, combs, lipsticks, and eyeglasses would be discreetly placed on a back shelf in Lost and Found after the holiday.

"Having a good time?" Watson asked Penny again. He mentioned that he wasn't what he'd call sober himself. He had trouble getting into a chair.

"Great."

When they were drinking again, Penny's expression grew pained. "I mean," she said, "I don't want to be superficial on a complicated subject at a party, but I don't think black people are right when they think every white person is against them." Penny swallowed more Scotch, and it made her feel queasy. The paper cup was going limp. She needed to go to the john, but the black man was answering her, and he would misunderstand if she left now. She fastened her eyes on his face, pressed her thighs tightly together, and kept sipping from the leaking cup.

Ted Watson was saying, "I want you to get a couple of things straight because you're new here. I am not this agency's token nigger. Quite the contrary. The agency is *my* token—my token that in *my* eyes *I* am a *man* first and, as it happens by accident, a black man as it happens. Right?" He poured for both of them from the bottle. He separated each word now for emphasis. "A. Man. Do you also notice that I do not say to you, 'You dig?' or use similar expressions of the brothers, et cetera?"

"I understand," Penny said gravely.

"I hope you do because I like you."

"I like you, too."

"Don't get me wrong. If a dude wants to be African, that's fine. Like a Jew wants to be a Zionist? Okay. But don't start telling every other Jew he is automatically a citizen of Israel. Right? I do more good *my* way." Ted stopped suddenly, like a car with jamming brakes. His eyes were reddening with liquor. "Still, it took a great guy like Phil to hire me, you know."

"*Great* guy!" Penny said enthusiastically. "I just hope he keeps wanting me to stay. Every night I pray to God!"

Ted deadpanned, "You think the Old Black Lady will hear you?"

Penny had never heard that twist, and she giggled with delight.

They were interrupted by a female voice rising at the bar. "Simone de Beauvoir never said that, you beanbag!"

Jock Rogers' voice drawled. "You need to get your face lifted and your voice lowered, darling."

"And up yours, you fascist pig chauvinist!"

Ted laughed to Penny, "Hey, it's a party. Let's dance."

Penny wanted the music and the talk to stop so she could head for the john, but she followed onto the dance floor. Almost all the lights were out, she was held close. Penny felt the man's hardness against her. Ted Watson made no pretense. She thought she ought to move away, but his arms were strong, and she found that she didn't dislike it. She admired the way he looked, the attractive odor of his skin, like a secret Oriental incense. She enjoyed the way his bony-hard body felt. She felt dreamy with sleigh bells in the snow tinkling out of the accordion drifting billowy clouds around her. Everything was blurring pleasantly and she didn't know when they stopped dancing and the man was leading her out of the room. She felt the booze in her belly, the heat going down now to her crotch and feeling good there, like Mickey's fingers when he parted her bush and started to stroke her to open her up before they did it, and anyway it had been awfully hot in that room with all the people dancing. She was grateful to the black man for realizing she had to go. He was her friend. She let her head drop on his shoulder as he opened a door.

As soon as the door closed, his arms went around her. Like a thin, tall, dark toy bear, Penny thought with her eyes closed. She felt helpless but unafraid. She was Goldilocks leaning against this strong pole that was rocking her, rocking against her, rocking up against her so that she was drifting off to sleep and hardly felt her dress being lifted and the long fingers starting to explore her softness. Ted was doing it so gently, a feathery touch, it was part of the falling asleep, sweetly. It wasn't his hand there at all, it was soft music, soothing and spreading inside her like a lullaby.

"You're great," he was whispering ardently. "You're the greatest, honey." He was pressing her hand downward. The man's pants were open and Penny felt the skin of his hanging sex. Between his legs, it was his whole body she was feeling as her fingers, in her deepening sleep, went around his dream sex in this fantasy of tall handsome dark statues revolving hard under her touch. It was a dream and she wanted to stay asleep enjoying it, but the pressure she had been denying claimed her suddenly. She groped away in panic. "Laszhee's room! *Please!*" She saw the toilet thankfully, and fastened herself to the seat with her eyes shut tight in relief as the stream gushed forth.

Then she wanted to wake up, and something seemed very strange when she opened her eyes. It was hard to see clearly in the glaring light, but plainly the tiles were white, not pink! And there were strange-looking tubs standing on their ends. It began to penetrate. Urinals! *Good God, I'm in the men's room!* Despite her befuddlement, Penny O'Hara was electrified. It was, after all, a little girl's forbidden dream come true. Her first impulse was to scoot out, but dizziness slammed her back when she tried to stand. Her eyes were less blinded now, the room was coming into sharper focus. The urinals were somehow sexy-looking, and there was the black man urinating at the white porcelain!—a yellow stream flowed from the tip of his black thing. His eyes, shining hotly, were fixed on her. Penny sat stunned on the toilet in the open stall, thighs apart, fully exposed to Ted Watson's demanding stare.

She couldn't move, and her eyes were pulled despite herself to the black snake silhouetted against the white urinal. She couldn't stop the spasm of animal excitement it aroused. Her mouth flooded with saliva, like a reaching nausea, but this wasn't sick, this was—what? she thought in a panic—skydiving! being electrocuted! being buried in an avalanche of spiky feelings roaring down foreign, craggy mountains.

Penny's head was spinning so dizzily that she nearly fell from the seat. She shut her eyes, but the splashing sound from outside pried them open again. She saw his—body. "Body." Where had that word come from? she puzzled. The answer was in the white tiles, like the subway station she suddenly and crazily remembered. She had been coming home from school, and there had been this large black woman beating a short white man over the head with a shoe. The woman was shrieking, "He took his body out to me!" Penny had understood immediately what the woman meant. Her head started to clear with the memory, and guilt and anger cut through her head's spiraling. This was shameful! She tried to force herself up.

But the black man was there first, looming over a little girl lost in a nightmare. Penny wanted to scream, but she couldn't open her mouth. He was directly in front of her, his erection level with her face, his legs spread as if to straddle her.

Penny whimpered. The nightmare was real, was happening. She could hear her mother screaming at her, the way she had when she was a kid of twelve, home from a party with white grainy splotches on her best black skirt. She had been mortified then because, although she was innocent, she had really known what the boy was doing with his pumping hand and had watched with secret fascination. When he started to shoot, she had been astonished and put her elbow up to hide her eyes, as she had later warded off her mother's fists.

"Don't you know even the cleaner can't get that out?" her mother had kept screaming. No, she didn't know. And only long afterward did it occur to her to wonder how her saintly mother had come by that knowledge.

It was no time for rummaging back. This wasn't kid stuff. Ted Watson had his hands behind her head, pulling her forward. This was happening *now*.

Penny twisted her head so hard she heard her neck crack. She was in a whirl of churning emotions, sizzling with passions she had never felt before, and at the same time furious and outraged. She tried to struggle away, but she was farcically tangled in her clothes and fell back in despair. Ted kept saying, "Hey, take it easy. You don't have to do anything you don't want." The air was filled with his whiskey breath and she was choking.

"Let me out!" Penny cried.-Her turmoil was greater because something in her she despised did want this to be happening, wanted this man to pin her and do whatever he wanted to her, and she to him, wild and shameful and scream-free. She lashed herself: Was she just glands and juices? She kept pushing Ted away as he whispered in a hurt tone, "For Christ sake, I'm not gonna rape you. Jesus Christ, you come in the john with a man, what do you expect a guy to expect!"

Penny had no chance to respond. The outer door opened and there was a loud exclamation from Jock Rogers. "Hey, you son of a bitch, where I come from we lynch bucks like you!" There was a rebel yell and a drunken laugh. "But let's all play cozy house instead!"

Penny was horrified to see the man's hand on his zipper. The fight was savage. Ted Watson went after Rogers with drunken roundhouse swings. Rogers feinted and ducked wildly. It was a ridiculous grotesque, a circus of clowns battling. Penny was shaking with fear, yet she wanted to laugh at the sight of the two penises, one black upright, the white one limp, both bobbing and swaying between the zippers as the men flailed at each other. She felt cold sober, revolted at herself for getting into this situation no matter how plastered she had been. The office Christmas party! She had heard tales, but nothing like this! If it were happening to someone else it might even be hilarious, but it was happening to *her*— these two grunting, sweating, drunken hulks wrestling like swine. If either of them put a hand on her she'd scratch his eyes out, she'd grab his thing and twist it off the way she'd once seen a geek do with a chicken's head in a movie.

Suddenly there was vomit in Penny's throat, and she didn't try to stop its spraying out. It splashed both men. Good! Revenge for my black skirt, *all* you louses! They stank, every three-legged one of them! The alcohol spew made a high arc, spraying the men again. Served them right, she grimaced. They were regarding her dimly, panting in their own fog of liquor, frustration, and bruises.

Penny shoved Jock Rogers hard to get him out of her way. He slid and bumped into Ted Watson, who lost his balance and went prancing on the vomit-slippery floor until his feet flew out from under him and he skidded into one of the urinals in a sitting position. Rogers jerked the valve and howled with laughter as water cascaded over Ted Watson, sitting supine in the flow. Penny remembered other Christmas tableaus—of angels, tinseled trees, candy canes, toys, and the crèche.

Crying miserably, she made her way across the men's room. At the door she flung at the two of them, "Put your dicks back in your pants, you pricks!"

She heard Phil Reynolds say gently, "You can't go home like that." Penny accepted his hand like a child and followed him from her desk. At his bar he dampened a towel. She felt it cleaning her dress, stroking over her breasts. To her heavy-lidded eyes the big office was hazy and comforting. She was safe now, away from the boors, with the decent man.

"We could do a better job if you took the dress off," he was saying. Penny shook her head fiercely. She still couldn't bring herself to speak. As long as she was silent, she remained a little girl who had skinned her knee, run to her father for help. One word spoken would turn her into grown-up Penny O'Hara in the unthinkable situation of a man like Philip Reynolds cleaning her puke. She squirmed with self-disgust.

"Hold still," Reynolds ordered.

She'd have to quit now, no question of that. How could she ever face him again, to say nothing of Ted Watson and Rogers. Tears ran down Penny's flaming cheeks. Served her right. What had the Sisters always said? "If only it was as easy to pay for mistakes as it is to make them!"

"I mean it." The strong voice came muffled through the misery that kept closing Penny's eyes. "Can't get you cleaned up this way." She felt his fingers pulling at the zipper behind her neck. "Don't worry, I have a daughter almost your age," he was laughing. Of course, Penny knew. She had met Selma at the award dinner. She bent her head, eyes still shut tightly, an obedient daughter.

Reynolds' hand was soft on her shoulders. How could one man be as wild as he had been earlier in the afternoon and so kind now? How complicated people were. She could be engaged to Mickey Connor and yet be standing here with practically a stranger taking off her dress. If she opened her eyes she would see the man viewing her in the bikini panties and flimsy bra she had worn for this day. Penny's arms crossed her chest primly, and she shivered with the cold of her shame.

She didn't see that Reynolds had turned to spread her dress along the bar and wasn't even glancing at her.

"Never mix champagne and Scotch," he said.

Penny pinched her arms white. If Phil Reynolds knew what had really happened, he wouldn't be trying to put her at ease. He'd be sending her to walk the plank. Still, he had gone hairy himself, hadn't he?

"I guess you're not used to heavy drinking," Reynolds kept up a conversation over his shoulder. "Now this ought to dry pretty fast over here."

Penny found she could mumble one choking word. "Thanks."

"It'll get you home decently, at least."

The girl cried to herself suddenly, "I don't want to go home!" Not to Mickey's gravel voice and his big paws, not to her mother's scolding. I want to stay here in this beautiful office forever, Penny prayed silently. She opened her eyes to take in the modern elegance once more, and realized that Reynolds, working on her dress, had not been seeing her at all. She felt cheated. It proved that to him she was, even near-naked, only another piece of equipment!

Well, wasn't that the way she had told herself she wanted it? she frowned. But standing behind Reynolds in her flimsy nothings, it was different. Penny pouted to herself protestingly—she was *not* just a dictating machine, a typewriter, a telephone. She had an urge to let her panties drop and call his name. She rebuked herself immediately. God, she must still be ape-drunk to think a thing like that! She swore a silent, fervent vow to the Lord. If only He would let her sober up, stop her heart racing at the sight of Philip Reynolds turning to her now, she would never touch another drop.

She could not help seeing his eyes move over her body, widen. She could not deny the thrill of his gaze. It was as if he had touched her flesh, touched her in her secret place. The wild music she had throttled burst out in her. Despite herself, her eyes gave Reynolds an openly bold invitation.

Reynolds was saying, "I'll get you some coffee" when, her eyes locked to his, Penny moved to him deliberately. It was one motion, her fluid step and her arms lifting around his neck, the murmuring sound of her surrender, mindlessly searching for his tongue with hers.

Reynolds felt himself swell. For one surging moment he thought how it might be to lie with this enticing girl. But she was drunk, clearly. The Penny O'Hara he knew would never behave this way. He'd have to be even sicker than Duncan Talbott thought to take advantage of her.

Reynolds tried to move away, but Penny pressed herself against him tightly. His body had its own response, he could not deny his full erection. He realized that Penny must be feeling it against her nakedness. He heard her gasp, and saw that the sensation was inflaming her past all discretion. Her hand moved at once to touch him. As her fingers went around him, squeezing hard, his body shouted that there was no reason to stop. Penny wanted him. It was a day when everyone forgot inhibitions. From long experience, he knew what had gone on outside all afternoon. Why not him? O'Hara was inviting him more and more passionately with her wet lips, her panting breath, her rising breasts, and her fingers at his crotch shuddering hot new desire through every nerve of his body.

But he put his hands on her shoulders and nudged Penny away. It was up to him, old enough to be her father, to take charge. His own flaring demand gave him no excuse; it would be as bad as molesting a child. With all his will, he went to the door, saying, "I'll get that coffee." He was out of the office before the tears of loss and mortification welled up in Penny's eyes.

When Reynolds returned, Penny was gone, as he had half expected. Maybe it was because he was getting old, but he had seriously considered cutting out the Christmas party and giving toys to a kids' hospital instead. People should be home trimming Christmas trees, not playing stink finger in the stockroom.

Well, he should be home too. He'd leave soon, just have one more drink to get his heartbeat back to normal and slow the wheels Penny had started whirling.

He sat in the rocker drinking and thinking. He'd finally found a great secretary and she'd had to get herself smashed. He'd bet that Monday she'd resign, he knew the type.

They did these things better in Latin countries—fiestas and carnivals where people could let off steam without a conscience-hangover.

God, how he had wanted to let himself go with those long legs of Penny and that great, hot body she had exhibited. He grew hard remembering. He owed himself another drink for resisting! Not many men would, he'd bet.

Reynolds toasted his maturity and with a barking laugh, boozy around the edges, told himself he was a fucking—no, a *non*fucking—idiot. In his imagination he could see Penny again, standing just there near the desk, gorgeously nude in her bra and panties, with the heavy dark bush frankly visible. He could feel the youthful breasts and hard nipples that had been waiting for his hands, his mouth. He could visualize the smooth young thighs curving over his back and locking him with their secret, moist heat in steaming, lush, rocking desire such as he had almost forgotten.

Reynolds gulped his drink and poured another to drown the image.

As he filled his glass, he started to chuckle, recalling a story he had often heard his grandfather tell—the grandfather with the yarmulke, the pious watery eyes, and the wound on his Jewish face from the day when his daughter married Clarence Reynolds.

The story was from Russia—or Poland. Reynolds could never get straight where his mother's family had come from. They hadn't seemed to know themselves, and he had been too young to make sense of the strange names, Latvia, Galicia. An-y-way, as his grandfather would chant in a singsong cadence, the story concerned a certain Shmuel, an immigrant house painter who one day without warning tumbled off his scaffold to drop several stories and break his legs. For some reason, this was said to have taken place in Montclair, New Jersey.

The painter's partner, visiting the injured man in the hospital, asked how it was possible for such a thing to happen to a man experienced already over twenty years. Shmuel explained as follows:

"Years ago when I was a young man in the old country, I had to travel a long way one winter night. My sled got lost in a terrible storm. Thank God, through the blizzard I saw a light. An inn—"

His partner interrupted, "Excuse me, but I don't see the bearing on your falling off a scaffold in Montclair, New Jersey."

"If a person will listen, he will understand. So to make a long story short, the innkeeper's daughter is opening the door. Everybody else was fast asleep. I see a girl? Like Marilyn Monroe, only more so! She gives me to eat and takes me to a room. I'm so exhausted, I fall down the bed a dead one. But all of a sudden is a knock. Who? Marilyn Monroe! Only now she is got on like a nightgown, you could see through it from Minsk to Pinsk—and what a 'Pinsk,' believe me! Only I couldn't keep my eyes open. She asks would I like another blanket? So she brings and tucks in and she's patting me here and there, but I only want to go to sleep, so good night.

"I am falling asleep like a baby, is a knock again. Who? Of course. 'Sir, I brought a hot brick for your feet.' So she puts, and again is with tucking and patting, and my eyes is closing like stones from exhaustion from the storm. I tell her I only want to sleep, please. But in a minute she is here again, a glass tea maybe I want? I tell her I appreciate but no thanks, again—"

Once more the partner cut in, with exasperation. "All right already! So what is this to do with Montclair, New Jersey?"

Shmuel spoke indignantly from his bandages and traction: "On the scaffold last week I was remembering that night and I realized what a stupid *yold* I was, and my head started to turn around so dizzy I fell off the scaffold!"

Well, God knew, Reynolds spoke to his empty glass, his own scaffold was shaking enough in storms of his own; it didn't need another shove from Penny O'Hara. No way. About Penny's invitation he felt, not like Shmuel, but like a *man,* a man who had done the right thing.

And a man who ought to stop drinking and head for Connecticut.

As if reading his thought, the radio's Christmas music was interrupted by an announcement that the snowstorm had closed down train travel to Connecticut.

Christ, he'd better see about a room at the Yale Club before they filled up.

Then the phones to Connecticut were jammed, of course. When he was finally connected, Helena said that of course she understood. Her voice was the same gray neutral tone it had assumed since the "accident" with Selma, but there was a touch of pique in it when she added, "Too bad for the girls you couldn't have left the party while the trains were still running."

"I wasn't at the party, damn it! I was working!" Unfair of Helena to dig at him when all he had done was turn down the most beautiful lay in town! He didn't intend the eruption that followed, but a match was at the fuse and the bomb went off, outside his will, as it had with the clerk that afternoon. "Goddamn it, Helena, *I* have a fucking business to run here! Don't you think I know the fucking tree is waiting?"

He knew how the foul language sickened his wife. He didn't want to talk this way, but an unstoppable force kept Reynolds shouting thickly, "It's not my fucking fault the fucking trains aren't running!"

He heard the telephone click off but his precipitate need for violence was so compulsive that he kept shouting into the dead instrument. The part of him that knew he had slid into drunkenness again was drowned in the boiling anger of a surging righteousness. *What did they all want from him?*

He drank again, and his irascibility took the form of an intoxicated exchange with himself. He had intended to reach home in time. It wasn't his fault it was snowing. He *was* a damn-fool Shmuel for not taking what Penny had offered! The real trouble was that men like him were caught in the Trap, with a cap T. The Trap was Wife-Children-Family-Obligations—work your balls off to care for *them!* Need *Men's* Lib!

The fact that Helena had come through with needed money didn't change the fact that he was Caught, cap C. To be Caught was to feel the way he was feeling now—contrite and lousy because he wouldn't be home this Christmas Eve where society said he was *supposed* to be.

Men like him were Caught because the feeling of blame, of culpability, of criminality, was inside themselves. Conscience was the steel of the Trap. Step off the straight and narrow by a quarter of an inch and the jaws were sprung—your conscience fractured your heart.

What the hell was his sin that he should be feeling so guilty now? He had drunk too much, yes, but it was the holiday season. He had started out on the wagon, but things had happened one after another. Was he supposed to get home on snowshoes now?

But he'd had no right to talk that way to Helena. She didn't deserve it, no matter how justified his own anger, irritation, and annoyance with her unfairness.

He saw what he had done, all right—taken out his hidden frustration over Penny! Didn't need a psychoanalyst to see that! Okay, he'd call Helena back, apologize.

But the lines were busy, and Reynolds fell asleep instead.

When he woke with a start at a suddenly loud "Jingle Bells" on the radio, it was after ten. The night was black outside, and his head was pounding with the enormous amount of whiskey he had consumed. He remembered dimly that he was supposed to call Helena and went, staggering, to the phone. At his desk his eyes were blurred and he had trouble seeing the numbers. His hand was shaking above the dial, and he suddenly realized with a surge of excitement that he wasn't calling Connecticut. Instead, his finger was doing the old thing that hadn't happened for a long time—the forbidden act was taking place by itself, without any bidding from him. Instead, he felt like someone else watching from a distance, but it was his own heart that was hammering with a sudden, accepting current. He was drunk enough, distressed enough, salacious enough—whatever enough it took—to watch the dungeon cover lift, and to welcome the monster that waited in the fathomless depths of his murky blood-ocean. It was aroused now, red-eyed and growling in the tidal wave that swept over his head. The monster that not even Duncan Talbott suspected was stretching and grunting its long, avid hunger, a livid irresistible force, callous to any pain, swifter than any guilt, greater than any strength Reynolds owned to contain it.

The dark power rushed up to conjure the lurid, heart-smashing image of Penny O'Hara naked. The rogue in Reynolds exulted. His face was distorted as he arranged his handkerchief over the mouthpiece. Ah, the exquisite delight of the furtive game, the promise of the phone ringing now in the Brooklyn apartment, echoing the wild ringing in his head, the single-minded emptying out of everything from consciousness but this riveted, unspeakable, dirty joy. He was engulfed by his feral, long-starved hunger.

When Penny O'Hara answered, there was a split second of sanity when Reynolds nearly put the phone down, but Penny's unsuspecting "Hello?" brought an immediate, overpowering erection, and a plummeting surrender of all reason to the seething lava out of his sclerous volcano, as Philip Marcus Reynolds began, from his luxurious Madison Avenue office, in his masked voice, with his left hand already pumping away, to whisper his obscenities.

Part Two

"Through abysses unproven
And gulfs beyond thought,
Our portion is woven,
Our burden is brought . . ."

—Rudyard Kipling

4

Penny dropped the phone as if it were on fire. Alone at the small Christmas tree with the last of the ornaments dangling from her startled hand, Penny stood staring with unbelieving eyes. The lunatic phone call had shattered the stolid familiarity of the room. As if for reassurance, Penny looked around quickly at the framed Jesus, the fading beige sofa with the lace doilies, the worn Morris chair. The one painting was a brown copy of The Angelus, faded into the green-brown walls. She had never felt the contrast with the office more sharply, remembering the Mirós, Picassos, and Calders with their pulsing forms and colors. You realized suddenly how much you wanted *that* kind of security when something out of the depths came at you, that phone call like a black-gloved strangler prowling the night. Penny shuddered. She had been upset and humiliated enough by her lapses at the office party. Now she was shaking physically.

Her mother shouted from the kitchen, where Mickey and her father were drinking beer, "Who was that calling, Penny?"

Penny found her voice. "Nobody, Mom. Wrong number." She had heard about obscene phone calls, of course, but never dreamed one might happen to her. The language of that slimy bastard! His heavy breathing had pictured the disgusting thing he was doing to himself. What kind of maggot was that?

There ought to be some way to catch them, Penny thought fiercely. She'd prosecute all right, see the degenerate jailed like the filthy hyena he was.

But if you did get them arrested, Penny considered bitterly, judges let them off. The papers were full of "poor victims of society." Well, if she had this weirdo in front of her, she'd show him sympathy and rehabilitation—a hard kick in his family jewels!

Was everybody in the world sick? Ted Watson and Jock Rogers in the men's room? For that matter, she herself, getting so drunk at the party!

Penny put the decorations down and flopped into the Morris chair. Who was she to call anyone names? If she was honest with herself, wouldn't she have to admit that in her secret heart she had wanted to keep her eyes on Ted Watson's penis!

Her quick impulse was to deny it, but she went on to ask herself with genuine perplexity whether other women—maybe *every* woman—would not secretly feel the same way.

And wasn't it true too, just between herself and the Christmas tree, that something in her had stirred at the telephone call, had not wanted to hang up?

The holiday lights reflected like hot snake eyes on the telephone, eyes of evil, challenging her to admit her responses. The way she had felt that other time when she was eleven-twelve, the neighborhood boisterously celebrating the first visit of a pope to the Americas, Pope Paul VI in New York City to address the United Nations. And the drunken grocer, Mister Sullivan, had invited her to his storeroom for special cookies, only to fumble his pants open and take out a surprising, thick candle, offering it conspiratorially to her trembling hand. He had put his finger between her young girl thighs and nudged past her panties to her secret place. He had stopped at once when she had given a pale scream, and she had flown out, safe.

Safe? It still lay in her. People had dark cellars where things like that lay for life. Rotting rats. She had never told a word of that stink to anyone, not to her mother, not to Father Doyle.

That *stink?* Wasn't the stinking fact that she had been intrigued, had *wanted* to touch the man's— Though naïveté and guilt had alchemized into panic and fleeing then, hadn't she really yearned to stay and let Sullivan do the whispers of the kids in the alleys that she didn't understand?

The man's finger on that spot between her legs had made her shiver with an unbearable delight! *That* was the truth, like it or not!

But no, her mother's voice and Father Doyle's had roared up her spine to blow away Sullivan's whisper to save her soul. But, ah, later, alone in her bed, the little girl shook with the strange new excitement she had known that afternoon, and she let her fingertip explore the spot the man had discovered. Awakened, it would never sleep again. Just the touch of her finger, tentatively, to the little moist tip down there. Penny, the child, had screwed her eyes shut, the better to pretend that all she was doing was easing an itch.

Then all at once, as if her mother had crashed open the door and flashed a light on her, she heard the words she had never comprehended before—her mother's repeated admonition at bedtime: "Remember, Penny, God can see through blankets!"

And the Lord thundering: "You have no itch! You are a disgusting, evil little girl and you will roast in Hell!"

It was too late. It was impossible for her to take her hand from her inflamed, hungry clitoris. Flames had poured from her crotch and were wracking her immature flesh. She did not even know the word Desire, but her back arched of its own accord and her thighs pumped up and down convulsively. With her blanket lifting like a tent, her spread legs had flung into the air with primordial female instinct. She was lost in her discovery of her body's lust. She had rubbed her little nipples with one emboldened hand, and touched, smoothed, and caressed the erected bit of heaven uncovered down there until she had plunged into the delicious warm ocean of her first, shivering orgasm.

Then, she remembered, it was as if she herself was the hot red sun sinking at the beach, its heat sizzling the water into gorgeous plumes of sunset as the sea cooled and extinguished the fire in her belly, and the blanket dropped back and she could sleep.

Sighing with the memory, Penny left the Morris chair to finish trimming the tree. What had brought all that back? The liquor, the party, her shame before Phil Reynolds, the obscene call? Tossing strands of tinsel over the branches, Penny decided that, yes, everyone else *was* hypocritical. Other women would have the same responses she did, no matter what they denied. At least she was trying to be gut-honest with herself, which was more than could be said for most from what she observed.

Penny felt better, and baffled.

She was glad when Mickey came in from the kitchen. His big, oil-stained hands cupped her breasts possessively. "How about we shove off for a while?" Penny had known how tonight would have to end. Well, she would go with Mickey to his place again, to find out for sure how she felt. It was only ten o'clock, she'd be back in time for midnight Mass. They'd tell the folks they were going for a holiday beer with Dorothy-and-Bob, whose recent marriage was a comfort to Penny's mother, contentedly watching her own daughter walking the approved path with Mickey.

In his rented room, Mickey stood with his pants drooping, as so many times before, but tonight Penny noticed how the beer was going to foam-rubber on him. The lean, athletic boy to whom she had given her first kiss at fourteen had a beer belly at twenty-one. It was what she and the nice Brooklyn girls like her had been led to expect. "That's life. Grim and bear it," as her father said when he couldn't get work. But on this night, Penny was allowing herself to compare Mickey with another man. Despite their years together, despite Mickey's fair hair above the quick Irish face and the puppy eyes she had thought she loved, he failed. The room's patched curtains, the linoleum floor, the peeling walls, the noisy traffic outside, all failed.

Penny stopped with a stocking rolled halfway down. "Nice" girl? What was she doing in bed with a man before they were married? Yes, these days most of the kids made out when they were engaged and even Father Doyle looked the other way. But what did it make her now if she didn't marry Mickey!

It was a monstrous thing to be thinking.

Penny had a sudden nausea again, as real as the afternoon's. She jumped up to go to the bathroom down the hall, but Mickey leaped at her unexpectedly, yanked her panties down, and slammed into her body at once. He was huge, and hurting because she wasn't ready. His heavy beer smell choked Penny as he heaved above her. She twisted to get her head away, and he mistook it for passion. His thickness humped away harder. He was pitching and neighing like a horse with its tool in a filly.

That was it, Penny moaned. He would ride her like a horse for the rest of her life. Maybe the girls talking Women's Lib at the office weren't as foolish as they sounded.

Despite her unhappiness, Penny felt her body responding. Somewhere in her she seemed to own a contrary, rutting animal that Mickey's very brutishness drew from its lair. He was making her come as his choking cries grew faster. It was the crescendo of his motorcycle engine when they took off. He was a hot piston exploding in her, racing her loins to their motor-roaring finish.

The moment Penny genuinely believed she might leave Mickey was the instant of his jolting, molten shafting of tire-screeching triumph as their orgasm sent them flying together *and it wasn't enough!* It wasn't enough for her.

Penny lay quiet, panting. Nothing had ever been so clear.

It was like being lifted to the summit of the highest mountain in the world, and the height itself was magnificent, *but the view was all desert,* as arid and sere as the moon, nothing alive, nothing of the green and flowers she had now known in another place. And wanted. And could, she felt suddenly sure, reach out for on her own.

Catching her breath, Penny thought how everything would be so simple if she had only remained like Dorothy across the hall. Dorothy, who wore tight sweaters to show off her big boobs and then hung a cross around her neck as a "Keep Off" sign. Anyway, since Madison Avenue, Penny knew a secret about Dorothy and Bob, a fact that changed everything for her. They thought they were just beginning their lives, but Penny saw they were already at the end.

Literally, nothing new would ever again happen to Dorothy and Bob. They'd had their baptism, their toilet training, their first haircut, their first playing doctor, their first day at school, their first communion, their first doubts of the dogma, their first silencing of the doubts, their first graduation, Bob's first hard-on, Dorothy's first falling off the roof, their first dance, their first necking, their first ball game, their first liquor, their first trip away from home, their first paycheck, their first (terrified) fuck. Now they would have their first baby and first grandchild and then their coffin and funeral, their first and last.

Not for hers truly, Penny told herself in a quickening avalanche of rejection as she took in Mickey's bland, satisfied countenance. It was a cud-chewing face! She wanted more.

On Monday morning, there were flickering grins and knowing smiles all around the agency. How he felt himself, Reynolds wasn't sure. The trains had finally run on Christmas morning. He hadn't taken another drink though liquor flowed everywhere over the weekend. The town kids had come caroling in the snow, and had brought sentimental tears to his eyes as his daughters joined in. In a terrible contradiction, he had kissed his girls with the same mouth that had called Penny.

How could he be the same man?

Another trouble was that his "safety switch" wasn't working. Before this, every phone call he made had been wiped out of his consciousness, utterly. Apparently, there was a switch in his subconscious that erased the memory as a tape is erased—simply not recorded any longer. Before, Reynolds was able to pick up and go on *as if the call had never happened.* He wondered now whether that was how it was with people like the Nazis. Might a man be up to his elbows in human blood all day, then rinse off when the whistle blew, go home and kiss his family austerely and sit down to dinner as if he'd been driving a bus or selling shoes?

Penny interrupted Reynolds' thoughts, coming in with his morning coffee. Reynolds was sure Penny had not recognized his disguised voice, but without the switch working it was strange and disquieting to face a woman he had phoned that way. The girl seemed as troubled as he was, but that was probably just too much holiday, Reynolds told himself. She had been a mess coming into his office after the party. Still, he felt himself perspiring and flushing. What in God's name would he do if she *had* recognized him!

But Penny O'Hara seemed lost in thought as she said a noncommittal good morning, and went back into her office. Reynolds stretched with relief. He was glad he felt a prickle of fear. It might keep him aware of how degenerate those miserable calls were—he was like a masked rapist, no better. He had given himself points for not taking Penny in the office, and then done worse! Well, with the drinking stopped now, really stopped, that ugly, incomprehensible weakness would end too, he told himself. He scowled at his telephone. *Never, never again!*

In her office, Penny was thinking of Ted Watson rather than Reynolds. Ted had passed in the hall with a stack of morning galleys, and said immediately, "Hey, I apologize for the hairy stuff, I've been getting my kicks smoking grass and I'm not used to drinking. Okay?"

"No!" Penny said, unforgiving.

Ted searched her appraisingly, taking in the neat gray suit and the ruffle-collared white blouse she had selected for the occasion of her last day with Philip Reynolds. His smile stayed confident. "If everybody took that attitude, nobody'd be talking to anybody in any office in New York today."

It occurred to Penny that Ted might be afraid she'd tell Reynolds what he had done. She hadn't intended to, but let him wonder! Would do him good after the fantastic liberty he had dared to take with her! In the new morning, in the bright, yellow corridor lined with ads, it was doubly incredible.

Her language had astonished her. "Fuck off, Ted!" she had told him in her new Madisonese.

His dark face had sparkled into a grin of fellowship. "Right on, baby! You're getting the idea." He had turned cheerfully into his office.

It made Penny more certain she could never face him or Jock Rogers again.

At Philip Reynolds' desk, she said, "I have to give you my resignation." It came out tearfully, not starkly as she had rehearsed it.

Reynolds heard what he expected, with chagrin. He made himself smile and speak lightly. "The first rule of an office party is to forget it the morning after. Did you get home all right?"

"Thanks to you," Penny said shamefacedly.

Reynolds thought guiltily it was he who should be ashamed. In any case, he wasn't going to lose this girl. He straightened at his desk and gave an order. "I've considered your resignation and torn it up. Now let's get at this stuff." With a gesture of finality, he waved at the piles of papers stacked along his desk.

To Penny, it suddenly seemed possible to stay. She was standing where she had been undressed and somehow she didn't need the ground to swallow her up. Penny's last doubts dissolved when, a little later, Reynolds gave her a batch of galleys to conform. She understood that she had to transfer his final corrections to the "Master Set." Her eyes sparkled. She had memorized the standard printer's marks, hoping this day would come. He hadn't called one of Lillian's girls, as always before, for this responsible duty! You bet she'd stay, Penny vowed with excitement. *And* register for school at night. *And* make up her mind about Mickey once and for all.

Later, galleys flapping in her hand, Penny headed for the proofreading office. Passing the nameplates along the corridor, she saw in her mind's eye: PENNY O'HARA. She might be just a pipe-dreaming Brooklyn nobody, she told herself happily, but maybe not.

Penny hugged the galleys to her chest and half giggled. She would tickle her new plans and see if they laughed—hone them and see if they shaved—tune them and see if they sang. The one-liners were her own, a game she delighted in playing although Lillian had told her they were passé on Madison Avenue. With triumph Penny made up a fresh one on the spur of the moment: She'd give her plan a badge, and see if it arrested anyone! That might be even better than the old standard, "Let's run it up the flagpole and see if anyone salutes!"

Lillian Schuster asked, taking the galleys, "Who sent you roses this morning, kid?"

As she returned to the corner offices, Penny's exhilaration was tinged with anxiety. Was it really possible to contemplate not marrying Mickey Connor without being struck by God's lightning? She could already hear her mother and Father Doyle crying up to "Jayzus Keeroist" to bring the errant daughter back onto the straight, prescribed path she was so feckless to be leaving.

5

Over the New Year's holiday, Reynolds surprised everyone. Instead of pleading work, he took his daughters ice skating. Instead of reading alone, and imbibing, he played bridge with neighbors. On the Eve, the one night of license for everyone to get plastered, he drank only a little champagne, and made sure Duncan Talbott saw that he could take two glasses and stop. He mixed the punch, as always, for Helena's traditional New Year's Day reception, but took only soft drinks for himself. It was his first sober holiday in years. He enjoyed it, it was better than being in the too-familiar fog. With a private, soft drink toast to himself, Reynolds observed the neighbors' skeptical looks, Helena's wondering and pleased glances, Duncan Talbott's silence. Reynolds considered that not even his wife and best friend really knew him. The Christmas lapse was past. Duncan would have to swallow those scaly names he had called him.

As the days passed, the old protective system seemed to take hold too; the obscene call to Penny was fading out of consciousness. A week into the new year, by the time the phone call came from Rodney Graham, the memory was obliterated.

The two agency heads held their luncheon meeting. Reynolds left with a sense of elation. As he had hoped, Graham had extended clear feelers about a possible merger. It might be because he realized Reynolds was a sure bet for the Acadia business. It might be because the two young agencies fit neatly in terms of accounts and talents. Whatever the reason, the prospect was as electric for Reynolds as he had anticipated. The Graham bankroll would make his long-dreamed projects viable. He'd be able to pay Helena back sooner than had seemed possible, and that would be a very great satisfaction. He'd have the chicken and the egg in one basket for the first time in his life, and that would be merely wonderful!

Aspera ad astra. Aim for the stars. That's what his mother's parents had dreamed when they reached for Chicago from the shtetl in Middle Europe. They never expected streets paved with gold, only the opportunity to walk freely and to work hard. If one studied and labored faithfully, and didn't expect free lunch, a person could not only aspire to the stars but reach them! Believe it or not, you could even hope to become a star yourself instead of a pogrom corpse.

That was a country! his Jewish grandfather used to hallelujah. America! Utopia!

The first conference with Graham and his people went promisingly. Graham's troops could move right into the extra space Reynolds had taken. There were only a few duplications in accounts, unimportant. The lawyers and accountants frowned, cautioned, drafted provisos, and piled up giant fees. "If it works, we don't need all that gobbledygook," Reynolds joshed, pleased. "If it doesn't work, all the paper in the world won't make any difference. We want a deal, not a lawsuit." Graham reservedly agreed.

Helena's hopefulness transformed the atmosphere at home. With his business pressures now to ease, Phil would be his old self again, Helena was certain. The girls caught her confidence. Their eyes cleared and they stopped leaving the room when their father entered. Sharing his own excitement with them, Reynolds was a different man, no longer haggard and ridden.

But there was a bomb waiting to explode. At a meeting a month later, with final papers on the table, Rodney Graham's senior adviser asked a matter-of-course question he had taken for granted while details were negotiated.

"I assume," he said, "that the new agency is to be called Graham and Reynolds."

"Hell no!" Reynolds erupted, his voice flashing with astonishment that anyone might possibly have thought differently. "It's 'Reynolds and Graham' or forget it!"

When Reynolds called Helena to report that the deal was off, she had no sympathy. "I think you're just terribly wrong, Phil!" she told him flatly. "You wouldn't expect a company to be called 'Reynolds and Rockefeller,' would you?"

It struck an exposed nerve. Reynolds knew he was being bullheaded and irrational, but he had become physically ill at the sound of his name following second, and at the thought of the stationery and advertising that would give Graham top billing. For the first time, Philip Reynolds understood what Duncan Talbott meant by "compulsive." There was no way his mind and reason could overcome the repulsion and disgust of "Graham and Reynolds."

After dinner that night Helena pleaded, "After all, it is Graham's money. Everyone will know *you* are the brains."

Talbott watched Reynolds suspiciously. "You're booting the chance of a lifetime, Phil."

Reynolds sat rocking impassively by the fire, not looking at his wife or his friend.

Helena went on, "I know enough about the business to know this too. You don't turn your back on a man like Rodney Graham without making him look a little foolish, and I would guess that's one posture he doesn't like very much. You're not just losing a terrific partner, you're making a dangerous enemy."

"Screw them all," came dully from the rocker.

"Because you're the great genius, eh?" Talbott challenged, probing.

"I didn't say that."

Talbott continued, making no effort to mask his exasperation now. "Genius excuses everything. Drinking. Violence. Screwing up a deal another man would be on his knees thanking God for!" His voice altered. "Well, Phil, maybe I'm the only one in the world who knows you well enough to say this to your face, but I call it damn false pride, and a fearful mistake." The man's nose had to be rubbed in reality.

Helena saw her husband bristling, and tried to keep her tone neutral. "Didn't you tell me that Graham's family has a lot of clout in Detroit?"

"Rod doesn't play dirty pool," Reynolds grunted. "In fact, I expect to hear from Acadia tomorrow." He kept rocking, his jaws steel.

"I'm just suggesting you ought to consider—"

Abruptly, Reynolds was rushing out of the room, shouting at his wife, "You'll get your fucking money back, damn it!"

Helena winced, and Talbott put his arm around her shoulder as she reached for her handkerchief.

The next morning, Penny was watching over Reynolds' shoulder as he edited an ad with his red crayon. She lifted the phone on the first ring, and handed it to Reynolds with a tingle of personal excitement. "It's Detroit!" Everyone in the office knew Reynolds was waiting for this call. Penny was glad he was not motioning her out of the room.

She heard Philip Reynolds veer from his hearty "Hello, Jim!" to surprise. "A delay? What's happening?"

There was a long pause. Reynolds' voice tightened. "I'm afraid I don't understand, Jim. A week ago, you told us we were as good as in. Frankly, this sounds like a runaround to me." Penny saw Reynolds fighting forward in his chair. "Next week? I'll be glad to fly out right

now if there's anything more you need from us." A pause. He sagged.
"Okay, then. We'll wait to hear from you." The call ended.

"Damn!" Reynolds breathed loud enough for Penny to hear.

"Trouble?"

His answer was to break the red crayon in two and drop the pieces
into the ceramic tray near the telephone. Without warning, his hand
flew after the crayon and swept the tray off the desk. It did not shatter,
but ashes spilled all around, and the crayon pieces were like clots of blood
on the silver blue carpet.

A week later, when the chairman of the board of Acadia Motors called
again, Reynolds signaled for Penny to listen and take shorthand notes.

She heard Reynolds clear his throat. "Hi, Jim. What's the good
word?"

"I'm calling you personally, Phil, because I want you to know our
people think your team put on one hell of a show."

"Yes?" Reynolds' tone went dead.

"On balance, our people have decided to go with Graham's shop at
this point in time. They feel that Graham himself has more experience
and financial depth to handle our requirements."

Reynolds pressed uphill. "Jim, since we made our pitch I've rebagged
the central concept and I'd like to show it to you personally. It can knock
the socks off your competition, domestic and foreign. I'll grab the next
plane and—"

"Sorry, old boy. I'm afraid it will have to be our loss."

What had Helena reminded him about Graham clout in Detroit?
Reynolds' mouth was burning as if he had chewed pepper. He wouldn't
give up. "I just want to lay this one copy theme on your desk!"

"It's out of my hands, Phil," came the smooth, executive rationalization. "The boys downstairs changed their minds."

Reynolds made another attempt—flatter the man's gargantuan vanity.
"Jim, nothing is wrapped up so tight *you* can't change it. They know
who's boss."

But it was no use. The phone was syrupy at his ear. "I will keep you in
mind for some of our other stuff, Phil."

Reynolds wanted to say, "Your lie shits," but made the appropriate
noise instead: "I want you to know I appreciate your consideration."

"And, look, we won't announce for a couple of days, give you a
chance to feed back how you'd like it done. We understand your
position, and we'll track along with you."

"Thanks, Jim. That's very decent of you." Within the context of being dumped on, it was. Reynolds hung up. To Penny his face was a death mask, set in a grotesque smile. "Well," he said, "you win some and you lose some." And when you lose, he thought, no matter how unfairly, no matter how visibly the knife is sticking in your back, in business there is no court you can go to for justice. There had been nothing underhanded, nothing illegal.

You took a wave like this broadside and prayed you wouldn't capsize.

Penny saw the tragedy in Reynolds' eyes even while the unnatural smile stayed frozen on his lips. With a small gesture, he indicated her notebook. "We won't need that, Penny." She went out quickly. She understood that he wanted to be alone. It wasn't her place to have the impulse to hold his head against her breasts to comfort him.

Reynolds turned to stare at the telephone. No, this was something to tell Helena face to face, and face her "I told you so." He had been wrong. Dead wrong. No pun. Dead. It was at your peril that you offended Graham power, as she had astutely observed.

The triple irony of it was that he had just come up with a zinger to kick off the Acadia motor car. Reynolds took out the writing pad he always carried and studied the three words he had jotted down on the train that morning.

Yes, they stood up. The line sang. He'd caught just what the moguls had challenged him to come up with—a slogan which, by its brevity, would bespeak the compact car, and at the same time would subliminally imply status and class in a small auto. Three words. Reynolds contemplated them critically again, and nodded ruefully. They had the music and the magic. The slogan was a banger, grabber—Phil M. Reynolds, award-winner, at his best.

He tossed the page on his cluttered desk. "Frame it," he told himself bitterly. "It'll remind you not to box out of your division."

He looked toward the bar.

No. That would solve nothing.

He leaned back with his hands behind his head, squinting at the ceiling. Hell, he wouldn't be the first or last to go bankrupt, to "escalate down," as a young copywriter had quipped at a recent staff meeting when a client cut its budget.

Helena and Duncan had been right, he reflected with self-accusation. He had been indefensibly arrogant, and self-indulgent. What unholy difference did it make if Graham's name went first? Was it worth the disaster he now faced? Why had he had to run his act even though he knew the cost?

Reynolds knew the answer. He had been helpless. He would have to make the same decision again even now—though now he was beginning to get a new message from the vise tightening around his balls: If he could blow Rod Graham's deal for the sake of his billing, he ought to be giving serious thought to what Duncan Talbott, M.D., had been advising. It was a sick thing, no doubt about it.

Helena had invited Talbott to dinner, and the girls were helping and chattering in the kitchen. They were surprised when Reynolds walked in early. When he saw their pleasure, he determined to say nothing until Helena and he were alone. There was no reason to deflate their high spirits for a while anyway. He said he had a headache and would nap in the den. At his desk inside, he covered pads of paper with all kinds of figures—letting Jock Rogers go, subletting the space at a sacrifice, pulling in every possible notch on the belt. The numbers were implacable. There was no way he could keep afloat without an immense injection of fresh money. Aside from the Acadia collapse, the agency was paying out for preparatory work on three big new accounts. It would be months before their ads ran on TV and in print, and the clients would not pay the agency for months after that.

Helena wanted Talbott to stay after brandy, but he had noted the restiveness in Reynolds and made an excuse about having to stop at the hospital.

Reynolds let the whole spool run out to Helena at one time: the loss of Acadia, the new cash-flow predicament. Without Acadia, he could forget banks entirely. His wife listened sympathetically, clearly upset. "What can we do?" she asked. "We've used all the trust income this year. I suppose I can ask the lawyers about—what do they call it?— invading the principle again—" Her tone bespoke her doubt.

"No. You're right," Reynolds said finally. "I'm bushed." He started upstairs. "I'm going to fold, maybe we'll get a miracle idea in the morning."

Helena called to his back, "We can always sell the house. The way land's gone up, it ought to be worth a great deal."

Reynolds turned to wait for her, his eyes resentful at the injustice he felt. "It may come to that."

As they went upstairs together, Helena squeezed his hand. It was impossible to think of leaving this place. "You'll manage, Phil. I'm sure of it."

When he was in the bathroom, Helena heard a sound in the hall.

Selma was standing in the doorway. In her long white nightgown she looked like a small child, but the anxious look she turned to her mother was more than a child's. "Are we going to sell the house?" Her voice was trembling on the edge of tears.

Helena pretended astonishment. "Where in the world did you get that idea?"

"I heard you say it to Daddy!"

"You must have misunderstood. What were you doing out of bed in the first place?"

"Daddy's business is in trouble, isn't it?"

"Everything will be all right, and it's no reason to eavesdrop." Helena led Selma back to her room.

The girl kept hold of her mother's hand. "Daddy looked so *old* tonight."

"Not to worry," Helena said. "Nothing is going to change. Now get your beauty sleep. I won't be able to pry you out of bed in the morning." Helena smiled at Selma reassuringly, and kissed her good night.

Instead of returning to her room, Helena went downstairs again, wanting to be alone. Selma had been shaken. She could understand that. How impossible it would have seemed if she had ever sensed a possibility that she might not live all her childhood in the great house in Silvertown, Georgia. Even now memory brought back the sense of security, the certainty of permanence that made it possible to grow and change herself. Even this house, which she loved, could never mean what her father's house had been, sanctuary and haven, as this was for Selma, Dorothy, and Midge.

In her mind's eye she could see the white height rising stately behind the Greek columns of the wide porch in antebellum style. The spreading lawns down to the river were the measure of the world. Everywhere her father's booming laughter. Everything needed was on that land and in that house, with its servants and elegant rooms for every purpose.

As everything needed was here in this modern elegance in Connecticut, as long as there was love.

No, Helena corrected herself with a sigh. That was sentimental evasion. The family needed more than love. It needed Phil to be sustaining them with pride and his own fulfillment, and it needed an economic base that now was tilting disastrously. She had no doubt that Phil would land on his feet, but a splitting apart of their lives in the meantime could be agonizing, especially for the girls at their ages.

She had been rash to promise Selma there would be no change.

Children were tough and resilient. If it came to push and shove, she and Phil would be honest with them.

Helena stood by the mantel staring at the cold ashes. It might not have to come to that. There was one possibility she could try, distasteful as it would be. It came to her that it was no accident that her mind had gone back to Silvertown; it had been a way of gathering the purpose she could not avoid. She might yet be able to keep her promise to Selma.

It took a long while before anyone answered the phone. It was late and they would be sleeping, of course. That itself would help them realize she was facing a crisis.

The butler answered. She did not recognize the voice; he must be new. She was sure of it when he dared to speak querulously, as old Devon would never have done.

Her brother came on finally, hacking worse than she ever remembered.

"It's Helena."

"Well, for Jesus' sake! What do you want?" he snuffled. Cold, abrupt, distant.

"How are you, Gordon? How is Marylou?"

"You didn't call at this hour to make polite conversation!"

As usual, he bulldozed into command, thwarted the way she wanted to approach her question. She could see him at the phone, hulking and fat, with a fierce frown on his red-burned face. How different from her father, whose size and power had been tempered with an inner gentleness. Maybe you could own kindness only when you had proved your power was your own and not off a silver spoon. Before she could respond, her brother, Gordon Weslie, continued, "What is it, Helena? Has your splendid husband got himself into difficulty again?"

Helena checked herself. There was no point in showing her vexation. She had known he would try to make her eat crow. Let him spew his poison as long as there was a chance he would help in the end. She said, warily, "The girls and I—"

He cut her at once: "Oh, we have nieces, then?"

"As it happens," Helena lied, "I was just about to write to you all about our coming down for Easter, the girls and myself." Not Phil, of course.

"Well, well. What a coincidence."

His sarcasm pricked her as nastily as if she had been telling the truth, Helena recognized morosely. For a moment, she thought of hanging up. Her family had become strangers to her, and she to them. But Phil was in trouble and she did not have the luxury of anger. She spoke carefully. "Gordon, we have an outsize opportunity up here to swing a big deal. I could use the trust for capital, but I thought you might be interested. We'd pay high interest for a loan . . ."

He cut her again, with a coarse laugh. "Even if it were a good bet, which I doubt, the answer would be nix-no, dear sister."

Helena nearly sobbed out of her frustration. "I don't understand you at all!"

Gordon Weslie's voice went greasy with false brotherliness. "I take this view for your own good. My dear girl, I know you don't believe it, but it may, belatedly, open your eyes to the trash you married. And you know, Marylou and I keep praying you will come to your senses and leave that man and bring the girls down here to us where they belong."

A laugh close to a snort escaped Helena. "You're out of your mind, Gordon Weslie!"

His voice went mean again. "So you still haven't discovered your husband's off his rocker? Do you know he broke a man's nose at the office during his Christmas festivities?" He asked the question with loud satisfaction.

"You're out of your *mind!*" Helena repeated, stunned. Was Gordon making this up to upset her further?

"Probably cost you a helluva lawsuit, dear. But I suppose that doesn't bother Philip Marcus. He figures he'll be bankrupt by then anyway. You know their sort always has an ace up the sleeve." He went right on. "And by the way, dear, has he told you about Penny?"

"Penny?" The onslaught was so unexpected and relentless, Helena was lost in confusion.

"We are given to understand that she is quite a tasty dish. Apparently somewhat eccentric in her tastes, which include a frolic with an uppity Nigra . . ."

"What *are* you talking about?" Helena managed to ask.

The telephone gargled with his laugh. "About a trollop in the men's toilet with a rascal Nigra! At your husband's liberated office party! Do you want the toothsome details?" Gordon Weslie simpered.

Her brother had to be making this up, Helena told herself. How would he, eight hundred miles away in remote Silvertown, know what was happening on Madison Avenue? Yet he somehow knew Phil had a secretary named Penny, a black man on staff.

The voice pushed louder into her perplexity. "It seems that pretty Penny then wound up naked in your husband's private office. With mistletoe over his couch, I have no doubt!"

"You are disgusting!" Helena cried.

"And you are still the swamp fool!" came a blast that made the phone quiver at her ear. "And more the damn fool if you think we'll ever help that scum with a single copper!" There came a crapulous laugh. "Direct him to the United Jewish Appeal or his nearest rabbi."

Helena was sickened. "Disgusting!" she shouted, through tears of rage and loss.

The receiver was slammed down at the other end.

Defeated, Helena went slowly upstairs to bed. She was grateful that Reynolds seemed to be sleeping soundly. He needed whatever rest he could get. She lay down carefully, to avoid disturbing him, and apologizing in her mind for Gordon's foulness.

Her brother's crackpot stories echoed in her head. Penny O'Hara and Ted Watson! The nice Catholic girl in the *men's room?* And Penny naked in Phil's office? It couldn't be! If by some insane chance something like that had occurred, how in God's name could Gordon be aware of it? A light flashed. The night at the award dinner when she had commented about his accent to Phil's new man, Jock something—hadn't he said he was from Georgia? *Silvertown!* It was possible! They made auto tires there, and he was involved with Detroit. She would have to tell Phil, alert him he might have a rotten apple in the shop. If there was to continue to be a shop . . .

Helena woke out of a frightening dream. She was lost in a swamp. The Spanish moss was a mass of snakes hissing around her. She opened her eyes wide to take in the haven of her bedroom, and reached across to touch her husband for comfort.

She sat up fully awake with the realization that he wasn't there. It was half-past four. He wasn't in the bathroom. Had one of the girls called? Was Selly still disturbed?

Helena found Reynolds in the den. He was slack-jawed by the dead fire. An empty bottle lay on the floor beside his chair. His eyes were nerveless as he turned to her step. Well, Helena thought, this was one night he did have a right. She was grateful he had drunk quietly so the girls would not know.

"Come back to bed now, Phil. We'll talk in the morning."

"No," he said. The softness of his tone was ominous. Helena feared it was the quiet before a storm. She saw that he was jarringly drunk now, and she glanced apprehensively upstairs. She didn't want the girls to see their father that way again. "We have to do what we have to do," he was saying sibilantly. "We can't take any more out of the trust. And we don't want to sell the house."

"Absolutely a last resort."

Reynolds' words came heavily. "There is another 'absolutely last resort.' Your brother."

Helena said, "That's useless. I—"

Reynolds cut her off. "That fat pansy got you so buffaloed you can't even call him?"

Neither of them saw Selma peering at them from the top of the stairs.

Helena's voice rose in new frustration. "I'm trying to tell you I *did* call Gordon! It wasn't any use, of course." All it had gotten her was crazy tales about Penny, someone's broken nose.

"No use, of course!" Reynolds' storm broke. "Nothing would make him happier than to see us sell the house, see me go down the drain, the chicken-livered son of a bitch!" With a wild motion that released the fury he could not contain, Reynolds recklessly swept the whiskey bottle up from the floor and flung it across the room, where it shattered against the brick wall opposite the fireplace. Broken glass ricocheted and slashed Helena's cheek. In her shock she did not realize what had happened until Selma flew down to her, crying, "Mother! You're bleeding!"

Reynolds did not see or hear. His explosion had yanked open a hidden valve and all his pent-up wrath escaped. He slammed around the room in unrestrainable madness. Making insane, protesting noises, he over-turned lamps, crashed a chair against the bar, sent ashtrays flying. He was oblivious to the blood-soaked towel Selma was pressing to Helena's face, blind to Dorothy and Midge who came to the stairs clinging to each other in terror. He did not hear Selma's hysterical instruction to Dorothy: "Call Unc Dunc to get here right *away!*" or Midge wailing, "Stop it! Please stop it, Daddy!"

None of them could know that he, continuing his raging destruction, wanted to fall to his knees and, weeping, beg their forgiveness, make them know it was someone else whipping him to this ungovernable virulence. There was no way he could make it clear to them, or himself, that, like a drowning man seeking air, he wanted to stop going down but could not find his will.

In the morning, with Reynolds asleep under the drug he had been given, Duncan Talbott came in to check Helena's face. The girls, though still upset, had gone to school. The maid had packed after one look at the ruined room. "Living with a loony ain't my idea of pleasant, ma'am. Who knows what that man'll take it into his head to do next?"

Paying the woman off, Helena had thought grimly that she couldn't blame her. This time Phil had gone beyond any excuse in whiskey or circumstance.

"It looks fine," Talbott said, dressing Helena's wound. "Feel all right?"

"It stings now and then." Helena asked anxiously, "Will I have a scar, Duncan?"

"Nothing a touch of makeup shouldn't fix easily for the time being." Talbott started to close his bag.

"Coffee?"

The doctor looked into the woman's hurt eyes and sat down.

"I need your advice." His clear blue eyes told Helena she could always have anything he had to give. She turned from them as she said quietly, "I'm thinking of taking the girls away. For a while anyway—"

Duncan Talbott said at once, "I believe if you leave Phil now, Helena, it will be the end of him."

Helena answered out of the agony of the night's upheaval. "It's not just me, Duncan! Selma was so upset, I had to give her a tranquilizer."

Talbott said, "I know how patient you've been. But Phil needs you."

Painfully, Helena demanded, "How about what *we* need?"

"He didn't mean to hurt you."

"That makes it worse! What *will* he do next?"

Talbott said, "I believe he'll listen to me now."

Helena looked at Talbott uncertainly. "I don't want the girls to see another rampage!"

"It may be worse to break up their home."

"He's done that already!" Helena was gray with new hopelessness. "You know how long it's been coming on. Last night was the last straw."

Talbott wanted Helena's head on his shoulder, to give her the respite he wished her instead of this suffering. He told her instead, "If Phil goes into analysis now, you ought to stand by him. I don't say he won't be trouble. But look, if he'd been hit by a truck, you'd be with him, wouldn't you? Phil has got a runaway truck in his gut—"

Helena's cup rattled in the saucer. "I'm tired of it always turning out to be my fault somehow!"

"I didn't say that."

"My responsibility, then."

Talbott found it difficult to meet Helena Reynolds' eyes. "Well, that's what many people take the marriage vow to mean."

"God, Duncan, the last thing I need this morning is a lecture on marriage!"

"You'd be saying it yourself tomorrow if you left Phil now."

Helena needed her handkerchief again. "You know me too well, don't you?"

"I think last night was a crisis." Talbott had difficulty keeping his voice professional, wanting more than ever to let the woman glimpse his feelings for her. But he had long since made his peace with his position. It was intolerable for him to admit the spark of hope that had flickered when Helena spoke of leaving Reynolds. He went on as clinically as possible. "Phil has been putting his own handwriting on the wall, to prove to himself he does need therapy—"

"What if he still won't accept?"

The doctor said mournfully, "Then I suppose I'd have to agree with you." He could not deny the spark's flaring again, and despised himself for it.

Taking dishes to the sink, Helena said, "This isn't the first time I've thought of leaving." She touched the bandage on her face. She did not believe there would be no scar. She was filled with a female abhorrence of the man who had marked her. It wasn't simply vanity; something deep within violently rejected the physical assault, accident though it might be. Her body was the space in which she had her life. Its violation was felt as a threat to her very survival, especially coming from the person she had trusted more than anyone in the world. "I just can't deal with Phil anymore, Dunc. I'm going to take the girls up to Vermont for a week anyway. I need time to think things over."

"Fair enough," Talbott agreed.

Helena's next words came very deliberately. "I doubt it's ever going to work with Phil and me again. I'm not just angry with him. I hate him." Her head was high. She had as much right to her emotions as her husband had to his.

Talbott reached for his bag. There was nothing more he could say.

6

Philip Reynolds sat in Duncan Talbott's office with his head bowed. He was listening to his friend through a shroud of shame. The enormity of what he had done was an unscalable wall blocking the future. He would not make it worse by proffering lame excuses. The loss of Acadia Motors didn't matter. The agency didn't matter. Since there was no way he could expect Helena or his daughters to accept his obvious instability nothing had any point or purpose any longer.

Talbott smacked his palm on his thigh. "It's a *good* sign if you feel you've hit bottom, Phil. A decision to go into psychoanalysis usually comes when *you* feel your life is out of control."

Reynolds thought despairingly that Duncan was righter than he knew. He would give his life to halt the violence that had taken him over, body and soul, and hurt Helena.

"I've talked to an old teacher of mine, one of the best men in New York. His name is Aloysius Kohn."

Reynolds stiffened. Why didn't he simply agree? Why was there a storm of resistance in him blowing Talbott's words away? This wasn't just idle conversation now. He knew in his heart that Talbott was right. Everybody and his uncle was in analysis these days. What the hell. He said slowly, "I guess so."

Three words. A decision that might transform his life. Where were the sound effects, the thunder and lightning, cymbals and drums, trumpet fanfares?

The doctor came around his desk with his hand outstretched. "I'm glad, Phil. I can't tell you it won't be rough, but I can promise that you'll be thankful in the end."

Reynolds turned away, hating the temptation of self-pity that offered him solace, and despising what had to be said. "It's expensive, Dunc, and it's touch and go at the agency, as you know."

"I thought that was taken care of."

Reynolds shook his head. He was tempted to pour out the story of the empty bag he was holding. But that would sound as if he were trying to escape the full blame for hurting Helena. He could at least save whatever shred of self-respect was left.

Talbott's hand tightened on his shoulder. "I'll be glad to let you have whatever you need."

Reynolds covered the strong hand with his own. He could not speak because he was embarrassed to let the generous Scotsman hear how close he was to tears.

Dr. Aloysius Kohn wanted to accommodate his friend and former student Dr. Talbott but he would not have an opening for a month.

To his amazement, Reynolds was disappointed at the delay. Something in him had geared up expectantly, and he was let down. He was impatient to prove to Helena that his remorse was more than words. She had made it clear that she was remaining in Connecticut only on condition that he sought help. They had agreed he would move to the Yale Club in the city until they both could determine the future. Reynolds was not sorry to get away from the accusing bandage on Helena's face. His daughters' frightened eyes were a painful reminder of what he could only see as his obliquity. Taking his suitcases to the city, Reynolds felt relief as well as the guilt that was now a constant stone in his chest.

But the changes in his life generated a new energy in him. At the office, he set about a salvage operation feverishly.

The first to go was Jock Rogers, together with his extravagant team. Rogers was not displeased, told Reynolds that Graham had made him an offer he was about to take in any case. He added that he was going on vacation first—back home in Silvertown, Georgia. He made a point of saying he understood that Mrs. Reynolds had folks there, quite a coincidence! He'd be glad to take regards back with him. Reynolds wondered why he had never noticed before that Jock Rogers had a shit-eating smile, but he was hardly listening. The resignation was a relief in every way; it even meant the agency's merit rating for unemployment insurance tax wouldn't be loused up.

Lose some, *win* some. The dice seemed to have warmed up for Reynolds. The conglomerate for which his building was named made an acquisition and needed more space. Reynolds was able to unload his white-elephant floor at three times what he had pro-forma-ed. The two prospects who had enthused at the award dinner came aboard.

The Acadia news made waves, of course, but they remained small. Old clients stayed on, without questions. The ship had rocked, but it was far from sunk. Between reduced expenses and the loan Duncan Talbott had insisted on, Reynolds could buy enough time to turn around.

There were other developments, of a kind that moved Reynolds deeply. Ted Watson came in to say that Rod Graham had offered him more money but he wasn't leaving. And he did not ask for a raise. The same thing happened with an indignant Lillian Schuster.

Reynolds was in no mood for patting himself on the back, but, alone at night, he considered that such loyalty could not be bought. Through all his waffling, he must have done some things right.

Penny watched and listened sympathetically, kept quiet, and worked with all her strength. She was at Reynolds' shoulder when he wanted her, invisible when he didn't. No hours were too long, no demands too onerous, no piles of dictation too high, no traffic jam of galleys, TV boards, layouts too tangled. Penny read proof with Lillian, handled traffic for Ted, checkerboarded models and photographers, ran props for commercials, mother-henned account executives, and charmed clients. She had no time for school, and congratulated herself that she was learning far more on the job.

Best of all, she smiled herself to sleep in her dingy Brooklyn bedroom, her overtime pay was hastening the day when she could finally tell them all, father, mother, Mickey, and Father Doyle, that she was moving into her own apartment and her own life, reborn, in Manhattan.

It was her craving for learning everything from media-buying to public relations—the whole shmeer, as Ted Watson put it amusedly— that permitted Ted to make his peace with her. That, and the news she had heard of his refusing Rod Graham's offer. In the print department, Penny realized how superficial her knowledge was. She still had only a glimmer of typography, for example. Fascinated, she watched the art directors as they sketched a layout, made a comp, which mocked up the complete ad, specified the type for style, size, position, and laid in headlines, Veloxes, or photostats, of the art, and got back crisp repro proofs from the typographer. Overnight! It was magic. So was the way the bullpen artists could overlay colors for pre-press facsimiles so that Reynolds, Watson, account executives, and clients could double-check advertisements before the expense of printing. Ted even had a special light booth with the same lamps used by the agency's engravers and printers, so that everyone could examine color proofs under identical illumination to match every nuance.

Penny was enormously impressed by the super-care taken every step of the way. People reading an ad never suspected these jeweled mechanics.

And that was only on the production side. At the same time, Lillian Schuster and her department were checking facts, spelling, grammar, and there was even a lawyer Penny hadn't known existed. He reviewed every line and photograph for regulations of the Federal Trade Commission and other legal requirements. There was one hell of a lot more to advertising, it became clear to Penny, than getting a bright idea for a line of copy!

She nearly crowed with happiness when Reynolds looked up from his desk one day as if he had never seen her before, and bestowed the best award she could wish for: "You're coming on, Penny." Her cup overflowed when he added, "You look good in blue—" He was aware she was alive, not just a faithful robot! Penny thought with a new excitement that Reynolds' eyes seemed to hold the same interest she had noticed from men turning to admire her on the street lately.

After the Acadia torpedo, Penny had another reason for her growing admiration of Philip Reynolds. The shop had buzzed with dire predictions that the erratic boss would surely flip his lid now. Some employees started scouting for other jobs. Instead, Reynolds had come on like a general regrouping his troops. There was no sign of drinking or temper. Little by little, a new sense of confidence spread through the agency.

Reynolds called Helena to tell her things seemed to be getting back to normal. Her voice remained unreceptive. She said she was glad, nothing more. He felt it wasn't up to him to suggest returning to Connecticut. Dr. Kohn wasn't available yet, so he could not say he was in analysis, if that's what Helena was waiting for.

Actually, Reynolds had started self-analysis, using two books by Karen Horney. One was *Neurosis and Human Growth,* which Duncan Talbott had been urging on him for months. The other was *Self-Analysis,* which Talbott had specifically recommended against.

Reynolds was impressed by what he took to be Dr. Horney's central thesis—that every human has a healthy center striving to fulfill itself, exactly as an acorn "wants" to become an oak tree. Sometimes, though, the seed falls in poor soil, or the young plant is struck by storms that stunt or sicken it. Nevertheless, the potential for health persists. The task of psychoanalysis is to cleanse the poisoned soil, and to bring the stresses under control, so that the natural sun and air can nourish the seed and encourage its proper growth.

It appeared to Reynolds that it didn't matter in what *way* his own life had gotten messed up. What mattered was his new conviction that he desperately and urgently needed to escape the whirlpools threatening to drown him in a mysterious sea. And as he read the Horney books, he became convinced that he could save himself without any Dr. Kohn.

And it worked, Reynolds rejoiced. His new self-possession grew each day. At lunch with clients, he could let them drink the martinis while he nursed a vermouth on the rocks. When he felt his violence button being pushed, he resisted with a basic insight Horney gave him: Through the years he had created a Glory Image as a defense against the pains of his early life. It was a false, inauthentic self, but he had been defending it with all his might, mostly with immediate, flaring rage at anyone or anything that represented a challenge to his inner "perfection."

The logic of it became beautifully clear to Reynolds, and he had never felt more in control of himself, more at peace. It did not occur to him that his answer was simplistic and superficial, even though that was the message of the literature he ransacked in his new explorations: Freud, Jung, Adler, Ferenczi, Bergler, Erikson, Kelman, Horney, Maslow, Perls, Reik, and others. They made him realize that the unconscious had a mind of its own and that there was a body of knowledge he did not possess, both theoretical and clinical, but Reynolds believed books were therapy enough for him, since his own disturbances seemed to him minor in contrast to real character deviations, such as homosexuality.

It wasn't that he was no longer hypersensitive, quickly angered, or that he was no longer tempted to drink and even to make obscene calls. The temptations seemed mild, their teeth seemed to have been pulled. Reynolds judged too that there are "good cycles" as well as vicious ones. As his conduct became less provocative, there were fewer occasions when others responded with actions that galled him.

On a clear, springlike Sunday in March, Reynolds arranged to play golf with Talbott. Clear-eyed and vigorous, though his swing was stiff after his long layoff, Reynolds made his case. He told Talbott confidently that his self-analysis had cured the inward agitations that had driven him to the drinking that had led to the disasters. He was getting all his monkeys off his back. Did Duncan, who had been seeing Helena steadily, think she was ready to forgive and forget?

Talbott studied Reynolds as his friend spoke. The doctor recognized the clinical stage his friend was passing through. It was a classical pattern, technically known as the "escape into health." It took place, typically, just when a person was on the verge of recognizing that he was truly ill. The threat of therapy was so alarming to the sick personality that it quickly fashioned an illusion of wholesome conduct. Frequently, neurotic symptoms literally disappeared. The gambit often worked: *Who's sick? Who needs psychoanalysis? Not me, surely!*

This could take place before formal analysis, as seemed to be happening with Reynolds, or during analysis when the neurotic personality realizes that its desperate and wily attacks and defenses are not deceiving or misdirecting the analyst.

Reynolds continued with what Talbott feared was coming. "Dunc, I appreciate your setting everything up with Dr. Kohn, but I don't need him now. I think you have to agree with that."

"No, I don't, not for a minute!" Briefly, Talbott described the escape phenomenon and what it meant, but he observed Reynolds' skeptical smile and knew he wasn't getting through. In the end he fell back to, "As your friend, I'm asking you to take my professional advice. At least get started with Dr. Kohn, you can always quit."

Reynolds answered securely, "This is one time you're wrong." He waved his club toward the tee. "Your shot, fella. Let's see a good one."

Saddened, Duncan Talbott addressed the golf ball. As the doctor looked to the distant green, he thought, "The hole is so damn small and far away, and the green is trapped so cruel." He sighed and drove a straight, smashing shot. In any case, he could advise with a clear conscience, "I think it would be premature for you to talk with Helena at this point."

Late one afternoon the next week, while Reynolds was out of the office, the receptionist rang Penny to announce that Selma Reynolds was outside. For a confused moment, Penny thought it was Reynolds' wife, then she recalled meeting his daughter, the sweet child in pink at the Waldorf-Astoria.

The girl came inside with a studied self-possession through which Penny saw the hesitancy of a child in an unfamiliar situation. It touched her, as it did when the girl tried to hide the braces that inevitably showed as she spoke, explaining, "My class is here for the Museum of Modern Art, and my teacher let me come to see my father."

When Reynolds had moved into town, Penny suspected something must have happened in Connecticut, but she put it out of her mind as none of her affair. Reynolds had said he needed to be closer to the store for a while, and only she was to know that he could be reached at the Yale Club in an emergency.

With his daughter now, Penny put on her best business manners. "I'm terribly sorry, Miss Reynolds, but your father is out. We expect him shortly." She knew she sounded like a telephone answering machine and disliked it, but there was something in the girl's eyes—almost an accusing look—that unnerved her. "Can I get you something while you wait? A Coke?"

"Anything like aspirin," the girl said. "I've got my period." Her directness took Penny aback. They were doing everything younger these days, Penny thought, before she remembered that her own first terrifying sight of the blood running down her thighs had come at around thirteen, with her father bellowing his disgust at her mother: "Get the bitch out of my sight, damn it to hell, you goddamn women!"

Penny brought pills and water. "You can use your father's office if you like."

"I'd rather talk to you, Penelope," the girl said.

It made Penny laugh, and the girl smiled back. "It's just plain Penny. What we used to call 'five cents plain' in my neighborhood."

"You're not plain," Selma said, her eyes never leaving Penny's face. Her smile broadened. "I like 'Penny' not being fancy." She went right on. "I liked you the night at the dinner. Like, you really talked to the black man, I mean, you weren't just being polite like some of the others. And you're not skinny-freaky like the chicks making believe they're fashion models when all they are is file clerks hitting the singles bars for hunks and dates!"

Penny said, "How old are you, Selma?"

"I'll be fourteen soon."

"You sound as if you really know your way around."

"Oh, shee-it." Selma startled Penny again. "One reason I liked you is I thought I could really be upfront with you."

"You can. I only mean that—"

"That I don't sound like out of Jane Austen. In my school kids have had abortions, almost everybody but me is on pot or stronger, so, I mean, let's not come unglued about where it's at."

Penny thought, Holy God, talk about your generation gap! Compared to this kid I'm Siamese twins with my grandmother! Aloud she said neutrally, "Okay, where's it at?"

The girl turned grim. "Can I really deal with you?"

"You can deal with me." Whatever that meant in advanced adolescence.

The girl hesitated. "I mean, we don't really know each other, and I have to get into some heavy stuff."

Penny was about to suggest that if it was school or boy trouble it had better be saved for Reynolds, but Selma was going ahead: "It concerns you."

"Me?" Another surprise.

"Look," Selma added coolly, "I wasn't born yesterday. I just want to know the score because right now things in my family are cruddy to say the best."

Penny was disquieted. "I don't know what you're talking about."

The girl's look was unbelieving. "You and my father, and why he goes nuts."

Penny stared at Selma dumbly.

"Last month he really hurt mother. Threw a bottle at her, tore up the room." Suddenly the girl was very young-looking, twisted with her effort to stop tears.

Penny remembered the Christmas party melee, but Philip Reynolds hurting his *wife!* Something was way out of line, and it was not her business. She said so to Selma Reynolds at once and with emphasis.

The girl angrily patted at her eyes. "But you're part of it! That's just *it!*"

Penny spoke sharply. "I don't know what you're talking about, and this has definitely gone far enough." If it sounded cardboardy and theatrical, okay. That was precisely how she felt. She couldn't cope with this kid.

What the girl said next came at her like a gunshot.

"You're sleeping with my father, aren't you?"

Penny was too stunned to answer.

"That's why everything's been so mixed up, isn't it?"

"Where in the name of God did you get that idea?"

The girl said, "Personally I couldn't care less, but it's a mess, and he's supposed to go to a psychoanalyst but now he won't, and my mother won't let him back home unless he does, and she's right." For all the bravura, the wet eyes were those of a youngster out of her depth. "Maybe he'll listen to you!" It was a plea of desperation that tore at Penny although she still did not understand.

"For Christ's own sake, you don't know what you're saying!" Penny took the weeping girl in her arms, feeling awkward, sympathetic, and at the same time put upon.

The girl sobbed louder. "I *heard* it! I was on the upstairs phone when my uncle told my mother!"

Penny was lost. "Your uncle?"

"About the Christmas party here, and you and my father."

Penny wondered confusedly whether Philip Reynolds knew she was supposed to be having an affair with him. Certainly he had given no sign. Her head was spinning. "I swear, honey, that's a lie!"

Selma Reynolds stepped back, drying her eyes. "I suppose I do believe you. I kept wondering how Uncle Gordon would know, anyway." A small smile came out of the clouded face. "I guess my mother doesn't really believe it either. Oh, it's all so fucking screwed up."

The foul language out of the childish mouth was bizarre to Penny.

Selma was thinking hard. "My uncle really hates my father. I guess he concocted the whole thing." She gave Penny a shy, appealing look. "I apologize, Penny. Thanks for being someone I could talk to."

Penny could smile. Something about Selma Reynolds went to her heart. The girl wanted an older sister as badly as she herself had often yearned for a younger one. She wanted the girl to know how she felt. She said genuinely, "Come and see me when you're in town. I'm just moving into a place of my own, and you're welcome any time."

"Outasight!" Selma gave Penny a hug, just as they heard the door to Reynolds' office open.

Penny pressed the intercom. "I'll tell your father you're here."

She was interrupted by a furious shout from Reynolds, then in succession a loud slamming of a door, and a heavy stamping down the corridor. The commotion brought Penny and Selma into the hall. They saw Reynolds hurrying toward the production department, viciously slapping a newspaper against the wall with every angry step.

Penny started after him, and Selma followed. They heard him shouting, "Where the hell is Ted?"

They saw Watson turn from the desk where he was reviewing a job with an assistant. His white sleeves were neatly rolled up on lean brown arms. Penny heard him say under his breath, "Here come some of Phil Reynolds' cringe benefits!"

Red-faced, Reynolds pivoted toward the offices lining the area. "Lillian, get your ass over here!" Reynolds fumed at the startled faces around the production desks. "Does anybody here know the English language, dammit!"

The frail woman came out of her cubicle blinking and immediately concerned. She said, "What's wrong?" and moved to Ted Watson's side. Reynolds flailed the air with the newspaper. To Ted, he cried, "You get rid of that typographer!" Then he raved at Lillian, blistering. "Since when don't *you* know the difference between 'ITS' and 'IT'S'?" He threw the paper savagely at her face. Thunderstruck, the woman ducked, but it hurt her. Her frightened cry was covered by Reynolds' ungoverned shout: "In the fucking headline!"

Knowing eyes widened around the room. This was the blowup they had been sure must come. It was turning out to be quite a show even for Philip Marcus Reynolds, The Fireworks King.

Lillian's finger was at her reddened eye, and she was biting her lips nervously as she squinted at the advertisement. "I'm terribly sorry, Phil. I don't know how it got past me."

Ted stepped in front of Lillian to take the blame. "Hey, Phil, *you* know it can happen!"

Reynolds raged, "Like a man slipping on a banana peel, it's funny only when it happens to someone else!"

Ted stood up to him. "Hell, nobody's perfect. That shop breaks its balls for us!"

Reynolds lashed, "That shit out of *this* agency! In 144 point in a full back page in the *Times!*"

Watson said, "Let's take this into my office and cool it off!"

Reynolds flipped Ted's hand away, and roared at the department, "This is a lesson for *everybody!*"

Penny, with Selma watching tensely beside her, wondered what lesson Philip Reynolds thought he was teaching. It certainly wasn't any of the things she was grateful for.

Reynolds was back at Watson. "That type shop is *out!*"

Ted defended his supplier. "They give us the impossible every day, dammit!"

"Would you rather I fired *you?*"

A shock wave went through the others, as Reynolds moved in front of Lillian Schuster. She was staring at the ad, still pinching her lips in an agitated way. Reynolds' sarcasm was loud and savage. "You're responsible for your department! If you don't want to be, take your Master's and shove it up your ungrammatical ass!"

As the woman began to weep helplessly, Penny saw Selma wince.

Ted Watson came in strongly, "It wasn't Lillian's fault, Phil! That damn insertion was so hot I probably whizzed it past Proofreading! I sign for it, man, don't lay it on Lil!"

"Everybody who gets paid in this goddamn department is responsible!" Reynolds kept blasting. Veins were bulging in his neck and forehead. His eyes were rabid. To Penny it seemed that the man's anger was bursting out of him like tires blowing on a racing car, skidding and spinning and unstoppable until the final, flaming crash. People were staring at Reynolds with disbelief. Selma dropped her head, trembling.

Ted's expression was open disgust.

Lillian was taking a deep breath. Her eyes blazed suddenly as she straightened before Reynolds and shouted, "You haven't any right to talk to me like that!"

Everyone was on her side.

But Reynolds had no ears, no brakes. "If you don't like it, you can lump it!" Horrified, Penny thought of the films she had seen of Hitler screaming hysterically. "Get the hell out to Rod Graham if you can't hack it here! *Now!*"

The woman's lost expression of incredulity tore at Penny. Lillian's whole world was being shattered by Philip Reynolds—over 'its' for 'it's'! Impossible to believe! Penny hardly heard Selma's horrified whisper, "Jesus God, he's as bad here as he was at home!"

In his blind fury, and with the knife of inner guilt slicing at his guts, Philip Reynolds did not see his daughter fleeing to the elevators. He stomped back to his office without another word to anyone. He grabbed at the pile of telephone memos on his desk and roared for Penny. She opened her notebook stonily.

In half an hour, he had cooled down. He sent Penny out with his nonstop dictation, and leaned back unhappily. Aside from Ted and Lillian, something else was fretting him. In his state he could not have been sure, but had Penny said something about *Selma* being at the office? What would she be doing in the city?

If Penny hadn't gone into a deep freeze—the first time he'd seen her this way—he'd buzz her and ask. But better keep things strictly on a work basis right now, he counseled himself. He couldn't blame her for her withdrawal. He had put on a stupid display, let the old volcano loose again. He gave himself a crooked, frustrated smile. Despite Horney!

Hell, Reynolds told himself, Lillian and Ted knew how he blew his stack about typos, hated them with a passion. All he had to do was call the woman, apologize, and things would be back to normal.

On the phone, he told Ted Watson he was sorry and to forget what he'd said about the type shop, everybody's human.

Watson said, "I want you to know, Phil, I damn near quit, and if any more of that kind of shit ever hits my fan again, I will!"

"I don't blame you," Reynolds said sincerely.

"Okay. I can get along with that." Reynolds didn't have to know his real reason for staying, Ted Watson figured.

Lillian was more surprising. When Reynolds urged that she above all should know he didn't mean what he had said, she answered: "Phil, did you ever hear the story of Toscanini and the French horn player? One time, rehearsing a Brahms symphony, the horn burbled. Now, every musician knows the instrument can phoomph any time no matter how great the player is. So when Toscanini yelled, 'Out!' the man was furious. Just before leaving the stage he turned and yelled at Toscanini, 'Fuck you!' And Toscanini yelled back, 'It's too late to apologize!' "

An hour later, Reynolds learned that Lillian Schuster had phoned Rodney Graham and been snapped up. He had booted a big one, it was a genuine loss, again due to the infernal demon that got on his back without warning and rode him like a horseman of the Apocalypse. It looked as if Duncan was right again—self-analysis didn't seem any answer. He had done an unforgivable thing to Lillian, who certainly deserved better. She was right to leave. And she was irreplaceable.

Except for a possibility that occurred to him in a sudden new configuration: He could promote Penny.

It might be an ace idea all around even though it meant finding and breaking in a substitute Girl Friday. It would benefit the agency by giving Penny a chance to spread her wings, and it would also be sensible to put some distance between them. Since he had moved to the city, their daily closeness had developed disturbing overtones for him. He often had an image of her as she had stood without clothes on the evening of the Christmas party. It would be better for her to be down the hall, in Lillian's old office.

But it would be the healthy part of valor to wait a while, Reynolds considered. Given Penny's sensitivity, she would probably balk at taking over "before the body was cold." Also, he'd have to lay some groundwork to avoid resentment among "Lillian's girls." He swiveled to look out the window at the blue spring sky, showing fresh and clear over the skyscrapers. Nothing was simple in business. Nothing was simple in him. It was impossible to believe he had blasted Lillian Schuster, of all people. He'd better see Dr. Kohn.

The gossips had plenty of fresh-squeezed lemon for their whiskey sours at lunch the next day. It had happened on Madison Avenue before, they commented cheerfully. A fella who could be cool when he was working for someone else showed his true colors when he got out front—for Philip Marcus Reynolds, diarrhea brown!

Part Three

"It so happens I am sick of my feet and my nails
and my hair and my shadow.
It so happens I am sick of being a man . . ."

—Pablo Neruda

7

At the reception desk in Dr. Aloysius Kohn's outer office, the woman was wearing a bright print dress and not a nurse's white uniform. Reynolds noticed it with mild surprise, until he realized that an analyst might of course have a secretary rather than a nurse.

"I'm Mrs. Wheatley. Dr. Kohn will see you in a few minutes." The voice came from a long, horsey, but pleasant Vermont face smiling a genuine greeting.

The waiting room was unexpectedly large, since no more than one person would ordinarily use it at one time, Reynolds observed. It was painted flat gray, including the ceiling. Even the one picture, a Käthe Kollwitz mother and child Reynolds recognized, was without color.

At the gray metal desk, glancing at Reynolds who was sitting stiff as a ramrod, the woman thought again how—*pitiable* was the word—most of the patients were at the beginning. No matter how successful and/or sophisticated they were on the outside, they came into this office with a trepidation and an embarrassment they could not hide from her experienced eyes. As Reynolds' gaze went around the room, she saw that he, like the others, was questing for some reassurance in this strange, and to him forbidding, place.

Sometimes she heard, even through the heavy door of the inner sanctum, sounds of weeping and pain. Her heart went out to the patients—young, old, men, women, children, tycoons, housewives. Happily, Dr. Kohn knew what he was about. It wasn't the diplomas and citations stacked in the closets. It was the clear-eyed, vital, happy look with which so many patients, though not all, said their good-byes at the end.

Reynolds kept his eyes on a magazine he wasn't seeing. He was sure the nurse—secretary—was staring at him. Who came to sit in this office? *Losers!* People like him who looked normal on the outside but were rotted within.

Who else of unquestioned position and status, like himself, made obscene phone calls—or enjoyed filthy fetishes, or molested children, or abused animals, or acted out the apparently unending depravities of civilized man?

Lord, Reynolds indicted in a sudden, concentrated protest, You move in mysterious ways Your uglies to perform!

Reynolds' stomach turned. How could he admit his telephone calls to *any* man, doctor or not? This was hopelessly impossible! He rose from his chair, determined to leave, only to be held by a buzzer sounding, and the kind woman smiling encouragingly. "Doctor will see you now, Mr. Reynolds."

When Reynolds stepped into Dr. Kohn's office, the first thing he saw was a door opposite. He heard a chuckle. "Yes. The escape hatch, some of my patients call it. There's a bathroom out there, incidentally, if you should need it."

Dr. Aloysius Kohn, in a large gray leather tilt-back chair, looked nothing like what Reynolds had expected. He was no movie analyst, no dumpy old professor with bulging eyeglasses. He was of medium height, clean-shaven, wore no glasses. Dr. Kohn looked like a stout, well-contented banker, with short, wiry gray hair. He was wearing a blue vested suit. His face was lined and, with its years, it held the appearance of endless patience. And self-confidence. Above all, he exuded a sense of no-nonsense concentration. It was heartening. This man, to Reynolds, seemed inured to every kind of human frailty. It might not be impossible to confess to that waiting face. If the time ever came. The unthinkable time!

"I'm pleased to meet you, Mr. Reynolds. Won't you sit over here today?" The doctor indicated a chair beside the desk.

The couch was across the room. To Reynolds it seemed a mile away. Foreign territory—spies, traps, black secrets.

Reynolds forced his eyes away, but could not look squarely at the doctor. Instead, he stared at the jammed bookcases that rose to the high gray ceiling, the piles of books and magazines spilling over on the floor, an assortment of nondescript plants on the broad windowsill overlooking Park Avenue. There were two photographs, both inscribed to Dr. Kohn. One portrayed the doctor as a young man standing proudly beside a bemused Sigmund Freud. The other was of a stately woman whose large, intelligent eyes sent beams of love, understanding, and encouragement across the room. Reynolds knew at once that this must be the Karen Horney he had been studying so avidly.

Dr. Kohn was saying, "We have a mutual friend in Duncan Talbott, I understand. One of my best students, but he preferred general practice."

Reynolds nodded and cleared his throat uncomfortably. He was leaning forward too brightly, had too eager a smile on his face, and felt preposterous. What was he doing in this office for the mentally disturbed? It was immensely clear to him now that what he needed was Alcoholics Anonymous and that this whole analysis shtik was just another of his devious ways of avoiding that one basic fact. Well, he'd sit out this hour—it might even be interesting—and then go his own way.

The words that came from his mouth, sincere-sounding, astonished him. "I'm glad you were able to see me, doctor. I know how busy you are."

The steady brown eyes were not to be denied. Or lied to. "Why are you here?" The same was true of the voice.

Because I make obscene telephone calls—

Instead, Reynolds said, with a laugh he intended to be disarming, "Because I find myself living unhappily ever after, I suppose." He recognized that the flipness was tension, and out of place. But what the hell, he wasn't on the couch yet, and wouldn't be.

"I know that you are in advertising, but we try to avoid sloganeering in here."

The sword had come out of the sheath. Well, he deserved it. He wished he didn't feel so hot and, somehow, combative. "There are a lot of reasons, of course. Actually, I suppose I'm here to find out why I'm here."

He wanted to sound as firm as when he gave orders at the office but he found himself trembling. Did everyone get this rattled talking to an analyst?

As if reading his mind, Dr. Kohn said coolly, "If it's any comfort, let me tell you that the first meeting is difficult for me too. But we'll both manage if you relax." The doctor smiled encouragingly. "Tell me what's on your mind just as it comes to you. Yes?"

"Well, there are two main complications. I drink too much. And I have a miserable temper that sometimes goes haywire." Reynolds was making a genuine effort to be totally honest. "I do things I don't really mean or intend or want to. It's almost as if somebody else takes over. Yes. That's it."

"Somebody else takes over."

"Oh, I don't mean split personality or anything like that. It's me all the way. Just that I can't stop myself when I want to."

"You can't stop yourself when you want to. Can you give me some examples?"

Reynolds told first about turning Rodney Graham down against his better judgment. He stopped. Next would have to be his violence. His gorge rose. He couldn't talk about those episodes—the whiskey that might have blinded Selma, the crazy fury that had broken the man's nose, injuring Helena and wrecking the den, the way he had blasted Lillian so unfairly, and lost her. Dr. Kohn was waiting.

"Well, as I said, I drink too much."

"How much is too much?"

Reynolds was irritated. This fella kept repeating, and wouldn't let *anything* pass.

"A couple-three at lunch, and before dinner, and maybe afterward doing some homework and watching TV." Reynolds would be damned if he'd start counting.

The doctor's expression said maybe he'd be damned if he didn't. "Every day?"

"I guess so."

"Let's add up the drinks in a typical day, please."

Reynolds said impatiently, "I told you—"

Dr. Kohn interrupted, but his voice was kind. "Here we tell it like it is. You said two-three at lunch?"

Reynolds grew red, more annoyed. Schoolboy caught out in a lie. He resented it. "Well, it depends." His voice rose defensively. "If I'm with a client, I can't let him drink alone. We'll have some drinks, and a bottle of wine." In his mind he had been adding up, and was astounded to realize how much he had been knocking back—counting his standard doubles, he often put away as much as a full bottle a day. He was finally able to say so to the doctor, who surprised him by replying, "That's good."

To Reynolds' raised eyebrows, Dr. Kohn added, "It's good because you realize you were ashamed to admit it. I'd like you to stay with that feeling."

Reynolds became excited. The spool was suddenly unrolling the way the books said it should. "Yes! And I didn't like being ashamed so it switched inside. I got irritated at the way you repeat things I say. I see how defensive I'm being!"

"Slow down," Dr. Kohn said unexpectedly.

Reynolds was disappointed, the wind knocked out of his sails. He had

expected applause for being so adept a patient so fast. This psychoanalytic continuum had a logic of its own, eye-opening and disconcerting.

Behind his desk, Dr. Kohn discerned the all-too-familiar pattern.
Philip Reynolds would, with every appearance of cooperation and logic,
try to spin away from every insight. Now, for example, it was necessary
to bring him back to: "You just caught a glimpse of how much you really
drink, suddenly *realized* it. So for the first time you begin to be in a
position where you can think about what it's doing to your head, your
business, your family, your liver. Do you see what I mean?"

Reynolds said carefully, "I think so."

"Our job together is to bring *everything* into awareness. Some things
will come easily, most will not. My point is that you can't deal with a
problem until you become aware of it—in the way I became aware of
hostility you provoked in me when you became resentful a minute ago."

Reynolds was taken aback. Hostility? Wasn't an analyst supposed to
be strictly neutral? Once more Dr. Kohn seemed to sense his question:
"It's the things that happen between the two of us as people that will be
most revealing. You'll react to me as a person, not just a doctor, and the
same with me to you. We'll be traveling together over some pretty
bumpy territory before we're done. If we're honest and trust each other,
the therapy will work. If we're not, forget it."

Dr. Kohn leaned across his desk and went on forcefully. "I want to
make one thing plain. Many people think psychoanalysis is a kind of
detective story in which we chase clues back to childhood and finally
unmask a villain. That's only partly true. We're not dealing with a
jigsaw puzzle but with feelings, mine as well as yours. *Feelings* are what
count in here. You won't fully understand what I'm saying for quite a
while, but it's the ground rule of everything we'll be doing together."

The rest of the 50-minute hour was spent in a review of Reynolds'
biography. As at the award dinner, Reynolds felt that the facts were
about someone else, not just concerning his career, but even in describing what he knew were the crucial years of his childhood.

Dr. Kohn opened his appointment book and said he could see
Reynolds four times a week. Reynolds was shocked; he had considered
he would be coming perhaps once a week, for a few months. Dr. Kohn
saw his silent question and answered it flatly. "Yes, you are that sick."
And immediately, "You leave through the back door, please." When
Reynolds, feeling numb, had the door half open, the doctor added in a
low voice without looking up, "And Philip, before our next session, give
some thought to the symptoms you were too ashamed to tell me about
today."

Reynolds' head jerked as if punched, and he turned scarlet. He left as fast as he could. In the elevator he decided categorically that he was not returning.

Dr. Kohn lifted the new notebook from his desk. On the cover Mrs. Wheatley had pasted a neat label: PHILIP MARCUS REYNOLDS. On the first page, Dr. Kohn wrote in a heavy script, "*Severe* alienation." Then, sighing, he muttered to himself, "Here we go again." The psycho-analysis of Mr. Philip Marcus Reynolds, Madison Avenue wunderkind, was going to be a balls buster for both of them.

During session after session in the quiet, book-lined office, Reynolds could not get comfortable on the couch. He was accustomed to looking at people when he talked to them. Typically, eyes shut, he would begin the hour dutifully by inviting associative images as he knew was ex-pected, and then find himself sliding into sleep until Dr. Kohn would ask, "Falling asleep?" Then it was a guilty jolt to Reynolds to realize he had indeed been dozing off. It annoyed him particularly this day because he had come in with a vivid dream, anxious to know what Dr. Kohn thought of it, and now he had wasted five minutes. At a buck a minute!

Reynolds urgently began to report the dream but, to his amazement and chagrin, his lips did not move. What the hell was happening? He fidgeted on the couch and tried to do what he was supposed to—turn his mind inward. He was grateful when Dr. Kohn prompted after pro-longed silence, "What are you feeling now?"

"Sleepy."

"Didn't you sleep well last night?"

"Yes. No. I don't know. I had this dream."

"Oh?"

"I've been trying to tell you but I keep falling asleep." Reynolds yawned. His tongue was thick and his eyelids kept pressing down. His mouth felt as if his lips were sewed and tied to his eyelids, the two pulling against each other.

He recognized this as the "resistance" the books made so much of, but he seemed helpless against it. He was experiencing its physical power.

Dr. Kohn prodded, "Tell me the dream, Philip."

No one called him Philip, except his grandfather on the Ohio farm, the gentle old man who always made him feel wanted and important. The prismed memory spilled over to encompass Dr. Kohn. You *are* my friend, Reynolds thought dimly. You want to help me. You're not sitting in judgment like my mother and father. His thought braked to a stop.

"What are you thinking?"

"My mother and father. That you're not sitting there ready to slap me down as soon as I do or say anything wrong."

"Right and wrong are a long way off for us yet, Philip. Stick with what you're feeling right now."

But Philip was up in his head again. "I've read that analysis is the process of turning psychological problems into moral ones." That had struck him as a profound statement. "Is that what you mean by no right or wrong at this stage?" Reynolds felt easier, in control.

"Let's skip the philosophy and get to the dream, eh?"

"Well, look, I'm mixed up." There was genuine confusion in Reynolds' voice. "First you tell me to say whatever is in my mind, and when I do you put me down."

The doctor said patiently, "You came here wanting to tell me a dream. You're going to leave this session having talked about everything but the dream. Doesn't that tell you something?"

The doctor's authority came through. Why *wasn't* he getting to the dream? Reynolds answered himself with an impatient gesture. Because he had a dozen questions about this whole damned analysis process, that's why! If Dr. Kohn would only answer his questions, and stop interrupting, he'd get to the confounded dream!

Dr. Kohn was saying, "I want you to have the responsibility of your direction here, but just now I will tell you two things. First, you are avoiding the dream. Second, and more important, you are not aware that you are avoiding it. That's what I would like you to try to feel now."

At this, a torrent started. With a big breath, Reynolds opened up: "There was a red ferry near the shore of a big lake. I'm swimming as hard as I can to reach it but I can't and I'm going to drown because now I can't turn back . . ."

Dr. Kohn made a note that Reynolds had plunged into the dream quite hysterically as a way of avoiding a confrontation with his resistance. That too would be a pattern until—unfortunately much later—Reynolds would understand that where there is resistance there are insights. And, usually, the greater the resistance, the more significant the hidden kernel.

Dr. Kohn leaned back and let his eyes close for a moment. It was all so damned complicated, so Freud-damned predictable, and tiring. And necessary.

"Then in the water is this naked girl, beautiful." Reynolds was slowing, speaking more normally. "I have to pass her to get to the ferry, but I'm naked too, and I have a—" Reynolds stopped, feeling a strange blush. He laughed at himself. He wasn't a child, and this was the office of a psychoanalyst.

"You have a what?"

"An erection."

"Is that what you always call it?"

"Well—a hard-on, I guess."

"All right. Seeing the girl gives you a hard-on. So?"

"She touches me. It. The—my penis."

"Your what?"

"My cock! All right?" Reynolds sat halfway up in vexation. "Aren't we talking scientifically in here?"

"You mean clinically? You feel clinical here?"

Reynolds shouted, "Okay, I said she touched my cock, my prick! I thought the important thing was the dream, and you keep interrupting me!"

"The important thing is why you are so angry."

"I'm not angry! I'm just trying to get this straight!"

The doctor answered imperturbably, "It would be better if you recognized how angry you are."

Reynolds slammed the couch with his fist, objecting, "I told you I'm not angry!" He jumped up. "This is a crock of crap!" He made for the door. "Charge me for the hour, please."

"If that's what you want. But you are even sicker than I believed." The sentence came so softly that Reynolds scarcely heard it, but its steel held his hand from the doorknob.

"What do you mean?"

"*You* tell me."

Reynolds turned, feeling flustered. "When I said I wasn't angry? Of course I was angry."

The doctor thrust, "But you insisted you weren't! And you meant it! In other words, you are quite out of touch with your feelings."

Slowly, Reynolds returned to the couch, suddenly very conscious of the sound of the doctor's pen at the desk. He lay down with mounting dissatisfaction. "I run a considerable business, you know. I deal with all kinds of people. I seem to manage all right most of the time. And here I am, flopping around like a fish when all I want to do is tell you my dream and all you want to do is discuss whether I call a prick a cock or a tool or a bishop or—"

"A bishop?" Dr. Kohn asked with interest.

"You mean *you* never heard that? Flog the bishop, for jerking off?" Reynolds roared with a releasing laughter. "I tell you something, doctor. It shakes my confidence to have an analyst who never heard of flogging the bishop!"

"Interesting figure of speech."

Reynolds contributed at once, "I suppose it has something to do with celibacy in the church."

"Now are we to have church history instead of the dream?"

"You don't give an inch, do you?" Reynolds grumbled. "Where was I?"

Silence from Dr. Kohn. Not an inch, indeed. The responsibility was his, Reynolds'.

"The girl starts playing with me and I—I had a wet dream." He couldn't deny his embarrassment. Suddenly he recalled his mother shrieking at him, pointing to stains on his sheet. "Wait until I tell your father! He'll teach you with the strap!" He had been honest-to-God innocent. That time. "First time in years." He was apologizing to Dr. Kohn as he had quaked before his mother. Idiotic.

"Well, the captain stops the ferry to watch me through a spyglass. I start swimming again, I can make the boat now. But all of a sudden I see there's a bar of quicksand in the way." Reynolds halted. "Doctor, do you want me to go into details like that? Like the bar of quicksand. I mean, if I went into every detail, it would take all day."

Dr. Kohn said, "Tell me the dream any way it comes into your head, and don't be concerned about leaving things out. Anything that really wants to be aired will come along sooner or later, in one way or another."

Nodding, Reynolds continued. "I yell to the captain to throw me a rope, but he wants to know why I'm so desperate to get aboard."

With that, Reynolds sat up, beaming. "Got it! The whole damned bit!" he burst out. "I thought dreams were supposed to be tough to interpret."

Dr. Kohn said dryly, "Apparently not for you."

"Oh, come on, hold the needle!" Reynolds laughed, feeling good because once again the experience was what he had expected. "The ferry's my analysis. The water is my unconscious I have to cross, past all kinds of barriers, like sex, and, as I said, a *bar* of quicksand—the bar equals liquor, sucking me down!" Reynolds was full of pleasure at his sleuthing, he expected approval from Dr. Kohn. But the doctor was impassive. Reynolds frowned. Why couldn't Old Iceberg at least nod?

He pressed on. "The dream is telling me that without help from the captain—you—I'll be stuck in quicksand all my life. Hey, this really works!"

Dr. Kohn remained silent.

"And the girl, don't you see? The touching and fooling around in the water, it's not real sex."

The doctor questioned, "What do you mean, not real sex?"

"Well, it's not sexual intercourse."

"Sexual intercourse?"

For Christ sake, Reynolds swallowed impatiently, doesn't this Dr. Freud know what sexual intercourse is! Aloud, he clipped, "Fucking! Screwing! Making out! Balling a dame!"

"Oh," Dr. Kohn nodded.

"Hello?" Reynolds swung off the couch disgustedly. "We've been disconnected again, doctor."

"Not at all. I'm only suggesting you use real language instead of clinical euphemisms."

There it was again. Instead of a word of recognition that he'd caught the dream by the neck, Dr. Iceberg was lecturing him on language!

He had another impulse to leave, but put it down sharply. It would be another surrender to the childish taunting he kept hearing from some distance in himself. "May I continue with the dream?" Reynolds asked acidly. He started back to the couch, but stopped when Dr. Kohn said, "When you feel sarcastic, don't try to hide it."

"I wasn't aware of any sarcasm."

"Then I apologize."

"Oh, shit, yes, I was being sarcastic!"

Dr. Kohn spoke with force. "Look, Philip Reynolds. You *are* a grown man and a successful one. But in this office you must come naked, face everything, hide nothing. It isn't easy, especially at the start, but unless you understand you'll be here forever."

Reynolds was listening attentively. He knew the doctor was on his side. The only opponent in this room was himself. It was difficult, nearly impossible, to move to the tug of someone else's reins, but he had to do it. Dr. Kohn was right. If he fancied up his language, he would launder his feelings—they went together. It was all a way of staying away from the abyss he still felt he could never face—confessing his abominable calls.

But he wasn't going to quit. That was determined by now. Lying back, Reynolds started once more. "The dream tells me that—"

"This time I *am* interrupting," Dr. Kohn said. "But only because we have here another critical point. I must remind you of one thing about your dreams, to remember always. Your dream doesn't 'tell you'; *you* tell yourself! A dream is just one thing: you talking to yourself! It is *your* voice, your thoughts, your wishes, your frustrations, your myths, your desires, your conflicts, your deepest feelings expressing themselves. When you report a dream to me, it would help if you said, 'So *I* said to *myself—*' You don't have to put it in those words, but you will do better if that is your orientation."

Reynolds was impressed. "I hadn't thought of it that way."

"The other side of this coin is equally important," Dr. Kohn stressed. "Never forget that the dreamer part of you is just as really you as the part that meets the payroll! It is not somebody else, it is not some distant relative, it is no one but Philip Reynolds."

Reynolds was silent as the statement sank in. It made more than sense, of course. He realized he had been reciting his dream as if telling a story heard from someone else about someone else. It suddenly shifted everything. It wasn't clear to him yet, but he glimpsed that this was not going to be a game. He was going to deal with the deep truths of himself. And he was going to *change!*

Reynolds' heart thumped with abrupt panic. This was more than he had bargained for. Things could get out of control. There was an inchoate boiling inside of him that he couldn't identify, but it put his teeth on edge. The way to handle it, he knew already, was to try to work on the couch. He returned to the dream quickly, to a scene which he realized he had suppressed because, somehow, it was most disturbing of all.

"I'm on the ferry. The girl's gone. The captain sends me into a small cabin to get something—charts and maps. Hey!" Reynolds stopped, sure he had come upon a major clue. "The name of the ferry is on a chart, a crazy kind of name but I can see it right now: PHIRNO LEYPOLIS." Reynolds did not wait for Dr. Kohn. He had read about this sort of dream. He went on excitedly. "That's one of the subconscious tricks, isn't it? An *anagram.* Now, let's see—"

Dr. Kohn took the wind out of his sails again. "I don't want to stop for that now."

Reynolds disagreed. "It may explain—"

"Go on with the rest of the dream!" Dr. Kohn ordered. "Your anagram will wait."

Swallowing his protest at the rebuke, Reynolds continued. "Well, in the cabin there's a dirty table, and a terrible stink in the place. When I pick up the charts, they turn to dust. I pick up a bottle for a drink and then see it's not whiskey but mouthwash! *And there's a mousetrap in it!* A large trap that couldn't possibly have gotten in the bottle." Reynolds squinted at the ceiling. "Now what the devil can that mean?"

And with even more wonder, "You know, I forgot all about the mousetrap part of the dream entirely. It just came back to me this second!"

"Stick with that!" Dr. Kohn commanded at once. "Recognize the way it was *buried,* absolutely outside of your consciousness, and then all of a sudden it was there."

"Right. It was in there all the time!"

"Important experience . . ."

"Yes," Reynolds said slowly. It was an unsettling experience to have the forgotten part of the dream pop out that way. His skepticism about the reality of another realm of being, the subconscious, had persisted through all his textbook reading, Reynolds recognized. It vanished now. He told this to the doctor.

"Good."

"But I haven't the foggiest about that mousetrap bit."

"Take your time."

Reynolds concentrated. "Nothing. Absolute blank."

"Then what should we suspect?"

"Eh?"

"Why did you recall this episode if you weren't prepared to even start dealing with it?"

"I don't know." But there was a physical answer in nausea, which hurtled up. He had begun to feel ill from the moment he had thought of discussing the obscene calls. Now he saw the gear-to-gear mechanics: He had dredged up the dream to have something else to talk about, to delay that intolerable prospect! It had almost worked, but now there was a threatening black telephone coming at him from across the room, a mocking robot holding out the receiver. Surrealistically, the phone became an opened mouth, gaudily lipsticked. Seated on vampire teeth was a homuncular Dr. Kohn, beckoning jerkily like a mechanical toy. "Tell me you make obscene telephone calls!" Reynolds rolled on the couch in terror and panic. *Oh, Christ, will it be now?* he moaned. Will the impossible words come out of my mouth now and—

"I have to vomit!" Reynolds caterwauled. He sprang from the couch.

The next morning Reynolds was mortified. He said at once, "I'm sorry about yesterday." To his surprise, Dr. Kohn was waving him away from the couch to the chair beside the desk.

"Philip, we'll get to the couch later. I know you have been reading and studying all the books in the field, but I'm afraid little of it will apply here in ways you expect. In the first place, I am unorthodox. There are many avenues to the unconscious, and many ways to travel through it. I use whatever methods I think will help you, from any school or approach. Mostly, as I've told you, you must be prepared for me to react to you as a human being. I am *not* a surgeon in a sterilized operating room, and you are not under an anesthetic. I laugh, I get mad, I can like you or hate you or not give a damn about you. Do you understand?"

"You mean you react to *me—*"

"And to each of the other seven patients I'm seeing today."

God, Reynolds wondered, where does he get the strength? Suddenly Aloysius Kohn *was* a man.

"Frankly, I don't have time or energy for a con job. And let me tell you, neither do you. With your great cleverness, you'd like to use me as your father confessor, tell me your sins, pay your dues, and leave unchanged! No. Analysis isn't confession and shriving. Analysis is facing and understanding. And finally forgiving, though that's distant. Right now, analysis for you is being as honest as you can. It isn't easy, but it's the only way to deal with the mess that is stinking so bad inside of you that you finally couldn't stand your own stench and came for help. Now tell me—honestly—do you want it?"

Reynolds was shaken, strangely moved, and he saw that this was put-up, shut-up. He nodded, realizing he meant it.

"Not just lip service."

"I do want to try." The words were genuine.

"Then you'll have to work harder than you have ever done in your life, and I know how hard you have worked. We have to do more here than a polite spritz out of an air freshener. You need an operation that opens up your gut and drains the pus. It will sometimes be torture, but anything less is wasting time and money."

"I want to do it!" Reynolds said, with grim truth.

"Then get over there and let's start."

As soon as Reynolds stretched out on the couch, the nausea heaved at his throat. He swung up again, desperately swallowing the flooding saliva.

The doctor's calm voice saved him. "Philip, you will tell me when you are ready. I am not pressing you. When you are ready, it won't be too hard. Meantime, leave it alone." The nausea left as suddenly as it had come. Reynolds sat panting, limp, thankful.

"Now what do you feel?"

"How hard I've been fighting everything."

"Relax. Don't try to talk until you want to." There was an unexpected chuckle. "One patient said he kept talking because silence here was like sitting in a taxi with the meter running while stuck in traffic."

Reynolds laughed and felt better. Silence. Take space. Give things a chance. Yes. The dream was back, and it felt right to talk about it. "The captain isn't there anymore. Instead, I see a man and woman, sort of shabby characters. They take me into the cabin of the ferry, but now it's a stable. They give me a harness to put on an animal that's sleeping. I'm frightened. It's huge, enormous, like a bison or a buffalo, with filthy long fur. It has a shaggy head, with slimy eyes that glare at me. It starts moving to me, slowly, grisly. I want to run, but I'm paralyzed. I feel its stinking breath and see its sharp teeth, like a shark's. I scream to the man and woman to help me, but they stand aside, laughing. I hear the man encouraging the beast, 'Get 'im!'

"At that, the creature pins me down with an enormous hoof and I see it's swinging a dead mouse over me. I've never smelled anything so horrible, and I nearly faint when I see what it's trying to do—drop the mouse, with maggots crawling all over it, into my mouth! I gag, wanting to vomit, and I scream out so loud that I wake up."

Dr. Kohn saw that Reynolds was white and sweating.

"Hey," Reynolds breathed. "What's this mouse thing that's haunting me? Is it Jungian?"

"Now we're not going to talk about your books but about your dream, please!"

"Now shall you slap me on the wrist again?"

The doctor's answer came sharply. "Your father slapped you on the wrist?"

"Hah, he did a hell of a lot more than that."

"I remind you that I am not your father, but it seems you put yourself in the position of a little boy."

Reynolds reviewed what had just happened. "I guess it's another try at steering away from the dream? Anyway, okay, what's the monster?"

"Let your mind go blank and see what comes," Dr. Kohn gave the routine instruction.

Reynolds said with a surge of discovery, "I see a face in a mirror, me when I had a beard, one summer when I was tutoring in a camp near

New Haven. Beard, hair—fur?" He gulped. "You mean *I'm* the monster?"

"I didn't say a word."

"What a picture of myself! God, do I really stink like that?"

"Apparently, to yourself."

Reynolds made a retching sound.

"Get a good whiff of how you stink inside. It will help us go on."

The next words from the couch were so low the doctor had to strain to make them out. ". . . worse than I've told you." And a sudden, breaking cry, "I'm a goddamn creep, doctor!"

There was no sound from the desk.

Reynolds opened his mouth to divulge his crime, writhing in his tortured need to pour out what he had so long hidden. But his jaws held rigid. He was grunting like an animal.

Dr. Kohn said, "It's a pity you waited so long to see a doctor."

There was genuine sympathy across the room, and it brought Reynolds to the edge of tears. They did not spill. If only he could cry, Reynolds thought—like a woman, like a child. Crying might break the steel chain that bound him. But he could neither weep nor speak. He gazed in agony at the gray ceiling like a man felled by a stroke.

Dr. Kohn's voice was compassionate. "I know how hard it is, Philip."

Reynolds groaned. Impossible for anyone else to know how it feels to be drowning in your own contempt.

Softly, helpfully: "But we are here to get the poison out."

"We," not "you." Dr. Kohn was sharing the struggle, friend, doctor, expert.

Abruptly, the binding fell away. On the couch, Philip Reynolds suddenly felt himself to be a swollen, bursting rectum, exploding excrement. He was taking a pouring, reeking shit, his soul's peristalsis of impacted agony. He felt his bowels gripe into grinding pains that made him twist and turn on the couch as he cried out the terrible, unspeakable words:

"I make obscene telephone calls!"

Five words bursting out of his gut, shrapneling his body to bloody pieces. He felt butchered.

The doctor's silence became a blanket under which he could rest and regain his breath. When Reynolds finally opened his eyes, it was to see Dr. Kohn regarding him quietly, as if nothing extraordinary had taken place. It was amazing, and at the same time comforting. What did he expect, Reynolds asked himself—Dr. Kohn to be standing above him like

Moses with granite tablets on Mount Sinai?—waiting with a black hood and broadax like a medieval executioner?—or blowing a police whistle to arrest him?

For the very first time in his life, it occurred to Philip Reynolds that his acts were actual crimes for which he could be arrested, prosecuted, jailed. He shuddered. That was something else he would have to deal with.

"So you have made obscene telephone calls." Dr. Kohn spoke in a cool, unjudging tone. Hearing the appalling words repeated so matter-of-factly had the effect of searing them into Reynolds' brain. They were real, and so was he, and so was Dr. Kohn looking at him from across the room with accepting eyes, eyes that, like Sigmund Freud's and Karen Horney's, could visualize everything he had done. They all knew how he had disguised his voice, how he had whispered, the way he mastur-bated during the calls—every disgusting thing he had done!

They did not judge, but he did now! Reynolds doubled over in a physical torment of disgrace and humiliation under Dr. Kohn's steady gaze. Long, helpless sobs shook Reynolds' frame, and his fingers hung down from the couch touching the floor like the ends of frayed rope.

As months of analysis coiled by into summer, Reynolds kept as much to himself as possible. He was totally preoccupied with the convolutions of his psychoanalysis, and his life away from the office was anchoritic. He came to work early, left twelve to fourteen hours later, did no drinking, and worked or read in his room, catching television commer-cials until midnight, when his eyes closed on him.

To Penny's disappointment, Reynolds refused her invitation to a party she gave for office friends to celebrate the apartment she had found on Riverside Drive. It was small and a bit neglected, but it had a magnificent view of the Hudson River, and, though it was a strain, Penny's new position at the agency made it possible for her to pay the rent without a roommate. The job was a challenge, but Reynolds had guessed correctly. What Penny wasn't ready for she tackled with a dedication that soon corrected any lack. She was no Lillian Schuster, but her strong schooling, and Ted Watson's constant help, gave her enough competence to perform adequately. With her drive, everyone recog-nized that she would soon do better.

Reynolds watched from a distance, strictly an arm's length manager now. He wanted no close contact other than Dr. Kohn.

Dr. Kohn neither approved nor disapproved; only reminded Reynolds that he must try to know and be aware of what he was doing and feeling every minute.

Reynolds found satisfaction in working doggedly, both with Dr. Kohn and at the office. Living in town, it was not difficult for him to make the eight A.M. session he had been lucky enough to get with Dr. Kohn. "The closer you were to your dreams and fresh morning thoughts, the better"—that was a cliché of the analysands' world.

Reynolds phoned Duncan Talbott often to talk about his progress, and about his family. Talbott told him the girls missed him, but Helena was adamant about the separation. Unfortunately, the cheek had not healed well. The scar was small and could be fixed with plastic surgery after a time, but meanwhile it was an ugly daily reminder. Helena had insisted to Talbott that she would not risk Reynolds' return even though he was in analysis. Not yet, anyway.

In June, between the time her school ended and a junior counselor job at the club was to begin, Selma took the train to the city occasionally. Reynolds met her for a welcome interval away from both Dr. Kohn and the office. They went together to the Central Park Zoo, to the museums, to the Statue of Liberty. When Selma asked if Penny could join them one day, Reynolds told her Penny was too busy on her new job. Seeing her disappointment, he relented. They arranged a Saturday outing, and Reynolds approved the growing friendship he observed between his daughter and Penny. It would do Selly good to have someone Penny's age to confide in.

On Penny's birthday in June, they got Helena's permission, through Talbott, for Selma to stay over at Penny's apartment so that Reynolds could take the girls to dinner without concern for a late train ride to Connecticut. The three made an attractive ad-photo, Reynolds smiled to himself as he squired Selma and Penny to a famous restaurant—"Handsome Father with Charming Daughters." Had he been alone with Penny, some eyebrows would have gone up in the red velvet, crystal-chandeliered room: "Dirty Old Man with Prey."

As it was, Reynolds felt pleasantly *en famille.* And why not, he asked himself as he regarded Penny and Selma discussing the menu, both wide-eyed at the prices. He should never let himself forget that he was twice Penny's age.

As to his telephone call to her, the Off-Switch had clicked completely somewhere along the line. The analysis sessions had been concentrating on his violence and other disturbances. It seemed Reynolds was not ready to examine his obscene calling; the subject did not come up in his associations or dreams, and Dr. Kohn did not bring it forward. So it was possible for Reynolds to sit smiling in the restaurant with both Selma and Penny beside him, taking pleasure in their pleasure, with no shadows of his illness spoiling the occasion.

July brought an interval of panic. Dr. Kohn informed Reynolds that he would be leaving for the month of August. Reynolds knew vaguely that it was the traditional vacation time for analysts, but the event threw him when it occurred. The morning hour was curiously empty, and Reynolds felt a new vulnerability as he spent days away from the couch. He had not suspected how much the analysis had become a central structure in his life, and what a bulwark Dr. Kohn represented.

The summer weeks were long and hot. Reynolds was thankful when Duncan Talbott called to suggest he spend a weekend at the club, swim, play some golf. Reynolds asked about Helena; they would almost certainly run into each other, and he wanted to cause no embarrassment. "Helena knows I'm asking you up," Talbott said. Selma had been urging her mother to see Reynolds, the girls missed him. Talbott had lent his weight. It wasn't as if Helena would be accepting Reynolds at home. The club was neutral ground, and she could consider Reynolds still on probation.

Helena consented to have dinner with Reynolds and Talbott at the club. Reynolds could see the ugly mark under her makeup, and it made him awkward. Helena was pleasant but distant, as if she were being polite to a friend of a friend. When they danced to the Saturday night band, she kept a careful separation, but her scent stirred Reynolds. "I'd like to see the girls tomorrow," he said. "Would it bother you if I slept over in the guest room?"

Helena thought a moment. "Midge and Dorothy have been jealous of Selma's seeing you in town. I suppose it would be all right."

Reynolds guided the familiar car over the road he could drive blindfolded. Quick now to capture his feelings, he became aware of how knot-tight he had been inside throughout his separation from his family. There was an unhappy emptiness in the way he was living. His sense of loss overtook him sharply as he unlocked the front door and entered the large foyer. He didn't have to snap on a light or walk through the rooms to be home again. The quiet blue of the den was to his right, the bright expanse of the gold living room ahead, the silken green of the master bedroom upstairs. He could smell the faint odors of the house welcoming him—the polished furniture, the thick carpets, the immaculate kitchen and pantry, the stairwell bringing a trace of the girls and their rooms.

Helena said in one breath that the guest room was made up, she was tired and would see him in the morning and if he wanted anything of course he knew where everything was.

Reynolds wanted Helena to stay with him. He did not know what he could say or what could happen, but he did not want their meeting to be over this way. It was no use. Helena was gone, and there was no way he could call to her. He had half thought she would be asking about his analysis, but it was clear she did not feel this was the time.

When Dorothy and Midge saw Reynolds on Sunday morning, they were reserved and uncertain, but Selma's quick warmth brought them all together before breakfast was over. At the club, they swam together, played tennis doubles with shrieks of laughter at Reynolds' flubbed shots. He did not let on that, at least partly, he was clowning on purpose. Let them see that he could be fun as well as drunk and violent; reassure them that he would never be drunk or violent again. At lunch, Reynolds made certain his daughters observed that he did not drink even the white wine Talbott ordered.

They had dinner at home. At nine o'clock, Reynolds looked at his watch. "I'd better make the 9:38 if I want to get back tonight."

The girls chattered their disappointment. Helena said, looking away from her husband, "You could go in the morning if you like."

Selma leaped up from the rug where she was sprawled. "Oh, great! I can go down with you, Daddy, and visit with Penny!"

Helena said firmly, "You're not off tomorrow."

"I didn't know Daddy would be here! They can get someone else!"

"Not on this short notice, and you know it, Selma."

The girl flopped to the floor with a loud "Oh, shit!"

Helena said sharply, "You may apologize for that, young lady!"

Selma remained surly. "I didn't say anything."

"Don't be impertinent. You know we don't use that language in this house!"

Selma stood up defiantly. "What the shit is so special about this house?"

Helena, outraged, slapped Selma hard.

The girl's face broke. She shouted, "Oh, *shit!*" and made for the stairs.

Reynolds moved at once. He was still the father here. "Selly, you deserved that! Don't talk to your mother that way!"

Selma gave Reynolds a devastating look. "You said worse to that poor proofreader when you crucified her for *nothing!*" The girl whirled and flew up the stairs. "Shit, *shit,* shit!"

Reynolds had a dim recollection that Penny had mentioned Selma's being in the office that sorry day, but in his turmoil it had never really penetrated.

Helena was saying, very worried, "She's really becoming impossible!"

Reynolds offered, "All the kids talk that way nowadays. Let's not make a mountain out of a molehill."

Helena sent Dorothy and Midge upstairs. "It doesn't help for them to hear you say that!" she rebuffed him. "Selma has been entirely too independent lately."

Reynolds said, "It's the way we wanted to bring them up, isn't it?"

"*You* wanted—"

Reynolds interrupted, "They're great kids!" His voice went tight. "I really don't think slapping Selly helps anything!"

To his surprise, Helena was backing away from him with an expression of fear. "Please don't start another fight!" Reynolds was shaken to see panic in his wife's eyes as her hands went up to protect her face. He had not realized how deeply he had wounded her. He said quickly, placatingly, "I only said our girls are okay." He smiled to reassure Helena. He held out his hand in what he meant to be a friendly gesture. His wife mistook it for a threat and cried out, "Please don't touch me!— You'd better go now, Phil. I have to tell you that just now something *snapped* in me. I am *afraid* of you. Physically afraid, and you have to know it. I'm sorry, but that's the way it is!"

Reynolds needed to make another attempt to reach her. "Helena, you don't know how well I'm coming along with Dr. Kohn. We haven't had a chance to talk about it, but it's the most important—"

She cut him off. "Duncan keeps telling me. I want to believe you. But I can't." She lowered her head. "I'm really sorry, Phil. I tried. I even thought with you back in the house we might—" She stopped herself. "*Please* go now." Helena was trembling with an alarm her reason could not reach.

Reynolds waited again but he, wordmaster, found no way to say how much he wanted to stay in this house, with his wife. If Helena didn't feel it between them, he couldn't create it. The fear that was sending him out might be unreasoning now, but it was a force he himself had generated. He asked, "Will you drive me to the station or shall I call a cab?"

Helena remained with her back to her husband. "Take a taxi, please." She went quickly up to her daughters.

At the station where he recognized every post and crack in the

narrow platform, Reynolds stood by himself. There were only a handful
of people; the town drew few weekenders. The moonless night was
sticky and damp. Insects buzzed thickly around the green-shaded bulbs.
Reynolds wished it would rain and bring a breeze, wished Dr. Kohn
were back in New York, wished Selma hadn't picked tonight to stir
Helena up, and, though he was headed lonely to an institutional room,
wished the train would come. He peered unhappily into the empty black
distance and doodled in his head: A watched track never trains.

The train was a local. On the endless, bumpy ride, Reynolds came to a
conclusion. There was a point at which "temporary" became permanent. Living in a room at the club was tolerable as long as he expected to
be returning to Connecticut soon. Now he realized that Helena was far
from ready to end their separation. If it hadn't been the incident with
Selma, it would probably have been something else. The fear—even
hysteria—in Helena's eyes was as real as it had been unjustified. He had
never intended this, but apparently it was going to take a long time to
heal, if it ever did. For the first time, the possibility that Helena might
want a divorce crossed Reynolds' mind. He cautioned himself against
premature conclusions. At the same time, it seemed plain that he faced a
new situation calling for an important decision: Should he leave the club
and take an apartment of his own?

On the clacking train, Reynolds weighed it. The move would affirm
that his marriage was in far worse trouble than he thought, inevitably it
would add distance between Helena and himself. It occurred to him that
he ought not make so significant a change without waiting for Dr. Kohn.
True, the responsibility was his, but in analysis you weren't supposed to
undertake major decisions without working them through. He should
get Talbott's advice too, Reynolds told himself.

But the next day he asked Penny to scout small apartments. He still
believed he would be back with Helena, but he did not know how long it
would take and he told himself he could not go on living like a gypsy.

Scanning apartment advertisements in Reynolds' office that afternoon, Penny burst into laughter. The "Collectors Club" had waned
with Lillian's leaving, but she had found a worthy entry. Enormously
pleased, she showed Reynolds: "Outstanding studio for quick posses-
sion, with all enmities."

"Sounds exactly right for *me*," Reynolds smiled, and they went to see
the place together. It was airy and pleasant, and boasted a considerable
terrace overlooking the East River. Penny gasped at both the view of the

Fifty-ninth Street Bridge, and the rent, as Reynolds took the apartment at once. She watched him thoughtfully, suspecting what was happening to his marriage, but he volunteered nothing.

Remarking about the rent, Penny took the occasion to mention that inflation was straining her budget like everyone else's, and she wanted to carry her apartment without a roommate. Reynolds agreed to a raise at once. Not only was Penny O'Hara doing Lillian Schuster's job, but he had begun trying her on small writing assignments. She had a knack with consumer products, a sixth sense that anticipated reader response. Her salary had been hiked with her first promotion, but she was easily worth more now.

Walking back to the office, Penny thanked Reynolds sincerely. It wasn't just the money, she said solemnly. It was his willingness to give her opportunities. She wanted him to know her appreciation.

Reynolds squeezed her arm companionably. "You're a bargain, Penny."

He might be a bastard sometimes, Penny mused, but she herself had never known anything but comfort, kindness, and understanding from this complicated, fascinating man.

Crossing Park Avenue and Fifty-Seventh Street, Penny was glad she had been to the hairdresser, and was wearing a cotton print that contrasted crisply with the sloppy jeans on every side. She proudly identified with the better-dressed women on the street heading to Tiffany's, Bergdorf's, Gucci's. She liked her reflection in the elegant windows. She belonged in this scene, she thought with satisfaction, though the fantastically priced clothes were unreal to her. She didn't approve the cigarette theme "You've Come a Long Way, Baby!" It seemed patronizing, but it surely seemed true of her, she thought again, as she strolled in the heart of Manhattan beside handsome Philip Reynolds heading to her increasingly important job at a top Madison Avenue ad agency.

Penny heard Reynolds asking, "Didn't you once tell me you were engaged, Penny?"

Penny realized how impersonal their relationship had remained. She had never mentioned her breakup with Mickey. Now it seemed so distant from this new life that there was nothing to say. "Oh, that's been over quite a while," she answered casually.

Reynolds nodded. He had just been making conversation, but all at once he saw Penny O'Hara not as the Brooklyn kid he had hired almost two years ago, but as the woman she was becoming. Penny smiled at the sudden intensity of Reynolds' gaze. "Since we're both unengaged," he was saying, "why don't we stop for a drink, and have dinner together tonight? There's nothing at the office that can't wait."

"I'd like that," Penny said directly, returning the pressure of Reynolds' fingers she thought she felt on her palm, though it might have been only a restraining touch as the traffic light changed.

8

On Penny's second Christmas with Reynolds and Associates there was no office party. Reynolds made a contribution to a children's hospital instead. In the early afternoon, Talbott phoned Reynolds. "You aren't planning to surprise anyone up here for the holiday, are you?" Reynolds frowned. Duncan could always read his mind. But he had decided against a visit. The worst thing he could do was try to force Helena, and it went against his own grain to manipulate the sentiment of the season. Actually, his own back was up. He had told Dr. Kohn with growing conviction that, though he understood Helena's apprehensiveness, she had blown their difficulty out of proportion. He would be glad to go halfway and more, but she ought to show some sign of relenting.

Instead—and the purpose of Talbott's call became apparent—Helena had invited her brother and sister for the holiday season. If there had been any possibility of Reynolds visiting, that ended it.

It would be his first Christmas alone since his marriage but, hell, he told himself, he wasn't a character in a Dickens carol. He had sent a pile of presents to Connecticut, and Selma would come down to spend a day with him. It would have to be enough.

On ad alley, he was in front again, going flat out—edged on that hairline between the speed of racing wheels and the hiss of disaster. Racing drivers know how the bright pinprick in Death's eye circles the track, with the tip of the speedometer needle sticking straight up a man's ass, daring him to that fraction more, that touch harder, a final testing. That's how he was pushing the agency, Reynolds considered, looking at his crowded workboard with satisfaction. He was zooming to a checkered flag in the hottest performance Madison Avenue had ever seen, or crash and burn! He was bringing in more clients and staff every week. He assured Dr. Kohn it wasn't recklessness or foolhardiness this time. He had learned from experience. But he was feeling new power too, and was driven by a new single-focused need—to pay Helena back every cent of her advance. Through the year, he had sent checks whenever he could, but there was still a large balance. It weighed on him, and he wanted it cleared as quickly as possible. That, he judged, was straight, not neurotic.

His attitude had become bitter, he acknowledged to Dr. Kohn. It was one thing to have borrowed money from a wife who was rooting for you, another to be indebted to a woman who did not seem to care about the progress he was making. He admitted his original fault, of course, but, he told the doctor, the estrangement now was Helena's doing.

As for the loneliness he felt in his office after Talbott's call, loneliness was a pain like a broken leg, Reynolds told himself. He had tried to escape pain for too long and it had, ironically, cost him a large part of his life. He eyed his locked bar, and reached for a TV storyboard instead.

Penny knocked on his door before coming in. It was another of her notions he liked. She remained a curious combination of old and new. Reynolds was surprised to see her. The staff had the half day off.

Penny was carrying a large portfolio. "I was cleaning our storage bin and found this, Phil. The Acadia presentation. You want to trash it?"

"No," Reynolds told her. "Some of the stuff should be usable. We'll get a Detroit yet."

Penny sat down, lighting a cigarette. "A year ago!" she said. "I can't believe how time flies."

For you, Reynolds thought. For him the year had been the longest, most turbulent of his life. On the day Penny had brought in her champagne he would have laughed at anyone who said he'd be separated from Helena, would have dismissed any suggestion that he would be in psychoanalysis. What a year it had been, indeed. Flying high with the promise of Acadia, plummeting to the near reality of bankruptcy, his personal foul-ups, Dr. Kohn, and now back on the climb. Alone.

Penny was saying, "I haven't seen anything on Acadia out of Graham's shop, have you?"

Reynolds shook his head. "They ran into an engineering snag. It'll be a spring promo, I think." It was comfortable talking with Penny. The quiet of the office outside provided a relaxing air. The tension of his thoughts began to ease. Penny was not just an employee, she had worked more closely with him than anyone at the office, knew all his quirks. She, not his new secretary, did personal errands like buying new shirts, underwear, socks when his laundry had been lost.

She was telling him, "Speaking of Acadia, you'll never guess who called me this morning. Jock Rogers!"

Reynolds asked at once, "Is Graham after you again?"

Penny shook her head. "He knows I'd never leave you. No, Jock just wanted to say Merry Christmas." She recalled the year before and shivered. "He asked me for a date tonight." She refrained from adding that she thought he had one hell of a nerve even for him.

Reynolds asked, "You're going to your folks, aren't you?"

Penny shook her head again. "They're still flipped out because I'm living on my own." Her smile returned as she ground out her cigarette and stood up. "This year I have my own tree to trim." Then with the privilege of the closeness she felt to Philip Reynolds, she invited, "What about you, Phil? I still have that knockout view of the Hudson you haven't seen."

Reynolds considered for a moment. He did not have to pretend with Penny that he was having dinner with old friends, and it was not a time to be alone.

"Personally," Penny smiled, "I bet my view beats yours."

"Name the stakes!" It was suddenly a game and a pleasant prospect.

"Jug of wine—"

"Nothing doing. Dom Perignon. I'm going to win."

"Okay, but you'll have to pay for it if I lose."

Penny, brighter than a shiny copper, Reynolds thought fondly. It would be nice to help her trim her tree.

Without planning, they found themselves stopping in the crowded Zabar's store on Broadway and loading shopping bags with every kind of holiday delicacy.

It happened between them as naturally as the stars shining in the black Christmas sky outside of Penny's windows, with the jewels of the George Washington Bridge matching their brilliance—diamonds above, necklace below. With food enjoyed, the tree decorated, and Penny washing dishes in the tiny kitchen, Reynolds rose from watching television saying it was time for him to leave. When he reached for his jacket, he found Penny's soapy, welcome hands going around his neck.

Penny did not know that as Reynolds followed her into the bedroom he was smiling to himself, reciting an old family secret: *"Don't be a Shmuel!"*

How different Reynolds was from Mickey, Penny exulted. Shuddering, she remembered the sweaty pawing, the filthy words grating her ears and forced out of her mouth unwillingly. Reynolds was gentle, tender, held her long to play with her delicately and knowingly, caring for *her,* not just for his own quick release.

When at last the older man turned on top of her and she guided him unbelievably inside, feeling him become deliciously part of her body, it was a sliding caress, not a ripping. When he began to thrust deep and strong, it wasn't the violent pumping of her insides to a frothing moment of physical paroxysm as it had been with Mickey. Once she had dreamed Mickey was a bicycle pump shooting air into her unstoppably. With Reynolds, lovemaking was a slow curving wave of sensation that floated her up and over. She didn't really have a climax, she supposed, there was just the rising and swelling and subsiding, over and over, but it was beautiful and more than enough to have this beautiful man inside her, filling her wholly.

Sometimes, with an unexpected change of rhythm, Reynolds held himself just at her entrance, moving just a teasing bit—she began to realize there was a gorgeous pattern to what he was doing—the slight movements just inside her eager lips counting, one, two, three, four, five, six, seven, and then—when she couldn't breathe with a raving hunger for all of him—he would drive inside suddenly, in, in, in to her most secret place, occupying all her flesh to answer her yearning, as if he were the very air heaving into her desperate lungs, thrilling and satisfying her into unbearable delight. Ah, this is what it meant to have a real male, a mature, sensual man instead of a hot rutting boy!

Through half-closed eyes, Penny caught a glimpse of Reynolds' face. So close above her, she saw its deepening lines and grizzling temples clearly, and the sight inflamed her with new passion to give and receive. The man who sat so dominantly behind the great glass desk, the industry leader who stood at the lectern at the Waldorf, was, incredibly, hers.

Penny wrapped her long legs around Reynolds more tightly, feeling him throb between her thighs, like holding the world. She ground her body under his exciting weight, and collapsed to his strength in a transport of new emotions. This, this was her first night of love, her true loss of virginity. Here with this *full man,* yes, old enough to be her father, she was flowering from childish virgin to fulfilled womanhood. The other had been little more than masturbation, using Mickey's tool instead of her fingers.

It was a new passion to feel that a man like Philip Reynolds *needed* her, that she could be of such value to him. She took a new glory in her body, strange and rewarding because for the first time she was using it to give fulfillment to a man she—

Penny stopped the circling whisper.

This man she *loved?*

What if she said the word? What if he said it? Where would-could it take them? She did not know. It was enough that they were together now. This, *now,* was all there needed to be and it needed no labels.

Consummated, Reynolds and Penny lay with their hands touching lightly. Penny smiled to herself with her fresh wisdom, gratified and comforted as never by Mickey. Turning, she looked at Reynolds' face and tenderness shook her. The power was there, yes, and all the years of his hard work and experience, and his battling with himself, but there was also vulnerability. Not weakness, but need. Penny saw that Reynolds needed her as much as she needed him. She was content in body and soul.

For Reynolds, Penny in bed was a flame that fed his passion as Helena had done at the beginning of their marriage. Penny's young abandon made him aware of how mechanical sex with Helena had become. After his abstinence, Penny had brought his body vibrantly alive, and ended the shadowy doubts he had begun to harbor about his potency—questions that Talbott had assured him many men began to think about at his age even when there was no sign of difficulty.

As for the obscene call to Penny exactly a year ago this night, Reynolds' Off-Switch was working perfectly. He possessed Penny fully now, and did not require fantasy.

In Dr. Kohn's office the session after Christmas, Reynolds recited what had happened, and questioned himself immediately: "It's wrong, isn't it?"

Dr. Kohn countered, as Reynolds had long since come to expect. "Are you asking *me?*"

With a laugh, Reynolds said, "Of course not."

Dr. Kohn smiled. "You're learning."

Reynolds got more comfortable on the couch, thinking hard. "Okay. Society says it's wrong, being unfaithful to my wife, and—" Reynolds stopped. His mind was veering to a parallel thought and he let it come. He had learned not to rein himself in on this couch. ". . . *Is Helena having an affair with Duncan?*" The notion came from left field, and startled him. He paused to consider it. "No. It isn't like Dunc, though I suppose I've suspected he's been in love with Helena for years, probably why he never married. And it certainly wouldn't be like Helena!" Pause. Reynolds pondered, repeating, ". . . Wouldn't be like Helena?" What did he know of Helena, the woman *behind* the wife, the mother, the carpool driver? And she had a right to change too, didn't she? He was changing. He hoped. Why shouldn't Helena be changing? He took time to say it all to Dr. Kohn and to think about what it might mean.

Resuming, he said, "I suppose an affair is par for the course at my age." He gave a short laugh. "Why is the old man always dirty and the young girl always the victim? Is it just a stereotype of our youth orientation? Dammit, I think I've been falling in love with Penny since the day I hired her. She's a terrific *person*. Older than her years. Competent as hell, talented, warm. She doesn't say it, but I think she is in love with me."

His new thoughts wrinkled into other shapes. "Divorce, no, that would be premature. Everything doesn't have to be tied up in a neat knot. I'm trying to sort out something that should be open-ended right now. The crux is that nobody is hurting anyone else. As I see it, that's the answer. I want Penny, and Penny wants me, and Helena doesn't, at least for now. As for later, I just don't have any crystal ball. Is that wrong?"

It had been a long way around, but he had come to a conclusion, Reynolds thought with satisfaction.

Dr. Kohn spoke now, flintily. "Is it wrong? Is it wrong? Is it wrong? Does it occur to you that perhaps that isn't the question for this room at all?"

Familiar instant irritation brought Reynolds' head up, but he knew better than to ask the doctor what he thought the true question was. He dropped back to the pillow, closed his eyes again, and considered. By now he knew how to respond; relax, take the challenge very seriously, go with it instead of resisting. Kohn always had a reason. (Reynolds remembered with a fond smile a time when Selma was three years old, doing something messy in a corner of the living room. "Come over here," he had called. "No," she had refused. "Why won't you come here?" he had asked. "Because you'll give me a reason!")

"What are you thinking?" came from Dr. Kohn.

Reynolds let the annoyance through. "That you always see something I don't!" The analysis rubbed his nose in that truth every session. Well, it was one way of deflating his Glory Image. He waited a long time, turning it over in his mind.

"Where are you now?" Dr. Kohn prodded.

The answer took off in Reynolds' head like a flock of birds: "The question is why I'm so uptight about the one angle of whether it's 'right' or 'wrong' for me to be with Penny."

"Exactly."

Reynolds punched the couch with discovery. "Because to my father *everything* I ever did was wrong! Just my being *alive* was wrong!" Agitation closed Reynolds' throat painfully.

"What do you mean by that?"

Long-forgotten echoes began to sound: "I was just a kid, maybe four-five, but I remember the fights. He'd come home plastered and scream at my mother—oh, Christ, *you* can write the script. He would yell that he had no friends because he'd married a mockie Jew bastard, he'd have left her long ago if she hadn't fucked him up by sneaking a kid on him. Now he was in jail—what they ought to do was give the fucking kid away to one of those Jew places! And I'm hiding in a corner praying my mother won't listen because I somehow know in my gut that if it comes to him or me it's going to be him she chooses, and anyway I know how the fight is going to end up. He's going to grab me out of the corner and yell about *something*—I didn't eat enough or I ate too much or I left a toy on the floor—any reason to take off his leather strap, wrestle me over his lap, and beat my rear raw. My mother'd yell at him until he'd ask if she wanted a beating too, then she'd go out crying, but not lifting a finger to stop him.

"I've spent my life trying to prove I have a right to some fucking space on this planet! Proving, proving, proving! *My* name has to go before Rod Graham's so my father will see who I am!"

Reynolds' face was contorted, his eyes were broken glass when he stopped, panting for breath.

"Go on," Dr. Kohn encouraged. When the shit was coming, let it pour.

Reynolds choked, "Ikey! IKEY!"

"What?" Dr. Kohn wasn't sure what he had heard.

To his amazement, Reynolds was blasted with nausea more violent than the attack preceding his confession of the obscene calls. He sprang up gasping, with his handkerchief tight against his mouth.

"All right," Dr. Kohn said gently. The kindness in his face eased Reynolds again. His stomach stopped churning. "My God," he sighed.

"Tell me about 'Ikey.' "

Wonderingly, Reynolds said, "That's the first time I've remembered! How in God's name could I have forgotten that miserable crap I lived with so long!"

Dr. Kohn reminded him, keeping his voice low and sympathetic, "We repress things that are too painful to remember."

After a long pause, Reynolds started his explanation in a way that puzzled the doctor. "You know my name." He waited.

"Of course."

Reynolds said slowly, accenting the middle name, "Philip *Marcus*—"
"Yes?"

"Marcus was my Jewish grandfather's name. As early as I can remember, my father made fun of it. My mother should have called me Isaac, he said. Real Jewish. Then everybody could call me 'Ikey!' Because I was 'a lousy dirty kikey!' "

Reynolds' teeth ground. It brought a rare interruption from Dr. Kohn: "Your father called you a lousy dirty kike?"

Reynolds' "Yes" was a barely breathed whisper.

Dr. Kohn made the first judgment Philip Reynolds had heard from him. The doctor declared, "Your father was a slob."

Reynolds was grateful for the support. It made it easier to rip the scab off the rest of the wound. "I wonder why a man like that ever married my mother."

Dr. Kohn said quickly, "We are not here to be *his* analysts."

Reynolds nodded and went on. "Neighbor kids heard my father. At school I was 'Ikey-Kikey.' I fought with them every damn day but they never quit." He felt his jaws stiffening. He still wasn't going to surrender to self-pity, not even on this couch. It had happened long ago. Forget it.

He caught himself up. That kind of thinking was pure resistance. He wasn't here to forget but to remember, especially the agonies which, as Dr. Kohn said, were too painful to bear. He had caught a big rat here, he wasn't going to let it scurry into its black stinking nest without taking a good look. To Dr. Kohn he said, "How in *hell* could I have never mentioned all that after nearly a year with you?"

Dr. Kohn made no response.

"That's how deep I buried it, eh?"

The doctor spoke. "Are you sure Ikey was buried at all?"

Reynolds was startled. "What? I never had an inkling of it until just now!"

"You have to deal with my question."

Reynolds concentrated. Deal with it. Another technique of Dr. Kohn's. But it worked. It had helped Reynolds dredge up carloads of unsuspected garbage in these relentless sessions. Keep working. What had Dr. Kohn asked? Was he sure Ikey had been buried at all? What was Kohn driving at? This doctor didn't have an idle question in his body.

A glimmering began behind Reynolds' closed eyes. A discovery meshed. How often had he felt that a Mr. Hyde had taken over, robbed his will, stolen his mind, usurped his sense!

Who had become a drunkard?

Who had made the obscene calls, from the time he was in college?

Who had axed the Graham deal?

Who had estranged his wife?

IKEY!—the terrorized, cast-out child who had battled insanely for a place at home, in the schoolyard, in college, in advertising, in Connecticut, battled for his place in the sun by becoming his own terror!

The insight came pouring from the couch.

Ikey was not only not buried, but alive and stalking Reynolds' life every moment his guard was down. *It explained the drinking too,* Reynolds burst out with excitement. Ikey couldn't get out of his cage while Reynolds was sober, but alcohol dissolved the lock!

If Reynolds had looked up he would have seen the doctor doing an unusual thing—nodding.

But Reynolds was still turned inward. There was a live magnet in him now. He sensed that there was more, much more, waiting to be exposed. He was determined to stay on the track no matter where it led. Part of his elation was his feeling of new strength that he could follow now without fear, ready to face whatever ugliness he came upon.

"Yes?" Dr. Kohn urged again.

Reynolds spoke with soft intensity. "I see so goddamn many things. Wait till I get them untangled."

"Right."

Then, suddenly loud with new discovery: "Unconsciously, I've been using 'Ikey' as a cop-out! In my gut I've been excusing everything by telling myself that *he* does all the shitty things, and poor l'il ol' Philip Marcus is just one of his innocent victims!"

Dr. Kohn said genuinely, "That's *good!* Go on!"

"What I have to see is that Ikey isn't *in* me like a rat that gets out of a hidden cage. No! Ikey IS me! Whatever 'he's' done, *I've* done! I can't shuck off the blame and responsibility." Reynolds' voice rose. "There isn't any Mr. Hyde! There is only me! Me, myself, and I!"

"Right!"

"No Ikey takes over! I *invite* him in when *I* want to do the hairy numbers!"

Dr. Kohn said, "I am delighted you've seen all this without my help."

"Yes," Reynolds breathed, slumping into exhaustion.

"Don't quit now," Dr. Kohn said quickly. "I have a hunch there are more fish ready for the hook today."

Reynolds gave an exultant cry. "Yes!" The light that flashed was a laser burning straight through the enmeshed crud of a lifetime. It was concentrated, nonverbal truth. Reynolds had to brake himself so he could translate the piercing radiance into words.

He began slowly. "What I see is *how* Ikey's destructiveness has been working in my life." He borrowed psychoanalytic terms from the casebooks; they were appropriate now, no longer window dressing: "I see the dynamics of my destructiveness, in two ways. For one thing, the rotten things I've done all have one thing in common—they put me down! I recapitulated my father's attacks on me by making myself as scurvy and unworthy as he said I was!"

"Yes—"

There was a crescendo of insight. "But the important thing is *why* I would do that, *why* I would keep going into that ditch. I did it because it kept me in the position of the injured child!—who then had a *right* to whatever comfort he could find, in whiskey, or sex, or whatever!"

"Yes—"

"Wow."

"Yes."

There was a pause. The doctor continued, "You said you saw two aspects?"

Reynolds nodded. "The other side of the lousy coin. My father might think me a stinker, but I would show the world my power. In sex, I could have power over women with my calls! At work, I would be *boss* so I could have power over everyone I worked with! I would be a genius so I could have power over my customers! At home, I would be infallible so I could lord it over my wife and children! Everywhere, I would be Glorious so I could live by my own rules in my own world!"

Dr. Kohn nodded vigorously. "Two damn big fish! I think I see even one more. Try for it."

Reynolds shook his head to clear it. "I'm beat," he said, but with a bright smile. Inside, he felt charged up. It was Ikey who was trying to shut him down. Ikey was beginning to realize this was no joke, that he was being chased for his dirty life.

Sensing Reynolds' struggle, Dr. Kohn repeated encouragingly, "Keep trying."

Reynolds took a deep breath. He felt himself sliding into a cool pool, grateful for the reprieve for his sweating body. He was in a glade with leafy trees among which birds were flying, brilliant colors. They sang words, clearly: "I love you. I love you." Crashing suddenly into the idyllic scene came Reynolds' father, bull-like, bellowing, and shooting at the birds with a huge penis-gun.

Reynolds' voice fell to a murmuring echo of the birdsong, "Love. Love." He sat up on the couch and turned a puzzled look to his doctor.

"Something connecting Love and my Father? He kills the birds but I keep hearing the song." Reynolds' frown deepened, and his fist abruptly slammed into his palm. *"Big* fish—a goddamn whale!" He stopped for a deep, trembling breath.

"A whale," Dr. Kohn repeated very softly.

Reynolds enunciated every word with a feeling that he was chiseling letters into stone. "I did all those lousy things *because way down I have been trying all these years to win my father's love by being as despicable as he always said I was!"*

He stopped again, overcome. "How the hell about that? I've been trying to buy that sonofabitch's love by being a son of a bitch! If I proved he was right, he might not hate me so much!"

Dr. Kohn's voice was clear, loud, genuine applause. *"Yes!"*

"I twisted my life into a corkscrew, and he wasn't worth one damn minute of it!" There was a heady surge of freedom.

Reynolds was struck again by the seemingly tortuous way the analysis elicited the links that suddenly locked together into a great crane able to haul the leaden debris out of the muck below.

Dr. Kohn was saying, "This has been a hell of a day, and I'm sorry that's all we have time for now, Phil."

At the door, Reynolds pivoted. "You called me *'Phil'!"*

Dr. Kohn was smiling broadly. "I suppose that's the way I feel about you today."

Reynolds stood for a moment with his head high, his eyes shining, his happy smile returning the doctor's.

He wished he could go out the front door so Mrs. Wheatley could see his joy.

On Park Avenue, he stood for a moment looking up at the old building where Dr. Kohn had his office, rejoicing.

He'd caught his demon by the toe now! He'd chain him once and for all!

Among other wonderful things, it meant that soon he wouldn't need to be coming back here.

It was going to be a great New Year all around!

Drowsing with Penny warm in his arms, Philip Reynolds thought contentedly that the analysis was paying at least one clear dividend. He could go to bed with Penny without feeling guilt. He was not "cheating" Helena; he was having an authentic experience which—under circumstances Helena herself insisted on—concerned only him and simply had no relationship to his wife.

For a doubtful moment, Reynolds asked himself whether that was rationalization, but he told himself immediately the answer was in how he *felt.* In his gut, not his head. And being with Penny in bed felt good, and clean, and right. No seaweed.

Penny stirred and smiled in her sleep, and Reynolds smelled cinnamon, deliciously aphrodisiac he was now delightedly free to admit.

9

Reynolds and Penny settled into a pattern. At the agency, they went about the day's work without a difference, except that Reynolds might reach for Penny's hand when she came to his desk, or Penny might brush the top of Reynolds' head with her lips if they were alone. She might murmur her private privilege, "Sweetie." At first, Reynolds found it cloying, but he came to like the word as part of an ingenuous quality Penny still held beneath her growing poise and confidence.

Several nights a week Reynolds went to Penny's place. Although his studio was more convenient, there was a tacit agreement that Penny did not sleep with him there. It seemed more a courtship this way, and also an unspoken recognition that Reynolds was not entirely free.

But in the middle of a blustery March, almost exactly on the anniversary of the start of Reynolds' analysis, Penny moved out of her flat into his apartment. It was almost as if the winds whipping across the Hudson were pressing the two to a greater, more urgent intimacy. Penny surrendered wholly to her love and asked nothing more than to be with Reynolds. He responded out of a need to recapture emotions which, he felt with new and flaring resentment, the years had pillaged. At Dr. Kohn's, Reynolds pondered aloud, "I suppose this ends my marriage, doesn't it?" The doctor asked, "Is every married man living with someone else ending his marriage?" Reynolds felt foolish. "Of course not." And tried to redeem himself: "I mean in a *meaningful* sense."

The doctor rejoined, "We're here to find out what that means, aren't we?" Kohn was giving no free passes, Reynolds knew very well after the year on the unyielding couch.

It did bother Reynolds that he was unfairly keeping Penny from meeting men her own age. He was inclined to agree with G. B. Shaw that every man over forty is a scoundrel. Penny laughed at his misgivings. "I've got what *I* want," she said.

"I don't know about that," Reynolds worried genuinely.

"All anyone ever has is Right Now," Penny reminded him.

How true the sophomorism sounded, Reynolds thought glumly. But Penny didn't know life yet. Banks call loans. Wives call lawyers. Pipers present bills to dancers. He said, "That's the difference between our ages, my darling. *I* know there's a tomorrow."

Penny had stopped his doubts with a kiss.

To his apartment Reynolds now brought flowers and caviar. He put in a small wine cellar, introducing Penny to Châteaux Margaux and Haut Brion, Petrus and Ausone. 1961's. The agency double line was still lean, but, as Reynolds told Dr. Kohn: "I'm beginning to like myself enough to allow myself a few damned treats."

Evenings were quiet. They watched television to monitor commercials. Penny read furiously, begging Reynolds' guidance. While he avidly plowed through his psychology texts, she studied art, Greek literature, philosophy. She only half laughed when Reynolds joked that she ought to pay tuition if he was going to be Mark Hopkins on one end of their log and she on the other. She did agree enthusiastically when he told her the currency in which he wanted the tuition paid.

They made love often and long. Penny spotted a *New York Times'* "gobbledegookism," which she felt applied to them perfectly. The story read: "During October alone, the most popular month for weddings, one couple exchanged vows every 12 seconds around the clock." Grinning, Penny wanted to know when they ate or slept.

At the apartment as at the office, Penny was adroit and thorough. She tacked daily lists next to a calorie-counting chart. Reynolds had given her a note pad with the legend *A Faire Aujourd'hui* beneath a photo of a couple enjoying sex, and Penny gaily wrote her errands below it in large block letters: TAILOR, GROCER, BUTCHER, HAIRDRESSER, WINDOW WASHER, OPERA SUBSCRIPTION, EXTERMINATOR, HEELS P'S SHOES, LIQUOR STORE . . .

Reynolds observed her indulgently. He suggested that lists like hers should be placed in cornerstones. More than other artifacts they would tell future archaeologists how this age had lived. Penny agreed soberly, and added the vitamins and minerals she was now buying for Reynolds. He grimaced as she wrote them down. The difference between his shelf and hers in the medicine chest wasn't funny, he considered.

On a glowing Sunday morning in May, Penny happily loaded the white iron table on their terrace with the bagels, feta cheese, and smoked salmon Reynolds had brought up with the Sunday *Times*. As they ate, Reynolds watched Penny's morning-fresh radiance, framed against the backdrop of magical Manhattan—skyscrapers lifting into cloudless space, elegant townhouses visible on quiet side streets below, Miró silhouettes of water tanks, and a sleek silver plane catching the morning sun like an arrow as it curved toward La Guardia Airport.

There was still a young girl in the roundness of Penny's cheeks, and her wide mouth held a furtive giggle even in repose. But there was a woman's depth in her knowing eyes, along with her enlarging sense of her talent and power. Reynolds took her in with gratitude and some uneasiness. How long could this undefined relationship go on? he asked for the hundredth silent time.

When Penny went into the kitchen for more coffee, Reynolds followed her with a strange premonition of loss. He pulled her into his arms, breathing her name. She fell against him willingly. Whatever, whenever he wanted. Love is never having to say No, or Later.

Penny's robe opened and her breasts were thrumming to his seeking fingers, her nipples up and instantly hard for him. As his hand moved down her soft skin to her bush, her quickly moist spot waited hungrily for his first touch as if she had never felt it before. She went for his hardness at the same time, voracious again for his sex she could feel swelling. They crumpled to the floor together, entangled in their robes, their need, answering their uncertainties.

It was enough, Reynolds told himself when they were resting. He wasn't ready to make any new decisions, and Penny didn't want him to.

Later, when Reynolds stretched for the Sunday paper, Penny swept it out of his hand. "Come on and let me show you Central Park." It occurred to Reynolds that for all his years in and around the city, he had never been there.

It was a revelation. In the spring air the trees shimmered with new buds. Splashes of bright cherry and magnolia blossoms made a dazzling aura of pinks, reds, oranges against the young yellow greens of the trees, and fairy white dogwood blossoms punctuated the scene in a breathtaking urban lyricism. On the gray-blue lake, ablaze with reflected sun sparks, colored rowboats slid along as gay as whistled tunes. The sun in the east glistened diamonds on Central Park West windows, medieval jewels set in the brick walls of modern castles. All around Reynolds and Penny flowed good-humored people, walkers, joggers, hansom riders, bicyclists, in colored sweaters, caps, dresses, shawls, baby blankets. Reynolds said it was like a Jackson Pollock, a gallimaufry of living colors shifting on the great canvas of the park.

Penny wasn't sure she didn't think Jackson Pollock was a phony, but if Phil Reynolds said he was great, that had to give her pause. They had talked about it hard at the Modern Museum one Saturday afternoon, and she had felt ignorant, second-rate, and resentful. *De gustibus* wasn't enough, Reynolds had lectured. It had to be *informed* taste. She wasn't going to spoil this precious day with any of that confusion.

A genuine surprise to Reynolds was a folk group dancing enthusiastically to a tape machine playing every kind of music, Greek, Italian, Jewish, Irish, Polish. The melting pot danceth over, Reynolds smiled.

Nearer the lake the rhythms changed. Bongos sounded from the shore and from the boats. They shafted cross-beats over the New York water from Cuba, Africa, South America, the Caribbean. On a green slope, Reynolds and Penny were diverted by a crashing lively steel band that bejeweled the air. Reynolds watched with admiration and an ache of regret. He had always wanted to play an instrument, but his father— Now, ruefully, Reynolds could in imagination hear the lesson the young Jamaican was teaching with his hammers flashing on the steel drums in the sun:

"Mon, if you don't got nothin' to play on, you make it! You blow you a shell, whistle you a reed, stomp you a log, bong you a bone! Hey, looka them fat oilcans! Suppose a coconut drop one day, like that apple on Newton's dome—boo-ong! Beautiful! Hey, I saw me off a piece of that sassy steel, git me a hammer, 'sno doubt not a Steinerway piana but she can play soft and mellow or hard like your head! Like *this!*" The mallets whacked away joyously while other players danced around jauntily with furious bongos, bells, voices, and the jawbone of an ass. Middle-class bicyclists stopped to watch the virtuosity with self-conscious smiles, dismounting and holding their bikes politely. Their pleased eyes demanded of strangers: Isn't this great? New York isn't just dogshit and mugging!

Reynolds led the crowd's enthusiastic applause and contributed a large bill among the coins in the hat. He received a special eye-widened Thank *You* from the perspiring black boy.

But there was another kind of music in the park less ingratiating. Wherever Reynolds and Penny strolled, their ears were split by raucous radios carried flauntingly with volume turned as high as possible. Broken sound rasped miserably out of the cheap speakers. Reynolds felt the noise as a physical assault. He noticed that his disapproval of the strutting offenders was shared by a well-dressed black couple nearby.

Penny took it with a shrug. "Poor New York. Every kind of pollution."

"There ought to be a law," Reynolds grumbled. "Why do they have to play those things so *loud?*"

"I suppose it's a way of walking tall," Penny observed. "It's almost always poor Puerto Ricans and blacks, their way of saying, 'I hope this bugs you, tells you I'm *here,* man. Louder than you means better than you, I'm a *Big* Man! They can't afford the pimps' Cadillacs to show off. It's, like, they carry a thunder chip on their shoulder, daring us to do something about it. Sometimes I think it's like a graffiti of noise."

Reynolds' frown of distaste turned into a small smile. "That's an interesting way of putting it." She'd be a copywriter one day.

Penny was going on. "Another thing they do that kills me personally is the way they snap gum on buses. I'm sure it's on purpose to annoy people."

Reynolds said, "Those sets look pretty expensive." The size, gaudy chrome, and arrays of buttons seemed a status symbol.

Penny answered with an edged tone. "I'd bet most of them are stolen, or bought with welfare money." There was clear complaint in her voice as she added, "I work so they can buy stuff like that with my taxes to thumb their nose at me with their noise. It's a lousy joke."

Unexpectedly, Penny uttered a bright laugh. "I know one thing I'd like to do. I have a fantasy where I invent a gadget that can knock out these radios. I carry it around in my pocket, aim it, and press a secret button. I wish someone would really make one. I'd love to see the look on their faces when their machines went dead!"

Reynolds regarded Penny with fresh interest. It seemed she carried her share of intolerance. At the same time, though God knew he agreed with her absolutely, it was a little disquieting. It was appropriate and all right for him to be a curmudgeon about things like this noise, but he didn't expect the heat of her resentment from Penny's generation.

Penny's generation. He was back to that cloud over their relationship.

Before it could engulf him, Penny was going on with her indictment. "Another of their thumb-nosers is smoking on buses and subways. I once asked a girl to quit it, and she threatened she'd come upside my face with her knife if I didn't mind my own fucking business. No wonder people are afraid to complain." Penny shook her head unhappily. "It's the only thing I really don't like about the city—this feeling as if Attila the Hun is in these ghetto camps sending out these scouts until one day the hordes will overrun everything."

Reynolds, who knew this aspect of New York only from a commuter train passing through Harlem, said casually, "I'm sure it's not that bad."

Penny smiled. "Not today, anyway." She changed her mood and tugged him unceremoniously toward a hot dog stand.

Buying frankfurters-and-sauerkraut and sodas, Penny pointed above the Great Meadow. Kites of every color and shape danced in the sky. There was a contest, it seemed. Reynolds had never seen anything like it. The kites strutted, circled, skipped, slid, swooped, climbed, fell, fluttered, skidded, while their long tails swirled behind in a looping accommodation of their dances, a blessing and grace of air itself. Above them all, a police helicopter added a final holiday touch, as well as a note of reassurance. The green and white cabin contrasted gruffly with the rainbow tracings of the kites. The ungainly machine seemed to be imitating them clumsily, pirouetting like a clown stomping on his own feet in a grotesque circus ballet.

The kites made Reynolds think of his daughters. A prickle of guilt ran over his skin like St. Elmo's fire. There had to come a day when Penny and he would have to stop evading the question of where they were heading, a day when "Now" would not be enough.

Penny sensed the darkening of Reynolds' mood and said quickly, "Let me show you Bethesda Fountain, where the kinkies hang out."

The Sunday exhibition of freaky young and old astonished and dismayed Reynolds. One group approaching on the path was clearly made up of homosexuals. They were camping openly, with hands exaggeratedly on hips, and casting high squeals like fishing lines to hook whoever might take their bait. Reynolds put his arm around Penny, muttering, "Christ, they're disgusting!" Nothing sickened him more than fags who flaunted their degeneracy. He knew gays in advertising who hated these exhibitionists as much as he did. "Let's get out of here," he said roughly. In turning blindly, he bumped into a tall, thin black figure with blond hair. The man flashed him a bold, inviting smile and swished his purse in Reynolds' direction.

"I do have what you want, dear," the man lisped.

Reynolds knew it was foolhardy, but his fists came up. Penny grabbed him with quick anxiety.

The fruity smile turned ugly. "You tagged *me,* dearie. Now you don't want to play?" It was a mean mixture of insolence and sluttishness. The man's friends, black and white, made a quick, threatening circle.

Reynolds gritted, "You belong in a zoo!"

The clicked knife hissed a hair away from Reynolds' nose. The face was savage, but the tone was purring. From the group came a clicking, mocking laughter. "Suck my cock, eat my shit, and drink my piss, honky mother!"

Reynolds lashed out despite Penny's cry of warning. His blow was slammed aside, and the knife ripped his sleeve. Penny screamed in terror. A police whistle blew nearby.

"Split!" a high voice cried. There was a pounding commotion, then only the buzz of curious onlookers as two mounted policemen came clattering up to the white-faced couple.

Back in the apartment, still shaken, Penny stared at the ripped jacket. "They could have *killed* you." Her anxiety was compounded with rising consternation about Reynolds. Something withdrawn in his eyes held her from expressing it aloud. She wanted to ask him if he hadn't realized the risk. She would have expected a man like him not to invite that kind of trouble.

On his part, Reynolds was not saying to Penny what was consuming his mind. He had wanted to savage that man, murder those creeps! He assured himself righteously that the feeling wasn't sick or neurotic this time; it wasn't Ikey! This kind of resentment, Reynolds told himself, he *never* wanted to be rid of—not by caution, not by Penny's worried look, not by Dr. Kohn's eternal admonitions! If chance ever brought that homosexual cocksucker across his path again, he'd destroy him with his bare hands. With great joy!

Reynolds dreamed that night:

A grammar school teacher, Liliam W. Roughbors, has kept a boy of twelve after class. She lifts her dress, leans over her desk, and reveals luscious naked buttocks. The boy is afraid. She says, "Open your pants." He takes out a boy's dick, like a pencil, stiff as steel. "Stick it in me," the teacher pants.

The boy goes for her, but the buttocks sprout two fat nipples. He starts to suck them, and she reaches around and jacks him off, but a loud fart blasts them apart, and the room stinks so bad he wants to run out. But the teacher is holding his dick, and as he backs away it stretches and becomes a whip. She yanks it off the boy and starts hitting him with it, latah-jumping, and screaming, "Murderer! Motherfucker!"

With that, a thin black man appears, pushes the woman aside, glowers, "Don't hurt my little boy," and bites off the small pale testicles, crunching them daintily like delicate almonds.

Reynolds never remembered the dream, and so could not discuss its meaning with Dr. Kohn, or his unconscious.

Part Four

"A great lost river
  Crepitates
  Through dry cracks of his brain.
  Long-buried days
  Rise out of tombs
  With fists that unfold
  Lost powers they held . . ."

—Stephen Spender

10

The next morning's papers exploded different dynamite for Reynolds. A full-page ad for Acadia Motors' small car appeared in the *Times*. Reynolds lifted the sheet to Penny with disbelief. "The sons of bitches!"

The blazened headline was his own three words, the caption and campaign theme he had created on the train over a year ago:

The Good Ride...

Penny gasped. "That's *your* line, Phil! I saw it on your desk the morning Detroit dumped on you!"

Reynolds stared at the ad critically. "It works just the way I thought it would," he said.

Penny was incredulous. "I'd never believe Rod Graham would do a thing like that!"

"It couldn't be Rod," Reynolds agreed. "I can tell you who it was," he added grimly. "Jock Rogers! He could have seen it!" Reynolds slammed the paper down. "You can bet on it!"

Penny said, agitated, "He'll lie, of course, but it's his word against two of us."

"Get me Rod Graham on the phone," Philip Reynolds ordered quietly.

It had begun to rain heavily, but the Graham offices were only short blocks away and there was no sense taking a cab. Reynolds waited uncomfortably in the reception area. No one had taken his wet coat or hat. The obviously British, nose-in-the-air receptionist had announced Mr. Graham to be on a long-distance call, and returned to her magazine. If they had merged, Reynolds thought resentfully, *she* would be fired pretty quick. He studied the wood panels, the thick carpet, indirect lighting, and, conspicuously, no display of the agency's work. That was self-assurance, Reynolds considered. Still, if you believed in advertising, it made sense to display it the way his own reception room did.

When Reynolds was finally ushered to the expansive corner office, he remembered its elegance. It was impeccably furnished with antiques and held some fantastic old masters. Reynolds saw with renewed pleasure the Caravaggio, the David, the Fragonard. Graham was knowing as well as wealthy. Seated at his Louis Something desk, he looked like a portrait of himself, perfectly tailored, head high, eyes aloof, model all-time gentleman. "What did you want to see me about, Reynolds?"

"Reynolds," not "Phil." And his voice as cold as his stare. Helena had not been wrong about his reaction to the fiasco.

No prelude was necessary. Reynolds laid the Acadia advertisement on the desk and tapped the headline. "I wrote that." He couldn't help but add "Graham" in the same tone his name had been spoken.

"Eh?" Graham's chin came down, his eyes narrowed on the page. "Eh?" He was as astounded as if Reynolds had fired a gun.

Reynolds went on, quietly. "There's only one way it could have gotten here. Jock Rogers ripped it off."

The marble green eyes lifted to stare hard at Reynolds. "You have a reputation for being somewhat erratic, Phil." It was "Phil" again, Reynolds noted with satisfaction. "It's one hell of an accusation to ask me to sign for. Are you sure about this?"

"I wouldn't be here otherwise."

There was a silence in the room, then Rod Graham nodded. His face was grim. "It's a dynamite line. We tested in the Midwest. People got the idea you subliminalized—'the good life.' "

Reynolds said, tight-lipped, "It's what I was after."

"I gave Jock a bonus, dammit!"

Reynolds wished Penny were in the room to see how Graham had come across without a moment's hesitation, without question or argument. There hadn't been any need for corroboration. When a man is decent, he's decent. Their respect was still mutual. "I'm glad it tested out," Reynolds said. A man could be pleased even in these circumstances.

Graham said, "We won't use it again, of course."

"If it's working, that would be a shame."

"Well, yes, but it's unfair for my shop to get the credit, and the Acadia people certainly have to know. Can we work something out? A royalty?"

"I haven't thought about it."

"I'll fire that scum, of course, but we decidedly ought to do something for you. Let me sift this a while and see if I can come up with a viable recco."

Reynolds smiled to himself. The men whose background was furthest from Madison Avenue spoke its tongue like the natives.

When Reynolds left, Graham pushed a button on his intercom and barked, "Jock! Haul your arse in here!" When he grew really angry, an "r" crept into Graham's pronunciation.

Going down in the elevator, Reynolds held an imaginary discussion with Dr. Kohn. He was pleased with the way he had handled himself. Though he had been boiling inside, he had kept his cool. Much better than charging in like an angry bull as he would have done a year ago. It came to him again how his neurotic temper had constantly betrayed and injured him. He might have gained an apology, a royalty, but not what was more important—the new respect he felt from Rod Graham. It was a heady feeling to be in control, even though there was a frustrated itch inside, the itch to confront Jock Rogers. But that was Ikey stuff, and past. Let Graham handle the inflated banana-head. His life was moving in its own fresh currents. The only real answer to your enemies was to make yourself so immune to their poison that, no matter how powerfully or deviously they might strike, they could not injure you.

Through the rest of that day and all night a pebble that dropped into Reynolds' thought kept stirring ripples. By the time he reached Dr. Kohn's office the next morning, he was ready to say immediately: "You know, I'm just beginning to realize how damned neurotic-irresponsible it was to walk away from the merger with Rod Graham." He added that at this time it didn't make any possible difference to him whose name might be first. "How about that!" he demanded of Dr. Kohn rhetorically.

"How about that?" the doctor echoed with satisfaction.

In his new mood, Reynolds phoned Graham directly. "Why don't we talk again about getting together?"

Graham was just as direct. "Tell you the truth, Phil, I've sort of been spinning through the same idea."

Reynolds moved the rest of the way at once. "I was wrong to be so stiff-necked last time. I don't give a frog's toenail about the name."

Graham said, "Meet me at the Union Club for lunch, and we'll see if we can get our ducks in a row."

Bread cast upon waters. Virtue its own reward. The couch does give birth! With his red crayon, Reynolds drew a swift, elated line through his lunch appointment. He was electric with his hunch. It was going to work, and it was going to be good, because he was getting his old big feet out of the way instead of tripping over them as he had the time before. What was it the Zen master said to the stumbling student? "The path is smooth. Why do you throw rocks before you?"

Reynolds smiled to himself at the irony. What had seemed like a low blow had knocked open a new door. It was a somber burlesque that Jock Rogers, in trying to screw Reynolds and Associates, had brought Reynolds together with Rod Graham again.

The two ad men kept their preliminary talks private. Graham was impressed by the visible transformation in Philip Reynolds. To Dr. Kohn, Reynolds said gratefully that it looked as if the merger was going to work, thanks largely to the analysis that was changing his personality.

And thanks to luck, he added with a subdued smile. Isn't it a travesty, Reynolds observed to the doctor, that we plan our lives—we organize, forecast, schedule, arrange, prepare, weigh every kind of input, make critical decisions only after the grimmest soul-searching—and then find that almost everything important that happens to us in life comes about through sheer happenstance! Think of how a man meets his wife, how he gets his first job, how he finds his place to live—

Within a week, Reynolds and Graham had an agreement in principle. This time there was no bomb to stop the final signing.

Reynolds brought the day's excitement back to the agency after the meeting at which the last details were settled. He swept Penny out of the office. "Holiday time!" He did not answer her excited questions until he had her seated beside him in a dim bar on Third Avenue: "How would you like working for 'Graham and Reynolds Advertising?' "

Penny was overcome, then hugged him tightly. "Oh, God! Terrific!"

They toasted the first champagne bottle empty as Reynolds explained what had taken place. Penny lifted a cautioning hand when Reynolds ordered more champagne. She didn't like the glaze beginning to coat his eyes.

Reynolds assured her it wasn't the champagne he was flying on. It wasn't the merger either. That was only one proof of the *real* cause for a celebration—*the success of his analysis!*

"Dr. Kohn is absolutely the miracle worker," Reynolds said well into the second bottle. He did not hear that his speech was thick.

When he called the bartender again, Penny intervened. "Phil, you know you can't take it."

Reynolds bristled with a glassy anger she had not seen since the afternoon in the park. "Who the hell do you think you are—Dr. Kohn? My wife?"

The words swirled in the air above them. Penny got up. "You've had enough!" she said flatly.

Reynolds grabbed her arm. Her gasp of pain brought heads around to their booth. "Siddown!"

Penny realized Reynolds was drunker than she thought. She knew that in this state he could raise hell without much warning. She sat down again, wanting to cry, and quaking with her presumption. Why did he have to be spoiling his red-letter day?

As if he had heard her, Reynolds lifted his glass and said the drunken words loud, to the amused, curious strangers, "Red-letter day, folks! Drink up! I'm buying!" His expression challenged Penny to stop him.

Suddenly Reynolds looked an old man to Penny. She saw his eyes pouchy, his cheeks loosening into jowls. For the first time, Penny could not keep her own shadow at bay—*could* it really work between them?

Penny slapped the thought away impatiently. She loved this man. He loved her. They had headaches, so did everyone else. He was working on his problems with Dr. Kohn. He might be backsliding today, but he had big reason to relax. It was her place to stand by and support him. She wasn't a kid, she was a woman. If Philip Reynolds had to go through this shtik in this damned bar, she'd pretend he was sick, had a fever or something. It was true. This was his sickness. He was having an attack she had to help him overcome.

But she didn't have to like the way he was demeaning himself and her.

A picture of Mickey with beer dribbling down his naked chest came to Penny. This was different, she rebuked herself at once. This man might be slobbering a little across the table, but he *was* Philip Reynolds, new partner-to-be of no one less than Rodney Graham!

Penny's self-excuses turned into despair as Reynolds refused to quit drinking. She could not pretend she did not feel disgust as well as pity when his head finally dropped to the table. She gave the bartender an extravagant tip to help with a cab, and was furious with both the man and herself. The size of the tip revealed her self-doubt, and his exaggerated effort at discretion—acting as if pouring Reynolds into the cab was as ordinary as pouring a beer inside—made her feel like a patronized child.

At the apartment she managed to get Reynolds undressed. She listened unhappily to his besotted snoring. Who could understand a man with so damned many facets, she asked herself. Penny stared at the powerful face, flaccid with alcohol's erosion. Maybe she ought to have a visit with Dr. Kohn to help her learn about him. She wished she were older. She wished she knew more about psychoanalysis. She wished she knew what she wished.

She left a note beside the bed in case Reynolds should wake up while she was out. "Gone shopping, back soon." She was going to add "Love" but was too put out. Reynolds' snoring stopped. She turned. He had shifted in the bed, and was clutching his pillow the way a child clings to a doll. Philip M. Reynolds, advertising powerhouse! Penny sighed. Apparently it was true that all men were kids.

She picked up the pencil and added the reluctant word.

Reynolds coughed himself out of a dream, hacking for breath. He had been back in a large park, alone. Black night, trees looming like heavy pipes, ominous organ chords. A light was flashing Morse code. It was the faggot. He was braying with superior laughter and shining a flashlight on his open fly. Inside lay not his sex but a green balloon. It inflated and encased Reynolds' head. At the same time, Reynolds felt gummy fingers pressing his sex, strangely seductive, arousing him. But it was revolting too. There was a sickening mixture of whiskey and bowels. The stench became a heavy, doughy piston that rammed into his mouth to plug his throat so that he was suffocating.

Choking and trying to call out for Penny, Reynolds stumbled blindly about the room. He knocked over the telephone stand. Lifting it groggily, he knew at once what he wanted to do, must do, would do. He laughed drunkenly as he started to dial: "Come on, Ikey, ol' boy! It's okay to come out 'n play." His idiot laughter made him dizzy. "Nobody here to stop us, kid . . ."

Nobody to stop him. No voice from inside. No echo from Dr. Kohn's couch, no signal of the strenuous, aching months. There was only the old, rising heat that torched his brain away.

The first woman shrilled, "Drop dead!" and hung up. The second kept saying, "Who? Who do you want? There is nobody here by that name, sir."

She said it over and over again, more and more softly, while his voice whispered on. Reynolds and Ikey both knew she was listening with relish to every syllable, and they started the old thing with the obscene gloating.

A key clicked in the lock outside. The sound stunned Reynolds sober. He slammed the phone down and rolled over on the bed, pretending sleep in a curled knot. Inside, he was already berating himself. Why had he started it again, why let Ikey take over, defeat him and Dr. Kohn after all the bitter work? *And on this day of all days?*

Reynolds churned with the agony of his failure. He had dared to congratulate himself on how well the analysis had worked! He had paraded his "changed personality" before Rod Graham! Changed? From shit to shit! He could never face Dr. Kohn again! He wasn't worth the time of anyone's day! (His father had been right all the time!)

And if Ikey didn't stop leering on the bed now, he'd cut his stinking balls off. But *he* was Ikey, Reynolds reminded himself tormentedly as the alcohol urged him back to sleep and forgetfulness. He pretended not to hear Penny's solicitous, "Phil, are you all right?" God, she would despise him if she guessed how weak and contemptible he truly was!

Penny put her cool palm on Reynolds' forehead. He looked so defenseless sleeping. She had no right to censure him. It was cruel to be so quick with judgment. After all, the man was entitled to one afternoon off the straight-and-narrow, wasn't he? How easy it was to forget her own drunken office escapade with Ted Watson. Penny shivered. How easy it was to excuse one's self, how hard to excuse others.

$$11$$

On his way to Dr. Kohn the next morning, Reynolds was harrowed with self-contempt. His only consolation was that he wasn't trying this time to hide from what he had done. He would tell the doctor about both the drinking *and* the phone calls, no deceptions, no excuses. At least he was at a stage where he could face the realities despite the anguish they brought. If this misery was punishment, he deserved it all and should bear it without complaining.

On the couch, the execrable report grated out of Reynolds' mouth. In a new paroxysm of bewilderment, he demanded, "But why in God's name did I go hairy when everything was so upbeat?"

Icily, Dr. Kohn inquired, "Why, indeed?"

Long pause, wheels racing, gears slipping, catching. A shout from the couch: "I've never made a call when I was sober! Never!"

"So?"

"Don't you see? I have to cut myself down to be able to do it!"

"Cut yourself down?"

Long since, Dr. Kohn's repetitions had ceased annoying Reynolds. They helped him deepen and widen his insights.

"Cut myself down to kid size so I can do a kid thing!"

Reynolds seized the perception desperately. There was a swelling in his chest that told him he was on to a major moment in the analysis. The light brightened: "Most of the phone calls, doctor—they came right after I did something *successful!* Yesterday it was finalizing the deal with Rod Graham!" A flood of words, explanations, understandings was coursing up in him, but Reynolds fell mute. It was a time to let his insight penetrate more of the darkness within. He had finally learned from Dr. Kohn that his glib verbalism was a foe. He was coming to understand how he had used words all his life to avoid real feeling, to keep emotions superficial, to short-circuit his electricity into his head instead of discharging it through his heart. Life wasn't words, no matter how poetic, how powerful, how intriguing, how seductive. A man needs to feel through his veins, not through his tongue. That was where analysis worked—in the sense of "fermented"—as it was working right now. Ice was cracking in his spine, knobs were turning in his gut, tunnels were clearing in his bowels.

Reynolds breathed deeply, excited. He was seeing new links and chains:

When he did something successful, he had genuine proof that he was a grown man, BUT in his secret depths he did not want to be grown! Drinking reduced him to childhood, and less!

Link—

Like Peter Pan, he didn't want the responsibility, the final giving up of his childhood, maybe because he had never had a real one!

Link—

To be grown, self-reliant, mature, meant the ultimate loss of his mother. He had loved her as much as he had hated his father. As violently!

Link—

At the same time, he didn't want to confront the hatred of his father that was churned up by these swirling currents.

And LINK—

All these contradictions were charged with pain. He had had to find ways of concealing them, or he would have lived in continuous anguish, impossible. So that's where his Off-Switch had come from!

Link—

And that had turned him into a *zombie!* His ingenious device had backfired from the beginning. *You couldn't switch off only ugly acts and bad feelings; you turned off everything!* He paused to consider that blazing truth.

Link—

His glibness masked the fact that he lived as a machine, a computer clicking on old tapes and programmed routines. Reynolds' voice faded in amazement at his image.

"Interesting way of putting it," Dr. Kohn encouraged.

"I never thought of it that way before, but it's as if I haven't had any real emotions of my own!"

"No real emotions of your own—"

Reynolds' tone rang with discovery. "I see why my mind has so often gone back to that volcano in Hawaii!"

"This time you've lost *me.*"

"My 'Off-Switch'—it's really a lid, too, isn't it? Holding down the lava in my gut! To feel *anything* I have to explode, erupt, smash through with my violence, the 'shark frenzy.' " Reynolds gave an acid laugh. "I'm mixing a lot of figures, but that's where my short fuse comes from, doesn't it?"

Dr. Kohn provided perspective: "One of the reasons."

Reynolds raced down a new tunnel he glimpsed. "And back to the goddamn phone calls! *A way of having sex without real emotion!*" He waited, turning the facets of this new thought in his searching glass.

"That certainly seems part of it," Dr. Kohn said.

Reynolds and Dr. Kohn worked on this vein for weeks. It was a period to recall Karen Horney's wise admonition: The process of therapy is not having a radiant insight but rather coming back to it again and again, seeing how it relates to every relevant dimension and activity of your life. You widen old shafts and sink new ones each session, letting in more and more light.

Nor do you reach the unconscious by digging straight down, as Reynolds had supposed at the start. The shafts had to branch, curve, and cross in every direction. How, for example, could he tell Dr. Kohn that he was a zombie, a robot, when obviously he loved—had loved?—Helena, and certainly felt emotion for his daughters—and Penny?

Dr. Kohn had come forward with one of his rare answers. "Phil, if you weren't hooked into reality at some points, you would be psychotic entirely, in an institution instead of this office. It's true that even the emotions you do feel are anemic, so to speak, but let's stick with your problem in the areas where you say quite correctly that you are numb, or at least insensitive."

The doctor saw Reynolds struggling to follow. He added, *"Where* have you been obviously unfeeling, insensible, hardened?"

After a long pause, Reynolds whispered, "Jesus Christ, I do see it." The gate opened. For the first time, it came to Philip Reynolds that the women he phoned had never been real individuals to him. He had never conceived that his voice might be an actual assault on a woman, a violation of her sensibilities as vicious as physical rape. He had gloated on the few responses he had won, and never considered for a moment the far greater number of women who had been shocked and horrified. It had never occurred to him that, especially with younger girls, he might be doing lasting damage. The reality of the *other* person had never existed at all for him! That was why, he discovered now, he had never suffered shame or remorse.

For a moment, Reynolds felt sharp anger. It was another instance in which, by cutting away a neurotic construction of his private world, the analysis was robbing him of experiences that had stirred him to life. They might have been ersatz and chimerical, offensive and disgraceful, but they had heated and thrilled him.

Dr. Kohn had interrupted. "Was it 'heat' or fever?" He would not let Reynolds forget they were probing not a passing aberration but a chronic illness.

Reynolds' annoyance flared with a long-suppressed question. "Okay, I'm sick, but what are we curing me *to?* What's so great about becoming adjusted to the 'real' world with all its hypocrisy, bullshit, misery—"

Dr. Kohn gaveled hard with his fist on his desk. "Later! Right now the acorn doesn't need to worry about the kind of forest it will grow into! It needs to worry about starting healthy roots!"

Reynolds mulled that over and simmered himself down. He had thrown up resistance again precisely because he was working well. He could get along with what Dr. Kohn said. If he kept working patiently, his acorn would grow, find its own authentic destiny. But, God, the patience, and the strength, and the endless exhaustion of these endless sessions.

Reynolds commented on the "existentialist nature" of Dr. Kohn's interruption, and started to quote Kierkegaard and Sartre. The doctor hit his desk again, harder. "Please don't do that! We are still looking for an acorn, not a philosophy!"

Reynolds managed a smile, crooked. Good old Aloysius Kohn was right as per usual. The doctor had warned from the beginning that Reynolds would be a troublesome patient because he was "too damned smart." Reynolds still had not digested what the doctor emphasized: "To develop a neurosis as slick as yours takes enormous intelligence and cunning. A less agile mind can't bring as much creativity to the neurotic's battle against change."

His own worst enemy, as always, it appeared.

Reynolds was recognizing more and more clearly how he used his cleverness to deflect the analysis. He had spent full sessions on what he knew were false leads. He had used mental prestidigitation and flimflam of every kind, like a stage magician. Thank God for a doctor who wouldn't be conned.

As summer wheeled into fall, and the new agency began to function, Reynolds became more and more impatient for the analysis to be done. He was weary of the constant self-nagging, self-suspicion, self-doubting at every turn. He was on a new highroad in his career. By now, Helena had made it clear she wanted the separation to continue indefinitely. Perhaps, though Reynolds did not see how, she knew of his affair with Penny. On Reynolds' side, if Penny were not in the picture, he might have pushed for a reconciliation. As it was, he felt that if Helena was waiting for him to make the first move, the ball game had changed— although in fairness it should be recognized that he had not planned it that way, Reynolds observed to himself.

His life with Penny settled into domestic tranquillity. He had even made his peace with one underlying problem, his old telephone call to her. He explained to Dr. Kohn that Penny had just been one of the "mannequins" then. Now she was *real,* and they were in a totally different world from the one in which the call had occurred.

Still, Reynolds complained to Kohn that, nearing the third year of analysis, he still ran into trouble. Unhappily he reported that after a Thanksgiving Day of drinking, the telephone temptation had hit him again. It happened in a restaurant as he passed public phones outside the men's room. If someone had not come along, he was pretty sure that he would have succumbed. Was he doomed for the rest of his life? he asked the doctor with despair.

Dr. Kohn had been tolerant. "We'd need to be very suspicious if tough symptoms like yours disappeared easily. This one can hang on for years, but I promise you it will fade—if you keep working."

So keep on working, Reynolds grudged wearily, through the bleary-eyed early rising, the Sisyphean drudgery of the couch, and the chronic exasperation of never reaching an answer that would hold still long enough to become a conclusion.

"Because it's still mostly up in your head," Dr. Kohn answered the grouching. You *know* things, you *see* them, you discover and disclose and

ferret out and you hook up and link up and relate and UNDER-
STAND. But you don't yet really FEEL!"

In his heart Reynolds knew that once more the doctor had put his
finger on a basic truth, but it only increased his restiveness. As hard as he
could, he genuinely tried to translate his head trips into blood-truths.
Hour after arduous hour he experienced inner wheels whizzing in his
effort to connect the motor of his head with the transmission of his gut. It
seemed beyond his control.

"It's hopeless," he said one day.

Dr. Kohn counseled, "When you're ready it will happen."

"When I'm Methuselah?"

"When you're ready." Old Imperturbable.

"After all this time, I'm ready, dammit!"

"Apparently not."

The sword was back in his back. "Why not!" A long pause from the
couch, then his own tentative reply. "Because for me feeling is pain. If I
still don't want really to feel, I must be afraid of some pain I haven't dug
up yet." It sounded right, a step forward. But by now Reynolds was as
leery of his snow jobs as Dr. Kohn. He waited, thinking, testing.

What came was a dream. "Hey!" he called out in what had become a
signal of a turn in the road. "I had this dream I forgot. About—Christ,
remember that girl in the water when I first dreamed about the ferry,
way back? I'm swimming with her again, but this time when she pulls
me off, a million eggs come out of her cunt, and I fertilize them." He
stopped, and added slowly, "Without screwing!" He stopped again.

"Stay with that."

"Yes." Reynolds tightened his eyes with effort. He seemed at another
impasse, with the image repeating itself like the continuous film reels
used for displays, until suddenly he saw he was connected to the girl by a
tube. Umbilical cord? *His mother?* Incest? He was back to Oedipus?

"Your mother?" Dr. Kohn repeated the report in a doubtful tone.

"Well, the umbilical cord!" Reynolds said argumentatively.

"What color was it?"

What the hell did color have to do with it, Reynolds wondered with
annoyance. But he had learned to respond.

"Black."

"Any association to a looping black cord?"

Roughly now: "I told you! Umbilical!"

"Toy shovel!" Dr. Kohn clipped. "Let's *dig* after this!"

Reynolds squirmed on the couch with his eternal complaint. How could he tell Dr. Kohn what he didn't see? But okay. Be grateful that Kohn had apparently spotted something that was escaping him. He had long ago come to know that the doctor worked by hunches, a kind of ESP of his own that was often fruitful. So okay, back to the black cord—

What did the girl look like? That might be a clue.

Blank.

No, it was the cord, the cord, the goddamn cord of Dr. Kohn.

Black cord?—*Telephone cord!*

"Oh, Jesus, of course." Reynolds shouted his discovery.

"Hooray," Dr. Kohn muttered.

Now the quick question came clearly: What did telephone calls have to do with fertilizing fish eggs in the water?

Answer, immediate and convincing: Sex without screwing, again! *Exactly like his telephone calls,* a way of having sex without sex, without a real person, without a relationship!

And, notice, doctor! Fertilizing *fish* eggs ties in with treating the women as unreal, not human!

And, if you're removed from reality in terms of sex, you are removed from reality, period! Back to being a very sick man, but this time with a trembling queasiness inside that is bringing tears.

Phantom of the Phone Booth shaking and crying.

Dr. Kohn, watching approvingly, was saying, "That's all we have time for today, I'm sorry. We'll stay with this tomorrow."

Overnight the formless thought took shape. Reynolds came to the session shaken. "I know the girl in the water!" he began at once. "My sister!"

Dr. Kohn said, "Ah! You mentioned her once in passing at the very beginning. I wondered when she would come back."

"I've been working it through myself," Reynolds said, feeling a flow of confidence that he *could* do so despite the tough resistance he had had to struggle through. "How the dream relates to my sister, ties up with the telephone calls! It's weird."

No weirder than the other wild tangles of the shadow-skeins of his unconscious. Not weird, even—actually, the classical commonplace of sibling hatred, aggravated in his case by—Reynolds stopped. He needed to set this out for Dr. Kohn, and himself, from the beginning.

Enkindled, he told the story. "You must understand that my mother as well as my father wanted a girl, not a boy. Aside from the Jewish-Ikey thing with my father, boys were bad news. At least that's the impression

I got from the first day I can remember. As little kids, if my sister and I got into a scrap, my father would beat me, even if it was her fault." Reynolds nodded bitterly, remembering with abrupt, venomous clarity. "She was sugar and spice and everything nice, and boys—I—were shit. It wasn't just my sister, it was *all* girls. It wasn't just my parents. For everybody where we lived, *girls were good, boys bad!*"

A mounting sense of discovery: "Especially about *sex!* Sex equated with filthy, and *only* boys had sex in their minds. *Only* boys were dirty!"

Tunnels were hooking up unexpectedly.

"Here's what I see," Reynolds went on after a pause. "It's not just my problem with my father and Ikey. There I am, a kid who wants to be 'good' so my mother will love me, but the whole world around me pegs me as rotten and bad because I'm a boy. So I'm in a bind, but *I'm* smart enough to see a way out! *If I can show that girls are as nasty as boys, then no one can complain about me!* So my goal is to prove that girls have sex in their heads too, which makes them dirty too!"

Reynolds reviewed this perception with the feeling that he was drilling pay dirt. He followed the dynamics of the unconscious eagerly now.

Link—

"No matter how much a girl, a woman, might be a sexy bitch, she pretends she never has a sullied thought. But if I caught her off guard on the phone, then she might show her real colors! How about that!"

Reynolds was stunned by the multiple impact of what had just welled up. He faced Dr. Kohn. "So the damned calls did two separate things for me, had two separate hooks into my gut. First, they were a way of putting women down, which kept me up. And second, what I kept running into—sex without a relationship."

Dr. Kohn said, "And it's important to see the way these forces have kept combining in your unconscious—forming shifting alliances, so to speak—so you recognize how many different neurotic purposes a single symptom may serve."

Reynolds sighed with good feeling, and said, "Man, I could use a drink right now." He added at once, "I'm not serious, of course."

The doctor was upon him, astringently. "Of course you're serious! Why do you suppose you spoke of drinking just then?"

"Because I'm tired!" The doctor's poking stirred old defensiveness.

"No! Because you want to get on to something else!"

Reynolds yawned. "I'm really too beat."

He was startled by a guffaw from Dr. Kohn. "You have a quota of insights you are not permitted to exceed in one session?"

Reynolds couldn't help joining with a sheepish laugh.

"Let's get back to the drink you want."

Reynolds started to work by imagining he was in his own office. He saw himself rising from his desk as in the film effect in which a spirit leaves its body behind. He saw himself going to his bar, pouring a drink. He could smell the liquor, feel its warmth on his tongue and the comfort moving down his throat to his center, delicious, seducing.

Light glowed from the center. "Warm. Comforting. *Mother's milk!*" The light was bright but a shade went over it and Reynolds' eyelids drooped. His voice lowered to a drone without his realizing it. "Wanting to be an infant again? To be in the cradle is bliss." He was falling asleep. "Bliss. My mother with me always, taking care of me, keeping the world off me—"

There was an unexpected laugh, soft, from the couch. "My God, I can remember when she had me out in the carriage," Reynolds added to Dr. Kohn. "If kids were playing nearby, she'd start yelling at them, 'Don't skate near my baby's carriage!' If they kept it up, she'd scream until she was hysterical and they'd all be laughing at her, calling her a crazy witch! *'Don't skate near my baby's carriage!'* Christ, haven't I made that *my* theme song the rest of my life!"

Reynolds forced his eyes open. This time the new discovery came not with a bang but with a slow sigh. "Paradise Lost," Reynolds breathed. "Until my father broke it up, my mother made me the center of the universe, God Himself!" The building truth coursed faster through his blood.

Unprecedentedly, Reynolds got off the couch and went to Dr. Kohn's desk, his voice a pealing bell: "If whiskey links me up with that feeling, takes me back to that lost paradise, no wonder a man would drink himself deaf, dumb, and blind!"

Reynolds dreamed that twelve blue angels were pissing green off a cliff below which his sister was floating, drowned. He piloted a helicopter to rescue her, but the body broke into pieces as he tried to lift her, and the blue water was filled with pink bits—her arms, legs, fingers. Fish nibbled, and he tried to divert them by throwing out smelly chum, but he was himself diverted by a school of boys swimming wildly to see a girl exhibiting herself on a passing cruiser marked HILLERY REMN. The boy raced after the boat, but all he could see on deck was his mother suckling his newborn sister, who was whole except for a missing nose.

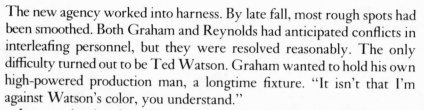

12

The new agency worked into harness. By late fall, most rough spots had been smoothed. Both Graham and Reynolds had anticipated conflicts in interleafing personnel, but they were resolved reasonably. The only difficulty turned out to be Ted Watson. Graham wanted to hold his own high-powered production man, a longtime fixture. "It isn't that I'm against Watson's color, you understand."

It was an ironic echo of Reynolds' early battle with Willie White, and again the stakes were high.

Reynolds stood firmly for Watson. "Guys like Ted don't get the chances they deserve. I want to keep him."

"Can't have two bulls in one pasture."

"Your man will find another spot easier than Ted."

"Well, if you care that much—"

"Yes, Rod. Absolutely on this one."

Watson heard of it, sought Reynolds out and offered his hand. "I've heard how you went to bat for me again, Phil. That's not shabby, friend. You're my man."

They clasped hands firmly. "I'll sign for you any day, Ted," Reynolds said, remembering the man's loyalty to him when he needed it.

It brought Lillian Schuster out of her distance too, and she accepted Reynolds' apology for what they could laugh at now as the Punctuation Explosion. "The thing that hurt was that you know I hate that shit worse than you do," Lillian couldn't help adding. Then she laughed, "If you want to start our club again, I've got a prize in my office." The goof was an enlarged reprint tacked over her desk. A headline from an Ohio State paper read: "Professor Calls Our Proofreading Abdominal." Lillian handed Reynolds another clip, a music review praising a women's orchestra: ". . . though weak in the bra section."

Reynolds found it good to be laughing with Lillian again.

The new team was meshing well throughout the agency. Reynolds did not bring his continuing tribulations on the couch into the office. Mishaps that would have sent him up the wall a year before found him quick to rein himself in. With solid gratification he told Dr. Kohn that each experience of self-control made the next time easier. Dr. Kohn nodded. By the new year, the G and R Profit and Loss Statement was comfortably in the black as a result both of new accounts and the spreading of overhead across the enlarged operation. Best, for Reynolds, was being out of the cash-flow straitjacket. He could "stretch," as Helena had once put it. Thinking about Helena, Reynolds blinked. Could it have been more than a year ago that they had separated? He sent her the last of the borrowed money. She replied with a proper note, conspicuously impersonal, but he had a new feeling that she would take him back now that he could honestly promise self-control. His trouble was that he was no longer sure, himself, what he wanted. He regarded himself in a state of suspension. It was enough to be content with Penny at the apartment, busy at the office, and indefatigable in Dr. Kohn's chamber. It left little time or thought for pressing the question of his marriage. If the wheel of his life was turning toward divorce, there was time for deciding; certainly, Penny wasn't asking anything but what they had. It was a new world, Reynolds told himself. He could be sure of one thing: Penny O'Hara would speak up for herself, loud and clear when she had anything to say.

Penny was having a ball. No longer needed in Lillian's slot, she had moved to a junior copywriter's office. It was tiny, but it had her name on the door. As the winter holidays came and went and Graham and Reynolds Advertising headed into its first spring, Penny kept proving to her group head that her copy had the clout that Reynolds had anticipated.

In the combined operation, Penny seldom met Reynolds during business hours, and no one at the agency suspected their private lives.

When Reynolds was invited to Connecticut for Selma's Sweet Sixteen party in May, he realized he was having a birthday too. It was the end of his second full year with Dr. Kohn. On the train, he wryly recalled his thought that he would be several months on the couch. Now he supposed he had at least another year to go.

His talks with Helena were difficult and only confirmed his negative thinking about their marriage. She let her voice sharpen when she said accusingly, "I know all about you and your secretary, Phil." He answered levelly, without correcting her about Penny's new status at the agency. "We're all adults, Helena. You wanted the separation in the first place. The question is how you feel about it now."

Helena said gravely, "I'd still be afraid to have you in the house. I'm sure that's unfair, but say it's something neurotic in *me*." Reynolds saw she was not being sarcastic. No, Helena would not have changed that much. "I'm not unhappy with the way things are," she added. "And I don't sense that you are."

Reynolds wondered again how she knew about Penny. "Maybe," he replied. "But after all this is my family." He heard the feebleness of his words, the formal gesture he apparently felt obliged to offer.

Helena gave him a tight smile. "Actually, when you said you'd come to Selly's party, I thought it was to talk about a divorce."

Like Dr. Kohn, Reynolds turned the question back. "Do you want a divorce?"

Helena shook her head. "I hate the idea. I suppose there isn't any special reason, at least for now. Unless you want to marry the girl."

Reynolds doubled his question. "Do *you* want to marry?"

Helena was genuinely taken aback. "What would make you think that?"

His thoughts about Talbott had been unfounded and unworthy. Inside, Reynolds felt a relief he had no right to. He answered evasively, "Penny doesn't want to get married."

Helena said, "Yes, I understand the new generation prefers shacking up."

It was a dig, unmistakably. To remind him that he was older than Penny? Actually, there was nothing more to say, although nothing was settled.

The trip to Connecticut did make a difference. It opened the way for a new commitment between Reynolds and Penny. Helena's mention of divorce stayed with Reynolds. As he took in Penny's loveliness every day, he felt his emotions stirring in ways long strange to him. It was exciting, he told Dr. Kohn, and edged with what he could only call fear.

"Fear?"

"Of letting myself go all the way in my feelings for Penny, opening myself to—being hurt."

"Did you open yourself to your love for Helena when you married?"

"It seems different now. I can feel *more* now, about everything—"

"And that frightens you?"

"There's our age difference."

"I know wider ones that are happy."

"But if I let myself love Penny—really love her—and then she wants out?"

"Let yourself love?"

Reynolds was annoyed. "We're not high school kids!"

"Commitment to *anything* is taking a chance of being hurt. That is why you have never committed yourself to anything," Dr. Kohn said flatly.

Reynolds protested. "Hell, just my career is commitment enough for a lifetime!"

The reply was curt. "On the surface! You have always held part of yourself back, away, distant, uninvolved. To avoid possible pain. We've talked about it a hundred times. Why don't you see it now?"

Reynolds pondered that session for days. His response was something of a surprise to him—a suggestion to Penny that they rent a larger, more comfortable apartment, on Park Avenue. Once again Dr. Kohn was correct. The studio had been a way of saying to Penny and himself that their relationship wasn't permanent. The apartment denoted they were entering a new stage.

Reynolds assured himself he was ready now for what Kohn kept calling "commitment." He would risk whatever pain might booby-trap him. He might be surprised and find only new and richer pleasure instead. He believed it would be that way.

Like a newlywed, Reynolds took a delighted Penny shopping for furnishings. Penny laughed with a bride's enchantment, "Out of a love nest into a home!"

Reynolds was more than pleased with this fresh chapter that seemed to be starting in his life. He almost hoped Helena would marry Talbott. Perhaps after a little more time he *would* suggest a divorce. He felt newly secure within. Between Penny's support and his new insights with Dr. Kohn, he was undergoing the kind of transformation psychoanalysis promised. With Penny he could let himself go. He could drink now without drowning. He could be put upon without exploding. He could face temptation and fight it off.

He was sorrier than he could say that he had injured Helena, and he would never forgive himself for unsettling his daughters as he had, but he had to draw a double line under his past somewhere. He was finished with Ikey. He could promise himself that he would never screw himself up again, he was through forfeiting another hour of the one life any man had to live.

These pledges Reynolds made on the day he and Penny moved into their new home. For the first time, Reynolds allowed himself to say to himself that he was in love with Penny, was surrendering to his love,

wanted it to thrive, and last. No reservations, no holding back, no
doubts, no detachment, no more alienation!

By ten o'clock that night, Reynolds' head was on his chest. Penny
turned off the television set, yawning. They had brunched-and-drunk,
and dined-and-drunk, and danced-and-drunk in their new living room.
She roused Reynolds with tenderness and they went to the bedroom.
Penny saw he had drunk too much to have sex, but instead of disappointment, she felt a pleasant relaxation. Married people didn't need to get
uptight about an occasional lapse like this. She snuggled beside Reynolds
with a contented feeling.

To her surprise, Penny heard a murmuring. Reynolds seemed to be
talking in his sleep, but when she turned inquiringly, Penny saw his eyes
open, regarding her sadly. He was whispering, obviously drunkenly,
that what he was doing to her was wrong. They should not have taken
the apartment, should not be here together this way. He was cheating
her of, yes, the best years of her life.

Penny held Reynolds and kissed his cheek, rocking him. She told him
again he was all she wanted.

"I want to make you happy," Reynolds kept mumbling. The air grew
heavy with his breath.

"I am happy, Phil," Penny whispered.

Then she realized he meant something else, for his head was moving
down her body, his hands lifting her nightgown, his lips seeking her
breast. For an instant Penny thought of stopping him; her own drinking
had left her with a slight headache. But then, with the thrill of abrupt
curiosity, Reynolds' intention came to Penny. He was licking her
stomach. It gave her goose pimples, and her nipples grew hard. She was
anticipating what she sensed he was going to do, for the first time.
Mickey had never done it, she had never had it happen to her, though she
had heard that in some ways it was the most sensational experience a
woman could have.

As Reynolds' lips took a first sucking taste of her clitoris, wet and
erect in expectation, Penny gasped with a thrill that galvanized her
body. She felt herself creaming as never before. Oh, God, yes! Don't
stop! she pleaded silently. She groaned and squirmed with fresh pleasure
when Reynolds' tongue played beneath her clit. She felt his teeth a
little—oh, divine tiny bites, pearl nibbles, not of pain but of pleasure. Ah,
how sweet teeth could be!

Penny felt Reynolds pushing a pillow under her buttocks, and she
helped him by arching her back, and spreading her legs wider. His soft
breath, velvet-warm, started into her body like rich whipped cream,

draping her insides voluptuously. She was giving birth to a thousand bubbly balloon-cunts, flying moist in all colors from her, dancing like kites in the sky of her passion. Then, paradise of paradises—sweet, knowing man—his tongue back on her clit, which was waiting in its moist nest ravenous for the wet touch, and the balloons started to crack in her never-before orgasm, her body jerking with each bang-jerk-bang-jerk, in an endless ravishment. Oh, Christ, she had thought that fucking was the living end—feeling a prick fill the hungry emptiness a woman carried—but this was beyond belief! With his tongue on her clit, one hand now inside her cunt, and the other playing with her anus, Reynolds brought her to a final climax.

"Oh, my darling," she choked, trying to catch her breath.

It was at that moment that she heard for the first time what Reynolds had been mumbling between her legs. It had sounded like an endearing murmur of his own passion, but now Penny made out: "Pussy-pussy. I love to suck your pussy-pussy." Reynolds was whispering the words intensely over and over again. "Pussy-pussy. I love to suck your pussy-pussy-pussy!"

Penny smiled. It was like a childish song, sweet and endearing, the sound of Reynolds' total surrender of himself to her. Oh, wonderful, to be so free, to know he could do or say anything to her, and she to him, from now on in their new oneness.

Penny froze, stupefied.

Those words weren't all that usual! It came to her that she had heard that singsong, that whisper just this way before! Where? When? How?

When it began to clear in her head, Penny moaned. She held it off, denying it because it could not possibly be true. Oh, dear Jesus Christ and Holy Mother of God, it had to be impossible!

But it was unmistakable, beyond coincidence or denial. It was that telephone voice saying those words she would never forget: "Pussy-pussy, I'd love to suck your pussy!"

Penny fell through space.

That slimy degenerate creep had been Philip Reynolds!

13

Penny sprang from the bed with a cry. Reynolds stared up at her with stony eyes, not comprehending.

"*You!* I'll remember those words till the day I die!"

Reynolds was blank, Penny saw. Nothing had penetrated; he was staring at her with the gaze of a catatonic. In her horror and distress, Penny realized she had never seen this person before. He was not a man. He was a mummy, a dead-eyed, empty shell.

Penny could not stop screaming. Her world was coming apart. If Philip Reynolds could commit such an abomination, nothing could be counted on anywhere. An unholy fear swelled with her disgust. Penny wanted to shriek every curse she knew at the dead-staring eyes, to wake them up to the pain she wanted to inflict. But as her hysteria diminished, she realized that Reynolds truly did not hear her. He seemed in shock, physically gone behind an invisible, impenetrable wall. He was deaf to the revulsion she had to pour out. "God, am I lucky I never married you, you unnatural freak!" She was dressing in a rush. "Something in me must have known what a degenerate you are! *Pervert!* Absolutely demented!" Penny closed a suitcase into which she had slammed clothes. "And don't tell me about your goddamn psychoanalysis! If you're that sick, drop dead, but don't dump your shit on other people!"

His eyes stayed empty, now following Penny mechanically as she picked through her drawers. In her frustrated need to pierce his barrier, Penny cried out, "I'm going to the police, friend! Maybe that'll wake you up! You belong in a cage!"

At the door, Penny O'Hara faced Philip Reynolds, her face furious, her mouth a slash of pain and outrage. "You dirty Jew bastard!"

Reynolds finally moved. He sagged on the edge of the bed, nude, his head bent. The outburst he had refused to hear was battering at his numbness. Hinges were creaking in his mind. The unthinkable was rising in him, he was understanding what had happened, and its enormity.

It was appalling enough that he had lost Penny, but she had also said she was going to the *police!* The horror of it began to be real for Reynolds, in his belly, not just in his head. He could go to *jail!* Penny was overwrought enough to press charges. True, he could plead she was mistaken, *but the stink would be out!* What a field day the newspapers would have—"Ad Tycoon Charged With Obscene Calls!"

Rodney Graham would love that!

He was in *trouble,* and there was no hiding now. In his fevered state, Reynolds imagined a pounding on the door. A policeman: "Complaint of you making obscene calls. You are under arrest!" He should have thought of that before it was too late.

What would he do if that did happen, Reynolds sweated in his nightmare. Cops jeering, "You had your fun-fun, now it's jail-jail!" He'd deny it, of course. They couldn't *prove* anything. Zillions of phone calls a day, BUT the leering Prosecutor saying: "Laze-gentlemen of the jury, this dastardly perpetrator believes he is on trial only for his contemptible call to the victim Miss Penny O'Hara, whom you have seen to be a lovely, innocent young lady. Little does he know that our new technology—ha, *ha!*—has been comparing his *voiceprint* with our secret file of dirty calls, and we have got him nailed same as if he left a trail of perfect fingerprints on every poor innocent woman he victimized!"

"Guilty!"

Christ, he *had* read somewhere that the telephone company had invented a voiceprint detector. He should have thought of that before too late!

"Guilty!"

Plea of all criminals finally nabbed: "God, oh, please, God! Just this one last chance and I swear by the heads of my children I'll never do it again! Just let me get away with it this one time!"

Should have thought of that before too late!

In his harrowing fantasy, Reynolds saw himself dragged naked to court, stripped down to the truth of his depravity. His enemies would have a field day, his friends would despise him, properly. How could he ever face his daughters again? Helena? His neighbors, his business associates? His name would stink in the nostrils of every decent person. He had sacrificed every meaningful thing in his life, all for a fleeting, lousy, sickie way of getting his jollies!

Panic scorched Reynolds. How could he not have realized there would be a day of reckoning?

In his head, he heard Dr. Kohn's answer: "Alienated! So far off in your own nifty private world that for you there are no rules, *no consequences!*"

That word again, now a sledgehammer shaking the structure of his life.

Reynolds clenched his fists, tried to clear his brain. Was there anything he could do? Bribe the police when they came? Beg them not to destroy him, make them see how much was at stake? Should he plead with Penny, have her talk with Dr. Kohn? Would-could Dr. Kohn sign for him at this point?

Perhaps, despite her fury, Penny would not carry out her threat.

Perhaps their happiness together would weigh in the scale. Perhaps she would not be able to be his executioner.

Heaving with a nausea of self-hate, Reynolds prayed for a reprieve. He vowed he would be worthy of God's mercy, would never, never, never make an obscene call again, would everlastingly remember the savage truths about himself that had tonight battered their way through the fortress of his neurosis and branded his drunken soul.

And the terrible loss of Penny and love would be a penance worse than any sentence a judge could pronounce.

Reynolds lay crushed, alone, on the first night in the new apartment.

14

Penny took a cab directly to the precinct station, but stopped at the door. Her head was in pieces. Philip Reynolds should not go free to victimize other women, but, she debated with herself, maybe her threat had frightened him enough. Anyway, she did owe the man something. And, even if she pressed charges, what would she be saying to the police inside? Tell them she had discovered "the perpetrator" of her obscene call by being in bed with him? Describe to a judge and jury how she had been living with Philip Reynolds for a year and a half, in (if she were to tell the truth, the whole truth, etc.) a state of happiness she had never dreamed possible? Testify how the man she had adored and respected more than anyone had turned out to be the Devil himself?

Penny shook her head. It was as ridiculous as it was revolting. She told herself the only sensible thing was to forget it and get the hell out of Philip Reynolds' life. She was no Dr. Kohn and didn't want to be.

Going back down the station steps, Penny felt the rusty iron railing cold and clammy though the July night was steaming. They had planned a weekend flight to Martha's Vineyard, she remembered with a pang. Well, as he had observed so many times, maybe it *was* time for her to check out men more her own age. Maybe it was an ill wind that— But Penny knew this was a melancholy that would never leave her.

Down the side street, Penny headed for Lexington Avenue, still incredulous. She had imagined the caller a cripple, a misshapen dwarf, a ratlike sewer cleaner!

Thankfully she saw bright lights ahead of her, a Chinese restaurant, a drugstore, late-hour grocery, a bar. Gratefully she kept her eyes on the

sanity of the neon signs, the people walking dogs, the traffic lights, a
graffitied bus rumbling downtown—a world that had not exploded.

It would have to be a new world for her now. She would have to leave
the agency. It would be impossible for her to be in the same room with
Philip Reynolds ever again.

Penny could not go on thinking. Her headache was blazing now.
Through her spinning confusion she felt loss and death; she was coming
from a dark cemetery where she had just buried forever the man she
loved.

15

In all his discussion of his obscene telephoning with Dr. Kohn, Philip
Reynolds had never disclosed the call to Penny O'Hara. Now he
struggled on the couch unable to bring himself to divulge what had
happened so cataclysmically the night before.

Instead, he droned on about a conflict with Rod Graham over who
should preside at the announcement of their acquisition of a Chicago
branch. It was a great step for the agency, Reynolds blah-blahed, and
was not surprised when Dr. Kohn interrupted with, "You're wasting
time today, you know."

Reynolds recognized the old enemy, Resistance.

"What are you blocking?"

Dr. Kohn's ESP. Reynolds heard the mixture of helpfulness and
suspicion in the doctor's question.

Not wanting it to happen, Reynolds found himself attacking. The
best defense. "I'm not blocking anything, dammit! Can't you let me
make my own pace?" Ikey to the fore!

Astoundingly, Dr. Kohn returned an unusual shout as loud and
impatient. "Shit or get off the pot!"

"I'm trying!"

"You started this fight as a way of *not* trying, and you know it!"

"Goddamn it, I'm not a five-year-old kid!"

The doctor's tone was granite. "Oh, aren't you?"

Reynolds sat up moodily. "I'm bloody sick of your scolding me as if I
were!" He knew this was more diversion, but couldn't stop himself; he
was afire, whatever the reason. Christ, he complained to himself, he'd

spent over two years in this office digging like a mole, and all old brass-balls behind the desk could do was keep shooting at his ass.

A sudden new sense of injury consumed Reynolds. *"Dr. Kohn, I think you and I have had it!"* The words astonished him, but they were out and ringing in his ears. The challenge was the last thing he would have expected, on this of all days. He didn't know where it had come from, but it was echoing in the room.

Reynolds was overwhelmed. A decision to end an analysis was even graver than a decision to start it. He had never dreamed it would happen this way between himself and Dr. Kohn, but he heard himself going on—in his office voice—assured, confident, executive: "We all know that analysis doesn't work for everybody. Maybe it's time I tried something else."

Dr. Kohn's reply surprised him by its casualness. "Like what?"

"Well, I hear interesting things about encounter groups—" Reynolds waited to catch Dr. Kohn's reaction. None came. "Frankly, in important ways I don't think you and I get along."

Dr. Kohn took Reynolds aback with a wall-shaking response, "I most certainly agree!"

Reynolds stood up, flushed. "Then why don't we quit?"

Dr. Kohn didn't give Reynolds a chance to say more. "Because that's one of the things you need to work through." And added a barb: "On this couch, not in any encounter group, or primal screaming, or meditation, or est, or psychosynthesis, or whatever!"

Reynolds knew he was floundering, but it only made him angrier. "Work through—" he repeated bitterly. *For what?* So that last night could happen? It was viciously unfair and futile. He hadn't made an obscene call for ages, but the past had risen to crucify him. It proved it didn't make any damned sense to try to change. If his old shit was going to keep on lousing him up, he might as well relax and enjoy his neurosis. If that's what it was in the first place! There were doctors like Laing who believed it was *society* that was neurotic and insane!

Reynolds' peevishness expressed itself bluntly. "Dr. Kohn, I can't work with you usefully any longer!"

The doctor's response came from the desk with unconcealed heat. "Because you still expect me to be a buddy, still want tea and sympathy instead of the truth?" The next words were bullets. "Because you've made me your father?"

Reynolds' teeth clamped. Was this more "transference"—projecting onto the doctor feelings he had about other people? He stopped to consider. Throwing down the gauntlet to Dr. Kohn was a critical move in his life. Maybe he was getting on his old high horse too fast again. Reynolds stepped back to the couch, although there was still a flood of complaint in him. "I've worn out your goddamn couch!"

"And you're wearing me out!" Dr. Kohn made no attempt to hide his own irritation. "Do you know what you really do here? We talked about it early on, and you're still playing that game—buying a ticket to indulge yourself! Oh, you're smart enough to camouflage it better every day, but you still haven't come to grips with your real problems, like whatever it is you're hiding behind all of today's nonsense about ending the analysis."

The doctor gave a sour little laugh. "You don't really want to walk out, you know. It would deprive you of the dandy answer you now have when you hurt people and can innocently say, 'Why, what do you wish of me? After all, I am in analysis.' "

"Oh, come on!" Reynolds protested with a growing sense of unjust persecution.

"You are using this analysis as a swindle to enable you to enjoy your hang-ups instead of fighting them!" The scalpel had to reach for the cancer, Dr. Kohn decided grimly. "At bottom, Philip, you are still out of the world, full of vindictiveness, violence, and self-glory!"

"Oh, come *on!*" This was intolerable, after all the honest effort on the fucking couch!

"And narcissism!" Dr. Kohn continued implacably. "Your all-consuming self-love that still does what you said your mother did—place you at the center of the world, King Shit!"

A bark of rejection came from the couch. "I've been the goddamn FBI chasing myself day and night! I've been tagging every screwball clue, booking myself for every obnoxious crime in the books, sentencing myself too!"

Dr. Kohn remained stern. "No, you haven't! You've used your infernal cleverness to play the Chinese box game I've pointed out a hundred times! You've got all the boxes neatly labeled with your casebook crap, but I still have to tell you that beneath your dandy labels most of your boxes are still quite empty!"

Reynolds felt paralyzed by Dr. Kohn's bombardment. He could only repeat, feebly, "Oh, come on."

"Nothing will work until it comes alive! Alive in here, with *me!*" Dr. Kohn leaned back, rubbing his eyes. "Believe me," he sighed, "I wish I could in conscience let you go. When an analyst sees one of you brainy professors of psychoanalysis enter his office, he should run for his life!"

Both men sat silently, letting the charged words resound.

Reynolds had too much respect for Dr. Kohn not to realize he had set off a genuine crisis. He faltered, "I'm still that far off base?"

"Philip," the doctor said, quietly now, "you came into analysis because you felt like a garbage can. I am willing to help you move your unconscious bowels, but I am not willing to wipe your ass. Is that clear?"

Reynolds closed his eyes in defeat, biting his lips. Of course he knew what he had needed to talk about today, and knew he had misused the time throwing up a smoke screen. And what a smoke screen!—announcing he was leaving! Dr. Kohn had caught him and rubbed his face in his evasions. He shook his head hopelessly. "God, I'm all tangled up."

"Untangle!" The voice was friendly at once.

Reynolds finally got it out, "P-penny!" and choked. No matter how much vileness he had confessed in this room, it never got easier. Penny's discovery of his foulness was the nadir, beyond expression. But his unconscious had been right again; the tragedy with Penny had brought him to a crossroads. He must quit the analysis unless he could find the honesty to tell Dr. Kohn the whole miserable story.

This time when Reynolds finally loosened the plug, the recital did not come out in a rush. Rather, it stuttered with his despairing sense of ignominy and dishonor, and his sorrow at the wreckage they brought. When he finished disconsolately, Reynolds suddenly erupted in resentment. "Why did it have to happen on our first night in the new place? Why did it have to happen at all? A stupid, drunken accident—"

Dr. Kohn was quick: "Accident?"

"Of course. I never went down on Penny before. I never said anything like those words—"

"By accident?" The doctor insisted on his point.

The question took Reynolds aback. "What else, for Christ sake? I shouldn't have gotten drunk—"

"Do you think there was a reason you drank so much?"

"We were celebrating! I told you—"

"You have 'celebrated' before without that kind of sex. You just emphasized that it was the first time."

"Yes. That's right."

"Well, it makes me suspect there might be a reason why you did precisely that sex act."

Reynolds said, nettled, "You suspect everything!"

Dr. Kohn clipped, "Now quit that game! I am asking whether you might have had a reason for *confessing* to Penny!"

"Confessing?"

"What else was it?"

"I *told* you—an accident. Too much to drink—"

"Still bullshit!"

All at once, Reynolds knew, sickeningly, what Dr. Kohn was driving at. It was impossible to accept, but it had the corona of blazing truth. Reynolds groaned.

"Yes?"

The words crept like worms out of Reynolds' mouth. "You mean I *wanted* Penny to know?"

"Think about that!"

Reynolds' jaws clenched. "But why? Why would I do that just when I've come to realize I really love her?"

"Why, indeed?"

The lightning struck.

"Because I was feeling a real feeling?"

"Go on!"

The air in the office became charged as always happened when there was new electricity from the couch.

"The apartment, having a home together, that *was* a commitment!"

Dr. Kohn sighed his assent.

"And commitment is what I still can't take! Oh, Jesus, you mean I *wanted* to break us up!"

"Yes."

"Because Penny was bringing me alive, and Ikey fights like hell against that."

"Yes."

The insight widened: "Because really *feeling* love for Penny would open the door to being alive about *everything,* and that would blow out the neurotic shit once and for all!"

"I think that is exactly right, Phil."

"Damn, damn, damn!"

"Yes," Dr. Kohn said in a tone that offered consolation.

Reynolds' head came up and his teeth ground. It was all true! It was a gruesome irony that he himself had forced his loss of Penny at the beginning of new happiness.

You had to be in psychoanalysis to see the perverted, life-sapping logic of the enemy in the mirror!

Dr. Kohn said, "That's all we have time for today." When Reynolds was off the couch, the doctor added, "Incidentally, you ought to know that it's not uncommon at your stage of the analysis for patients to feel fed up and talk about quitting, especially when they run into a crisis as difficult and painful as yours."

16

Penny O'Hara got a new job easily. Peterson, Fredann, Douglas & Mink, while not "Batten Barton Durstine Osborn & God," was one of the oldest establishments in the business. Penny made the move with a mixture of feelings. A dismal sense of death clung to her, but at the same time she was excited. There was a bright side. At Graham and Reynolds she would always be the gal who had been Phil Reynolds' secretary. There would always be something limiting about that. Here she had been hired on the basis of her track record, short but impressive. Penny told herself with new determination that she could go as far as her talent and hard work would take her, and now more than ever that meant the top. She didn't need Philip Reynolds or anyone else. She had learned her lesson about the unpredictability of a world in which a man like Reynolds could exist.

Penny firmly advised herself that the breakup was a blessing in disguise. She was still hurt and bewildered, but she now understood that whatever Reynolds was, he was too complex for her to deal with. To go on would be unthinkable. Even if she could find sympathy for him as a "sick" man, it would only drain her own energy. Marriage, formal or informal, made enough demands on a career without such an extra burden. Let Dr. Aloysius Kohn handle Philip Reynolds and his hang-ups. Let her own work now occupy her entirely.

Penny found another apartment on Riverside Drive, not far from her first place, with an equal view of the Hudson. She moved in with a sense of fresh beginnings. She was pleased when she ran into Ted Watson at a graphic arts gallery opening night. They resumed their friendship and saw each other with increasing frequency, sharing shoptalk. Their sticky Christmas encounter was two and a half years in the past, never spoken of.

During the first weeks in the new agency, Penny was additionally grateful for the knowledge Ted Watson had given her. It rounded out her tools for handling an ad as a whole. She understood the craft of typography more intimately now—how one type family, a basic design, offered many variations. With relish, Penny pasted up type charts of her own showing typical weights and widths:

Helvetica Regular and *Italic* **Helvetica Bold and *Italic***
Helvetica Regular Condensed   **Helvetica Bold Condensed**
Helvetica Medium and *Italic* **Helvetica Extra Bold Extended**

Penny lingered over the technical terminology, still colorfully esoteric to her. She learned the close relationship between her copy and the
type in which it would be set, and she began to think of the two as an
organic whole. She scoured type books and listed samples for her private
study:

For "light," or "elegant," ads, with quick female identification:

Bembo Italic   L & C Hairline

Bernhard Modern   Souvenir Light

Garamond Italic   *Janson Italic*

For heavy products, or to demand headline attention:

Cooper Black   **Plantin Bold**

Kabel Bold   Baker Danmark

Franklin Gothic Bold   **Stymie Extra Bold**

For decorative and ornamental impact, Penny sampled:

SOUTACHE   *Vivaldi.*

VINETA   MADISON

SUMMER   DAVIDA BOLD.

It boggled Penny's mind that there were literally thousands of such
faces, old and modern, and that contemporary designers were adding to
the type treasury every day.

Ted Watson had pointed out that super copy could be weakened by
the wrong choice of type, while an attractive design could strengthen a

pale idea. Penny shaped her own work accordingly, and made sure her supervisors noted her expanded skills. At the same time, she got along well with the type directors and art directors. They appreciated her approach, especially since she was careful to make clear always that she deferred to their more expert judgments.

On a Labor Day date, eating moussaka and spinach pie at a Greek restaurant on Broadway, Ted said, surprisingly, "You know, Penny, you're very much like me. You understand that opportunity doesn't come knocking. No, it strikes like lightning. Which means the way to get hit is to be sticking out, the way I did at school, et cetera."

Penny laughed, understanding that he was praising her and not himself. He smiled back, and sipped his resin wine with a toast he did not speak aloud: "Penny, baby, my sweet white chick just out of the egg, think you are so safe high up on your hoity branch out of reach. No hurry." Ted knew what Penny did not—those sweet pigeon feet were edging down the branch to him every time they were together.

Without fuss, on an Indian summer night a month later, when they were saying good night just inside Penny's door, Ted Watson unzipped his slacks, flipped out his sex and laid it in Penny's hand, whispering, "Remember, sugar?"

In the genuine innocence of her astonishment, Penny's palm held him. Protest rising in her throat was stoppered by a flooding truth. This was the nightmare that had plagued her after the party.

Nightmare? Or old secret wish?

Penny flashed her hand away. She tried to turn from Ted's insistent lips. "No, *please!*" But they both heard that she was ready.

Naked, Ted Watson's body was not much darker than a deep suntan, yet his "blackness" created a throbbing fear in Penny as he took her in his arms. She was breaking an ultimate taboo. Ted's black flesh pressing her white skin down on the bed was a blasphemy, the consummate antipode of the little girl sitting stick-straight in the parochial school with her hands clasped tightly in obedience, and her budding body rigid beneath wide eyes submissive to the tiniest order of Sister Claudia, of Father Doyle, of mother and father, of the neighbors on Flatbush Avenue, of Mickey, the policeman on the beat, the President of the United States, the Pope of course, and the God-Who-Sees-Through-Blankets. Oh, say, can't you see what a proper, decorous, and good girl I am? Love me and keep me for this. Now a *black* man was about to do *this* thing to *that* girl!

Sin of sins, unthinkable of unthinkables! To fuck a nigger!

What can God see now? There isn't even a thin blanket over the writhing couple. His omniscient eyes and omnipotent wrath are bearing down on the intertwined black and white bodies making the bed squeak.

As Ted spread her and entered her, Penny cried out harshly. She felt spitted with a blazing lust that charred her flesh.

With Mickey, sex had been explosive. With Philip Reynolds, she had known a different rapture, of a yielding and fulfillment she did not want to recall. When Ted Watson moved inside her, something else happened.

It wasn't that Ted's sex was bigger, it wasn't. Penny realized that the whispers she had heard were true—a black organ is large in its unexcited state and erection swells it without elongating it. The difference was that, to Penny, Ted *became* his penis, he existed only in the prick that was stretching her exquisitely. She felt she was a puppet, on hot wires that traversed from his dark tool to all her limbs. Now her hands were yanked down to press the man's hard buttocks closer to her steaming thighs. Now her legs were jerked apart wider than she had known possible, then tugged up high and clasping around Ted's muscular shoulders. She was in a grasping frenzy of raw sex that pithed her mind. It was unendurable and she wanted it to go on forever.

The ravishment of her body turned Penny's blood to a flaring gas that gleamed through her veins like lurid green neons, making her passion visible behind her closed eyes.

Then the black prick was a hard rake scraping her into a new nakedness of pleasure that dissolved everything but a throat-catching ecstasy. And with it there came a molten pouring of guilt at her sinfulness. If sex for a pigtailed child is a sin, then with a nigger it is Death itself! Oh, Black Cock! Penny twisted her head from side to side weeping with shame and exultation. *Fuck me hard!* Black snake! Whip! Wicked evil debased polluted! Penny wept to herself as she whipped on the bed, gulping for air. Ah, *this* fucking was the total everything that had ever excited her, the lewdness of filthy words on toilet walls, the boy jerking off his hot semen on her party skirt, her girl-finger playing in her hairless place under the blanket, pulling Mickey off to his grunting splashing. Oh, the only thing worse than this black cock in her body, Penny moaned, would be fucking her own father or Father Doyle himself! Ah, she was a wanton altogether, Penny castigated herself as she heaved under the panting Ted Watson with a surrendering despair to the blaspheming joy she was knowing. Wallowing in spasms of self-degradation, Penny flung through ring after ring of orgasm.

As the black man moved more fiercely and demandingly, Penny felt as if her bed was the toilet floor on the night of the Christmas party. Now that nightmare of being raped was happening. The time between had vanished. She was being screwed and ravished as she now knew she had yearned to be then. The impossible thought turned Ted's penis into a claw that was slithering through her cunt up to her belly, to her breasts, to her throat, where she choked and suffocated in an immolation of penance for this black devil roaming the foul Eden of her dirty desire.

The act, continuing beyond belief, emptied Penny's skull, rolled her eyes up like a doll's, again and again, skinned her down to her sex alone, until she was nothing but cunt as the end approached, as the man was nothing but prick. Cunt and Prick. Penny unleashed her wild woman's command with shrill unmasked craving for the first time in her life. "Oh, fuck me! Oh, FUCK ME, you filthy dirty scum shit black nigger bastard!" And then, crying out with all her might, "My father will kill you, kill you, *kill you!*" Her words sent them both to new frenzy.

Ted Watson rode Penny O'Hara savagely, with all his own rage fueling his lust to a heat he too had never known before. "White bitch!" he burst out, and slapped Penny hard as he pitched in her.

Penny climaxed not down there but in her chest. Ted's last violent stud lunge became an iron spike he drove through her heart. She broke apart and lay back away from the black heat-smelling body, mortified, defiled, and bewitched.

Later, alone, Penny could not believe what had happened. The old question surged. Was she abnormal, oversexed, obsessed, nymphomaniac? Was she nothing but a rutting female animal without self-respect or self-control? Was she "liberated" so she could follow her desires as guiltlessly as men (were supposed to?) or was she, simply, a slut?

Deeply disturbed, Penny pictured to herself the women she saw every day at the agency, on the city streets, shopping in the stores, and asked her question once more: If these decent women were to testify that *they* would never sleep with a black man, would they be lying? Or was she herself beyond the pale? Would she ever know the answer?

It did not cross Penny's mind that in seeking the honest truth about her reaction to Ted Watson there might be a seed of understanding and acceptance that should also apply to Philip Reynolds.

17

Two months later, in the middle of a freezing December, Reynolds was surprised by his new secretary—a pleasant, gray-haired professional who was carefully impersonal—bringing in a Christmas package with a note from Selma. His daughter wrote that she had been out of touch with Penny and did not know where to send her holiday gift this year. Would he please help deliver it so it wouldn't be lost or late?

Reynolds stared thoughtfully at Selma's neat, back-slanted handwriting. It appeared much like Helena's. Were handwriting characteristics inherited? he wondered idly. His mind was elsewhere. He was sure that if he telephoned Penny she would not see him. But if he appeared bearing Selma's gift they might talk, if only briefly. Penny would be over the shock of the disaster; six months had passed. She might be ready to hear him out, he might even be able to persuade her to meet Dr. Kohn.

His purpose was not so much to win her back. He did not expect it. But he wanted to be certain of her feelings before he went on with the plan that had been forming in his mind. Rattling around the large Park Avenue apartment, he had come to terms with his grief, and had determined it was time either to return to Helena or end the marriage. Dr. Kohn agreed that both of them had continued too long in their equivocal state. And Helena had responded positively to Reynolds' call suggesting that he come to Connecticut for Christmas this year. They agreed that if all went well, he should spend the full holiday week with the girls.

Reynolds wasn't sure where this new motion would lead, but it felt right to have started it. Dr. Kohn agreed again.

Reynolds' secretary found Penny's address from her agency. That night, stamping snow from his feet, Reynolds determinedly pressed Penny's bell. Opening her door, Penny gasped with surprise. She stood like a statue holding the packages he thrust at her.

The rest happened in surreal fast motion, like a crazily speeded-up film.

Reynolds: "May I say Merry Christmas inside?"

Penny: "What are *you* doing here?"

A man's voice at the same instant: "Who is it, sweetie?" The voice was unmistakably and incredibly Ted Watson's. And *"Sweetie!"*—

Penny's old, private endearment! To Reynolds it was like a head-on auto crash.

Ted Watson, naked under a robe, appeared at the bedroom door. He blinked his own surprise, saying, "What the hell" at the same moment Reynolds blasted Penny with, "You whore!" and slapped at her face, all his new control dissolved in his searing discovery.

Simultaneously with Penny's cry of outrage, there was a punch from Ted Watson that sent Reynolds reeling to the floor. "You ever come near Penny again, I'll cut your balls off!"

As Reynolds, dazed, struggled to his feet, he heard from the closing door, "That motherfucker hurt you, sweetie?"

Trembling with mute fury, Reynolds pulled his overcoat around him and made his way down the hallway to the stairs. He had Penny's answer to his unasked question. In spades!

18

Anticipating what he would be telling Dr. Kohn, Reynolds was slashed with new confusion as he walked through deepening snow the next morning. A New York blizzard had paralyzed traffic, the streets were a fairyland of cottony buildings cleansed by the snow falling out of a black sky. The contrast of brightness and gloom was Reynolds' own mood. He felt funereal about Penny; he had believed he was past that Ikey violence. And Penny was gone, irretrievably. He had read somewhere that a man could survive without love, but could not live without hope. It seemed a sore truth.

And yet, in his heart Reynolds had to acknowledge a sense of release he had not felt in all the time with Penny. It was a lightness like the snow's flakes powdering his eyelashes: Release from hope is a kind of freedom itself, he recognized.

His smile to Mrs. Wheatley was genuine when she said he looked like a snowman and handed him a towel. "It's fine out, really," Reynolds told her.

Serving him hot coffee, the woman reported, "The storm's delayed the doctor. He called to say he'll be here in half an hour if you want to wait."

Reynolds smiled again. "Half a session's better than none." He had important matters this morning.

Mrs. Wheatley turned to her work, and Reynolds scanned a magazine. Curious, he thought; he had been almost three years in the deepest intimacy with Dr. Aloysius Kohn, and he didn't even know where the man lived, where he was coming late from. It was as if he had believed the doctor existed only in the heavy chair behind the desk, with no other life. The only glimpse of personal activity had, in fact, come at just the last session, when Reynolds learned that Kohn would be speaking at a seminar in San Francisco in January. They would have to take a two-week break. The prospect of a hiatus no longer upset Reynolds; on the contrary, he had a proposal that fitted right in.

The door admitted another snowman, this one wearing a large fur hat. Rosy-cheeked and blowing, Dr. Kohn greeted Mrs. Wheatley and Reynolds heartily. "I think I was on the last train that made it." Ushering Reynolds into his office, the doctor laughed, "You know, if I were an enemy of this country, I'd spend all my munitions money on research for making snow. Then I'd push the button over New York, Washington, Boston, Chicago, and so on, and take over without a shot, eh?"

It wasn't such a far-out idea, at that, Reynolds considered.

On the couch, he expected to be racing on about the violent scene with Penny and Ted, deploring Ikey's take-over again. Instead, with amazement, he found all his attention focused on what he believed a complete irrelevance. The result was an extended silence.

"We have only half a session today, Phil," Dr. Kohn reminded.

Reynolds got out, "With all the important stuff I want to cover, why am I hung up on your tie?"

"My tie?" The doctor's voice was alive with fresh interest.

"Your red tie, the first thing I noticed when you took your coat off." Reynolds applied his experience and book-reading knowledge. "Of course I know it's significant when a patient catches something like that first thing in a session, but I'll be damned if I can see any connection to *my* problems."

Dr. Kohn said, "If the tie isn't a red herring, you will. Let's see what else is on your agenda."

Reynolds unwound in the familiar technique. By now he began with the image of a blank television screen. If he waited patiently, grayly, it would begin to light up, as it was doing now. What did he see?—a ghost movie figure?—Dracula?—No, it was Frankenstein?—Why?—A clone. Puzzling, but stay with it. A wipe-out on the screen, and, crazily, a toy store. A toy he had bought for Selma many years ago? Yes, a doll with a record inside that metallically said, "Momma." The image altered to a metal, square body, batteried lights for eyes, mechanical head rotating spookily with antennae quivering. ROBOT!

Reynolds said to Dr. Kohn, "Robot. What the hell?"

"Robot?"

The picture was replaced with a circling montage of the old flat in Chicago, the house in Connecticut, his apartment with Penny, his offices. The settings of his life were tumbling together like toy houses in a tornado. Reynolds told it to Dr. Kohn and said, "I'd better slow down."

The next image did not have to follow logically, not on this couch, Reynolds well knew by now, so he was not surprised when it was Helena's face, and he heard himself saying, without apparent connection with what had gone before, "I've wondered why the separation from Helena didn't bother me more. I thought I loved her, and I certainly love the girls. I did love Helena, she was even more exciting than Penny at first. But now I see it became—what?—the usual marriage?—convenience, comfort? Oh, I went through the motions, husband, father, breadwinner. But did any of it really matter?" Reynolds paused, waiting for the new thought to find its form. When it came it was with a shouting affirmation: "There was no *me* to reach!"

Reynolds rolled over. "Ha! Robot! I cut off my emotions so I wouldn't be hurt. *Amputated* my feelings! I'm back to *that!*"

Reynolds left the couch to emphasize his enlarged understanding. Amputation was precisely what he had done, he repeated. With Helena he had sliced away love. With his children he had masqueraded in a father's role and they felt the phoniness. Worse yet, as a father he had been a nice guy one day, a bully the next, a drunken bum the next, and a genius and a hero after that! This *inconsistency* could screw kids up, he knew from every book.

"Screw yourself up too," Dr. Kohn injected.

Reynolds continued, "With Penny it was the opposite of Helena. At first I wasn't in love at all. I used her. She was convenient and she wanted me. But then *that* changed. Where I fell out of love with Helena, I began to fall *in* love with Penny." Reynolds paused again. "So where am I now?" A new configuration clarified. "It goes back to my 'confession' to Penny. I was afraid of feeling then, as we saw. But when I decided to take Selma's gift to Penny, I was apparently ready to accept it—"

The ugly incident had a bright side, he saw suddenly. In terms of the analysis, he was ready—and able and willing!—to come alive more fully.

"Important!" Dr. Kohn assented.

"New ball game, dammit!" Reynolds exclaimed.

"Very possibly," Dr. Kohn said, but his expression remained neutral.

Reynolds laughed aloud. "If you weren't so stiff-necked, I'd offer to buy you and your damned tie a drink this evening."

It earned a smile. "We haven't quite reached that stage."

"I was only testing."

"I know. Now shall we get back to business?"

"I'm exhausted. But there is one thing I want to talk over before we quit." Reynolds handed a brochure across the desk. "It's a place up the Hudson called 'Center for Existence.' Ever hear of it? I'd like to go while you're in San Francisco."

Dr. Kohn scanned the booklet. "I know the doctor in charge, Silas Frank. He's a sound man for this sort of thing, but I do not recommend it for you."

"Oh?"

"I assume you understand that these self-improvement activities are not therapy as psychoanalysis is."

"I understand that."

"They're useful with people who aren't functioning on all their cylinders, but they don't deal with neurotics like you."

Typical of Dr. Kohn to leave off any varnish, Reynolds observed. "I understand that."

"An encounter can get pretty intense, Phil. This might churn up material you wouldn't be ready to handle."

"I'm willing to take the risk."

"The others might not be."

Reynolds evaded the challenge. "Some people at the agency say places like Esalen have changed their lives. I'd like to see for myself. This workshop is nearby, the time is convenient, and—"

Dr. Kohn made his decision. "Well, if Dr. Frank doesn't mind playing with your fire, I'll drop him a note. You've come a considerable way, and it's possible that the exposure will put you in touch with material we can use here when I get back."

"That's what I thought," Reynolds said with enthusiasm.

Dr. Kohn harrumphed. "Did you? Let me suggest we have plenty of stuff here you leave untouched. Example, you never got back to my tie."

"I can't believe it," Reynolds ejaculated. "My whole bloody life is rollercoasting and all you can think of is that confounded tie!"

Dr. Kohn counseled, "Let me tell you, my red tie can be the most important thing that's happened in your 'nearly three years' on that couch, if you can figure out why it caught your attention this morning!"

"You have got to be kidding," Reynolds was saying as the buzzer sounded from Mrs. Wheatley.

On his return to his office, Reynolds found a sealed memo on his desk from Ted Watson: "For personal reasons I hereby resign from Graham and Reynolds effective immediately."

Reynolds grimaced. If the mother believed that concluded the matter, how wrong he was! All night, Reynolds had stewed over how to teach Ted Watson his lesson. He wasn't going to sit by and watch anyone take advantage of Penny O'Hara, much less this black harpy. He had settled on a way that would make the presumptuous bastard sorry for the rest of his life.

Throwing the resignation in his wastebasket, Reynolds reached for his telephone. Within half an hour, he had dialed private numbers up and down Ad Alley. He spoke to the agency principals with top-man assurance, in sworn confidence. His tale was the same each time: "I think you ought to know I've just sacked Ted Watson. We have some reason to believe he's been on the heavy take with our print suppliers."

That was cool, not a flat accusation but enough of a smell so that no significant agency would touch Ted Watson with an NAACP flagpole as the word spread around. It would teach the cocksucker to move in on Penny and throw punches at the man who'd given him his start.

Only one man hesitated, saying, "I'd never have believed it of Watson." And added immediately, "But you can never tell about them, can you?" The street always relished believing the worst of people. Given Ted Watson's high-stepping air of self-assurance, that would be doubly true in this case, Reynolds guessed.

It did not occur to him that he had just made one of the most obscene of all his obscene phone calls.

Part Five

"I saw a man pursuing the horizon;
   Round and round they sped.
   I was disturbed at this;
   I accosted the man.
'It is futile,' I said,
'You can never'—
'You lie,' he cried,
   And ran on."

—Stephen Crane

19

Driving his rented car along the New York Thruway on a Friday in mid-January, Reynolds felt completely at ease for the first time in years. Heading for the encounter workshop, he was released from Dr. Kohn's couch for two weeks. There was no longer a flapping loose end with Penny. His Christmas visit home had worked out well, gratifyingly well all around. Everyone understood that the week was a test. After the first day of strain and doubtfulness, the girls relaxed with him. They knew he slept in the guest room, and with an innate tact did not indicate that it was a strange situation. Helena remained calm and pleasant.

Reynolds did not drink at all, and Helena observed that he did not seem to miss it. On the road now, Reynolds recalled with satisfaction that they had all seemed genuinely sorry when it was time for him to leave for the workshop. Best of all, Helena asked him to return to Connecticut rather than go back to New York when the week was up.

Reynolds was more than ready to come home if Helena wanted to try. He realized it would be a time before Helena accepted him as husband again, if ever. But he was closer to her in the guest room than he was on Park Avenue, which spelled only loneliness.

Right now, he wanted nothing more than the tingling freedom of his shoe easy on the gas pedal, with the snow-flurried road ribboning beneath his wheels as he drove along carefully. The surface was dangerously slick, and the January sky was an enameled Georgia O'Keeffe vault promising more snow. Against its metallic clarity, the trees on distant hills traced a delicate Japanese scroll of bare boughs. Reynolds smiled at the two poetic fallacies, comparing nature to art, the real to the artificial. Hadn't that in a way been the deepest flaw in his character?

But he was off the couch and didn't have to analyze every wisp of thought. He turned to enjoy the scenery again. He would like for the denigrators of the New York area to see this lovely countryside, only a few miles from the core of the Big Apple. The rolling hills bore dense forests, and there were still large tracts of open land not Monopolied with toy houses of developments. The Hudson Valley, toward which he was headed, held as much grand beauty as anywhere in the world with its majestic river, towering cliffs, and natural battlements.

On an impulse, Reynolds turned off the Thruway to make for the Bear Mountain Bridge. The panoramic views on the twisting road east of the river were fantastic, he remembered. It would be tricky driving in this weather, but worth it, and he was an expert at the wheel.

The sun went suddenly, except for one rent in the gathering clouds which dispersed rays in a fan of benediction. Without warning, hail was drumming on the hood. It pelted so hard Reynolds could hardly see ahead. Cars were pulling to the side to wait it out, but he went on at reduced speed. He had allowed ample time, but had a considerable drive ahead, and did not want to be late for the first session at the workshop.

Reynolds gave himself over to the road, to the click-clack of the windshield wipers and the sh-sh of the wet tires. The rhythms matched his heartbeat. He quickened with a sense that he was headed for a new adventure, open ideas, different people. He didn't know who they would be or what they would be like but he was ready for whatever lay ahead, and Dr. Kohn needn't worry about his being thrown. He had invested too much of himself on that damned gray couch to turn quixotic at this point.

Reynolds needed his bright lights now, and squinted through the snow-streaked windshield. With a jolt, he saw Ted Watson's face mirrored back. He cursed. The sounds and rhythms had hypnotized him, he told himself. But even as the image faded, Reynolds recognized it was his conscience stirring again. He knew Ted Watson had gone on vacation after leaving the agency, but the man would be back in a couple of weeks, and then the telephoned story would hit him. What Reynolds had done in a fit of vengefulness disturbed him now. In the car, pondering the calls he had made, he realized starkly that he was ruining the man's career, and unfairly. Watson had worked too hard for his success to be screwed out of it, no matter what reason Reynolds had personally.

As if he were talking to Dr. Kohn, Reynolds added, almost aloud, that he wasn't only hurting Ted Watson, but setting back his own new personality. A clear resolve came to Reynolds. He ought to and would undo the damage. It wouldn't be difficult; he could call around again, say he had made a bad mistake, that he had been fed a lie about Watson by some sick turkey out to get the black man. The people would buy it, he was sure, though it would leave him looking foolish. That was a small price to pay for putting things straight.

Reynolds glanced at his watch. No sweat. If the weather let up, he'd have time to stop at the Bear Mountain Inn and begin phoning the agencies before five o'clock. Ted Watson might still pick up some gossip-static when he returned, but the important thing was he'd have no trouble finding something. And Philip Reynolds would be able to look at himself in the mirror with respect once more, after giving Ikey another well-deserved boot in his neurotic asshole.

Reynolds felt better again. Dr. Kohn would be pleased. It was a good feeling not to be a screwball bastard. He was sorry only that he couldn't undo the other phone calls as easily. That was something he would have to live with, in shame and regret. Okay, he told himself—punish yourself for it, but not forever, and not more than the crime demands. Even a disordered neurotic has constitutional rights, Reynolds smiled wryly. Justice Freud: No cruel und unusual punishments, please! *Nein?*

The car was approaching the narrow road, blasted out of the mountain, that climbs steeply to a peak before descending to the Hudson in a series of near-hairpin turns. Reynolds was glad he was going west; it meant he was on the inside lane, next to the mountain. Across the road there was only a low rock railing, probably high enough to keep a car from plunging over the cliff, but not reassuring on a day as slippery as this.

At the crest, before the road dropped to snake down the mountain, the view burst rewardingly. In the white gray of snow and ice, the lifting Bear Mountains across the river were a glistening sheen, a mighty fanfare of silver trumpets for the eyes. Unfortunately, Reynolds could savor the spectacular scene for only a moment. The steep decline demanded all his vigilance immediately. No sand trucks had been through yet, and the road was becoming sheer ice. Cautiously, Reynolds shifted into low gear and let the car ease itself down. He guided the wheel gently, applying just a brush of the brake as he negotiated the tight S-curves that uncoiled endlessly through the thickening snowfall.

Reynolds found himself tense, but enjoying the road's demands on his skill. The easy highways make drivers fat and lazy, he thought, as he anticipated a skid and kept delicate control.

The urgent beep-beep of a horn hit Reynolds like a blow on the back of his neck. His foot responded automatically to the brake and his rear wheels skidded at once. It took all his will to force his foot off the brake to feed gas. He accelerated gingerly, fought the veering car, and brought it straight with choking panic. He glanced in his mirror, expecting to see a long-haired leather-jacketed brass-belted hoodlum in a souped-up hot rod who didn't care whether he killed everybody in sight, including himself.

Instead, Reynolds was astounded to glimpse a matronly-looking woman. He could not see clearly through the snow-pocked rear window, but she had gray hair under an old-fashioned bonnet. The horn did not quit. Desperately darting his eyes from road to mirror, Reynolds made out a schoolteacher's face, twisted into Medean fury. What the hell did the old witch want? he grunted to himself. She held her hand on the goddamn horn though she must know there wasn't anything he could do to let her pass. She must be out of her mind riding his tail this way! Hadn't she seen him skid? He'd gladly get out of her way and let her commit suicide, but did she expect him to dig a hole in the mountain rock or crash the line of drivers crawling up the left lane?

White-knuckled, Reynolds cursed silently. That old bitch wouldn't take her claw off the goddamn horn! The irritating beep-beep (it always seemed to him that small-car horns had a whine like a spoiled, demanding child) was like a dentist's drill on raw nerve. Christ, Reynolds swore, when they got down to the bridge he'd stop her and knock her honking brains out! His outrage incandesced when he felt the bumper of her car nudging his. Jesus, the old hag *was* out to kill him! If he tried braking now, they'd surely both fly right off the goddamn mile-high precipice.

Reynolds tried to hold his car at a deliberate pace around the treacherous curves, but shee-it, she was *pushing* him! Reynolds groaned. It seemed she had her unholy demon hoof on the fucking gas and unless he took a chance braking she would force him faster. Talk about your Nantucket sleigh ride, he thought virulently, where the whale might sound and pull the men to drown unless they could hack the harpoon rope fast enough. He had a whale on his ass and no possible ax!

Reynolds swallowed nervously as he watched his speedometer needle climb from 25 to 30 to 35. The curves were rushing at him faster as the decline grew steeper. It couldn't be real, this headlong nightmare, taking all his skill to nudge the wheel, feather-touch the brake, outguess the tires. Forty, 45—he choked, gulped for air. Impossible! That bug (always the goddamn bug-cars, road hogs, scooting in and out of lanes like the unruly cockroaches they were!) ought to be taking off like a fucking plane at this speed on this ice. He glanced back again. The old Fury-out-of-Hell was still on the gas and the horn!

It had to be a bad dream, Reynolds sweated. He'd drunk too much and this was the punishing hangover. Hell wasn't fire and brimstone, it was being on this ski jump with the curves coming at you Ziz-ZAZ-ziz-ZAZ-ZAZ-zip-zip-ZAZZOOOOM! and a final wrack-up into the boulders, and the startled eyes of unbelieving drivers seeing the two locked cars speeding down to the open mouth of hell.

As Reynolds hissed around a sizzling curve, just missing a jutting rock, his eyes widened with new terror. He was bearing down on a station wagon that was inching along below. It held a group of small children in gaily colored snowsuits and hats with bobbing red pompons. A modern Currier & Ives print that would be a carnage in moments. Frantically, Reynolds pumped his window down and desperately sig-naled the driver behind, pointing to the car ahead. But the witch seemed to see only the horn she kept pounding.

Reynolds saw he had no choice. They were nearing the bottom of the incline. If he could hold the bug back for another half a minute, they might avoid the looming smashup. He touched the brake, and felt the wheels rebel instantly. The car was skittish as a colt, but he kept microing the brake down carefully. For a moment the speedometer wavered and eased back, but the push from behind was relentless. The station wagon ahead was growing larger every second; it would disappear around a U-curve, and reappear visibly closer.

Reynolds began to pound on his own horn with frantic blasts, hoping Mrs. Stationwagon would wake up and see the doom racing down on her. People ought to drive off the rear mirror, dammit, any neophyte knew that, Reynolds cursed. Even when you had to glue your eyes to a snake road like this.

The woman below lifted her head at his horn. Reynolds saw her back stiffen with consternation as she got his message. She started to speed up a little. It gave them a few more precious seconds, but, Reynolds knew desperately, not possibly enough time for all of them to get to the bottom safely.

At that moment, with a relief so great he could not experience it, Reynolds saw the turnout. The station wagon hadn't caught it in time. Reynolds saw he had one slim possibility. He might overturn, he might burn, he might bounce off the edge of the road to eternity, but there was a roulette chance to beat the certainty of disaster below. With his last ounce of control, Reynolds braked softly and then, just before the turnout, jerked the wheel around while slamming the brakes with all his might.

As he had anticipated, the car spun crazily, banged into the hillside, jounced, jumped, careened—but scraped to a screeching stop against rocks and trees. Reynolds cracked his head, the steering wheel plunged his breath from his chest. He glimpsed a red streak flashing by just before he blacked out.

When Reynolds came to, he realized he had been out for only a minute. He looked for his driving spectacles. Fortunately, they were unbroken, on Helena's side. In the jaggedness of his shock there was a momentary shimmer of comfort in the thought of Helena that somehow tied in with his prayerful relief at being alive, and apparently not seriously hurt. He leaned back breathing heavily, checking himself out. His head and chest ached, but he seemed whole. There were no pains when he tried moving. In a few minutes he was able to get out to check the damage. The car was battered, but the motor worked and it seemed drivable. Reynolds saw the expressions of shock and sympathy in cars grinding up the climb, eyes that told him they'd like to help but had no way of stopping for him. He nodded across the road to show he was all right and appreciated their concern. God, he'd been lucky! Except that—with an inexplicable recurring niggardliness about small expenses that often led him to take a bus instead of a cab—he had this one time declined collision insurance. His assumption of the risk would now cost a pretty penny. So what else is new, Reynolds asked himself grimly. Kicking the tires, he again felt his fury at the harridan driver. She'd pay, he swore under his breath.

As his car limped down the last of the road, Reynolds saw, shudderingly, the accident below. Fortunately, the station wagon with the frightened children was safe. The mother was crouched over the front fender, vomiting. But the red compact was tangled upside down around a cement traffic stanchion. Its skid marks, like livid black scars in the white snow, showed the woman had hit one side of the road, rebounded into a concrete wall opposite and then, turned turtle, had whipped into the stanchion. The car was literally wrapped around the steel and cement base. Wheels in air, the compact was a mangled monster-movie insect that looked as if it had been through a giant crusher. Bloodied traffic signs were scattered helter-skelter staining the snow in ugly patches.

With a turning stomach, Reynolds made out the old lady. She was caught inside, torn and gory, her head nearly severed. With the gray hair now stained bright red beneath the prim bonnet, it hung like a puppet face grotesquely guillotined.

The anger in Reynolds evaporated before the dreadful sight. The accusation he was prepared to make to the police became an overwhelming pity that quivered through his body to his toes, particularly after he heard one trooper explain to a newly arrived officer: "Her brakes went out up there."

Reynolds' knees turned to water.

The woman had not been the hag-out-of-hell that he had tagged her with furious, unthinking hatred. She had been a poor, plain old lady in trouble, in peril. She had been pounding her horn not to torment him but calling, pitifully enough, for his help!

It penetrated monstrously to Reynolds that he had never for an instant considered the possibility. All *he*—star performer on Dr. Kohn's couch— could imagine was a madwoman. All *his* response could be was conjuration of demons! How sickened Dr. Kohn would be!

One of the troopers eyed Reynolds' walloped car. "You look like you had some trouble yourself. Need any help?"

Reynolds shook his head mutely. If he tried to speak, he would weep. Did he need help? Oh, God, yes! he castigated himself. *He* endlessly demanded that others understand and forgive his frailties and the evil in him, but toward others he still seemed to own only meanness, an uncharitable readiness to believe others wicked, and a contemptible quickness to condemn people out of hand.

Alienated? He was *inhuman,* Reynolds lashed at himself with fresh despair.

As his motor sputtered to a new start, Reynolds looked at his watch. With this delay, and now needing to change the car in Newburgh, he would have no time to stop to make the Ted Watson calls. And tomorrow was Saturday. Well, there would be phones at the workshop, and he would do the job first thing Monday. Reynolds made his vow more solemnly as he stared again at the crushed little car. He might have found some way to save the old lady if he hadn't been so occupied cursing her. He might have tried harder anyway. Now he'd have this monkey on his back just when he was getting Watson off. He was in a hell of a mood for starting a new experience, Reynolds mused as his car shook and rattled slowly across the high-arching, icicle-bedecked Bear Mountain Bridge.

20

After transferring to another car, Reynolds found himself on country roads winding through snowy pastures and woodlands. Distant explosions of snowmobiles dirtied the otherwise heady air. It reminded Reynolds of the blaring radios in Central Park. He wished he had a machine like Penny's fantasy to shut off the ugly sounds. He wished he had a device to shut off the disturbing thoughts of Penny, like this one, that still intruded when he was off guard. He was glad to see he was near his destination, where he hoped for a fresh look at everything he was thinking and feeling and doing in his life. Just ahead on the right of the road there was a sign, broken, announcing CENTER FOR EXISTE—. It was drawn in a fancy high-school hand that did not augur well. Through the bare trees on his right Reynolds made out a ramshackle farm dwelling that looked as unpromising as the sign. He had been assured by an honest-sounding female voice on the telephone that his accommodations would be modern and comfortable, though modest. Reynolds scowled at the bleak prospect. There hadn't been anything like a motel for miles back. What kind of discomfort had he let himself in for? It occurred to him that he ought to talk to Dr. Kohn about the role which the-importance-of-comfort played in his life.

He parked near the farmhouse. Most of the cars were old and shabby looking. Students? A large bright Cadillac stood out. Someone else like himself "adventuring"? Nearby, incongruously, stood a converted hearse painted in rainbow colors—van to heaven, Reynolds smiled. His new companions would be a varied lot if nothing else.

There wouldn't be anything like a bellhop, of course. Carrying his imported leather bag self-consciously, Reynolds approached the sagging porch, where a weathered sign announced OFFICE. Along the porch, in a variety of slouching postures, were hippie types of both sexes, dressed alike in faded jeans and huddled under army blankets against the bitter cold. It was a great deal colder here than in the city, Reynolds observed. He trusted that his room had heat; they wouldn't be that primitive. As he passed the unsavory characters, noting their matted hair, the frayed look of most of them, Reynolds thanked God they weren't his daughters, though it would be a safe guess that most of them were rebelling against middle-class families much like his own.

Heads turned to follow Reynolds without expression, as if the man were a stone that had rolled in the snow from the pasture rising behind the building. Later Reynolds would learn that these applicants were part of the tradition he had always before associated with Zen monasteries, where seekers awaited acknowledgment without a gesture to call attention to themselves. Here, when a person was hired for the kitchen, grounds, or room-cleaning, Reynolds found, he or she would be bathed, combed, and laundered. At least everything was clean inside the office he entered.

Including the reception clerk, a bright young lady with an open, raffish smile. Yes, they had reserved a single room for him. No, it was not in this old building, but in a new row of cabins beyond. The girl gave Reynolds an amused, tolerant look, which said she understood he was past the dormitory stage of life. Reynolds guessed she was little older than Selma, seventeen, perhaps a little more. Country-wholesome, an ad for "farm-pure" butter—a perky face with cheerful eyes that were taking him in steadily, not in the unsure way he was studying her. Her presence made Reynolds feel better about staying. She was milkmaid, with her neatly brushed hair falling like a golden shawl over smooth young shoulders. There was a fresh bayberry smell Reynolds liked. He saw that it came from candles for sale on a counter, but it might have been the girl.

As Penny had been cinnamon—

Reynolds banished the obtruding thought impatiently. He was here *only* to work with Dr. Silas Frank and a serious group "seeking to raise the individual's sense of self-consciousness and personal authenticity," as the brochure put it.

The girl told him her name was Mary Humphrey, just Mary to everyone. Anything he needed, any questions, she'd be glad to help. Her nubile breasts were half exposed in her low-necked gingham frock. When she sat at a table to fill out Reynolds' form, he saw her short dress lift over swelling thighs, no stockings, the flesh firm and sweet going up to the private place. He chopped at his thought again. Now did he want statutory rape on his dossier too? Hadn't he had his lesson about consequences? He was *not* going to forget the terror of the night waiting for the police knock he truly expected. If Penny had given him a reprieve, it certainly wasn't so that he could stick his neck (or cock) in another hang noose.

As Dr. Kohn had explained, temptation would probably always be around him, but he was more than a sordid Ikey now.

The girl was saying, "Here's your schedule and directions. We don't have any phones except this one." Reynolds noted the pay phone on the whitewashed wall. He would use it Monday, he reminded himself. "Dr. Frank will start your group right after dinner tonight. In the Red Barn."

Even, white teeth showed in a welcoming smile. "Glad to have you aboard, Phil. Hope you brought boots, this snow will last."

Reynolds' thank you was off-balance. It was her calling him "Phil," and the frank curiosity in her expression: What was squaresville doing on this side of the tracks? No long hair, no whiskers, no jeans, and obviously over forty! Reynolds was glad when the phone called the girl away.

Reynolds stopped to look at the literature displayed on a green oilcloth. Zen subjects, parapsychology, Gestalt, Esalen authors. And a large sign: ANYONE USING MARIJUANA OR DRUGS OF ANY KIND WILL BE EJECTED FORTHWITH! "Forthwith!" Good! Reynolds did not want to be dealing with mind-blown spooks.

To the right of the door a freshly painted bulletin board carried notes and announcements. To Reynolds it made a fascinating collage of forms and colors, particularly one message selling exotically-named incense packets. The ad was in the form of a snake that wound among the other messages. The signatory was a "Barney S." Reynolds considered that Barney had advertising talent. Mostly there were requests for rides, to as far away as San Francisco, Reynolds observed with surprise. There was one that brought a snort from him—Montclair, New Jersey. *Hi, Shmuel!*

A tacked-up page torn from a Bible caught his eye. In the margin, lipsticked graffiti blazened, "Seek and Ye Shall Find." It was followed by writings in different hands: "I sook, didn't find nothin'. " "You sooked in the wrong place." "I sook behind the Red Barn, midnight daily." "Fook you, sooker." It wouldn't be dull at the Center, Reynolds smiled.

Reynolds' room turned out to be small, clean, and warm, with a hooked rug, fresh blue curtains of homespun, and a multicolor quilt that seemed authentic patchwork. Sort of fun way to rough it, Reynolds considered, yawning as he unpacked. He could use a nap before this new experience began. The drive up had been brutal in every way.

Stripped, Reynolds tried the bed. Hard but not uncomfortable. The bathroom, with a prefab shower, was tiny but adequate. He would manage nicely enough, though it was a far cry from Park Avenue and Connecticut. He tried to doze, but he couldn't shut down the pulse of what was for him a venture in an alien world. Eyes closed, his mind went back to his first train ride alone, from Chicago to the farm near

Cuyahoga Falls in Ohio. For a seven-year-old, such an interval of aloneness is a literal suspension in time and space. Excitement coupled with trepidation generates a new beat in the body, a quickening of self-awareness and identity. Everything ahead is possible and desirable, and everything is charged with doubt and fear. There is the child's ritual of worried questions: Am I on the right train? (Reynolds had deeply distrusted the conductor, a greasy-looking man with ashes graying his uniform.) Where did mother put the ticket I can't find? (Frantic search, visions of being put off the train, deserted in a strange place with no relatives or friends, and only the sweat-wet dollar bill crumpled in the small palm.) Thank God, in the band of my hat! If I go to the toilet, will someone steal my suitcase? Is that the toilet back there where the (nose-wrinkling) smell is coming from? (And phantoms of what children are told about lurking men near toilets, like the pigtailed Chinee in the dark restaurant, who do awful things to kids!) Will the grandparents be at the station? Suppose the train is late? Or early? Suppose somebody made a mistake about the time? Suppose there is a different timetable in Ohio than in Illinois—after all, they are so far away from each other!

How his heart had pounded with anxiety that first night, even though he arrived in one piece and happy at being on the farm with its spreading fields and orchards and the friendly (good-smelling) barnyard animals. Away from his parents for the first time, Reynolds missed even his father's drunken abuse. Comfort had come by accident that night. In his tossing about, the boy somehow slid the pillow between his legs. A strange tingling began to happen. He did not know why, but a thousand birds seemed to flutter over his body and roost with trembling wings where his legs joined . . .

Reynolds opened his eyes, blinking back to the present. He picked up the sheet Mary Humphrey had given him, and studied the schedule. Dinner in about an hour now. Then the first session. Then the baths. That would be the nude bathing hour described in the brochure as a basic element in the workshop. Reynolds had wondered about it before, but now that it was only hours away the question became concrete. Would he get an erection?

Thinking about it, stretched out nude on his unfamiliar, narrow bed in his cubicle at the Center for Existence, Philip Reynolds' hand moved automatically to his crotch as it had that long-ago night of disquiet in Ohio. Was it possible to be among naked women and not get an erection if you were normal? Hell, Reynolds answered himself, men didn't walk around with hard-ons in nudist camps, and they weren't homos necessarily. He guessed it would be the same here, except that the thought of naked Mary Hump-Free moving her luscious buttocks before him was bringing a hardness under his fingers. The scenario was as clear as if it was happening before one of his television cameras right now. In his imagination, he directed the scene. The girl would turn to look at him and stare at his sex, and he would swell even thicker as if her eyes were fingers playing with him, the way he was doing now, her proxy, rubbing the silken skin for the comfort it lotioned over his still perturbed reaction to the prickly day.

At once he jerked his hand away. What the crazy-damn was he doing? He wasn't that skinny scared kid with the pencil cock shaking the Ohio bed.

But Reynolds suddenly felt cold and alone as if the world held no Madison Avenue, no Helena or daughters, no Duncan Talbott, as if he were loose in space; and his hand went back to the waiting place for the warmth he needed to kindle him back to earth. Was this sick? Well, maybe, Reynolds told himself, but not as disordered as responding to that girl would be—and what made him think that with all the young horns around she would even be interested in a senior cocksman? Anyway, it just felt plain-unapologizing-private good, and he would bet his half of the agency that it was done not infrequently by every type of young, old, poor, rich, single, married, neurotic, and whatever.

As growing excitement caught at his chest, Reynolds tried to talk himself out of the hovering feeling of guilt that was spoiling his enjoyment. Why was it wrong to be doing this? he demanded of the ceiling. When he was a skeleton in a coffin this pleasure would be impossible. Oh, the truths of life everyone ignores!

His blood began to race, and Reynolds' mind trailed aside. He was suffused with the goodness of his cock, big in his hand as he continued to stroke, evenly and gently, with his fingers pressing easily here and there, giving his own answers to the secret language of his body, withheld, in the end, from everyone but himself. He relished being so big that even his large hand could not hold it all. Here, alone, he could admit his pleasure in its size and potency.

Women, he mused, did not really know how to pull a man off properly. They tended to yank and tug and squeeze, sometimes they hurt. At least at first, you wanted to take it slow 'n' easy, sometimes clasping all around, sometimes just playing up and down with thumb and forefinger or, nicely, thumb and pinky—ah, yes, *that* was neat. Sometimes you wanted to titillate the spot near the tip that sent shivers up your spine, must be what a woman feels from her clit.

Women played with themselves. Most women, anyhow. The books on Women's Lib were full of encouragement, with graphic directions on the use of vibrators and dildoes. Did Helena? It was one of the things he'd always wanted to know about her but been afraid to ask. Afraid? No. People owned a space of privacy that should not be trespassed. It wasn't just decency or good manners. It occurred to Reynolds that a woman like Helena lived in her privacy the way an astronaut needed his space suit. It was a life-support system not to be punctured. His scarring her had been such a puncture, he understood at last. But right now he had another preoccupation . . .

He began to pant with mounting heat. Now, now was the time to start the pumping, to enfold the gorgeous throbbing organ with a full palm, your other hand under your heavy balls, and get it going good, up and down, up and down, up, up, down-up, with the lusting beat of the sex rhythm he had felt pulsing from the sugar-candy farm girl in the office with her red-checked dress (old-fashioned schoolteacher fabric) riding up her thighs, where his fantasy hotly saw she wore no panties and was exposing her sweet bush to him purposely, as he had envied Bloom masturbating when he was a teen-ager lost in Joyce, with her legs spreading apart wider so he could see better the juicy red secret. The golden crotch of hair was sweet fruit in honey to suck, drink, gorge on as his body was gorging with its own flooding climax. Ah, jerking off was better than getting laid, some ways. You could slow down, hold it, wait to prolong the essence of every singing muscle and nerve. You could touch the right spot, squeeze harder there, the way no one else could know you needed, needed, needed this glorious tautness, delaying its release in an agony that was the greatest jubilation. You could finger your tender anus, where the spasms of delight began. As this instant! Oh, so few women did that! They demanded men to know all about playing with their clit, but few ever understood about a finger ringing softly around the tender, waiting, grateful anus.

Reynolds' hand pumped wildly. It was getting away from him. Now, he was going to shoot! He moaned aloud through clenched teeth. He was the seven-year-old boy and the forty-odd man, and ageless, and a stallion, a bull, a peacock with a fanning burst of his uncontainable energy, hydrogen of cum blasting the quantum of sex, God's true sign to man that he was made in an Image.

Utter abandonment jerked Reynolds' body as infinite pleasure coursed from his ass out with Onan's flame and thrill.

Reynolds could breathe again. His brain was beating like his heart. God, that was the first time in years he had done it sober. He was not sorry he had let himself go. The days were over when people pretended the body did not own cunt, tit, cock, balls. Good riddance to the old hypocrisy that printed sex passages in Latin, and terrorized little kids with threats of hair-on-palms or going blind or crazy. What he had just done was as natural as eating when you are hungry. It had been, Reynolds suddenly realized, a very long time since he had had a woman. No wonder he had been carrying such a load. He grinned to himself. He had hurt no one and even Mary Humphrey had, in his scenario, had a good time.

Reynolds mocked himself with frank glee. How innocent could you pretend to be, Middle-Aged Goat? Anyway, *penis erectum non conscientum habem!* Should it be "conscient*um*" or ". . . t*am*?" he frowned. God, he had forgotten the Greek and Latin he had loved so ardently. He'd return to that happiness some day when he retired. That happiness, and writing poetry again. If he lived that long. If he ever graduated from Dr. Kohn's couch.

"Couch" brought guilt flaring back. With a start, Reynolds realized he was going to be ashamed to tell Dr. Kohn he had masturbated, pulled off.

His mind wheeled stubbornly again. It was *not* wrong! He had wanted-needed the comfort. If ye will not comfort me, Mother, if you will send me great distances alone, I shall comfort myself. Could he have been only seven or eight, even nine? Didn't puberty arrive later? Reynolds tried to calculate back, and abruptly recalled that his sister had died when he was nine, but had been alive that summer, so he must have been younger than nine. Could boys that young masturbate? He'd have to ask Dr. Kohn or Duncan sometime.

Reynolds told himself it was stupid to feel the guilt that would not fade. The annihilated red car flashed into his head. It could have been *his* brakes that failed. If that poor woman had died a virgin, who had gained, in this world or any other? Everybody should have orgasms! Satisfied in groin and head, Reynolds slept.

He did not waken until after the dinner hour, and had to rush to make his group's first session. He was hungry, but that was secondary. He was full of curiosity about the people he was about to "encounter."

Reynolds counted ten women and nine men, including himself. They all entered the Red Barn as he did, expectant, watchful, and nervous. They sat on folding chairs set in a semicircle in the large space. Uneasy and wary, some held mechanical smiles, others examined the building with a show of self-possession. They saw a high, crossbeamed, well-lighted structure that had been scrubbed and whitewashed but still held an odor of cattle and horses. Reynolds saw some of the women sniffing with distaste, but he enjoyed the smell, another reminder of Ohio. ("Rustic" perfume—good name for a new product? No, too bald.) Reynolds shifted his attention to the people he would be living with for the week. Total strangers now, how would they seem to him by this time next Saturday after the intimacies of the encounter sessions, and the nude bathing?

It helped his uncertainty to recall a relevant gaff in Lillian Schuster's collection. A small-town paper intended to announce that the Rev. W would address the ladies of the Bible class in the basement of the church on Sunday night. The item appeared: "Rev. W will undress the ladies of the Bible class—"

Silas Frank, M.D., Ph.D., came in, a giant of a man. He wore farmer's overalls, heavy-duty boots, and a rough wool cap that he kept on, tilted to the back of his skull and showing a shaved head which, with his heavy moustache, gave him a walruslike face. His wide-set, large eyes projected a man with no capacity or care to pretend or contrive. He had a bulging stomach that bespoke some indulgence, and he bore an expression of permanent satisfaction with himself, the world, and his fellow men. You could like this person easily, Reynolds thought, but you also had to be wary of that knowing, nobody-cons-me gaze under the shaggy brows. Like Dr. Kohn, this was a person who could flush you out of any hiding place. Those eyes were hammers that could smash dishonesty like an eggshell.

Dr. Silas Frank uttered a spectacular belch as he lowered his length into his seat, and everyone broke into laughter. Much of the tension went immediately as the leader looked around with obvious pleasure. "Lesson number one," Dr. Frank said, joining the laughter. "Most of you wouldn't have let that go. Right?"

"Right," some voices ventured.

"Well, I know enough not to do it in polite—that is to say, hidebound—society, but I can share with you that it felt real good. Okay." His deep voice turned as authoritative as his bearing. "How many of you have ever been to an encounter group?" One person raised his hand, a beefy young man who looked like a football player. "Bo Evins," he introduced himself with the air of a veteran. The others observed him with interest as Dr. Frank grinned at them and said, "Good, the rest of you won't spot the mistakes I make." Tentative smiles appeared around the circle.

To Reynolds' surprise, Mary Humphrey came into the room and

slipped into a seat. Apparently she was to be a participant. "Sorry I'm late, Si. I had to close the office," she told the leader.

"Okay. But not again." A tight ship was run here, his tone made plain at once.

Reynolds felt vaguely disturbed by the girl's presence. He had fantasized her in the baths, but had not expected her to be in the workshop. He was stern with himself immediately. He *had* to stop tracking every notion that prowled his head. What he should be doing was listening to Dr. Frank:

"Our purpose here is to learn—personally and directly—how far we get out of touch with our true feelings, because mostly people act as they think they are *supposed* to act. In daily life, we mostly suffocate our real feelings, the legitimate ones as well as the illegitimate. Instead, we run an act that helps us survive and win approval. Of course, that's not all bad. Civilization requires order, and we all have to make our contracts with society. Freud himself emphasized that.

"Still, though we don't want anarchy, many of us do go too far in self-suppression. Justice Holmes once said that my right to swing my cane ends where your nose begins, but that doesn't mean I have no freedom to swing my cane at all, does it? By holding back *too* much, from early childhood, many of us lose our authentic feelings and live out false personalities.

"This week, we'll be asking two embarrassing questions about the phony acts you are running. One, what does it *cost* you in terms of screwed-up relationships? And two, who are you making wrong with your act? The answers will give you good clues to getting back in touch with yourself and what *you* really want out of *your* life."

The encounter veteran, Bo Evins, interrupted. "Isn't that 'est' language you're using there, doctor?"

Dr. Frank nodded. "Partly. Psychosynthesis and others too. We share some common concepts. We apply them quite differently. Any other questions?"

No one responded.

Dr. Frank continued, "After people establish false personalities they often buy into habit patterns that support them. As a result, the authentic self gets buried completely.

"Now what this workshop aims at is, no, not to try to break those habits—which would be impossible in one week—but to try a sort of end-run around our emotional ruts, so to speak. We do this by relating *with scrupulous honesty* both to the people around us and to ourselves. One example right now: You don't expect to see a distinguished physician like me," Dr. Frank chortled, "in clothes like this. Okay. I hope it does throw you a little, starts breaking down stereotype reactions. That's a key, you see. No stereotypes, no stale labeling. If we shuck that off, we have a chance to catch our authentic feelings by surprise. We stir them up and, if we're lucky, we claim them strongly and honestly enough to take back home, where they improve the quality of our lives.

"Hopefully, by the end of this week you will all have a clearer line on where you're coming from, and that will help you get your shit together. Do you dig me?"

The man's language was a new surprise to Reynolds. No stereotypes, right on!

Dr. Frank said, "We'll begin now. I want you all to relax. Close your eyes, please, and place your feet flat on the floor. Let's take our shoes off, eh?" After the bending and shuffling, the leader continued, *"Now* close your eyes, and just let your hands rest, let them just fall in your lap, and breathe deeply, slowly, out slowly, like this, right, and just we all relax, get rid of the tension so we can begin the first exercise together, eh?" After a long hush, during which Reynolds began to feel the early drowsiness of Dr. Kohn's couch, Dr. Frank roused the group. "I will count to three and we'll open our eyes, and you'll feel fine, just fine. And take a deep breath, in, one—two—three—open and flex our muscles a bit, nice and loose and, fine, now, feeling fine, face each other in couples." It took a moment of jostling to pair off. Reynolds found himself partnered with a man, under thirty, with hair so blond it was almost white. His small face was fragile-boned, he had long lashes, and a soft, smiling mouth. A new schoolboy eager to make friends.

Dr. Frank instructed, "Now I *don't* want you to talk, or move, or touch. Got that? Just look at each other, eh? Anywhere your eyes go, hands, feet, anywhere, but finish up by looking into each other's eyes. Right? End up by looking into each other's eyes for as long as you can. And no speaking, please. Just look." The leader fell silent; the room was pin-drop silent.

Reynolds took in his neighbor. He seemed slender as a girl, but muscular under his tight T-shirt. His blue flaring slacks were tight around the crotch. Reynolds raised his eyes and, suddenly, the way a fish takes bait, his gaze was hooked by the man's stare. It was a palpable pull. The man's scrutiny seemed to hold a fugitive cast, somehow secretive, knowing, sardonic. It made Reynolds a little uneasy. He wondered what the man was making of him.

And so the week started, with the group following the doctor less and less hesitantly. His weight alone instilled confidence, helped the people accept the new experiences of touching strangers, going limp inside a circle and falling backward with full confidence that your fellows would catch you, and similar exercises calculated to introduce personality on a nonverbal level, and to start building an environment of mutual trust.

After about an hour, Dr. Frank introduced a change of pace that intrigued Reynolds at once. The leader placed a white canvas chair beside him, calling it the "hot seat." Anyone who felt like "working" could come forward, he explained. If you took the seat, that meant you were willing to let your hair down, be open with the group, tell it like it really was with you. Understood?

Heads nodded all around the circle. Like puppets on a string, Reynolds observed with a private smile, and quickly damped his thought as defensive jitters and unwarranted snobbishness. He had no reason to feel superior to anyone in this room. He didn't know who they were, as they knew nothing about him. There was excitement in being incognito. How would he come across to people who didn't have his Who's Who calling card?

There was an encouraging laugh from Dr. Frank. "It isn't as easy as it sounds. Who wants to hack it first?"

No one moved.

Dr. Frank took off his wool hat and passed his hand over his shining dome while he looked around the circle. He stopped at the football type. "You, Bo?"

"Not yet." The man seemed not so much to speak as to growl.

The dome turned slowly again and came to rest at Reynolds. Reynolds' heart tattooed in his chest. "I understand you've been in psychoanalysis, Phil." Of course—it was on the application, and Kohn had undoubtedly spoken to Dr. Frank. Reynolds could only nod. He knew he was reddening. Why him to start? Was it a test—to see if he could "deal with what might be churned up?" Well, this was what he had come for, wasn't it? What was he afraid of? What seat could be hotter than Dr. Kohn's couch?

Yes, but in that office he dealt only with Dr. Kohn. Here there were a score of people. Suddenly the sound of their breathing was like a crouching animal's. Reynolds wanted to say "Not yet" like that fellow Bo, but he found himself drawn to the white chair. As he sat, not knowing what to expect, he felt insects crawling up his spine and sweat running down his back although it was cold in the barn. Looking around, he was grateful to see an attentive nod of support from the man who had been his first partner, whose name he now knew was Harold ("Hal") Basser. He noticed too that Mary Humphrey was leaning forward toward him with clear interest.

Reynolds heard Dr. Frank saying, "Before Phil begins, I want to explain that when you take the hot seat you can tell us about your work or not as you please. Our whole point here is that we care less about what you do for a living than what you do with the living you make. Okay?" He paused to let the words sink in. Reynolds' eyes widened. That was a bull's-eye with 14-karat clout. It would make a helluva slogan if they ever wanted to advertise this place: *We care less about what you do for a living than what you do with the living you make!*

Dr. Frank had turned back to Reynolds. "Just start by telling us what you are feeling."

Reynolds said uneasily, "I'm hot."

"It's cool in here," Dr. Frank offered.

"I know it is." Reynolds aired his confusion. "I feel foolish," he confessed, trying hard to cooperate.

"That's par for the course. Good."

Reynolds did not share the image that came across his mind, though he knew he was supposed to "tell all." It was the girl, Mary, moving naked into a pool. He repeated, inanely, "Hot as hell."

Dr. Frank addressed the group. "I want everyone to understand the methods we will be working with, so just let's take this very easy now." He returned to Reynolds. "I would like you to go around the group and tell each person."

Reynolds was puzzled.

Dr. Frank spelled out, "Tell each one what you feel."

"That I feel hot?" It was doltish. Reynolds ran his tongue over his teeth in a new tic of discomfort, but he rose. If this was the encounter game, okay. He stopped at the first person, Bo Evins. The husky face lifted professionally, the pig-like eyes challenging. The man was eager to play his full role, to show his experience, and to get his money's worth.

Reynolds had trouble getting the two words out. "I'm hot."

Bo Evins rumbled, "You ain't sayin' it to *me*, man!" The accent was heavily southern, the sound truculent. Reynolds thought of Gordon Weslie and Jock Rogers.

Reynolds said louder, "I'm hot." But he could hear the conviction trail out of his voice. Bo Evins sneered at him with a nasty superiority. "It's cold in here, man. Don't lay your number on me!" It was more of the special lingo. Reynolds despised the fellow, but liked the jargon. Harlem out of Esalen?

Reynolds shrugged away from the man and moved around the circle, repeating, "I'm hot." He felt more stupid each time until he came to a woman, about forty, dressed in a soft gray wool sweater and gray slacks, who touched his forehead with her palm and said gently, "I know. You're sweating, Phil. I'm glad you're showing us how it goes." The touch of her hand, her use of his name, her support, flowed through Reynolds. When he thanked her he wanted to sit beside her, but Dr. Frank was telling him to go on.

The next person was Hal Basser. When Reynolds went through the short routine, Hal smiled up pleasantly. "I feel like Mrs. Caldwell here. You're helping us all, and I know it's tough." He reached to shake Reynolds' hand. The fingers were limp and clammy. Reynolds dropped the hand and said, "I appreciate that."

By the time Reynolds reached the last seat, Mary Humphrey, his turtleneck was soaked with perspiration. He recited dutifully, "I'm hot."

Mary Humphrey looked up at the tall man, so obviously "somebody," and so obviously feeling out of place, and said brightly, "You sure are hot."

The room's contained nervousness ignited into titters. The girl's quip had opened it up. *Hot-horny.* Reynolds went along, with a laughing noise. It appeared to him that this was idiotic; he might as well pack and drive off tonight. Resistance? Dr. Frank cut his thoughts with a question, "Do you want to tell the group what you do, Phil?"

Reynolds considered for a moment. "Let's wait," he said, feeling in charge of himself once more. If he stayed, now he was sure he wanted the feedback on Phil Reynolds the man, not the advertising executive.

". . . what you do with the living you make!"

"Okay, thanks," Dr. Frank said. "I just wanted a first start. We'll check you out again later." To the group the doctor observed, "Well, you see, nobody bites *too* hard, and you might even run into something pleasant."

Across the room, Mary Humphrey winked openly at Reynolds, with a welcome-to-the-club smile. He stiffened against the magnetism he felt from her, but was pleased inside that he was now an initiate of sorts.

Dr. Frank was asking him, "How are you feeling?"

"Okay." Yes, he did feel okay. "Cooler," he added, laughing, and liked the sound of the approval he heard from the group.

"Good," the doctor said. "I don't want to leave you hanging."

The woman in gray, Mathilda Caldwell, took the hot seat next. After an uncomfortable silence that brought fidgets around the room, she unexpectedly broke into tears. The group bent toward her. She sobbed to them, "My divorced husband keeps calling me, and I don't want to see him. It doesn't matter why. But I can't make him quit. He makes me so miserable I don't know what to do."

To Reynolds it seemed a plea for help from any of them, and he heard himself responding in that spirit, "Why don't you just hang up?" (Shades of his own telephoning!—his old excuse that anyone could hang up if they didn't want to listen.)

"I don't want to hurt him any more than I have."

Reynolds went on. "He's hurting *you*, isn't he?" (It was a Dr. Kohn-type observation.)

Reynolds was brought up short by a rebuke from Bo Evins. "Stop helping her!" Puzzled, Reynolds turned to Dr. Frank for support. Wasn't this kind of exchange—this "feedback"—what an encounter group was all about? But what he got from Dr. Frank was a soft, *"Don't* help. Not yet anyway, and not that way." And to the group. "People need space. Let's keep that in mind. We have to give people their own space, everyone."

Evins' heavy voice came again. "He wants us to get how smart *he* is!"

Reynolds faced the man, lecturing. "It's a sadomasochist thing, don't you see?" Why waste time when it was all so clear? He pivoted to Mathilda Caldwell, disregarding what Dr. Frank had advised. "Don't you understand you're playing into the man's hands?" (Christ, he was an expert on *this!*)

Dr. Frank corrected Reynolds, "Nobody will see anything, man, if you intend to be our seeing-eye dog all week!"

Reynolds felt unfairly whipped, and resentful. Their rules were asinine, and disrespectful. He had only been trying to give them the benefit of what he had learned painfully himself.

At the same time, he was disconcerted. At the back of his mind, Reynolds recognized that he was doing for Mathilda Caldwell what Dr. Kohn adamantly refused to do for him. And being arrogant about it. And Glorious. That damned Evins fellow might be right. Reynolds eased back in his chair, lips tight. Okay. Let them slog through their own confusions themselves.

His upset faded as he watched with growing fascination when Dr. Frank offered a fresh technique. Placing an empty chair before Mrs. Caldwell, the doctor said, "Now pretend your ex-husband is sitting here. Talk to him as if he were right here now."

Immediately, the woman launched into a heated recital of wrongs the man had done—drunkenness, infidelity. Dr. Frank intervened after a while. "Okay, now switch places. You move to this chair and be your husband, and talk to *that* chair as if you, as his wife, are sitting there. Got it?"

Nodding, the woman shifted. It took only a few moments before the roles became real, both to Mathilda Caldwell and the group. Playing her former husband, the woman gave an impassioned speech of misunderstanding, of love and loss. Her voice took on strong emotion. When she stopped, she was clearly shaken, and so were the people in the room.

Dr. Frank said, "I think we all heard how much you feel this man still loves you. How did that go down with you?"

Mathilda Caldwell said, with wonder in her voice, "I have got a lot of thinking to do."

Reynolds nodded. Yes, he saw what could happen with these methods. Now the woman had raw emotion to deal with instead of poached manners. An important lesson for him to learn and relearn (echo of Dr. Kohn) . . .

After a coffee break, Dr. Frank had the people stand and face each other as they had done for the eyeballing. "When I give the signal, I want you to pretend you are children. Jump up and down, yell nonsense, any kind of sound except words. Got it?" He himself began with a pachyderm leap and pounding dance, while issuing a string of barks and garbles: "Lo la lee-oh plocky wocka hoboabob shmeeklo shmeeklo kama kola lama loma polpopolopolopoyeeee!"

The group became a giggling, hopping mob, dervishing and bouncing, hands flapping like wings, blabbering, jabbering, gabbing, googling, cawing, mooing, clacking, hooting.

All except Reynolds. He was trying with all his might, but could not utter a sound. He had started to hop, wanting to join in, but had stopped dumbfounded. His jaws were locked; he could not even hum. He was looking into a mirror of silence and getting back an empty skull.

It came to Reynolds that there were more disconcerting challenges in this workshop than he had suspected.

Nobody seemed to notice, so Reynolds volunteered nothing when Dr. Frank called the exercise to an end. He would discuss it with the doctor in private, Reynolds decided. The leader was saying, "Okay, that should get rid of some of your inhibitions, eh? Loosen you up for the baths. It's time to go."

"Loosened?" Reynolds felt wound up tighter than ever. Dr. Frank

could announce the baths as casually as a coffee break, but this might well
be a confrontation he could not handle. Reynolds took in the nervous
smiles flashing around the group. He wasn't the only one wondering.
People were hanging back while Frank herded them like a camp
counselor: "*Okay* everybody, let's *go!*"

Well, Reynolds thought, the Japanese have been doing it for
centuries.

The group formed a straggling procession on the snowy path to the
farmhouse and the waiting baths in the basement. Mary and Dr. Frank
were in front, throwing snowballs at each other. Reynolds was at the
rear of the line, with Mathilda Caldwell coming up beside him. She
whispered anxiously, "I don't think I can go through with this. What
happens if you don't?"

"I don't know," Reynolds answered. "I think you must leave the
workshop."

"Oh, dear. I'm getting so much out of it." The woman slipped and
Reynolds quickly gave her his arm. She smiled her thanks and said,
"Hell, if everybody else can do it, I can try."

"Right," Reynolds said encouragingly. "Take space." He liked the
new language, would bring it back to his shop.

The woman said, "I want to thank you for trying to help me. They
shouldn't have jumped on you the way they did."

"I guess it's part of what we all came here to learn." It was his turn to
skid on the icy path, and he had to grab Mathilda Caldwell's arm. He felt
the support of her strength, and it was a comfort.

Going down creaking steps, the group was met by a warm gust of
damp air that felt like the tropics after the brittle cold outside. The
whitewashed walls were decorated with Eastern-looking esoteric sym-
bols that Reynolds did not recognize. He admired their graphic expres-
siveness; it was a talent the agency could use. He'd check it out when he
went to the office to make the Ted Watson calls.

Downstairs there were clean gray lockers and freshly painted blue
benches around a large cement-block room. Through a wide doorway
Reynolds saw a dim cavernous space and made out three pools, each
about ten feet square.

There was no division into men's and women's sections, but the group
split automatically with women clustering at lockers on one side and the
men on the other. Dr. Frank laughed, "Hang yourself anywhere, folks."

Starting to undress, Reynolds locked his eyes front, feeling as if his head was in a vise. As he tugged his turtleneck over his head, he remembered with a touch of guilt that it was one of Helena's Christmas presents. Maybe he should have stayed at home mending his fences with Helena instead of coming here . . .

All around the room there were sounds of clearing throats, vague humming, small issues of jittery laughter, people saying speechlessly: "This isn't *me* stripping naked—"

Reynolds unbuckled his belt. He assured himself that, just as he was looking at no one, no one was looking at him. He chided himself for the disquiet he could not overcome. He was a grown man; they were all grown people. This wasn't an orgy. His fidgets were exactly what Dr. Frank had emphasized at the beginning: In the Center's parlance, his nervousness was a "trip laid on him by society." Yet it was a nose-rubbing irony that he, who could so easily make dirty phone calls, was embarrassed to expose himself to these women. With his mind darting in all directions to escape his confusion, Reynolds found himself remembering one of the prizes of his typo collection, a retail store advertisement: "Closeout Sale on Name-Brand Pajamas for Men with Tiny Flaws."

Reynolds yanked his pants down. His fingers fumbled at his briefs. Finally, he glanced right and left. Some of the men, stark naked, were beginning to turn into the room.

And nothing was happening, except a sudden hush.

Dr. Frank stood in the center. He had a forest of black hair curled on his barrel chest, and a mountain of black moss for a bush, from which a long penis hung plump against a great sack of testicles. His legs and thighs were thick and straight. "Let's go, everybody," he led them again.

Reynolds tugged his briefs off. Every instinct pressed him to cross his hands before his crotch, but he turned to the group fully exposed.

His reaction astonished him, he would tell Dr. Kohn later: "There I was, doctor, in a roomful of nude women, stark-naked, a dream out of *Arabian nights*, and all I got was *a sense of everything being so natural, so normal, so everyday-ordinary that, actually, I felt cheated!*

"I couldn't believe it, especially when I looked at Mary Humphrey. She was ravishing, sexier than Penny. Full breasts pointing up, with young nipples like cherries on vanilla ice cream. A body like Botticelli's Venus, long perfect legs, my afternoon's fantasy come true, only better. And I don't have a semi-demi-quaver of a sex reaction! The *one* feeling I don't get—and nobody else seems to either—is *sex!* I can't believe my eyes, my brain, my cock!"

That was the incredible truth he would be recounting to Dr. Kohn, Reynolds reflected with abiding wonder as he followed Mary Humphrey into the pool and sat in the comforting warm water between her and Hal Basser. Naked and innocent. The pre-apple Garden of Eden rediscovered!

A story his young daughters told came to Reynolds' mind. Two three-year-olds are playing near a fountain and the little boy suggests to the girl that they strip to bathe. As the girl climbs over the ledge, the watching boy says, "I didn't know that was the difference between Protestants and Catholics." That was the sense of innocence he would, beyond belief, be describing to Dr. Kohn when he returned to the couch.

Then the second surprise occurred. Dr. Frank called out, "Come on in, Mathilda. It's all right."

Reynolds realized with a start that the Caldwell woman had not entered the pool with the rest. Dr. Frank said softly what seemed unnecessary, "Just go on, everybody, with what you're doing." Some people had their heads back, eyes closed, with dreamy expressions. Others were conversing softly. Reynolds saw Mathilda Caldwell come haltingly through the doorway. The light behind her was haloing her hair beautifully, and the glowing outline of her body was a mature loveliness that made him think of Helena. Walking slowly toward the group, she was holding her head even higher than Helena did, and Reynolds felt that she was straining for self-possession.

Hell, Reynolds thought with irritation, they had all made it, why the sudden drama? What did the woman have so special that the others didn't?

Then he saw it as she came out of the shadows. One breast. The woman had only one breast.

An involuntary cry of shock and protest and self-revulsion almost escaped Reynolds' throat. At once he was totally on her side. Lord, what courage every one of her faltering steps must require, he thought with a soaring respect. He had never suspected anything like—

Reynolds berated himself. As he had not suspected the old woman in the brakeless compact? As he had not suspected the truth in an incident that flooded his mind now. When he had first come to New York, late for his job one morning, he had cursed silently at a jam-up on the subway steps. Hearing a train approaching, he had shouted impatiently at a man down front who was taking his own sweet time in disregard of everyone else. He had pushed his way down and nearly bowled the man over before he saw the crutches. It knocked the wind out of him. The amputee was ashamed and apologetic, and Reynolds felt sicker. He had wanted to weep, as he did now, averting his eyes from the hurt woman. It was more than he could bear to see her sheer bravery as she stood at the edge of the pool trying to smile.

Then, suddenly, as had happened with the sex thing, the tension was gone in the room, and Reynolds' own steel coil snapped.

So this woman had needed the operation. So what? So the mastectomy was probably part of her complicated problem with her husband. So what? It came to Reynolds that there is no human being in the world who is not in some way crippled.

In the quieting warm water, sitting opposite Mathilda Caldwell, Reynolds experienced again how much he was at fault in jumping to conclusions about people, never giving others the space to be whatever-it-was-they-were, always seeing things through his eyes only, as if no other viewpoint ever existed.

Tolerance, sympathy, understanding of *others?*

If he learned nothing else in these perplexing encounters, the week had already paid off by bringing those long-lost words back to him, Reynolds considered with humility.

The water was soothing. The brochure had promised natural hot springs. Everyone seemed relaxed, with arms around shoulders, beginning to chat easily. There were small ripples in the water, but bodies could be seen quite clearly. More mysterious to Reynolds was that he felt no difference between the touch of Mary's wet skin and Hal Basser's. *They were both simply human beings.*

Dr. Frank made that point as soon as the group was settled. "As I started to say earlier tonight, our encounter workshop is about only one thing—coming to accept our *natural* selves. *And,* now I add, to accept others the same way. As we are all doing right now. In our sessions this week, we will come to feel how people have pretty much the same emotions, good, bad, and indifferent. This should lead both to greater self-acceptance and tolerance of others."

Reynolds nodded silently.

"Right now, we are undergoing a fundamental experience. We are experiencing each other as humans *who are basically alike,* rather than as sexual creatures who are basically different. In a sexual frame of reference, vive la différence! In this frame of reference, vive la *sameness!*

"So you see the logic and importance of the baths to our ongoing group. We build mutual confidence by seeing how little charge there is in even our sex differences, which usually carry so much dynamite. Since this is true, we find it easier to form a steady center and to open ourselves to ourselves and to others throughout the sessions, and then, hopefully, on the outside when you go back home."

Dr. Frank looked about him with a broad grin, showing crooked teeth beneath his moustache. "I'm sure most of you expected this communal bathing to be a sensational business. Now you understand why I, personally, sometimes wish it were a little more fun!"

In the good humor that followed, Reynolds ventured a contribution to the group. It was an item Lillian Schuster had found in a San Francisco newspaper. The manager of a nudist camp had complained that a hole was cut into the fence around his park. The paper reported that the police were looking into it.

Even Bo Evins broke up, and Reynolds enjoyed the new acceptance he felt coming his way.

21

When the bath session ended at eleven o'clock, the group went upstairs for a snack. Mary Humphrey signaled Reynolds to a chair she was saving in a corner of the dining room. Over a beer, he asked the girl whether she sat in with many of the groups. She told him she had done some weekend marathons, but not a full week's workshop like his. "I use the baths all the time, though." She gave a bantering laugh that reminded him of Selma's, adding, "It's a neat fringe benefit."

"What about school?" Reynolds asked.

"I'm finished."

"You dropped out?"

"Oh, no. I graduated."

He showed his surprise. "How old *are* you?"

"Seventeen. I skipped some. Around here the schools are geared to the dumb-dumbs. If you have half a brain, you're a genius. I thought I might go to college, but these days that's sort of dead end." Mary Humphrey gave Reynolds a direct look. "I'd like to try advertising. I saw on your form that's your field." Her eyes were earnest. "That's why I wanted to talk to you alone."

Reynolds was taken aback but liked the girl's frankness. Another Penny, indeed! "I don't even know you, Mary—"

She turned saucy. "Well, let's go to your room and lay my trip on you. I could use some Scotch instead of beer for a change anyway."

Reynolds had to share her smile. "How do you know I have Scotch?"

"What else would a man like you drink?"

"Maybe tomorrow," Reynolds heard himself say stiffly, as if reading a cue card held by Dr. Kohn. "I've had a helluva day and I'm tired." He wasn't ready to be alone with this girl in a convenient room with a bottle between them.

"Come on, you aren't *that* old—" Now she was laughing *at* him, as if reading his mind.

Reynolds was out of his chair, saying good night brusquely, admonishing himself sternly to remember *consequences*.

Trudging to his cabin, Reynolds enjoyed kicking up sprays of snow along the path. He felt elevated, respectable, and virtuous. In his room, he saw the lamps darken outside as he drew the curtains. The moonlight sparkled on the spreading snow. The sky contained all the space Dr. Frank wanted to give all the people in the world. The air was still crisp in his lungs. A drink *would* go good. He had a great deal to absorb, the hot-seat experience, the baths, the one breast of Mathilda Caldwell, the pass the girl was making at him—it was pretty transparent.

But Reynolds did not take the bottle from his suitcase. Better get to sleep, he told himself. They would be getting up before six thirty according to the schedule he had tacked on the inside of the bathroom door.

Brushing his teeth, Reynolds was newly aware of the gray stubble the mirror showed in his beard. Reality. Mary Humphrey is a kid, hardly older than Selma. Forget it. He nodded. Keep testing reality, and abide by what you find. That was the name of the game on Dr. Kohn's couch, and up here at the Center, and in the real world outside. In his pajamas, Reynolds was feeling righteous and sleepy when the knock came. He opened the door reflexly.

"It's me. I want that Scotch, please." The girl had her parka off and was loosening her hair before he could respond.

Reynolds got the bottle out and poured a small drink into his bathroom glass, the only one in the room.

"Thanks. Where's yours?"

"I don't want any."

Mary held the glass up for him to share it. The smell brought the bird beaks open, as always. He turned abruptly. She drank in one swallow, shrugging. "You're sure stingy with it."

"You're not old enough," he said.

Her look was mischievous. "I'm old enough."

"Good night," he said.

"You know, until now I felt we were on the same wavelength." It was a taunt.

Reynolds tried to make it into a joke. "I'm old enough to be your father and that's a long way for some waves to travel." Well said, he thought to himself. This girl must want a job awfully bad.

The girl wouldn't be diverted. "I checked you out in the bath and I liked what I saw. I never had an older man." She went on plainly but somehow not brazenly, "If you didn't turn me on, you could drop dead trying, job or no job. Lots of men try. If you do turn me on, what's to yak?"

With that, Mary let her dress fall to the floor and, naked, raised her lips to Reynolds.

The young body that had somehow been neutral in the baths was fire now. Reynolds could smell the offer of the fresh, eager sex, pungent below. But to take her would be unconscionable. This was no Shmuel joke!

But, oh, God, the girl—the *woman*—naked and waiting before him was the anointed bloom of the Song of Songs. Her lips were petals opening to him, her breasts were music enticing his tired head. O temptress, O Delilah, O Lilith, O Jezebel!—don't come to my bed *now* with Dr. Kohn, and my wife, and my conscience reminding me, reminding, reminding, reminding me! I am not drunk now, I am not irresponsible, I am not an outlaw!

Right versus Wrong. Tomorrow versus Now. The endlessly exasperating conundrum, the horns of life's dilemmas bayoneting Everyman's ass! (Only live once! *Take* her!) (Shut up, Ikey!)

Damn Freud and the Superego! Damn Kohn and Frank and the Authentic Self! What could be more authentic, Reynolds raved inwardly, than what was happening inside his pajama pants?

But that was just it, an inner voice insisted. If he slid back, he might as well quit his analysis. That would make no damned sense. He had to be reasonable as well as horny—he had invested too much of himself in the agonizing climb out of the Stygian cave. He was *not* going to be Sisyphus. *Fuck Sisyphus,* he was not going to fuck Mary Humphrey!

Right now he needed to remember: *"The task of analysis is to turn psychological problems into moral ones."*

He was not going to forget that. He had battled his way into the moral arena now, and there he had choice, not compulsion. He could wrestle his old self-indulgence, and beat it down! If this naked siren before him was a crisis of temptation, he would get past it.

But Mary Humphrey stepped closer, put her seeking arms around

Reynolds, and pressed her nakedness against him. Through his thin pajamas he felt her as if he were nude. She nudged her crotch against the hardness he could not control and gave a perverse laugh. "Good-o! A mile long!"

Reynolds shied like a shot animal. His wild *"No"* astonished him as well as the startled girl. He hopped into the bathroom and slammed the door in Mary Humphrey's disbelieving face. Turning the lock with shaking fingers, Reynolds swore at himself. What a fucking Mack Sennett farce this was! Mack Sennett? No, Alfred Jarry and Antonin Artaud—*absurdity!*—he shaking with lust in a tiny bathroom with a hard-on sticking out of him like a fishing pole, frantically locking himself away from a steaming nymph who wanted a hot fuck! Was he adult or dolt? Man or dithering putz? Hero or bum?

A word new in his vocabulary rose to answer: *Self-respect!*

Through the door Reynolds heard the girl's incredulity. "Shee-*it*, you really mean it!"

There was a pause. "Man, are you ever in the lost and found! Do you ever need to get in touch with your feelings! You are too *much!*"

Reynolds held himself stiffly behind the bathroom door. *This* was being in touch with himself. He felt his new strength. He was no longer disconnected, he could take charge, decide.

Outside, the floor creaked. Leave, dammit, Reynolds cursed under his breath. Leave before all this great self-control is pulverized by the furious, frustrated pole making a ludicrous tent out of my pajama pants.

Thankfully, he heard the door close. She might be tricking him—she was bizarre, that one, unpredictable. Reynolds opened the bathroom door a crack and peered into the room, conscious again of the comical figure he was cutting. Mary Humphrey was gone. Or should he look under the bed? All at once, Reynolds roared at himself and the situation, relieved that it was over. I have met the enemy and I have won, though a Pyrrhic victory, he mocked himself, regarding his erection.

Reynolds flopped on the bed, his head hammering. "God," he addressed the heavens through a space where the curtains had separated, "chalk one gold star up there for me, and hang it on the biggest pair of blue balls You ever saw!"

Reynolds' dream was of a group of beautiful Greek boys, with pointy, uncircumcised penises, who came alive off an amphora when the clock struck midnight. They dived like dolphins into an Olympic pool at a gay party thrown by a rich automobile executive in Grosse Pointe, which was somehow in New Jersey and not in Michigan.

Everyone drank ambrosia, ate peeled grapes, danced and cavorted, but no one touched. It was as if each person was enclosed in an invisible force field that prevented contact, much as in television sci-fi shows. Private space made palpable.

A storm broke suddenly, to Debussy's wind-lashed *La Mer*. Lightning avalanched sheets of fire that melted everyone like wax, the Greeks and Michiganites, male and female, clothed and naked, drunk and sober, laughing and howling. The huge lump of wax then heaved and shaped itself into a sculpture, which turned out to be Michelangelo's David, wearing a thin red tie that hung like a rope down to his penis.

Reynolds, not invited to the party, spied on all this sulkily from bushes of hairy plants. He was angry and felt forlorn that he had not been part of the wax mass, and so could not be enjoying the festivities now going on inside the hollow marble of the David. He knew there was a party within because when he crept to the figure and put his ear to the matchless buttocks, he could hear ravishing music, lutes and flutes and horn, bells, and a soprano singing "Yankee Doodle."

It was a brilliant cold day with the sun dazzling out of a cloudless, cerulean sky. People were clustered in front of a bulletin board on which Dr. Frank had listed the subgroups. These "quartets" would meet separately "to process" the experiences of the full sessions. Mary Humphrey came up behind Reynolds as, with mixed feelings, he read her name in his group, along with Hal Basser and Mathilda Caldwell.

Mary was beaming a roguish smile at him. "See? Even Dr. Frank can't keep us apart." She saw that Reynolds did not expect her friendliness, and she laughed again. "Sure I'm sore about last night, but I don't hold grudges. I've got a lot of energy invested in you, Phil, and I stick to my agenda. Do you read that?"

"I read you," he said unenthusiastically. *She* had better read *his* agenda, which was to keep his distance.

"And I've packed a picnic lunch," Mary went on securely. "Unless your ancient bones will need a nap."

He would not respond to her badgering. Reynolds said quietly, "I'm sorry. I have some business calls to make."

"On Saturday afternoon?" the girl scoffed.

Of course Ted Watson would have to wait until Monday morning, Reynolds reminded himself.

Reynolds' quartet met in his room for convenience. Dr. Frank had listed Hal Basser as the leader. The slight man started out diffident and uncertain. "I don't know why he picked me. I've never done anything like this before."

"Maybe that's why," Mary taught.

"Do you want to work first?" Hal asked her. His watery eyes were a plea for assistance.

The girl considered for a moment, then inclined her head. "Yes, I feel like taking some room."

Mathilda Caldwell sat down on Reynolds' bed. Reynolds slid to the floor, leaning against the wall. Hal came beside Reynolds.

Reynolds watched the girl intensely. She had her eyes shut tight. Slowly her hand stretched out and she spoke, in a sepulchral tone that recalled high-school dramatics: "I see a cobra." Mary started to sway, and her hand stroked the imaginary snake in a curving motion that was clearly sexual. Reynolds stopped smiling. There was an undeniable stirring in his groin despite his genuine wish to be only a clinical observer. Mary's bra-less breasts were nudging under her tight sweater to show her nipples off. A man had to be sick *not* to have this male response.

Reynolds glanced at Hal Basser for his reaction. The man's face was a pale mask showing nothing.

Unexpectedly, Mathilda Caldwell broke the silence. "What's happening, Mary?"

Hal moved into his role as leader, using an expression picked up the night before. "Yes, where are you coming from, Mary?"

The girl intoned, "I am coming from a picture in my head. Of my father." The pose broke. Her hands whipped to her face. "He died last year." The weeping came like rain, she was a heartbroken child making no effort to stop the tears or the lament. "Why did you die, Daddy? I loved you so much, Daddy!"

Reynolds was put off by the theatricality. He was suspicious of the obvious sexual implication of her "beat," and at the same time unsettled by a sense of prying. It was well and good for people to come to the Center to let their hair down, but it didn't mean opening every secret crevice of one's life. That was tough enough on an analyst's couch. Reynolds remembered how uncomfortable he had felt as a boy when it had occurred to him that a surgeon walking down the street might be seeing everyone opened up, not clothed but naked, guts and gizzards— X-ray eyes! Here he was looking inside of Mary's head. How soupy could this stuff get? Mary's tears were clearly moving the others, but they grated on him. Why? Because superficial answers weren't enough any longer, he replied to himself, and he felt she was putting on an act. But he shouldn't be playing amateur analyst. Maybe everything was exactly as it seemed. He had an example of that in the two psychoanalysts he described for a laugh in some of his speeches. The doctors meet one morning on the street. One says, "Good morning." The other nods and walks on, asking: "What did he mean by that?"

Hell, Freud himself had once said, "Sometimes a cigar is just a cigar!"

At lunchtime, Mary came to Reynolds. "I do want to ask you about advertising. I reserved two snowmobiles, but if you don't want to be bothered, I understand."

Reynolds looked at her now-obedient young face, and around at the snowy expanse and tall trees going invitingly up the mountain. He had never been in a snowmobile. In a way, it was flattering that this attractive wench kept choosing him when she could have any male on the premises with a crook of her finger. Was it really a job she was after? Well, it couldn't hurt to talk, and his batteries could use a recharge from the girl's boundless energy.

The snow motors climbed quickly to a plateau from which the Center was small dots below, and the Catskill ranges reached majestically across the distance. It was an Alpine landscape, and Reynolds contemplated once again how the world held no scenery more varied or breathtaking than the United States.

Mary tidily set out their food on a checked tablecloth over a flat rock, reminding Reynolds of Penny on the terrace over the East River. He didn't want the memory, and was glad to listen to Mary saying, in one breath: "In the summer this field is full of wild flowers, you never saw so many colors, I come up here a lot to be alone. Phil, my father didn't really die, I don't like Hal and I just felt like pulling his leg this morning. I saw you were out of the whole thing, but Matty—" (Mary apparently brought everyone into intimacy at once) "—took it seriously, so I told her the truth too."

Reynolds, puzzled by the girl, said nothing. His thought was that if God had meant people to be simple He wouldn't have given them parents.

Suddenly Mary was on her feet, waving at two figures hiking toward them across the wide ridge. Reynolds eyed the couple with curiosity as she made the introductions. "This is Phil. He's in this week's workshop."

The young man probed Reynolds skeptically with hazel eyes above a wispy brown beard. "Barney," Mary named him. She turned to his partner, a short, heavy female of about twenty. "Terry." Fat peasant face, unpleasantly pimpled, a wart on her left cheek, and small eyes that spit arrogance as if she were a royal princess instead of an uncomely dwarf. She suddenly pivoted into a quirky dance that whirled her cape out to display flamboyant letters of bright orange spelling "FUCK YOU."

Disregarding his companion, Barney was holding a stained envelope to Mary. "The candles Terry made," he said. Mary glanced at the letter and passed it to Reynolds. He read: "Your shitment come broke. Fuck you for pay." It was written in block letters, almost illiterate in form.

Barney said, "I ought to sue the motherfucker, you'd be a witness, Mary. You saw Terry pack the fucking corrugated and all that shit."

Again it struck Reynolds how casually these young people used profane language. He supposed that, among other things, it was deliberately intended to offend squares like him. They needed their private tongue as slaves had needed their field songs. Ironically, he reflected, they defeated their own purpose. Their overkill took the sting out of the words, and left the rebels seeming stupid. More important, it left the language without dirty words, which are required for outrage, protest, separation. If the trend continued, Reynolds conjectured, society would have to create new profanity to fill the vacuum. He wondered what the new words might sound like. Go *schmoof* yourself? If he ever got back to writing poetry, that might be a helluva project, inventing fresh scurrility and maledictions.

This Barney seemed a bright youth, the more the pity that he had to express himself so churlishly. Selma would never become a slob like these two, certainly not if he could help it.

Mary was asking, "Are you guys still into Zen?"

Barney said, "Nah, I had my bellyful of Stuffed Karma at my Bar Mitzvah."

Reynolds laughed, liking the fellow and his humor despite his hang-dog manner.

Barney turned to him boldly. "Can you lend me some bread, man? We're naked."

Mary said at once, "Phil, Barney will pay you back!" Barney's head lifted. "Man, I am not a beggar."

The girl Terry sidled back to them. "Tell him your *ideas!*" She stood in front of Reynolds. "Barney's going to buy masks like doctors wear, you know? And I'm gonna paint stuff on them, like for Gay Lib, and

Women's Lib, and all the good shit, you know? And we sell 'em so people can protest their thing *and* protect against the pollution at the same time! Don't that go down great, man?"

Barney said, "Terry, this man doesn't want to hear all that diarrhea. I'll tell you when to talk!"

That raised a storm. Terry shrieked, "Listen shit-o, don't you chauvinist me! You split any fuck time you want! I have a great lover of my own!" She waved the middle finger of her right hand under Barney's nose.

Reynolds smiled at the young man. "You really do have wheels in your head, don't you?"

"Not the way you think, man. I'll be a millionaire if I feel like it, but with *my* jive, not your kind of crap."

Mary's amused eyes moved from one face to the other as Reynolds responded conversationally, "And what's your jive?"

Barney decided Reynolds was not being sarcastic or superior. "No, see, the way guys like you and my father are into 'business,' I mean, you're like in *jail*. Like you always have to be in a certain place at a certain time, so the whole shit-network can keep on dumping. Like my father is a lawyer, okay? So when he picks up the phone to call you, it's predictable your end will be there, you or your surrogate. And vice versa with him, and all your banks, airlines, printers, whorehouses, grocery stores, steel mills, and condom manufacturers. I mean, man, you are just a Bug in the Web. So let's say one of your employees decides to go rowing in the park on a sunny day, such actions are truly inimical. Because they disrupt the network. And that is true in Russia and China and Cuba as much as here—even more so!"

"Interesting theory," Reynolds conceded.

Barney's head moved in commiseration. "I'll make mine without burying myself every day in the grave of responsibility. That's why my old man is a joyless sad-puss. Sure the world stinks, but why waste your life uptight?"

Reynolds' smile was genuine. "Well, I leave it to you people to change the world."

Barney smiled back. "Old Zen saying: If your bladder is full what good if *I* piss?" He added, with respect, "I tell you one thing. My old man would never have the itch or the guts to come to a place like the Center." He offered Reynolds his hand. "And that's not just because I'm still asking for some bread."

Reynolds said, "Will twenty help you out?"

Taking the bill, Barney smiled disarmingly and lifted his pack. "I give you a true parable as interest on your twenty bucks, sir. When I was a boy we had a big locust in the back acre. Squirrels were up and down that tree all day long. One year a hurricane knocked it down. Well, for weeks afterward, there were still squirrels that would tear across the lawn and race up the stump right on up into the air like a fucking Walt Disney cartoon, until a puzzled look would hit their tails—squirrels think with their tails, you know—and they'd fall on their dumb asses.

"And the moral of my story is this: *People who climb ladder of success are on tree that isn't there!*"

Reynolds' reply surprised the young people. "Do you know the story of the two Zen monks who came upon a beautiful girl unable to cross a muddy road?" he asked. "One monk lifted her up and carried her over. The companion monk was scandalized but said nothing. Finally, hours later, he was unable to contain himself. 'It was wrong for a pious man like you to touch that girl!' The first monk answered, 'Dear friend, I put the lady down hours ago. Why do you continue to carry her?' "

Mary chortled, "One on you, Barney!"

Barney retorted to Reynolds, "I give *you* a quote. 'The mistakes of youth are preferable to the successes of age.' Said by *your* Disraeli."

Reynolds enjoyed tilting with the young irreverence. "But mistakes have a future," he countered. How well he knew that truth. "Your kind of anarchy leads nowhere."

Barney answered with finality, "I have seen the future, and it grunts!"

He started away. Terry ran after him, calling out, "Barney, why doesn't God make colored snow? I mean, after all, he can make a dumb thing like a rhinoceros. Who needs a rhinoceros?" Her voice faded in the distance.

Watching the two cavort down the mountain, Reynolds heard circus music in his head. They were two clownish silhouettes rollicking on white tanbark, flitting between tent poles of trees holding up the blue canvas of sky. Their merry cries to each other made a calliope music, free-flying in the frosty air. Beguiling.

That young man had something, Reynolds repeated to himself. If he ever cut loose his albatross of childish rebellion, he'd go places.

Mary brought him from his thoughts. Packing up, she said again, "Barney will pay you back, Phil."

Reynolds' eyes were friendly on the receding figures. He didn't believe Mary, and didn't care.

Gathering speed downhill, Mary swerved her machine in and out of

the trees like a slalom skier. It took all Reynolds' attention to keep the
snowmobile under control as he raced after the girl across the dizzying
shafts of black tree shadows and threatening rocks kaleidoscoping in the
sparking snow to awl his eyes until he could hardly see. Thinking of the
tragic race with the woman in the red car, Reynolds wished he could
slow down, but it would be a griping defeat to let the girl pull away as she
was doing.

He pressed harder, swerving by inches past a boulder, skidded, tilted
perilously, but fought the machine back and sped for a shortcut he
spotted between two giant rocks. It was narrow passage and clearly
dangerous, but he'd show that young Mary!—who was yoicking like a
foicking fox hunter, Reynolds guffawed. He felt invigorated as the snow
sprayed wildly around his speeding machine.

Without warning, Reynolds' snowmobile, yawing sickeningly,
plunged blindly and turned over, slamming into a rock with a crash that
brought Mary Humphrey around in a frantic return. Slipping and
falling in the deeply piled snow, the girl was crying hysterically, "Are
you all right, Phil? Are you all right?"

With the wind knocked out of him, Reynolds could not answer. His
head was an explosion of fireworks that would not stop. Above him,
Mary looked like a crone. His breath was coming back, though his hip
hurt badly. He wheezed, "I'm okay." The girl pressed him to her,
crooning, "Oh, please. Please. Please." There was ineffable terror in her
face. It occurred to Reynolds that, floundering in some undercurrent of
pain she could not handle, this convoluted girl had lied to him about *not*
losing her father. Maybe she needed a Dr. Kohn more than a Dr. Frank.

Reynolds was able to get to his feet. "Nothing broken," he said. They
righted the snowmobile, and Mary led the way down at a snail's pace.

Following grouchily, Reynolds thought the accident might be another
sign that the Center was not for him. He had looked to the workshop to
help his developing sense of self, and to give him improved insight into
his relationship with people. What he had gotten so far seemed mostly
tension, trouble, and trauma. One vow he made now as the snowmobiles
tracked to a stop behind the farmhouse—Mary Humphrey would remain
far out of bounds!

In the afternoon session, several people worked on the hot seat before
Reynolds had an impulse to take another turn. He felt the group's special
curiosity about him. It was clear by now that he was the only participant
from the business world. The others were graduate students, social

workers, teachers, or guidance counselors. By and large, Reynolds felt he could trust them. He began with the standard procedure: Press stockinged feet solidly on the floor—relax hands in lap—bend head over, eyes closed, and take three breaths as deep as possible, held as long as possible—open your mind, gut, body, soul, will, emotions, thoughts, fantasies as far as possible.

What did he feel, Reynolds asked himself.

His head came up. "When we did the jumping-around bit last night, I couldn't join in." Reynolds could not have explained why this was his preoccupation; he was following the rule to go with the first thing that came to mind. "While you were all hooting and stuff, it was as if I had lockjaw."

Bo Evins megaphoned, "Only words of wisdom may pass those lips."

Everyone laughed. The sound was good-natured, but it came to Reynolds as a cheap shot. Here he was, trying to level with the group, honestly trying to share, and that clod was trying to make him look foolish. Anger, blazing out of nowhere, fed on itself. Reynolds tried to tell himself that his rage was out of all proportion—that this was the kind of overreaction he had learned to check—but he was suddenly possessed by the same blind fury that had sent him battering at the clerk years before.

He was able to hold himself in the chair but, unhinged, he snarled at Bo Evins like a cornered animal. He saw and spurned the stunned eyes of the group as a savage growling issued foreignly from his throat. He despised himself for what was happening but could not halt it, though he was shouting at himself inwardly that he would not let Ikey take over.

That, he saw, was what Bo Evins had somehow triggered. "Only words of wisdom may pass those lips." The man had attacked his deep Glory Image, and fang-bared Ikey had leaped at his throat.

But, Reynolds thought desperately, it *was* different now. He had the strength of the years with Dr. Kohn!

With enormous gratification, Reynolds felt his features begin to relax. He hoped the group would pass over his lapse, but he half expected it when Evins witlessly came right on with, "Don't lay your hostility trip on us, Phil!"

Reynolds glared at the man with a renewed seething, visible hate that brought gasps of consternation around the room.

Dr. Frank took over promptly. "If you're angry at Bo, tell him, Phil. Let it out. That's what we're here for. We can't deal with it—*you* can't deal with it—unless you get it out."

Reynolds still could not answer. He was using all his force to rein himself in. It was wrong, unfair, for the group to see him this way. Ikey had betrayed him unexpectedly. He had to get back to himself. He began to breathe more normally, felt his throat open. He would be able to speak now.

Dr. Frank was asking him, "What are you feeling, Phil?"

Reynolds felt trapped. There was no way he could begin to explain the complications. He should never have taken the hot seat. Why the hell was he continuing to overreact so crazily to a half-witted comment? He said to Dr. Frank—and in a way it was totally honest—"I don't know." (Thank God Ikey was letting him do more than grunt. He'd get that sonofabitch locked away again in a minute, and keep him locked up the rest of the week!)

Dr. Frank appealed to the group. "Anybody buy that? Phil doesn't know what he's feeling?"

A woman called, "He's off on his head trip again."

A man said, "I'll own a piece of that!"

Dr. Frank said, "Phil, how do you feel about *that?*"

Reynolds tried to find total honesty as his rage cooled. "That I'm getting a message but I don't know what it is."

It had come out *dis*honest. He told himself he knew damned well what it was—his same problem with Dr. Kohn. Everything *was* up in his head, except anger.

He wanted to say it to the group, but it seemed too mixed up.

A woman objected, "I think he's hooking us on a side trip."

Hal Basser's voice came to Reynolds, a soothing tone obviously trying to help. "Phil, isn't it true?"

Reynolds said diffidently, now aiming only to get off the seat, "I guess."

Unexpectedly, Mary's voice: "Can you lay that out?"

Reynolds went blank. The numbness frightened him, until he quickly decided they were fishing too hard too fast. He needed space! Was that another cop-out? Bo Evins said so, with an exaggerated groan: "You're dragging me down." And to the group, complaining: "We can't deal with this guy." Other voices agreed.

"I feel bad about that," Reynolds said sincerely, using another of the standard phrases. He did feel bad, did not want this sense of strangeness—old alienation?—that had crept over him, asking himself what he was doing here, why he was subjecting himself to the slings and arrows of these people who did not even know who he was. At the same time, he could hear Dr. Kohn, accusingly: "Narcissism! King Shit! Glorious You! Are you telling *me* you're past all that?"

Far from leading him away from analysis, Reynolds fidgeted, this damned encounter seemed to be heading him straight back!

"I hear you," Bo Evins was going on, "but I don't read you. You still haven't got your shit together and if we let you go on we'll all be in a time bind."

Reynolds answered defensively, "I'm trying to buy your feedback, dammit!"

A voice called, "But you're not tracking it!"

Reynolds protested, "You're leaving me hanging!"

"You're hanging yourself," someone shouted.

Dr. Frank intervened with a wave of his hand. "Hey, people, *give* the man some space, eh?"

The group settled into a grudging silence. Reynolds told himself that he had seen others go through a baptism like his. The group wasn't here to be conned by any of the members. They were quick to spot phoniness. That was good for him, not bad. In this workshop a person was guilty until proven honest.

Dr. Frank prompted, "Well, Phil?"

"I'm sorry." Reynolds' voice was firm now. He could handle himself again. "I apologize to everyone, I guess I'm not ready for this yet, and I don't want to waste your time." He looked toward Bo Evins. "You're right about the time bind."

The man jeered, "Now what are you trying to do, smooth our ruffled feathers?"

Dr. Frank's big hand was on Reynolds' shoulder before the fuse lit again. To Evins, the doctor enjoined, "There's a difference between feedback and needling, guys." To Reynolds, he said, "Before you get off, Phil, I want you to tell me this. Say, 'I am blocking my feelings.' Say it here to me, and then around to everybody."

Desultory: "I am blocking my feelings." He would not tell them that his only feeling was aching frustration. He had tried, had wanted to try, had not wanted an episode like his fury at Bo Evins which, he saw, had genuinely frightened the group. And himself. Apparently, he was still hung up, worse than he had suspected in Dr. Kohn's office. As soon as he got into a situation he couldn't control, with people he couldn't command, his main reaction was irritation, and either an attack or withdrawal! Yes, he was seeing things here that he could not see or test with Dr. Kohn. In that sense, the encounter was valuable, but right now he was annoyed by his discomposure and his vexation at Dr. Frank, who was demanding that he repeat the cliché/injunction: "I am blocking my feelings."

"Louder."

Reynolds said it louder, with growing annoyance. Jesus, he was glad there wasn't anyone here from Madison Avenue to see this tommyrot. Nobody at his office would believe this man standing like a scolded schoolboy could be Philip Marcus Reynolds of Graham and Reynolds Advertising . . .

"Louder!" Dr. Frank commanded, and suddenly Reynolds was bellowing at the top of his lungs. *"I am blocking my feelings!"*

"What does that feel like?"

Reynolds withdrew. This screaming bit—primal type?—wasn't for him. To get off this Guignol stage as fast as possible, he said what he thought was expected: "It feels like a stranger locked up inside of me trying to get out."

Hearing his own words, Reynolds realized he had tossed not a bone but a truth. Something was happening inside he had not experienced even with Dr. Kohn. It was a stirring of gaping enemies circling him terrifyingly. He would have dashed away from them out of the barn, but Dr. Frank's question held him. "A stranger?"

The force inside was a bellows that blasted the shout from Reynolds' lungs. "No, of course not. *Me!*"

Peremptory from Dr. Frank: *"Let yourself out!"*

Panic. "I can't!" And a cry of a terrified animal: *"He'll kill me!"* It was a dream, it was the shafting lights like the fireworks in his head against the rock, it was not real, a scenario somewhere distant, out of space, all happening to someone else, someone else. From outer space Reynolds heard Dr. Frank saying quietly, "You mean the real you will kill the false you—the animal you showed us a moment ago?"

Reynolds stood panting, silent.

"You don't have to answer, Phil." The voice was gentle. "Thanks for letting it all hang out. You can go back now." Dr. Frank added, "We'll talk later."

Reynolds felt drained as seldom in his analysis, but to his own bewilderment, he remained in front of the hot seat and said to Dr. Frank genuinely, "I *am* sorry. I *want* to let go, to get out of my head, but I *can't!*" He felt a ripping inside, the way he had when his father beat him, and despite unbearable mortification could not stop tears that suddenly rose out of this unanticipated surrender to despair.

Even as he wept, abashed, Reynolds felt the hush of the group's sympathy, their quick support. When Mathilda Caldwell moved across the floor to put her arms around him, he was a child again, and the others felt it. They did not know what his anguish was, but it washed into the river of their own pains and stirred their hearts. Standing against the woman's warmth, Reynolds heard people sobbing with him and for him all around the room, and it was a shriving and a reconciliation such as he had never known. His shame fell away. It was all right for a grown man to surrender and cry.

Later Reynolds thought how different, indeed, the encounter experience was from the couch.

When the afternoon session ended, Dr. Frank motioned Reynolds aside to the small room he used as an office. It had clearly been a horse stall; books lined the bin where oats had once been poured. "How do you feel now, Phil?"

"Ashamed and embarrassed."

"You don't need to be, you know. A lot of yelling and crying goes on. The sessions wouldn't be working if it didn't. Still, I agree it *is* coming across a little differently for you. You know, of course, that Dr. Kohn and I had a talk. Today you almost couldn't handle the material you generated, and the feedback got to you. Yes, they can be cruel, it's part of the heat that helps you understand the kitchen you're cooking your life in. I believe your therapy is working well with Dr. Kohn, but I also think you need a different kind of space than the group provides."

Reynolds was dismayed. "You want me to leave?" He was resentful. This was a trapdoor he had not considered.

The doctor said, "Not necessarily. We just have to keep you off thin ice. I'm sure Dr. Kohn would agree it will do you good to finish the week. But hold back more, see yourself more as an observer than a participant. You can keep on with your quartet, but duck the hot seat there too."

"Won't that be conspicuous?" Reynolds suddenly wanted to argue himself back into full membership.

Dr. Frank gave his broad smile. "These people are more concerned with themselves than with you, believe me." His expression was jovial as he patted Reynolds on the back. "You can still have a very useful week. Just try not to talk so much."

Reynolds felt reprieved, and upset with himself for caring, and angry at himself for being upset. He shook Dr. Frank's hand and used their terms: "I'll make the contract."

"Good. And try a little method I sometimes use to help verbal people like you."

Reynolds waited, curious.

"For the rest of today and tomorrow, before you speak to anyone, I want you to say out loud, 'Now I, Philip Reynolds, am talking.' "

For a moment, Reynolds believed Dr. Frank was being mischievous, then the dum-dum exploded: "Now I, Philip Reynolds, am talking!"

Reynolds guessed he wouldn't be saying very much except to ask for the salt and pepper, if that!

Pondering it, Reynolds had new admiration for Dr. Frank. He was going to take Reynolds' bull by Gestalt horns and stymie the glibness and intellectualizing that Dr. Kohn kept deploring.

It was a ridiculous technique—and he would be forever grateful if it worked, Reynolds knew.

Later, new snow was streaming down outside. Why *didn't* God make snow like confetti? Who was Philip Reynolds to call Terry a fat slob?— her concept was a lovely poem. Would he ever write again? Why did he have such a disconsolate ache of envy when he saw Dr. Silas Frank surrounded by his chattering flock? Why was there a stab in his chest when Bo Evins appeared with his arm around a laughing Mary? Why did he resent their tramping up the hill together, hatless and open-collared while he needed to tighten his woolen muffler (a Christmas present from Selma) around his neck?

Reynolds looked for Mathilda Caldwell. She was hanging on Dr. Frank's arm, giggling like a schoolgirl. Hal Basser was in a tumbling snowball fight with a band of others. The quartet was supposed to be an instrument of support and consolation, especially when someone had taken a beating, but he wasn't getting a hell of a lot of attention from his band. It appeared to Reynolds that he had been gullible to take any of the hogwash seriously. Insufferably, he had made a fool of himself; he had not cried that way before anyone in his life, not even his mother when he was a boy.

Leaving the group, Reynolds went alone in the snow to his cabin. Looking up at the vaulting sky he made his decision. Perspective. Let the others have their conviviality. He would take a shower, ease his bruise with a drink and aspirin, then leave.

But as he opened his door, he remembered that only minutes ago he had accepted a contract with Silas Frank. Something in him did not want to dishonor it, something Reynolds felt as a friend, not foe. He rejected with scorn the tug of self-pity that seemed always so ready at his elbow. He would stay. Nothing worse could happen now.

22

Every Sunday night at the Center there was a community dance. It gave the various workshops a chance to come together. In the converted, dimly lit dining room the air was thick with incense. Reynolds coughed, entering from the icy air outside. Music was issuing from a weird-looking assemblage. The men wore striped togas of bright green and blue, the women were in yellow saris covered with purple stars. All had orange headbands with the Yin-Yang symbol in red and white. To Reynolds, they seemed in a trance as they activated flutes, recorders, guitars, bells, castanets. With bare feet shuffling back and forth in little circles, they looked like toy figures on a bizarre music box.

The sound was amateurish and unskilled to Reynolds, and he found their self-regard offensive. The guitarists seemed to know only two or three chords, which they plunked endlessly without regard to the monotonous scales the flutists happened upon. Occasionally there would come an aleatoric flurry of plucking, whistling, and barking, at which the drummers would whack away with frenzied energy, and mouths would open in chants that Reynolds took to be imitation Sanskrit. To him it was a pretentious rip-off of Indian ragas, which he admired greatly in their pure form.

Reynolds deeply believed that the real renaissance of the twentieth century lay in jazz. He himself used jazz in his commercials whenever he could find an excuse. He understood and loved the complex, stirring improvisations, and always wondered at the uncanny musical intuitions of the players who could seesaw together without notes, and often without having met before. What *these* far-out weirdos were doing had nothing to do with any real music, Reynolds criticized.

It was self-arguing time again. Reynolds asked himself impatiently why he was making his assumptions. Why did these people need a license from lofty Mr. Grim? They were having a hell of a trip with the plucking, tooting, knocking, chanting, and the crowd was eating it up. The milling dancers crowded the floor in Brownian movement of their own. Why did he always have to be so ulcer gulch? Because he had kept his mouth shut all day, under Dr. Frank's injunction?

Reynolds tried to laugh at himself. He was here to have a good time. He didn't think he could manage to dance to the caterwauling, and his hip hurt, but he decided on Mrs. Caldwell as a suitable partner. She was standing alone, seeming as ill at ease as he felt. He went to her, smiling, and invited her to the floor. Her reply was another revelation. Her words came fast, as if she feared she wouldn't get them said before she changed her mind: "Thanks, Phil, but up here we're supposed to be scrupulously truthful, aren't we?—and I'd really rather dance with the younger people because I came up here for *new* experiences and I don't want to get pigeonholed, like, and I appreciate you wanting to help me when I was on the hot seat and I'm sorry you had such a bad time and you're a real nice man but I have to say you don't appeal to me particularly and I'm here to find my own space and I don't want to start any relationship with you on that basis, so I'd rather not—" The woman faded, exhausted by her unfamiliar effort of honesty.

Reynolds was flabbergasted, then went along. Fair enough! The woman knew what she wanted, and was finding the courage to stick to it. Wasn't that what the workshop was all about?—to help him take a real look at his receding hairline, the wrinkles in his forehead, among other things. The woman wasn't wrong, and she wasn't the first one over the years to give him his walking papers. It was healthy to be reminded. He had been so tremblingly shy with Helena on their first dates because she was exactly the type that had always snubbed him. In college, sometimes he had even smelled his armpits to see if it was body odor. For a moment, Reynolds stood on the smoke-filled, noisy dance floor and knew again the sinking-heart feeling of being rejected. Back when he was eighteen, nineteen, he had asked himself if it was because he was half-Jewish, or awkward and unsophisticated. He had not then thought to examine whether he turned people off by what he and Dr. Kohn now called the glorious-King syndrome he used compensatorily. Thank Mathilda Caldwell for the kind of perspective he wanted from the workshop.

A figure leaping into the air caught his attention. It was Hal Basser, with a trio of hippie-type young men swaying somnambulistically around him. Hal was in his usual tight jeans—black tonight—and a bright pink turtleneck.

Glancing again at Mathilda Caldwell, Reynolds saw a heavy-bearded man in a studded leather jacket yank her unceremoniously into the melee. She followed, without choice. It upset Reynolds. Why should that sausage-head feel free to do *his* thing without regard for the woman's wishes?—the eternal conundrum of the anarchist's philosophy.

But perhaps the woman secretly wanted it. *Don't help!* Let people do/be their own thing!

Reynolds saw Mary in the arms of Bo Evins. She was wearing a brocaded grandmother gown that should have appeared ridiculous, but gave her, paradoxically, a carefree air. He supposed it was because she looked like a child playing dress-up in an attic. Unlike the other dancers, mostly hopping about frenetically, Bo Evins was shuffling lazily, his hips grinding slowly against Mary's body. Reynolds saw the man was obviously dry-fucking the girl, and anger built on anger in him. All at once, he didn't feel tired or out-of-it-all. Abruptly it very much mattered that the girl should not be molested by the beefy loudmouth.

Reynolds' blood suddenly responded to the charging music. What had been phony became urgent and irresistible. For a puzzled moment, Reynolds thought it might be the marijuana he recognized in the air, but, whatever it was, he was drawn into the current of the drums. In a flurrying explosion now, they engulfed him completely, and sent him pounding across the floor. People from his workshop slapped him on the back with encouraging shouts. "Let it all hang out, man!" He brushed past them, dug his fingers into Mary's shoulders, and swung her around the way the burly man had grabbed Mrs. Caldwell. The girl was startled, and Bo Evins' eyes popped open.

"My dance!" Reynolds claimed the girl.

"Fuck off!" Evins said.

"I saw you, scum!"

"Look, Sir Big Shot, I'm sure you can buy and sell all of us, but we don't work for you, and you don't give orders around here!"

Mary separated the men, with a bland look at Reynolds. "Maybe I was enjoying it."

Floored, Reynolds moved on without another word. If the wench thought of herself as just another piece of ass, it was none of his business. It appeared he should have taken the whore-sex she had peddled the night before.

Disgusted, he left the dance, regretting again that he had given his word to stay the full week.

Nearing his cabin, Reynolds turned at the sound of a shrill laugh. He made out Mathilda Caldwell and the burly man coming from the dance hall. They had their arms around each other, obviously on their way to a rendezvous.

Good for Mathilda Caldwell, Reynolds thought, and another lesson learned for him. She was opening her own space. Where was his?

Reynolds was suddenly overcome with loneliness and thought of Helena with a pang of physical yearning.

With his key in his door, Reynolds stopped again for another breath of the frigid air to clear his head. The snow was ending. The sky was moonless, studded with the ranging stars. A step behind him brought Reynolds around, startled. It was Hal Basser. The man said, "I saw you leave. You okay?"

"Just tired, I'm turning in early."

"You've sort of been in the meat grinder, and I feel kind of guilty. I mean, our quartet is supposed to help each other, but we've all been into our own thing. Listen, I've got some good shit in my room, Acapulco Gold, if you'd like to turn on."

"I don't use it, thanks." Reynolds appreciated the friendliness. "If Scotch will do, I have a bottle here."

Over the drink, the man said, "That Bo sure was drilling it to Mary, wasn't he? It's lucky he wasn't with us when she did the snake bit. Would have blown his mind. It reached me, you know." The man sat down on the floor, leaning against the wall as he had done at the quartet session. "Did it get to you?"

"I guess," Reynolds replied noncommittally. He didn't want to be thinking of Mary Humphrey or her snake, and somehow being in the room alone with Hal Basser was sending an uncomfortable prickliness up his spine. He didn't know why, but he felt an unfamiliar agitation. Maybe it was because he detected what sounded like the hint of a simper in the voice, which was going on: "I mean, you could just see a big penis there, couldn't you? The way she was stroking it, a prick plain as day." To Reynolds the voice held an innuendo of confidentiality, and he wanted none of it. He yawned loudly, sitting down on his bed. The man ought to take an old-fashioned hint.

Reynolds was relieved to see Hal Basser get to his feet. But instead of going to the door, the man turned to the bed, his words now an entrapping, creamy invitation: "I swear I could see a big cock right there in front of my eyes." His smile was tremulously frank in its now-unconcealed expectation. The bulging slacks plainly disclosed the man's erection.

What came from Reynolds was a cry of discovery and a rasping laugh that took the man aback. What he could not know was the picture that suddenly projected itself into Reynolds' head—*Dr. Kohn wearing his red tie.*

LINK!—

Red tie equals penis, cock, prick! Kohn's prick, father's prick, his own prick, everybody's prick!—including this Freudian Frail with his hard-on and fatuous, pleading expression on his goddamn pansy puss!

Reynolds couldn't stop his laughter. It became a series of hysterical hiccups that had him pummeling his bed. This fairy cucumber-head thought *he* was gay or acey-deucey!

Gasping for breath, Reynolds jumped up to slam at Hal Basser's fucking faggot face.

But the man was gone.

Lucky for him! As lucky for that nigger faggot long ago with Penny in the park. He'd have murdered the fuck if it hadn't been for the knife.

Reynolds poured himself a drink, stiff this time. He wanted a shower to wash away the cologne odor the man had left. He turned the water to ice cold and forced himself to stand shivering under it for a full count of sixty seconds. He still felt dirty when he got into bed.

Too restless to sleep, Reynolds picked up a book on Eastern religions he had borrowed from the Center office. But he couldn't concentrate, found his mind wandering. He recalled a story, told as true, about a guru who was asked one time whether he had ever taken LSD. "Yes, once," he replied. "Why did you stop?" "Because it was like a telephone call. I got the message, and hung up."

If only psychoanalysis gave you such a message so that you didn't have to keep holding the receiver forever. Nothing did, not religion, not literature, not philosophy, East or West. As long ago as Yale, Reynolds recalled, he had balked at the Eastern views. To him, they ran against the grain. To dissolve your self in the infinite seemed bad, not good. For free men, the ideal was the opposite—to evoke and celebrate the individual ego, not to submerge it.

Reynolds could readily see how today's young rebels would seize the Eastern stance because it legitimatized the copping out many of them sought for other reasons.

At Yale, he had written a paper on the Faustian man. It argued that the unfolding of creation was *particularization;* movement from the infinite to the finite, not the other way around. To Reynolds, history and evolution traveled from species to genus to individual, and from the claims of society to tribe to clan to person.

He would put that a little differently now, Reynolds thought. He'd say, "Accepting the premise that we are all one with the universe, still, it is my *difference* that gives me my identity; it is my uniqueness that identifies *my* life and defines *my* being. My task is to fulfill my unique function as part of the whole, because my part has a particular purpose in the ultimate scheme. Therefore I am to cherish and develop my separateness rather than suppress and deny it. Only in this way can I make my destined contribution to the Whole, which I take to depend on its parts for its own fulfillment."

Regarded this way, you don't fulfill a human life by drowning it in a Ganges of the Universe. On the contrary, you celebrate the ego. Just as the submergence of the individual in society is political totalitarianism, so a surrender of self to eternity is religious totalitarianism—both fatal to freedom, progress, and human dignity. Didn't the new enthusiasts-of-the-East know the too-obvious fact that those religions had flourished where life was cheap and humans were fatalistically resigned to suffering?

But it was popular to condemn everything American and to see good only elsewhere. No wonder things were so out of joint. Including himself, Reynolds thought jaundicedly, dropping the book to the floor with a thud.

What was bothering him, he knew, wasn't any pilpul of philosophies, but the picture of Hal Basser's bulging pants he could not erase. The mental excursion had been one of his typical efforts to escape the lingering image of the exhibited erection and big balls showing in the jeans of that cocksucker with the sweet pale eyes and the girl-kissable mouth . . .

Reynolds got up to pour another drink. With horror he realized that the thought of the man had brought his own erection. Jesus Christ, what was he getting into now? He had a sudden knife-stab in his belly, and was sweating with new nameless terror.

Was it remotely conceivable that he might have even the faintest homosexual inclination?

Impossible!

Walking about agitated, drink in hand, Reynolds swooped together his evidence with a kind of hysteria. Look at his obsessive wish to see girls naked when he was just a kid. Count the girls he had necked with, played stink finger with, been masturbated by all through high school. Add the townies he had slept with in college. Account his love for Helena!—his desire for Penny!—even his goddamn phone calls! They were to *women*, weren't they?

Yet Reynolds could not deny his erection. It mocked him—a *man* had given him *this* hard-on! Not Mary Humphrey, not Mathilda Caldwell, not any woman at the Center. And it would not go down, as he could not drive away the picture of the man's sex offered, as he could not deny the trembling of his hands as he stood, unnerved, in this damned room that was turning out to be an entrance to hell!

Could *this* be what Dr. Kohn kept implying was buried under his resistances? Christ, had all-knowing Dr. Kohn anticipated this might happen, and that he would *not* be able to deal with it?

Reynolds went into the bathroom and looked at himself in the mirror. Angry. Distraught. Suspicious. And on the attack, answering his unsettling doubts: "What the hell is the matter with you?" he demanded of his countenance, aloud. "You know that *every*body has homosexual feelings at some time. A thousand books say so! This crap hit a nerve because you're uptight and in a freaky situation here, but you can deal with it if you don't blow your stack!"

Reynolds came out of the bathroom for another drink, still muttering to himself. "You can damn well handle it without Kohn or Frank or anyone else!"

A knock at his door interrupted Reynolds, sent him rigid. *Had that queer dared to come back?* Hastily getting into his robe, Reynolds called, "Who is it?"

The only answer was a more demanding rapping.

A *Walpurgisnacht* of demons in Reynolds suddenly wanted it to be the man, so he could beat him, kiss him, destroy him, fondle his penis! He had never felt anything like the knives shredding his sanity. He almost screamed out. *Wasn't there any bottom to this hell, Dr. Kohn?*

In desperation, Reynolds flung the door open, his fists tight again. He shivered immediately in the cutting night wind.

It was Mary Humphrey, smiling as if nothing untoward had happened. Closing the door, Reynolds stared at her, silently demanding what she was doing at his cabin. She said at once, with her usual directness, "I think Bo Evins is a bag of wind. I was trying to make you jealous so you wouldn't turn me down tonight." She looked at him with unfrivolous eyes.

Christ, Reynolds thought, this girl was indeed too much for him. He had been through enough of a wringer for a while. "Go on home," he muttered.

But now he wished she would not leave. He was enormously grateful for her presence, the female voice, the female scent. She might help put out the crazy flames Hal Basser had ignited. It was evident to Reynolds that if it had been the man at his door instead of Mary, he would have gone stark, literally mad. It brought a stunning and horrifying knowledge that he could rupture, could jump the tracks, could be swept all the way to actual insanity.

Reynolds' self-confidence began to fall apart. Stingingly, it came to him that his mind could be blown as a conch was blown, the flesh emptied out, the skull left a hollow gourd. His mind was jumping like a Mexican bean as he watched Mary pour herself a large drink and start to undress. Offering him a "honey-fuck"—a young-girl screw—she was silently telling him the one thing he wanted most in the world to hear— that he was a *man,* a honcho, a macho, a stud, a cocksman, *all* man and nothing but *man!*

When the girl eased down naked on the bed and lifted her arms to Reynolds, there was only one thing possible. Her age no longer mattered, Penny didn't matter, Helena didn't matter. Mary Humphrey's touch, her odor, her crooning sighs, her passionate lips on his were the answer Reynolds craved with all his soul. She swept away whatever was left of denial and conscience. The girl was all over him nimbly and wantonly, using her tongue, her fingers, her nipples in and out of him, all around the world, no place forbidden, no touch unexplored.

Panting, Reynolds rolled on top of the sweet-sweating body to ride out his new, imperative need. He was fiercely proud of the size of his penis now. What had Mary said the first night? She had "checked him out," and had "liked what she saw," and she had added something about never having lain with an older man.

He would show her now what it was like.

Reynolds opened his eyes, wanting to see the girl's expression as he started to enter her. Here! This is what a real man is— And Reynolds shuddered unbelievingly as the nightmare struck. The face he saw on the pillow was Hal Basser's, and it was gagged with a red tie.

The impossible vision disappeared in a split second, but it took Reynolds' erection with it.

Beneath him, Mary Humphrey was a wide-open, dripping flower, impatiently arching for him. And he was wilted.

In despair, Reynolds pressed hard against the hot young flesh, praying for the girl not to suspect. He sought her eyes blazing with lust, lips wet with young rapacity. *Turn me on again!* he silently implored. He kissed her ferociously, tasting her sweat, her salt. He went for her nipples, hoping to circuit their electricity through his lapsed body.

At the touch of his lips on her breasts, Mary made meowing sounds of pleasure. She pulled him tighter, bit his ear, and whispered urgently, "Now! *No-ow*, darling! Oh, put it in, now!"

For Reynolds, the agony of this first impotence was like no other torture of all the torments he had known. This was a man's watershed failure. Would he ever be whole again?

His mortification before the panting, demanding, cheated girl was the least of it. The dread specter of impotence that looms universally with a man's passing years had suddenly become real for him, with a steel grip strangling *his* throat. Worst, the red tie, which he could no longer deny, had become a dagger turning in his chest, flooding the room with blood that gushed out of him with the stench of slaughterhouses in his nostrils.

Through the engulfing red mist, Reynolds heard Mary's consternation. "Phil! What's the *matter?*"

He wanted to cry out, "Ask Dr. Kohn! Get Dr. Kohn!"—as people cry mindlessly in a disaster, "Call an ambulance!"

But this was another catastrophe he had to weather. Some inner reservoir of strength spoke to him sternly: "Handle this now or you will crack up entirely!"

Reynolds got off the bed, keeping his eyes away from the accursed limpness. He pretended a seizure of pain. "The accident," he fabricated. "My hip hurts like hell! I can't—"

"Hey, I'm sorry!" The girl was immediately contrite. "I didn't realize—"

"It's all right." Reynolds struggled for self-possession. "I'd better just get to sleep."

Mary asked, "Would it help if I massaged your hip?"

Just get the devil out, Reynolds cried to himself. He shook his head with an exaggerated grimace, pretending again to wince with a spasm in his side. "I'll take a hot shower." He went into the bathroom and closed the door again, remembering the first night with the girl. But tonight held no jot of farce or absurdity. Tonight was total tragedy and disaster.

The girl's voice came through the door. "I'm truly sorry. It was being so beautiful." There was a pause. "Tomorrow night?"

Reynolds turned the shower on full blast, pretending not to hear.

Although he took two sleeping pills, it was hours before Reynolds slept, and dreamed:

He was in a funeral home. The casket was closed, but with his X-ray eyes he could see the corpse was Hal Basser. Reynolds saw his own mother weeping. Reynolds kept telling her that the body was a stranger, a man none of them knew or wanted to. A rabbit appeared on the pulpit

and shouted at Reynolds, "You are a megalomaniac!" At which his
mother cried a protest: "He is not! He sleeps only with women!"

Two little old Jewish ladies met at the coffin. One started boasting
about her sons. "My son the doctor is head of the biggest hospital, my
son the lawyer is from the Sewpreme Court, my other son is—" The
woman stopped herself, not wanting to be too overbearing. "And *your*
son?" she inquired politely. "My son?" the other answered proudly.
"My son is a *homosexual!"* "You don't say?" came the response.
"Where's his office?"

Everyone at the services burst into laughter, and the funeral parlor
was suddenly a large theatre. Reynolds sat on a toilet eating popcorn and
watching a cartoon comedy. The film showed Minnie Mouse swinging a
blue plastic baby, while singing in a deep bass voice, "When I am lay-id,
am lay-ay-ay-ayd in earth, remember me, remember me, but a-ah-ah-
ah-ahah, for-geuht my pay-in—" Reynolds recognizes Henry Purcell's
Fido und Anus.

The baby falls off the swing, and Minnie Mouse is angry. She shoves
the doll back up into her womb, as if a film of birthing were run in
reverse.

Superman appears and announces he will give her another baby. He
mounts Minnie. She blows hysterically on a police whistle, and Mickey
Mouse comes in the nick of time, riding on a pink elephant, Dumbo.
While Mickey Mouse and Superman struggle, Minnie dances near a
fancy calliope, with DR. CLANCY E. RELESON painted on its side in gold
letters.

Superman overcomes Mickey Mouse, and turns to attack Minnie
Mouse again. She runs about squealing, "Clancy, save me!" The
elephant aims its trunk at Superman and shoots a cannonball that slays
both Superman and Minnie Mouse. From the earth where their pieces
drop, little colored mice spring up like flowers.

The dream explosion woke Reynolds. In his half sleep, the images
seemed an impenetrable mishmash. Was there a clue in the name on the
calliope? This anagram solved itself in a flash—his father, CLARENCE
REYNOLDS! instrument of all his woes.

Reynolds came alert. It was always useful in analysis when you could
catch a dream as fresh as this. What about Superman, usually the hero,
coming on as a rapist? Well, the unconscious often switches roles to
confuse the mind. But Mickey Mouse was a hero too (this was a Jungian-
myth dream?), so he, Reynolds, had pitted two heros against each other.
Dead end. Also, why *mice,* always mice in his confounding dreams?

What about Minnie Mouse? Who was Millie? Hey!—interesting slip!

"Millie" for "Minnie." It led right to his mother's name, TILLIE! Yes, it was opening up. The *blue* baby was *boy,* and his mother was pushing it back inside because she, like his father, had never wanted him!

And Superman was his father! wanting to make a girl! While he, Reynolds, was Mickey trying to stop the act! (Oedipus!) Immediately, Reynolds saw there was more. A dream could of course have many facets of meaning. What about the elephant? Why, sure, *"Dumbo!"*— *dumb,* stupid, outcast, *himself* for not being a girl in the first place. So he, as Dumbo, slays his father! *And* his mother! No, wait, something wrong here. Underneath everything, he had loved her too much. And Mickey was always Minnie's lover, as he had Oedipally wanted to be. Okay, but then who was killed in the dream?

Flash!

His *sister!* Being with Mary (young girl!) might stir such a dream if subconsciously he had wanted to violate his sister—*which would tie back to his needing to prove that girls were as dirty as he!* If his *sister* wanted sex, he would have the ultimate proof!

He would have to take this one back to Dr. Kohn. There was a great deal more to be dug out of it, Reynolds guessed sleepily. The unconscious gives up its secrets reluctantly, not only because it is jealous of them, but because it knows how potent are its mysteries. To see them all too clearly too quickly would be like looking at Medusa's head.

He had seen enough snakes this night, Reynolds asserted to himself. Gratefully, he felt the sleeping pills take hold again.

Reynolds asked Dr. Frank to transfer him out of Hal Basser's quartet. As for Mary, aside from everything else, Reynolds was not about to risk another fiasco in bed, whatever the cause of his failure had been. His hip continued to be a convenient excuse.

The days at the Center passed quickly with a packed schedule that continued to rivet Reynolds, even though he was now mostly an observer. There were not only the workshops, but Esalen massages, dance-and-body building, meditation training, lectures on transactional analysis, seminars on Yoga. There was seldom free time, and something always prevented Reynolds from calling New York. When he did manage to get to the office, there was always a long line waiting at the phone.

Reynolds considered driving to a telephone, but he recalled that Ted Watson would still be on vacation when he returned. There was no urgency.

As the week drew to a close, everyone had been on the hot seat except Hal Basser. On Saturday morning, he was prompted by Dr. Frank. As the man perched on the edge of the chair, Reynolds watched him with contempt. The fellow was uncommonly quiet.

Hal darted an ingratiating smile around the group, a silent appeal: "Don't hurt me." There was a long pause. Dr. Frank used the familiar routine. "Hal, go around the room and tell everyone you're embarrassed."

"I can't do it." The reply was barely audible even to those next to the hot seat.

Complaints sounded at once. "Can't hear you!"

The man whispered to Dr. Frank, "I don't know why, but I can't speak any louder. My voice is gone. I'm sorry."

Impatience seized Reynolds, nearby. "*We* have to come to *him!*" He wasn't supposed to intervene but, hell, his feedback was as good as anyone else's—maybe better in this instance, he considered.

Bo Evins, for the first time, was on Reynolds' side. "Phil is right, and I buy a piece of that!" Reynolds liked the man as he attacked Hal Basser. "You want us to think you're shy. I say bull*shit.* I say this is your way of thumbing your nose at us. That's the message you are really sending, man. Do you read it?"

Reynolds remembered Penny seeing the blasting radios in the park as thumb-nosing. Whispers could be too. Interesting.

Forget Penny.

Dr. Frank asked, "How does that go down, Hal? Is being quiet your way of attacking the group?"

"No."

"Then what?"

"I don't want to lay my trip on everybody, that's all."

Bo Evins was strident. "Talk the hell up or get the hell off!"

Hal started to rise, whispering, "Yes." But Dr. Frank stopped him.

"Doesn't that make you feel bad?"

"I don't care!" There was petulance in the whisper now. "I'm in touch with my own feelings and that's what counts."

Support came from all directions: "Unlock it, Hal, you'll feel better." "Tell us where you're coming from!" "Don't let it fester!"

Meant as encouragement, the calls came to Hal Basser as a badgering he could no longer stand. He uttered a high cry that startled the group: "Because I fell in love with someone and he won't give me the time of day!"

Dr. Frank was up at once. "You're right, Hal! That's too private! You can go back to your seat."

Mathilda Caldwell whispered excitedly to Bo Evins, "He said he's in love with a *man?*"

Evins rumbled, "So what else is new? It boggles my little finger!"

Hal Basser suddenly erupted. All the shackled pressure of his tense days poured out in a frenzy that took the group aback. The man whipped around to confront Reynolds. "You're cold! You're dead! You're *nothing!*"

Reynolds stared at the man with his mouth open.

"You want what I want, but you're locked into your closet with all your middle-class shit!"

It penetrated to Reynolds that the man was calling him a homosexual, even hinting to the group that they had had some kind of intimate contact. It was too hideous to bear. Old violence ripped Reynolds open, searing away reason and probity. In his outrage he leaped at Hal Basser.

Dr. Frank and the other men lurched forward, but before anyone could reach Reynolds he had checked himself. His face was scarlet, his veins bursting. He glowered at the cowering homosexual for a moment, then knew his own danger. If he laid one finger on this man, he would go all the way to murder. There was no question in his mind. Nothing would stop him. He bolted out of the barn. There was going to be no more mindless violence.

It was freezing outside without his coat. The cold sobered Reynolds further. His lips were twitching, and he ached to feel the man's bones break, see the blood for vengeance.

But the ferocity had faded, and what was left now drained out of Reynolds. It had come to him in that instant that violence like his was empty. Savaging the man would accomplish nothing.

Hugging himself with new emotion as well as against the wind, Reynolds was amazed at how, all at once, he had been able to hold himself in check. He was no longer compelled to act out his rage—and this was a rage that was entirely justified. Apparently, there were some lessons he had learned better than he knew.

Mary Humphrey came outside looking for him with his hat and coat. "Nobody blames you." She laughed. "Two types of people you can never trust—a dame who never got laid and a gay who wants to!"

Before dinner that evening, Dr. Frank visited Reynolds' room.

Taking off his fur parka, he said he had come to apologize. "I try to watch out for nuts, but Hal Basser got away from me. My fault. Sorry, and thanks."

"Thanks?"

The doctor said, "Considering the havoc we both know you're capable of, I salute your self-discipline."

To Reynolds the obviously sincere praise was a cheering and welcome recognition of his progress.

"I realize it was a crisis point for you. I was afraid you'd really go after him. I know you'll be discussing this with Dr. Kohn. Meantime, my congratulations, and I'll have a drink on that if you have any booze left."

Reynolds smiled to himself with pleasure as he poured. Not only had the bottle lasted all week, he had gotten at least one doctor to have a drink with him!

Mary Humphrey said good-bye in the parking field. She pecked Reynolds' cheek and gave him a flaky smile. "I'm sorry your hip stopped us," she said. "It could have been so great-o."

Reynolds ducked. "It wasn't in the stars." He wished he didn't smell bayberries.

"Can I come to see you in the city?"

"I don't think there'd be much point in it, Mary." For the first time he felt like the stuffed shirt his starched words bespoke. It was the ambiguous moment, he decided—leaving the Center, not yet back in his own world—an interval of time without any suitable language.

The girl's eyes darkened. "I was serious about wanting a job."

"You'd need a lot of training first. I'll send up some school bulletins that might help."

He saw the skepticism as she shook her head. "That's a crock. Anyway, I'm not into running errands for some ego-honcho."

Reynolds tried a reasonable smile. "You can't start at the top."

Sadly, Mary added, "I thought we could get to fuck."

Incorrigible! Reynolds said, "I've got to head out now," feeling as inadequate as the night he locked himself in the bathroom against her. There was no way he could deal with this girl and keep any dignity.

Mary Humphrey searched Philip Reynolds' face and turned from him sighing. Trudging away slowly in the snow, she called over her shoulder, "Be mellow, Phil."

He had a plunging sense of loss. It would be wonderful, wonderful, but there was no way, no way. "You, too," he said the necessary words. For a moment he wanted to jump out of the car and follow her, but he twisted the key fiercely in the ignition instead.

Somewhere Reynolds had read a western description of certain pastureland being "good for passage, not for fattening." That about summed up Mary Humphrey's place in his life, Reynolds concluded. Helena was for sustenance.

If he still had a right to a wife, he thought somberly as he warmed up the motor. He'd have to talk to Kohn and Duncan about it. He *couldn't* be impotent at his age. His hip *had* bothered him. The episode with Hal Basser *had* upset him. His fiasco with Mary was surely just a onetime fluke. Yet, as he thought of returning to Helena now, Reynolds wondered whether just the fear might not lead him into lapsing with her too. That prospect itself was a sudden heavy belt fastening over his groin.

Reynolds drove away from the Center full of fleas he had not bargained for. Melting snow had left the now-familiar fields rock-pocked in a thaw promising spring. The road was wet in the sun. Treacherous, Reynolds thought. Beautiful now, ice later. He checked his watch, and figured he should be home safely before the sun went down.

Part Six

"When you are the anvil, bear—
When you are the hammer, strike."
—Edwin Markham

23

After the week of close intimacy with the workshop group, Reynolds found it pleasing to be in the car alone. He felt new enthusiasm in his conviction that at least some reins of his life were back in his hands. He had withstood his violence—that was an important trophy to be bringing back to Dr. Kohn. Good things were happening as well as bad.

When Reynolds stopped for coffee, he opened the glove compartment to check the rental contract. He was puzzled to find an envelope he did not remember. It was Center stationery. A note from Mary? He opened it with curiosity, and turned livid. Not Mary at all, though the hand was feminine with a backward slant:

> Phil, I am sure you are sincere in the way you think you feel, but my instinct is seldom wrong. It is only a matter of time until you will recognize in yourself what I *know* about you. I am not laying my trip on you, but only urging you to let your feelings out of the straitjacket. You will be happy for the first time in your life! It's the most beautiful experience in the world. I am only sorry it won't be with me when you discover it at last. With love, Hal.

Reynolds viciously tore the paper into tiny pieces, infuriated that the rat had presumed to take such a liberty.

At home, the maid had a message for Reynolds. Helena had taken the girls to Vermont for a ski weekend since there was no school on Monday. They would return Monday evening. Reynolds was not displeased that he would have this night alone to unpack, decompress, and get himself reorganized for "the real world."

On Monday morning, Reynolds strode whistling through Graham

and Reynolds Advertising, nodding genially to the staff. In his buoyant mood he did not notice his secretary signaling to him from a copying machine down the hall. He swung his door open and was halfway into his chair before he did a silent-movie double take. Penny O'Hara and Ted Watson were waiting side by side on his white leather sofa. Penny was stark beauty in Reynolds' eyes, grown to maturity and a new assurance, and—now—clear, blazing anger.

She greeted Reynolds with, "How could you do a thing like that to Ted!"

Reynolds defended reflexly, "Now just a minute!"

Penny's eyes were scornful. "Don't make it worse by insulting our intelligence. Are you so far out you don't realize at least *some* of your buddies would tell Ted about your lie?"

Reynolds frowned to the tense black man. "That's how mad I was, Ted, and I'm sorry. I was going to fix it, call around first thing this morning. I've been away, and I thought you were too."

Penny glinted at Reynolds. "I couldn't believe it. I don't care what reason you thought you had!"

Unspoken words of the fight at Penny's apartment were crawling among the three of them like roaches.

Reynolds said, "I don't blame you. It was Stinksville. It was tough to get to a phone where I've been all week."

Penny's mouth compressed with more distaste. "Don't give us the sudsy, Phil!"

It was hard for Reynolds to think of anything but her appealing loveliness. New winds blew around his churning head—jealousy, regret, resentment. Those confusions were not gone, as he had believed and hoped.

Ted Watson stepped forward. His eyes were like the tips of his just-shined shoes, spit-polished and ready to kick. "Man, you poisoned my well once and for all! Once you bum-rapped me as a taker it doesn't matter *what* you say now! Anyone who might still hire me would be on my ass with a magnifying glass morning, noon, and night! You think I can work that way? Old friend, old chappie, you sandbagged me, and no *way* it can be fixed!" Ted Watson leaned across the desk, spitting his bafflement and hatred at Reynolds. "One thing I thank you! You make me see my brothers have been right and I've been honky-wrong! You shafted me because I'm *black!*"

Reynolds argued back, "I didn't ask your color when I hired you, did I?"

A dark fist circled in the air. "And don't hire me *because* I'm black! That's another way you whiteys cut our balls off!" The fist slammed on the glass desk scattering papers. "You imply you hire me out of your bleeding heart, not for what I can *do!*" Ted's voice sizzled hotter. Let everyone in the agency hear this now. "Man, you dumped on me because I had your girl! You and your hairy psychoanalysis, as if that excuses anything! Oh, I could knife you or sue you—which I am having a *black* lawyer look into—but mostly you are a waste of time! You know, when I was a kid I used to bite my nails. Later on, I wanted them to grow, so when I jerked off I would spread the gism on my fingertips. I mean, if *that* stuff couldn't make my nails grow, what could? Well, that's about as much sense as there is for my people to try to grow understanding in you honkies. Oh, one in a million there's a Penny, but I want you to know I am out to get the rest of you for the rest of my life!"

In his wrath, Ted Watson could not stop. He had to repeat the injury that had castrated him. "What I worked for all my life, you wrecked with one motherfucking lie!" His tone said he still could not believe it had happened, and then turned ominous. "Man, I tell you one thing not to forget. You will not know when, where, or how, but I will hand you my chit one day!"

In Graham's office, after Penny and Ted were gone, the first words were frigid with restrained anger. "It's a bummer, Phil."

"I know. And Ted is right. It's gone too far to fix. I tried to get to a phone all week but—" Reynolds' voice trailed off. He didn't have to sink lower by lying. He could damned well have tried harder, driven out to a phone, he recalled. Had he secretly wanted Ted Watson to swing slowly in the breeze? And let him face his truth—it wasn't the doing of any Ikey. It was he, himself, who had waffled, the same Philip Reynolds sitting opposite Rodney Graham, ashamed, embarrassed, and regretful. There was nothing he could say. It would only demean him further to plead a case on the basis of "working with Dr. Kohn."

Rod Graham, in his direct way, put the same thought into words. "I'm sure you had your reasons, Phil, and I know you're in analysis and all that. But this is too serious." The green eyes were unrelenting, judging, censuring. "I have to tell you my confidence in you is gone, and that creates a situation there is only one way to deal with, I'm afraid."

As Reynolds took in Rod Graham's meaning, the word consequences reverberated loud in his head again. He'd never dreamed his unthinking deed could lead to what his partner was declaring.

"Let me put it this way, Phil. If you had syphilis, I would be glad you were getting treatment, but I would not want to count your germs, hold your hand, or be your partner."

Reynolds tried to match the unyielding eyes, tried to take Graham in without flinching. But what did it mean to face consequences "like a man"? This sick feeling? Your insides twisting, your brain centrifuging out of your skull? It was like being run over by an endless train.

Rod Graham was going on, "I haven't had time to think this through, of course, but I would like to suggest that you talk to your lawyer about an arrangement for me to buy you out."

Reynolds found his voice to disagree. "Look, Rod, what I did was lousy, and I admit it's bad for the company, for us, for everything, but, look, let the punishment fit the crime! You're blasting me out of my business!"

Rod Graham was unyielding. "Isn't that what you tried to do to Ted Watson? I would have to say the punishment fits the crime precisely!"

Rage swept up in Reynolds. He gripped Rod Graham's fragile old desk so that it shook. "Christ, it's so easy for you holier-than-thous to lay it on! What the hell do you know about how hard I've worked—" He stopped himself abruptly, trembling with the effort. How hard he had worked on the couch was irrelevant, it wouldn't get Ted Watson a single paycheck. Rod and Penny were right, of course. His being in analysis had no bearing at all.

Rod Graham softened a little. "I know you've had your personal problems, Phil. That's just beside the point."

Reynolds tried stubbornly. "Suppose I don't agree to a buy-out?"

The eyes went arctic. "You'll wind up with considerably less money than I am willing to pay you right now. Think it over. I just can't team with you any longer. You'll have a kitty to start another shop if you want to—"

"After you've made my name mud?" Reynolds challenged bitterly.

Graham let the question answer itself.

Reynolds glowered. It was exactly like a session with Dr. Kohn. How clear, and warranted, the implication that *only he, himself,* was responsible for this shattering result. It was hard to accept, but his partner's straitlaced morality was consistent. Rod had been quick to grant Reynolds' claim to the Acadia campaign, now he was as quick to condemn and dissociate himself from Reynolds' offense against Watson. If Reynolds was on a slide back to the bottom, he only had greased it.

As for what it would mean to start a climb up again, Reynolds was too overwhelmed and disgusted with himself even to think about it. All Ad Alley would know, and be delighted to see a mighty fallen.

Leaving Graham's office, Reynolds felt the bondage of his sickness anew. It appeared to him that his efforts were always one step up and two or three backwards. In his latest disappointment and new self-disgust, it seemed to him that he no longer had the will to try again. Hopelessly, he told himself that if his "syphilis" had sprung this trapdoor to a new dungeon, he would lie in it and rot. It was what he deserved. Sorrowfully, he reflected that his sick vagaries had cost him not only Penny, irrevocably now, but probably his family and his career. *Quo vadis?*

The books said that neurotics held on to their sickness because they drew pleasure from the disorders. What pleasure was he enjoying now? He found not even masochistic joy in this anguish. He had sowed bad seed and the harvest was rotten.

As Reynolds lifted the phone to call his lawyer, his fresh grief was a pile driver beating his brain to mush. And Dr. Kohn wouldn't be back for another week.

That afternoon, after sending his representative to sit with Graham's people, Reynolds was alone in a quiet corner of the Yale Club nursing a soft drink. The more he thought about the new disaster, the clearer it was to him that he could have taken Watson off the hook in plenty of time. He fully deserved the doom he had brought on himself.

Why? he asked himself. In God's name, *why?*

It came to Reynolds slowly that all of it was a way of killing himself. Freud's classical death wish did explain much of his otherwise inexplicable conduct through the years. He had always thought of the theory as hyperbole, a literary metaphor. Now he felt the cold breath of its reality seeping out of his subconscious. For the first time in his life, the notion of suicide crossed his mind.

Reynolds' thoughts split in two, like a dream. Behind one eye there was a lane fragrant with funeral flowers. It led to a grassy dell where a satin-lined coffin was waiting. It wasn't frightening; on the contrary, it promised peace—healing silence and eternal peace. He found it had enormous appeal.

But behind the other eye there was Dr. Kohn's office, and Reynolds imagined himself lying on the couch, speaking aloud: "Well, yes, but dying is the ultimate evil. If a man is ready to accept death, any kind of living has got to be better!" The logic seemed irrefutable.

Reynolds got up to go to the men's room. When the bladder calls, even a life-and-death debate can wait.

Not since he was a boy had he paid as close attention at the urinal as he found himself doing now. Watching the light yellow stream gushing out strongly, he found himself experiencing all at once *how wonderful it felt* in his belly and balls to be relieving himself fully. It was a pleasure that brought a delightful contraction of his sphincter and a grateful grunt of awareness. He might still have to worry about losing his potency, but at least his prostate seemed okay. Duncan Talbott had brought back a story from a medical convention that told of a stuttering patient who complained of difficulty in voiding. The doctor prescribed a prostatectomy. The man resisted, "B-but d-d-doctor, s-s-suppose I d-d-on't w-want an op-op-op-operation?" The doctor answered, "You'll piss the way you talk."

It made Reynolds laugh aloud again. Washing his hands, he liked his face in the mirror. So he was back down in Crudsville City once more. Okay. He was not going to lie down and die. Rocks are hard, water is wet, and he was on his ass. Well, as his Jewish grandmother would have said: *"Abi gezunt—"* "As long as you have your health—"

Behind his image in the mirror, a hazy death skull seemed to be beckoning him. Reynolds stared it down. "No, not yet!" he laughed with a sudden tide of energy. "I've changed my mind!"

A man coming out of a stall stared at Reynolds as if he could not possibly be a member of the club.

24

By the time Reynolds headed for the train that evening, his mood had firmed. He was still sick at heart, but a new resolve was crystallizing. His lawyer had already determined that Graham would be fair, and more. There would be money to fill in the skeleton of a plan that was feasible, and even exciting. Why couldn't he simply open a small office, hang out a shingle as a specialist, accept particular assignments only? He wasn't really a team player—he had chafed under the yoke of shared decision-making, even though Rodney Graham was an ideal and considerate partner. Maybe everything would turn out for the best (what had he once observed about chance determining life?). Getting business would be no problem, and his pulse quickened at the prospect of a new freedom, working alone and without the burden of running an agency. (Out of Barney's "web," at least partway?)

To use a Penny O'Hara one-liner, it seemed decidedly worth putting a quarter in the idea to see whether it came up lemons or bars.

Reynolds straightened in his seat, pretending to be reading the newspaper as the other commuters were doing. The best thing he would have to report to Dr. Kohn was that the blowup had not thrown him. The test was murderous, but he was facing into it, not turning to whiskey or telephone calls or tempers. He felt a new surge of gratitude for the strength Dr. Kohn had helped him establish. Without it, he knew, this crisis would have led to calamity.

Suddenly Reynolds was looking forward to seeing Helena, though earlier in the day he had cursed at the agency upheaval coming just when he and Helena would be crossing their own shaky bridge. His decision was to say nothing of the split with Graham until he had formed his plan more concretely. Helena and the girls would be tired anyway after their drive from Vermont.

It proved wise for another reason: Helena was disturbed about Selma. She told Reynolds at once that she was glad he was at home to talk to the girl. There had been a very unsettling incident over the weekend.

The night before, she recounted, Selma had asked permission to attend an après-ski party at a nearby chalet. Helena had consented—all the youngsters were friends and "good kids." She had awakened at three in the morning to find Selma still out. She knew no telephone number to try. Deeply concerned, she had dressed quickly. It was snowing heavily. The kids might have gone for a drive and met with an accident. Every kind of fear assailed her, except the one she found.

The house she entered was full of supine bodies, and thick with marijuana smoke. Worse yet, her outraged questioning elicited that the "grass" (Helena said the word as if it were broken glass in her mouth) had been brought in by Selma! Selma denied it stoutly, but others insisted she was the one.

"Where would Selly get marijuana!" Reynolds asked in consternation.

Helena said, "She could pick it up in New York."

"New York?" Reynolds was doubly puzzled.

Helena jolted him again. "I don't know. Around Christmas, Selma got a call from your old secretary to thank her for a present or something, and Penny invited her down—"

Reynolds interjected, "Penny would never give Selma marijuana! I'm sure of that."

Helena went on sternly. "And Selly has a picture in her room of Penny and her in front of a Christmas tree with *Ted Watson.* I think that's quite odd, don't you?"

Reynolds thrust aside the stab of uneasiness he felt. Most kids experimented with pot these days—

Helena cut short whatever comfort he was selling himself. "Phil, I think maybe Selma's into drugs. You only saw her over the holidays, when we all stayed pretty close together. But in the time you've been away, there have been weeks on end when she hasn't been herself, and absolutely refusing to see Duncan. And we're not naïve, you know. I don't like the way Selly's taken to wearing long sleeves all the time."

"It's winter," Reynolds muttered, more disturbed.

"It's warm in the house!"

"I'll talk to her."

Helena nodded thankfully. "Yes. She needs that."

It was the next night after dinner before Reynolds could get Selma alone. In the library, the girl dropped to the floor slackly and said, "We're glad you're home."

"So am I," Reynolds smiled. How do you ask your daughter if she's on drugs? It had been pleasant to sit with the family at the dinner table again, to be in his own chair in the familiar room, to feel a father. But this was the other, rough, side of the coin.

The questioning came from Selma: "You don't see Penny O'Hara anymore, do you, Dad?"

Reynolds blinked at the pale face and downcast eyes. His daughter was just making idle conversation, he concluded. Certainly Penny would have been discreet. He answered casually, "Oh, Penny went her way some time ago." He tried a step out on thin ice. "I delivered your present, you know."

"Yes, she called me."

"Did you get to see her?"

"Yes. She had Ted Watson in to dinner one night, and asked me down."

"I see." She couldn't very well lie, probably knowing that Helena had seen the photograph. He took another careful step. "When Ted was at the agency he let everyone know he smoked pot instead of drinking. He and Penny ever turn you on?"

A look of innocence formed on Selma's face. *"Penny* and *Ted?"* she gasped. She was on her feet, her eyes wide. "I know Mother's told you about Vermont. I'm sorry. I never did it before. I was curious. I won't ever again, I promise."

"It wasn't you who brought the stuff?"

Selma's eyes flashed. "John Baker said that, the skunk! He was trying to make out with me the whole weekend, and of course I wouldn't!"

"Make out"—the words echoed in Reynolds' ears. Surely Selma and her friends didn't go that far.

His daughter was telling him, "I had it with that jerk last summer too. He took me to the drive-in one night and asked if I'd like to get in the back seat. So I gave him our standard answer all the girls use—"

"What's that?"

"I said, 'No, I'd rather sit up front with you.' That steamed him for real. He drove out in the middle of the picture."

Reynolds couldn't help but laugh. It wasn't easy to be *any* age. The kids were okay, Selly was okay, he wanted to believe. Anyway, it wasn't a time to press her too hard. He had been away from the family too long. He would talk to Duncan and Dr. Kohn about how to handle his fast-growing daughter when he had reestablished himself as the father in this house.

In their concern over Selma, Reynolds and Helena talked late into the night. When they went upstairs, Reynolds automatically turned to the room he had occupied through the Christmas holiday. There was no signal from Helena. One step at a time. It was too soon. And, upset as they both were about Selma, this was probably not the night in any event for the test he could not put out of his mind.

25

Helena was surprised when Duncan Talbott, a week later, asked her to see him at his office. Her heart sank when he said it was about Selma. But the broad, familiar grin reassured her at once when she sat by the polished desk.

"Selma is fine," Talbott started. "She came in on her own for a checkup. She wants me to talk to you because she's not sure how to deal with a problem she has."

"Deal with what?" Helena asked with quick anxiety. She had worn a scarf against the February wind. Now she removed it and loosened her blonde hair. Her pale eyes on Talbott's craggy face were puzzled and vulnerable.

"Let me lay it out the way Selma did. First of all, she's really happy that Phil is home again, even as a 'guest.' She respects your reasons for that, but at the same time she's concerned that she may be causing some friction between you." The doctor slowed and tilted back in his chair. "Apparently, she's heard you talking about drugs and how upset you were over the marijuana incident—"

Helena said without hesitation, "There is no friction between Phil and me about that! We're both very worried."

Talbott reported, "Selma assures me the fellow in Vermont was lying. I think she's telling the truth."

"I'm afraid Selly's learned how to be pretty glib," Helena said.

"I'm not easy to fool."

"Well, I hope you're right. But Phil and I *have* noticed she wears only long sleeves, Duncan."

Helena did not expect a smile in response to her dark concern. The doctor was saying, "To make a lousy pun, I think Selma wants to needle you a little for your suspicions. I've examined her from top to bottom, and there isn't a sign of anything except growing pains. She's been having some menstrual irregularities and that leaves her tired and irritable sometimes, but I've prescribed for it and she should be okay in no time."

"That's good news!"

"Well, I'll accept a reward in the form of a dinner invitation for Friday night."

"Done!" Cheerfully now, Helena rose and started to replace the scarf on her head.

"Hold on." Her friend lifted his hand. "While you're here, Helena, there's something else I'd like to talk about. Phil."

"Phil?" Helena sat down. One end of the scarf dangled, giving her a young-girl appearance.

"Well, now that he's back home, you ought to know that I've been talking with Dr. Kohn right along. We both feel Phil has made important progress, and that there are lasting changes in his personality at this time."

Helena wanted it to be true. "Yes. I think that's so—" Phil had been nothing but a pleasure at home, both during Christmas and since his return from the week at the workshop. There had been no drinking, no tantrums, and no pressing her about sleeping in the guest room. She knew they must end the ambiguity of their arrangement some time.

"Probation" could not go on forever; there was a point at which temporary became permanent. She appreciated his willingness to wait for her to be ready.

Helena was glad that Duncan Talbott was in effect saying the same thing, indicating it was time for a fresh start. But the woman was startled by her friend's next comment. "You face a difficulty, though, Helena, and I'm going to level with you because there's no other way to avoid an almost sure breakup again—"

"What difficulty?" The scarf was off now.

"Ironically, the problem is that Phil is doing so well."

"I don't follow you."

"I don't blame you." The doctor continued after a moment, "I want to give you some perspective on where Phil stands now. The only way to say it is to repeat what I've told you before, that Phil is literally in a war, *literally* in a daily battle with the neurotic disorders in his personality. Right now his healthy forces are winning, although not a day goes by without some seesawing."

The doctor was speaking with professional gravity, and Helena was concentrating, wanting to understand.

"The neurotic personality is a dirty fighter, Helena. It lies in ambush, it sets traps, it lulls the patient into a sense of false security, it seduces with every kind of temptation. Then, just *because* the healthy growth wins new territory, the sick army strikes with a counterattack. The more threatened it is by the patient's growing health, the more violent its drive to overcome him. That's why I say, though it sounds cockeyed, that the lapses we may still see in Phil are signs of improvement!" The doctor looked at Helena Reynolds with sympathy. "I'm sure you follow me. The question is whether you can accept it."

It was a new configuration for Helena, and gave her new pause. "I don't know. I suppose it depends on what you mean by 'lapses.' I couldn't take it if Phil ever raised his hand to me again."

Talbott spread his fingers. "I don't expect violence, but sometimes we have to anticipate severe regressions with a man of Phil's sensitivity. You see, aside from the counterattacks, Phil is heading into another buzz saw. As he improves, he begins to leave his old, neurotic cocoon, and he moves out into a world he has spent his life avoiding. He gives up all the neurotic shields and defenses he has used for years, and he has to face all the slings and arrows without them. We must never forget that his old, sick life did *work* for Phil. In its own way it provided him with safety, familiarity, like the narcosis of his drinking.

"So. The intelligent patient inevitably asks what kind of bargain he is making. This starts another inner conflict, which perfectly suits the neurotic gang within, and a new round of battles is on!"

"My God, I knew it was complicated—" Helena murmured.

"Unfortunately, yes," Talbott nodded. "It's difficult for us to understand that Phil isn't neurotic for one or two reasons, which can then be 'cured.' Phil is sick because of this AND that AND that AND God knows how many more tangles in his life—"

Helena said, "I still think a person with willpower can control himself."

Talbott answered sharply, "Dammit, Helena, don't be naïve. I've explained to you about compulsion." He wasn't going to get into the nature of Philip Reynolds' obsessions—Dr. Kohn did not share those confidences, and he did not need to know. "Helena, when I was studying with Dr. Kohn, there was a patient who was a voyeur. He told me that one time from a hotel room some twenty stories up he noticed a woman undressing about ten floors below, but the view was blocked by his angle. He told me his compulsion was so great that he nearly flung himself out of the window *convinced* that he could fly down like a bird rather than drop like a stone to his death. He told me it took his last ounce of sanity to realize he could not really fly. Even in my office, there was regret in his voice that he hadn't tried it!"

The doctor continued. "In psychoanalysis we recognize that a compulsion is as real and potent a force as gravity itself, nothing less. All the common sense and willpower in the world are useless. That's why the struggle is so brutal. Phil is wrestling with devils the rest of us never confront. His lifetime defenses are masks that have become his very flesh. When he tries to get rid of them, it's like ripping off his live skin. I'm not exaggerating. It takes enormous determination and courage. It takes an inward heroism."

Helena moved uncomfortably. She was ready to give her husband credit for the painfulness of his analysis, but it did seem a mockery of everything decent for Duncan Talbott to be talking as if Philip Reynolds were some kind of brave hero fighting against dragons for the Holy Grail. At best, she could see her husband as a knight in rusty armor. She said with some impatience, "Duncan, I keep reading about chemical treatments—"

"Phil isn't in those categories," the doctor replied at once.

"What about this lithium carbonate?"

Talbott shook his head negatively. "Lithium carbonate is decidedly useful, but only for what we call manic-depressives. That's a specific illness characterized by wide mood swings up and down. It's not Phil's problem at all. Even in manic-depressives, we find lithium ineffective in twenty to thirty percent of the cases. And there's no significant proof that it works at all for other types of depression or disturbances. Also, I might add, though lithium poses little danger when properly monitored, it can be dangerous if it's fooled with. One possible 'side effect' is death, and I'm not joking."

Helena sighed. "Well, obviously I'm only a helpless layman. But I hear about all these groups and methods that don't take so long. Why does Phil have to go through this whole *Freudian* thing?"

"Helena, it isn't the label that counts. Therapy has got to break through ground that's hardened over a lifetime. It doesn't matter whether one doctor uses rakes, another shovels or dynamite. What matters is to turn that ground and make it friable again. We can depend on Dr. Kohn. At this stage in Phil's progress, the question is how much you can depend on yourself. That's a rough way to put it, I know, but if you stand by him in the next year or so, he should be home free. If not—" Talbott shrugged.

Helena interrupted, her voice aggrieved. "A *year* or so—"

"Maybe longer."

"But it's already three full years this April!"

Talbott nodded and held his peace. Neither Helena nor Philip Reynolds—especially Phil—ought to be told now that the usual prognosis in a case like his was at least five years, and more likely seven. It had to move a month at a time, a year at a time, with acceptance and forbearance born of increasing knowledge and understanding, both in the patient *and* his family.

Helena's hand moved to her cheek. "You're saying I'm just to go on never knowing—"

Talbott said with conviction, "With the progress he's made, it's extremely doubtful that Phil would harm anyone again, much less you." An edge appeared in Duncan Talbott's voice. "I don't want to psychoanalyze *you,* but I think it's time you faced your own reasons for not doing the plastic job I've recommended. It's a nothing procedure, and there wouldn't be a trace—"

"Reason?" Helena fumbled. "I've never had time, with the girls, and—"

"Crapperoo-hoo, my dear! I haven't pressed you before, but it's important now that Phil is home again. Shall I tell you why you've resisted?"

Helena blinked. She was aware of Duncan Talbott's feelings for her, knew he wanted only her good, but she did not want this probing into some unknown he saw and she did not.

"I've told you why," she balked.

Talbott shifted. "We've talked about how painful it is for a patient to keep digging at his guts in analysis. Here you have a small sample you can experience for yourself. Let me tell you, Helena, straight out: You want that mark on your cheek as a *badge* of one deep, symbiotic aspect of your marriage." Talbott went on quickly. "Symbiotic describes people fitting together like jigsaw pieces. Sometimes it's all to the good—the mother's wish to feed her child is matched by the child's hunger for her breast. But it can be bad too—like the pairing of a sadist, who enjoys inflicting pain, with a masochist, who enjoys being hurt. Where two people play into each other's weakness, you have an unhealthy brew."

Helena's brows were high-arched. "I haven't the foggiest of what you're suggesting, Duncan!"

Talbott came back with, "One of Phil's troubles is that he is a bully. And, symbiotically, you have played the role of his willing victim— enjoyed it!"

Helena scoffed. "Why in the world would I enjoy being bullied?"

Talbott felt this was a time to prick Helena's "perfection" and move her to greater tolerance. He said flatly, "Through the years you deferred to Phil in damn near everything, including every conceivable embarrassment. You had a great excuse, you were buying peace at home. But you had a subconscious reason as well, which was that your marriage echoed your daughter-father relationship."

"My father?" Helena gasped. "He was the gentlest man!"

"The way your brother, Gordon, is?"

"Of course I've told you a hundred times he's a terrible tyrant."

"In whose image? Oh, I believe your father was gentle with *you,* but that was probably because he had no trouble dominating you!"

"But if that were so, why on earth would I want to remind myself?"

"Because you loved him, as you love Phil. The scar reminds you of the role you played with both men. In its own way it ties you to them, and that ties them back to you."

Helena sighed wonderingly. "It's too far-out for me, Dunc."

"Not at all. Just takes a while to percolate. Maybe you can see it more easily in your acceptance of Phil's drinking for as long as you did."

"I accepted it because there was nothing else I could do without bringing down the house!" Helena defended with asperity.

Talbott tested her quietly. "Don't give *me* the answer to the question I'm about to put; answer it to yourself, but answer it: When drink turned the great Philip Reynolds into a helpless bum or baby, did you enjoy the feeling of superiority you had in taking care of him like a samaritan or a mother?"

Flinching, Helena said, "Duncan, if I didn't know you well and truly, I swear I would say that is absolutely disgusting and outrageous! To say I enjoyed the sight of Phil when he was a mess! To suggest I am in any way to blame for *his* self-indulgence that has hurt us all so abominably!"

Talbott did not like the direction Helena Reynolds was going, but he had brought her too far to turn back. "I am saying just one thing, Helena. In all innocence, you did in some ways further rather than hinder Phil's illness." He said at once, "It happens all the time. When people try to placate a neurotic, they don't realize it but they are playing into his weakness, and that only reinforces it!"

"My God, you *are* witch doctors!" Helena was as deeply hurt as she was astonished. "You are saying that I *hurt* Phil by trying to be a good wife?"

"I'm sorry these things aren't simple. But I'm telling it to you like it is, and you'll also see that keeping that scar is a way of punishing Phil."

It was a risk, Talbott conjectured, but he was betting that by showing Helena Reynolds she shared some of the psychological trouble her husband was in, the chances of their getting together were improved. At worst, he considered, the misgivings he had introduced might delay the reconciliation, but it would be the more solid when it came. In any case, Helena and the girls ought to know what might happen next. Too often, families were not prepared for the convoluted course of an analysand's ups and downs so that the inevitable crises were met with new panic and rejection rather than the understanding which could support the patient through to higher ground.

Helena Reynolds got up stiffly, arranged her scarf quickly, saying, "Thank you about Selma. It's a relief to know *she's* all right." At the door, she turned back to Talbott. "I've been reading a book about Australia," she surprised him by saying. "Have you ever heard of a drongo?"

Duncan Talbott coughed. "A what?"

"A drongo is an extinct Australian bird," Helena told the doctor with a wintry smile. "It slept with its eyes open, and flew with its eyes shut! Absolute truth! That's the kind of upside-down world you're telling me I have to live with!"

She banged the door shut going out.

Talbott knew it was her way of saying she would try. She continued to be a remarkable woman, and ever his loss.

While Helena was with Talbott, Reynolds had his own surprise. It came to his new office, forwarded from G and R. The letter read:

"Dear Bug-In-The-Web, we send you our condolences for being back in the spider-world. We know you like it the way a horse likes its harness. Mary tried to show you different, but you thought it was only sex and you missed her Zen message all the way. She was saying what Dr. Frank says about the baths. Just as you there see men and women are more the same than different, so Mary was saying young and older are more the same than different. Your problem is mind-fucking, you never get out of your head. Sex does get you out of your head, but only until you come, and that is not enough. Man does not live by orgasm alone.

"Up here you got a lot of theory data and input, but no real getting your shit together. Too bad. Anyway, we're glad you didn't blow away Hal Basser when he tried to lay his trip on you. It's a good thing you kept your cool because (1) the man has a right to screw any way he wants, and (2) you are locked tight enough in your world not to be afraid he might have a key, and (3) maybe you got so mad at him because you *would* like to fuck him, which we could all care less, a hole being a hole being a hole, etcetera."

Turning the page, Reynolds was astonished to find a check taped to the paper. "So here is the money you thought you'd never see again. Your loan to me, plus interest—better than you'd get in a bank. So we're not just scruffy rip-offs, right? So take this as some important feedback.

"Mary really wanted to give you her feedback, but *you* think feedback comes only in words. No! It comes in eyes and fingers and kisses and kunts and tongues and rektums and hot coffee down your cold cut in the morning and throwing snowballs.

"But you are out of that world, where the truth lies. Like you think and believe that Mary wanted to screw you because of some kind of sick. Jesus, take it up with your shrink! DID IT EVER OCCUR TO YOU THAT MARY *LOVED* YOU, that you made her flip, that you turned her on-on-on-on?

"No, no! YOU could not think THAT for the REASON that it had to be IMpossible! BECAUSE Mary is a 'kid' and you are an 'older man' and so on! See how you have trussed yourself all up in labels. Shit, when will you comprehendo that all there is is *people?* And who knows why anybody falls in love with anybody?

"And, man, don't ever look at ANYBODY again with the shiteye you gave me when I asked you for the bread. You know, if I had your kind of false pride I would have torn up the bill and shoved it up your asshole. But after my Zen, I understand you too well. You see, I experienced my disgust for you, but ALSO my PITY. Yes, pity. Pity, pity.

"You think you're getting someplace with your headshrink shit, but that just keeps you tapping around your pigeonholes with a white cane, man. The only way to get out of your head trip is to hang loose, but that is the one thing you don't. Guru says: *Man who don't learn hang loose never learn one motherfuck fact of TRUE.*

"For your bread, thank you. Don't be surprised at my politeness. When I seem rude, that is Zen. (When I seem polite, that is also Zen.) And Mary says be sure I send you her LOVE. She tried to write you herself, but she stopped because she was crazy-surprised to find out it *hurt.* How about that? She didn't think she would miss you (any more than the others) but she does, and it bothers her. She hasn't got time for such mosquito bites on her transcendental tits. She doesn't want anybody so close that she would MISS them. (About her father, let me level and say even *I* don't know if he's alive or dead or what.)

"Anyway, right now Mary is fucking Terry and they both seem to be having a ball, so why not? It takes their mind off us. I am into a new stage of Zen where Terry can't come, so everything is all right. Mary, too, because I am teaching her that you are only a fragment of God's imagination and her feelings come out of *her,* not you. As the master says: *The trigger is not the gun, and the bullet is not the victim.* I hope you dig this.

"On one thing we agree, I think. It's too bad that God is such a stupid turkey. Any one of us, even Terry with her colored snowflakes, could do better."

There was no signature.

Reynolds chuckled. He was right about Barney. It was too bad their trips were so far apart. He reread the letter, and smiled reflectively. Barney might be right at that. Mightn't it be a better life to write bad poetry than good ads? Ought he to think seriously about kicking over all his buckets and going native? No man could deny the temptation of that Promised Land, a life of abandon, little responsibility, anchored in the poetry for which he wanted more time.

Reynolds coughed. It was too late to change his spots. Anyway, time and the need to eat (much less support a family) were great persuaders of even the most profound anarchists. On the couch he had long since learned of his own need for structure and security, and there was nothing wrong in that.

Still, Reynolds speculated, would he hang loose Barney's way if, say, he knew he was to die the next day or week? Would he then, so to speak, try opium, just to have the experience once before death? A new view of "morality" occurred to him. Yes, he would "try opium" under those circumstances. He would not feel it immoral to do *anything* that did not injure anyone else. Then why wouldn't he take opium now? Because he expected to live many years yet. *But that turned morality into an actuarial computation!*

It was a fascinating concept, Reynolds mused. He would like to chew it over in an old-fashioned bull session with Duncan Talbott.

Reynolds tore Barney's letter to pieces. He wanted no reminder of Mary and that dismal, disjointed night. Watching the last scrap drop into his wastebasket, it came to Reynolds frighteningly that the night with Mary could have spelled another kind of disaster. He had cautioned himself that the girl was "SQQ—San Quentin Quail." If he hadn't fizzled, he could now be open to a charge of statutory rape!

The nightmare of police arresting him for his obscene calls dirtied Reynolds' head again. Although it was in the past, he knew the same wrenching sickness, and the despair of seeing his entire life sacrificed. Ah, Penny would not have let him off if she had known what he would do to Ted Watson! *And* for all he knew, if those kids needed money, Mary could still say he had raped her! Who would believe him?

How, Reynolds asked himself again, did he get himself into such messes? Would he, could he, ever be free of the wretchedness his sickness kept visiting on him? What possible pleasure did he get out of it that made the miserableness worthwhile? Well, there was nothing old Ikey would like better than to see him become a basket case—which would happen if he surrendered to the devils constantly reaching for him out of his gut.

Reynolds gathered his willpower. When he resumed with Dr. Kohn the next day, he was going to straighten this out once and for all, he promised himself. A man did not forever have to dance like a puppet on the wires of his obsessions. He could will himself out of that slavery! And he would!

Part Seven

"If thou has lived in despair—
whether for the rest thou dost win or
lose—, then for thee all is lost, eternity
knows thee not, it never knew thee or—
even more dreadful—it knows thee as
thou art known, it puts thee under arrest
by thyself in despair . . ."

—Kierkegaard

26

At the first session after Dr. Kohn's return, Reynolds took the couch with a head full of news. He felt as if he should have drawn up a bulletin, but as a veteran he waited for his inner television screen to light up, let a picture take shape. And there it was—colored worms wriggling into a title. (He would commission a trumpet fanfare here if it were one of his commercials.) The sharpening letters spelled what could be a detective program, and came as no great surprise: "The Red Tie!"

A wipe. And a vivid close-up of Hal Basser's bulging pants.

Reynolds was ready for it. There was no way this would not come up. But to Reynolds' astonishment, before he could speak of the image to Dr. Kohn, it was superseded by another, totally unanticipated, picture that commanded all his attention. It was a photograph album opened to a sepia snapshot that could never have been taken except in his head, and Reynolds recognized at once that it represented another signal event he had totally suppressed until this moment. He immediately described it to Dr. Kohn:

A locker room at a bathing resort, he a skinny boy about seven, naked and drying himself clumsily, with his wet bathing suit on the puddled floor. His father is sitting on a bench. His chest is hairless, but there is a forest in his triangle, which the boy peeps at from the corner of his eyes. To the boy, his father's sex is like a curving bull's horn with a sharp point. It is threatening, an ominous weapon. Still innocent, the boy does not know whom the weapon threatens. He has a vague notion his mother is involved. It has some mysterious connection to the taunt that had started a savage fistfight in front of his house, when the neighborhood bully had mocked, "Your mother fucks!" The boy did not know what the word meant, except that it was an intolerable insult. He knew he would be beaten up, but that did not stop him from flailing at the bigger kid. *"Your* cockeyed mother fucks!" he yelled back. Whatever fucking meant, it was a secret sin that others might do but never *his* mother. He had wound up on his back in the gutter, his nose bloodied, and moaning in misery "My mother fucks" as his arm was twisting to the bone-breaking point. That night his father had beaten him up for tearing his clothes in the street.

Reynolds told Dr. Kohn he thought he remembered quite clearly looking down at his own water-shriveled member and wondering how he could ever grow a huge sausage like his father's. How much piss a hose like that must be able to hold!

Reynolds waited now, aware of his tendency to talk insights away. (Ah, wise Dr. Frank—"Now, I, Philip Reynolds, am talking.")

The album became a moving film. Reynolds couldn't believe what he was watching. It was flickering and grainy, and the people moved jerkily, as in old Chaplin movies, but the scene was clear and graphic. In a poor but respectably furnished living room his father was at the door waiting for his mother. They were dressed up to go to a wedding, it seemed. How beautiful his mother was, with her fragile, oval face, the small mouth that seemed never to know whether to smile or cry.

The picture showed the mother being held back desperately by a boy of no more than four, weeping his heart out and begging her not to leave. Behind the boy, a crony grandmother stood, with a tattered, unclean shawl around bony shoulders.

Reynolds' father is tapping his pocket watch angrily, shouting irascibly, "We are late now, Tillie!" The mother tries to comfort the child. "Grandma will put you to bed and before you know it we'll be home." The grandmother bobs her gray head, with a grin that shows her gums, and spittle runs down her hairy chin. The boy wails mindlessly, "I don't want you to go!"

The mother turns to the man, torn. "I don't want to make him sick again, Clarence."

"I'll make him sick!" Reynolds' father comes at the boy loosening his belt and shouting, "You'll wake up the baby, damn you!"

Ah, yes, the sister! The infant sister asleep in the crib in his parents' room, the hallowed place that had once been his, now stolen from him, the evicted, disowned, spurned.

"I don't care!" The boy challenges the giant in his torment. "I *want* to wake her up!" And screams at his mother. "You won't stay for *me,* but you stay for *her!"*

The doom descends, the belt whistling with all the father's rage. The blows make the boy jump and howl. The mother tries to stop the man, but he keeps flailing at the child until the boy is prostrate on the floor, beaten to a frazzle, but still shouting his defiance as the man roughly shoves the woman outside and slams the door, muttering, "That Ikey-kikey brat should never have been born!"

The granny comes to comfort the boy but he shoves away from her, shrieking, "You stink, you smell bad, I hate you!" Not so much his father's belt as his father's words have murdered the boy. He vows he will kill that man some day. Some day he will put that man to death.

There was a stillness on Dr. Kohn's couch. Reynolds felt the child's anguish and frustration all the way to his own feet as if it were happening now. This was no "mind-fucking," this was a real, long-wished-for plunge into the searing depths. The knife-edged incident came back forcefully across the years, a phantasm materializing out of a long-sealed crypt.

Reynolds whispered to Dr. Kohn, "My grandmother is yanking at me, her hands are like claws. I scream that I hate her. She did stink, vilely. I used to hold my breath when she was near me, hold it until I would nearly suffocate, and then it was disgusting to breath when I simply had to. Phew! I can smell it now!" Reynolds' face screwed up, and he caught his breath with another memory that zoom-lensed at him out of that night—his grandmother taking him into the kitchen for bedtime milk, *and blowing into the glass to clean it.* "She *always* did that, and I had to gulp the milk without breathing. I used to choke. . ."

Reynolds turned his head from the ceiling to Dr. Kohn, his eyes incredulous. "The things that happen! I can see how much of my violence, my drinking problem, goes back to the pure accident of that old witch." Reynolds uttered a cracked laugh: "My whole life might be different if my grandmother had bathed and brushed her teeth!"

Dr. Kohn said nothing.

All at once, the voice from the couch was that of a terrified child, screeching, "There's a mouse! A *mouse!*" Dr. Kohn saw Reynolds press against the wall involuntarily. The mouse was so real to Reynolds that he could swear he had seen one skitter across the gray office carpet as plainly as it had appeared on the worn kitchen linoleum that distant night.

In the instant, a rocket of understanding launched inside Reynolds . . .

That early, recurring dream of mouthwash, of mouse, had been pointing like a straight arrow to this central episode of his life! Pointing to it right from the very beginning of the analysis! (Christ, what a wonderful, if devious, network of hidden staircases and secret panels the unconscious prowled down in the subterranean cellar of the soul!)

Excitedly, Reynolds explained: "What happened next is the important thing, and I had forgotten it entirely!" He sat up to face the doctor,
overwhelmed by the flooding memory, needing to share its too-clear
meaning with his doctor, mentor, friend. He made himself tell the story
quietly, slowly, resisting the pressure behind the cracking lifetime dam.

"That night, as soon as my grandmother left me, I got out of my cot
and ran into my mother's room. *I vomited on the bed.* I opened the closet
and forced my vomit on her dresses. I remember thinking that now my
mother didn't smell so sweet, now her things stank like my grandmother. Now he could have her!"

Reynolds wiped his forehead with his wrist. "So that's what Oedipus
feels like, eh?"

"Skip the labels!" Dr. Kohn commanded. "Go on!"

Reynolds' mind was spinning, as well as his emotions. It was fantastic
how everything meshed, just as the books described. He saw how his
love, hate, violence had alternated with his parents, and had become
paradigms for a thousand other conflicts throughout his life. They
formed a witch's cauldron in which he steeped the venom of neurotic
"double toil and trouble" that had contaminated his years. The inad-
missible passions and violence he could not discharge against his mother
and father he vented against an office clerk, a Lillian Schuster, Ted
Watson, Hal Basser, Selma, Helena!—And himself!

Breathing heavily, Reynolds rested. Thank God he was beginning to
tilt the cauldron a little, the poison starting to pour out. He was
approaching his final, buried ghosts to exorcise them at last.

And apparently there was another one, suddenly pounding on the
door of his consciousness. It made itself known physically in an attack of
knifelike cramps that bent Reynolds over and made him cry out with
excruciating pain.

"What?" Dr. Kohn asked quickly.

Reynolds was gripped by a physical seizure that drove out his breath.

Dr. Kohn spoke encouragingly. "It's the double bind again, Phil.
You're afraid of what you will reveal to me, and what you will reveal to
yourself. This time you have got to break through it."

It came as an instruction Reynolds wanted to hear. He twisted back
on the couch, and shouted, "My sister!" The throbbing in his chest
turned to a panicky hammering. The hidden apparition had taken on
flesh and come through the door to stand accusingly beside him. "My
sister! That night I went to her crib in my mother's bedroom and I
vomited on her face. I wanted her to choke on my vomit, and die. When
she started to kick and scream, I put the pillow over her face—"

Reynolds shivered with the vivid memory. "I said to myself that it wasn't me killing her, it was the pillow doing it! That's what a shit I was! Then I heard my grandmother coming, and I ran out of there."

Later, when his agitation eased, Reynolds came off the couch to sit near Dr. Kohn. It was necessary not to be alone across the room. He wished he could touch the man on the other side of the desk. It would make it easier to face the terrible truths roiling inside of him.

"My sister always acted afraid of me after that. As if she remembered!" He asked, muted, almost in a tone of pleading, "She couldn't remember that night, could she? She was only a year old!"

The doctor was silent, and Reynolds knew the appalling answer himself, as clearly as he now had an awareness of the times his mother had pulled her sore nipples away, leaving him ravenous and squalling.

The exhumation of what was perhaps the deepest of all Reynolds' buried guilts was so shattering that he could not focus it into reality entirely, though it was all too obvious how it reached into this room, into every chamber of his life, at work, at home, asleep, awake. When his sister had died at seven—of pneumonia—he had been ten. Secretly convinced that his early wish for her death had killed her, he suffered a guilt too heavy for a boy to confront. Like the other boulders of his self-condemnation, it had sunk to the bottom of his River Lethe, there to obstruct the flow and create new, turbid currents in his cavernous unconscious. No wonder he had raging torrents within, constantly eroding the banks of his life, and shredding his misshapen roots into tangles of disease and degeneracy.

When Reynolds paused, spent, Dr. Kohn said quietly, "An unusually clear example, isn't it, of how absolutely you have repressed key parts of your life."

Reynolds nodded in the wonder that always came with these revelations. "As if it never happened at all! Yet in me all the time, of course, working away like cancer." He paused again, seeing a new aspect. "You can't bury part of yourself without everything rotting—the maggots get going, they take over! And that's what I was doing without knowing it, *burying myself alive!* That was part of my violence too, wasn't it? Banging on my coffin trying to get someone to help me get out! Thank God Duncan Talbott heard me, eh?" Reynolds gave Dr. Kohn a steady, grateful look. "And thank God for you, or I'd still be down there with the maggots and the ghosts."

The doctor said, "Yes, but I have a feeling you can take this further."

Reynolds was jubilant with the relief he felt. It made it easy to go on. His insights were gravid. His voice rose again, as it always did with new discovery: "All these years, I've been despising myself for things that weren't really my fault! For not being big enough to fight my father. For being afraid to love my mother. For denying that I hated my sister. How about that? I mean, I even hated myself for being a boy in the first place, and there was certainly nothing I could do about *that!*"

LINK-CLICK-LINK—a long and major hookup here:

"And by this kind of self-hate I could get into a *martyr's bag!*"

Dr. Kohn observed that, although Reynolds was not aware of it, he had thrust his lower lip out in the pout of a hurt child.

"*I* hadn't done anything bad. Everybody was hurting *me*. Poor me! Oh, how sweet the feeling of righteous self-pity is, *and how much it excuses!*"

"Yes."

Reynolds took space, until a meteor question crashed into his brain. He knocked the heel of his hand against his forehead and asked Dr. Kohn, a word at a time: *"What made my mother and father do those things?"*

Dr. Kohn's chair creaked as he leaned back. "What made your mother and father do those things?"

Reynolds proceeded cautiously, with a fresh feeling that he was opening still another new door, an entry into a new place promising air and light. "I mean, here I am in psychoanalysis, basically asking everyone—Helena, my girls—to understand me, and forgive the lousy things *I've* done. I excuse myself by saying I was compelled, couldn't help myself, by things done to me before I could be responsible.

"But what about my parents, then? Were they just as helpless in doing what they did? Can I really hate my father if he was, in his own way, just as compelled?"

"Or as responsible!" Dr. Kohn interjected forcefully.

Reynolds objected. "Responsible at four years of age, younger?"

The doctor stood up, and walked about the office for the first time in all their sessions together. "This may be the most important single thing I ever tell you," he said. "The infant is already responsible! Yes! Not for the events, of course, but for how he chooses to respond to them. Now you have read this ad nauseam in all the books, but you have never until this moment been in a position to accept it. Do so. It is granite-foundation truth. And it means that, although we well understand compulsion, in the end you *are* responsible for everything you have done." Kohn went back to his seat. "Take that in, Phil. Take that all the way in."

It was difficult for Reynolds to accept. "An infant is just a bundle of instincts." His argument gathered force. "You can't talk meaningfully about an infant having free will!"

"Stay out of that philosophical quicksand," Dr. Kohn said at once. "We are talking about one irrefutable point: *The act is its own responsibility!*"

Reynolds pondered the statement. It kept enlarging in his head with the powerful persuasion of newly comprehended truth. "I see what you mean," he replied finally. "I can't excuse the lousy things I've done by 'being sick.'"

"Right!"

"It's what Rod Graham said," Reynolds continued thoughtfully. "If I have syphilis, he could care less about where or why I got the disease, he just wants no part of it." Reynolds followed the new spotlight with pulsing conviction. "The women I phoned—what the hell could they care *why* I was sick? If I myself read about a ten-year-old girl being raped, I want to cut the guy's balls off, and I don't care that his mother didn't love him!"

"The act is its own responsibility," Dr. Kohn echoed, nodding. "And, incidentally, we ought to observe that a surgeon opening up a peritonitis is revolted by the stench as much as anyone else. I can tell you at this stage that, yes, I always understood your obscene compulsion but that didn't prevent my feeling the same disgust your victims did. And notice I said victims. The difference is that as a doctor I keep my eye on the cure, while others are more concerned with the bucket of blood. In the rapist case, we need to pity *and* condemn. Our condemnation is part of the reality the man has to face if he is to have any hope of rehabilitation. It is unreal not to condemn such a man on the plea that he is ill."

Condemn *and* pity, Reynolds repeated silently. That might bring a cleansing fire out of which a phoenix might arise.

"Of course," Dr. Kohn added with a compassion he felt for all his patients, "the judges and accusers might also think to say, 'There but for the grace of God go I.'"

Reynolds took this in gratefully, with a sense almost of absolution. He was guilty, and he had committed despicable acts, done wanton evil. Although there was no excuse, and he remained accountable, there was *extenuation*—the human condition itself.

It came to Reynolds at the same moment that he had never told Dr. Kohn his atrocity against Ted Watson. Apparently the ignominy of it was as great in him as the first, early block against confessing his calls to

women. He turned toward the doctor now, and tried to tell the ugly
story, but could not get it out. It was cowardly, but apparently it would
have to wait, along with Hal Basser and other still-unfinished business.

Reynolds dreamed a slow-circling montage. There was a very clear
picture-postcard view of the Ohio farm. A sign on the red barn was
lettered in yellow: BARANTA VOGEK. All the cows were in the barn.
Instead of eating hay, they were sucking up great jugs of milk, and
shitting green grass.

Leaving the barn, Reynolds saw a boy flying a high banner: "VOTE
GOD!"

The boy turns into a Chinese kid, saying, "Wanna fuckee-make-
fuckee my motha, fucka?" When Reynolds says no, the kid opens his
pants. His cock is a square piece of black wood with a large hole. "Chow
men more better to eat," he offers, then laughs. "You catch splinters-
syphilis, you no syphilized!" A radio advertises, "Family Dinner—35¢."
The family goes in. Sister gets all the white meat out of the Show Mein.
Mother dips a chopstick in the hot mustard and paints a Star of David on
Reynolds' head. The cows moo Hatikvah. Reynolds searches the menu
but there is no Bar Mitzvah in Column 1 or Column 2. Sister hands a
fortune cookie, slit like a cunt, to her brother. It reads, "Confucius say
Chop Pussy velly good, why you no eat Chop Pussy-Suey no more,
foreign devil?"

A second dream that night was unusual in that it was not a fantasy but
recalled an actual event. Soon after coming to his agency, Penny had
brought Reynolds an issue of *World Catholic Review* which told of a sign
at a convent gate: "Trespassers will be prosecuted to the full extent of
the law. —Sisters of Mercy."

It applied to him, all right, Reynolds considered in the morning. It was
just about what Rod Graham and Dr. Kohn had both been saying.

27

The country club held a fund-raising dance on Washington's Birthday.
It was still a new experience to Reynolds to be at a party without
drinking. It was like removing dark glasses, taking plugs out of his ears.
The music, the gowns, the faces of young and old, the dancers, all were
bright and new to him in their unfogged reality. Reynolds gave it back at

his table in his fresh, spontaneous pleasure. He enjoyed Helena's open approval, and found himself wondering how he had ever taken pleasure in the sickening anesthesia of drunkenness. He smiled at himself for the zeal of the reformed.

Reynolds was dramatically aware too of the difference between this dance and the Center's. The contrast was summed up in the good taste of Helena's simple black dress against Mary Humphrey's outlandish costume then. It was in the easy tempo of the band's "Star Dust" against the theatrical cacophony in the marijuana air.

He belonged here.

He belonged with Helena, and he wanted her.

After the party, when he took his wife's arm in the portico between their garage and the house, Reynolds trembled with his desire. When he helped her off with her coat, her scent reached him, heightened by the heat of her dancing.

But on the landing he said good night quickly and turned again to the guest room like the visitor he still was. Their relationship had arrived at a delicate pivot point. Reynolds knew that Helena and Talbott had talked about him, and that Helena had a new acceptance of his working with Dr. Kohn. She also had accepted his explanation of leaving Rod Graham. He told her nothing of Ted Watson, only that he now wanted to work on his own, and have more time to return to writing poetry. Helena had seemed pleased, he thought. Money was no problem, and she had encouraged his writing from their first days.

Tossing in the guest bed, Reynolds remembered the past when he had brought Helena home after a party. He could not wait then. And though Helena made small gestures of protest, her own hand was not unwilling when he pressed it to his swollen crotch. Standing in the foyer, he would lift her dress as her fingers closed around his erection, and a small sound in her throat would echo his flaring sex. He would draw her down on the floor despite the caution she murmured about the sleeping girls. And they would do it to each other hotly and wetly there.

In the guest room Reynolds pressed his hands over his ears like a child, with a sense of fearful loss. How much more must his sickness cost him! He tried to erase the memories, but they would not leave. Should he take a chance that Helena might be ready—*and* that he would be able? What if she rejected him? What if she accepted him, and he couldn't?

His body was answering even while his mind was uncertain. He tiptoed across the hall. He could smell the flowers Helena had cut in her greenhouse, a fresh scent he did not recognize. The scent of a wedding?

It was a strangeness. Reynolds lifted his hand at Helena's closed door, but dropped it silently. It took three attempts before he knocked. Then he waited in the quiet. Would the key turn?

Instead there came Helena's soft call. "The door isn't locked."

Reynolds and Helena came together with honeymoon tenderness and seeking. Her hair was down as he liked it best. Her eyes from the bed were wide and yearning.

As Reynolds took Helena in his arms, praying he would be a complete man, he thought how blessed he was to have this wife, this—what was the lovely archaic word he had called her, to her giggling delight, on their first night?—*nobsey!*

Lovely nobsey in his arms again at last, her breasts still high and full, with the large rosette nipples he remembered so well. As she spread with a sigh to receive him, Reynolds felt himself responding to the strength of her thighs and the invitation of her woman-broad hips. Helena held a voluptuousness different from the litheness that vaulted you high over the bar of orgasm but dropped you as quickly to the ground.

Best, she was kindling him to a fullness in his sex that dispelled his lingering doubt at once. Gratefully, he felt his virility gathering in his loins, as powerful as ever.

As Helena moved beneath Reynolds, wetting her lips and swallowing with unconcealed passion, it was a yielding that inflamed Reynolds as neither Penny nor Mary had done. And, taking fire from her husband, Helena found a lust in herself, not just wifely obedience but her own long-denied avidity, flowing and demanding.

Helena grasped Reynolds between her legs with a starved heaving. All their years together fueled this new exchange of their bodies—their daughters, their business worries, their accomplishments, their failures, their laughter and pain, Reynolds' drunkenness, Helena's patience and her perturbation, Reynolds' years with Dr. Kohn, and Helena's skepticism and gradually growing understanding.

Reynolds exulted. In Helena he had, yes, come home! She engulfed him now, and more.

Ah, Reynolds rejoiced, if youth should not be wasted on the young, *neither should age!* He came soaring in his creaming wife.

Helena slid into a half doze, deliciously released. She thought with unexpected happiness of her husband, warm in his place with her now. Yes, she wanted this, to be filled with him again, to have him in this bed, not across the hall, not across the gulf of his sickness and whiskey and violence. She had been at fault too. At the beginning she had been afraid of sex, the veritable cartoon of the "nice" girl to whom lust was indecent, who let her husband put it in, of course, but didn't *enjoy* it. You might even have your own orgasm, but you weren't to be randy-raunchy about it, slamming around like a whore. Maybe, she thought in the dark, her sexual illiteracy—for that was what it had been—was part of his drinking and wildness. And could she honestly blame him if he sought from other women what she had lacked or refused to give? In this night's new honesty, Helena faced the fact that she had never been able to go down on her husband even though he had let her know it was important to him. Maybe some day she would herself go to Dr. Kohn—

Helena's smile of pleasure stayed on her scarred cheek as she fell asleep holding her husband's hand.

Reynolds had another dream:

He was on a farm with Dr. Kohn. Helena rode out of the barn, not on a horse but a zebra. She was Godiva naked. Dr. Kohn pulled her from the zebra, took out a long, striped penis, and mounted Helena rearward. She cried out, "Sodom and Gonorrhea!" The zebra then mounted Dr. Kohn. The three of them cackled like roosters when they came happily. Then they were in a canoe on the farm's pond. A black boy was playing Handel's *Water Music* on oilcans, reading music set in 72-point Souvenir Bold. They left Reynolds alone on the shore. He went into the barn to get a zebra of his own, but the place was empty, not even a mouse. A sign read: "KEEP OFF THE ASS—Jock Rogers."

Outside again, Reynolds saw his sister on Selma's swing. She was dressed in the clothes Helena had discarded. Sister had a long, striped whip she kept whistling before her, shouting, "Even Roman Remail declares you-all a filthy, mucky pig, Boy! You stay 'way from me or I calls ma Pappy an' he cut you balls right off! Y'hear? Y-all stay away from my clean-clean dress an' my spotless, spotless cunt!" The swing catapulted the girl to heaven amidst blazing rainbows. The echo came clearly: "Ma cunt-hole do *not* stink, you putrid boy! It ain't-not-neither no bleeding sewer. *You*-all made out of Godshit, *I* am made outta his pearly teeth and his golden hello!"

Reynolds woke up laughing. The hell with what the echoing dream might mean. He reached for his wife with a reborn sense of felicity.

Working in his studio at home, Reynolds enjoyed being at a drawing board of his own again, making his own first layouts, uninterrupted by agency clamor, his own man again for the first time since he could remember. It was good. When he looked up from his work it was pleasant to see not the punched-out rectangles of skyscraper fenestration but God's sky, and birds establishing their territories with bright songs in budding trees.

One exercise at the Center had been to concentrate on his fingerprint. "It's typical of how we live that we look but don't *see*," Dr. Frank had taught. "Mostly we take in our preconceived ideas of what things are like, and miss the excitement of their separate *reality*. You don't have a preconceived idea of your fingerprint, so this will help you *experience* the act of seeing-when-you-look, the way a child takes in the world. You know," the leader went on, "it's not Wordsworth's cloud of glory children come trailing into the world, but the glory of reality before they become blinkered, bespectacled, and bemused with the stereotypes of adults."

Like the glory of the springtime trees Reynolds was seeing with new eyes. For the first time he perceived that spring was not the green that poets hailed; it was pale umbers, magentas, delicate reds, hues of promise, not yet "colors." Looking across his great lawn to distant trees, he was sensitive to fresh images. It was not a metaphor to say the lifting branches were smoke rising gently above the still-brown earth. This was the nature of early April.

Reynolds watched yellow green come to the trees in later weeks, darkening to May and June as buds opened to delicate tendrils and they opened to leaves. The fragile colors of Reynolds' relationships inside the house altered too with the passing months. The girls came more frequently into the studio to ooh and ah over the tissues Reynolds scotch-taped over the pine walls. They were tickled when they recognized the name brands he worked on. They had always taken pride before their friends in ads "made by my dad!" particularly on television. It was almost as good as having a celebrity for a father. And now they were intrigued by seeing, day to day, how his work was accomplished. Reynolds felt their new spirit inwardly, and was happy. For Helena, the family was a well of happiness once more.

With Dr. Kohn, Reynolds' sessions were reduced to three times a week, an acknowledgment of his improvement.

In the city office he maintained for convenience, Reynolds received an unlooked-for telephone call. "Phil, this is Jock Rogers, and don't hang up. My new shop has a special account we'd like you to handle—"

"Not interested!" The thieving, swindling bastard.

"You'll deal direct, I'm out of the picture. You can name the fee. Let's say that in my own way I'm trying to make up a little for the Acadia screw-up."

A year ago, Reynolds would have told Rogers to fuck off. Now he was able to tell himself that throwing stones did no good, and after all he lived in his own, very thin, glass house.

He said, "They'd have to wait. I'm over my head right now."

"We know how busy you are. They want your particular savvy."

"Okay, then."

He could not bring himself to say thank you to Jock Rogers, but he considered there was no reason to turn down the business if he didn't have to deal with the man.

"Their telephone is 312-45—"

Reynolds interrupted. "That's Chicago?"

"Right. Fly out, get the dope, do your thing, get the bread—one, two, three, four."

Reynolds wrote down the number and the name. He knew the company. Prestigious. An account was an account was an account whether it came in over the transom, a hundred-dollar lunch, or via a garbage can.

"A birthday present," Reynolds had laughed, when, in April, Dr. Kohn had agreed to the reduction in their hours. It was hard for Reynolds to accept that three years had passed on the couch, though in terms of the bruising he felt it seemed he had been with Dr. Kohn all his life. On the balance between doggedness and hope, hope was finally tilting the scale. As his neurotic demands eased, Reynolds found new energy, and began to tap a wider range of his talent, including his return to poetry. He knew he was rusty and out of the mainstream, but it was a pleasure to be in touch with this neglected part of himself. An extra dividend was Helena's growing respect. His new writing, when he showed it to her with some of his old shyness, moved and touched her by its efforts toward rediscovery and rebirth.

Helena was not sorry she had heeded Duncan Talbott and given her husband "more space."

With Dr. Kohn, Reynolds began to consider whether they might talk of termination. He argued that he had fished every reluctant creature out of his dank unconscious. To himself he rationalized that if he hadn't yet worked through Hal Basser and Ted Watson with Dr. Kohn it was because they were no longer significant lesions. But Dr. Kohn insisted that if, indeed, his monsters were all beached, they should examine the evil collection more closely after the trouble they'd had netting them.

Evil collection, truly, it appeared to Reynolds, but stripped of their power now! Now passing his mid-forties, Reynolds could at last declare that he was a better human being, more outward, less imprisoned by his own narcissism. He was no longer a drunk, a bully boy, a shark, an obscene caller. Indeed, an obscene call seemed simply impossible for him now. The compulsion was gone because the need was gone. His marriage was improving every day as trust and security developed more firmly with Helena. The girls were thriving normally again, happy at school and with their friends.

On a balmy morning in late May, Reynolds went over this record with Dr. Kohn, but added a dream that, he made so bold, he understood all too clearly. It had been a short dream but powerfully depictive, like a trompe l'oeil painting. In a glossy magazine carrying some of his new ads, Reynolds had come upon a jar of cream. The artwork showed a looped metal zipper lying above the jar, which was labeled with a red skull and crossbones.

"You understand it, you say?" the doctor asked. "I don't."

"As soon as I woke up! The jar is ointment. The zipper is *fly,* as in trousers! Fly in the ointment! And something dangerous about it, something deadly—the skull thing."

"It sounds right."

"But why in red? Usually a warning is in black."

"Well, why red? What else is red?"

Reynolds felt the old electrical jolt that preceded vision. He was not disappointed. The ad appeared before his eyes as in his dream, but this time the facing page showed a photograph of Hal Basser and his expanded fly.

Red skull and bones—*red tie!* The fly back in his ointment! In his heart Reynolds had known all along that he was hiding the Center incident from Dr. Kohn.

The fact finally admitted shook Reynolds physically. He felt as if he were sliding down a greased chute from the couch to Dr. Kohn's desk. The doctor's face looked contorted, blurring into Hal Basser's. It was a gargoyle head of spite now. Without realizing it, Reynolds was pounding on the couch and crying out, "It is not resistance! I just don't want to waste time on something that doesn't have a damned thing to do with me."

"All right, what does have a damned thing to do with you?" Dr. Kohn persisted.

Reynolds snapped back vehemently, "I keep seeing your confounded tie!" He stopped, feeling he was abruptly at the entrance of an unsuspected labyrinth; it was almost as if a brackish breeze was coming out of a cave hole. He had goose pimples. Bewildering words started to pour, out of a crooked mouth not his. "Your fucking tie! A tie doesn't fuck, a cock fucks! *You* fuck!"

Aghast, Reynolds saw another unspeakable picture in his throbbing skull. It was Dr. Kohn with his pants zipped open and his sex out, erect and inviting! Reynolds started to moan, twisting his head from side to side. Had he finally gone raving mad? "I want to make you come!" he cried out. And at once: "No! No!" It was Hal Basser's sex, and then black, Ted Watson's—a boa snake coiling to crush him.

Suddenly Reynolds was flailing on the couch, blasting, "No, I'll bite it off you! I told you I'll kill you someday!" He leaped from the couch to attack his father behind the desk. All his fuses blew out. *"Kill* you, bastard!"

Dr. Kohn slapped the desk with his notebook. "That's enough, Phil!"

The order was icy spray. Reynolds dropped back, hunched over, heaving.

"You never let go like that again! Here or anywhere!"

Reynolds nodded in terror of himself. He breathed in disbelief, "I was really going after you!" A vague tingling spread from the back of Reynolds' head over his crown, then his mind went blank.

"Get back on the couch, stop talking, and try to realize what has happened!"

Time did not end Reynolds' numbness. He tried: "Well, I suppose violence like that, it lets the pus out—"

"Shit!" Dr. Kohn shouted sternly. "Acting out that way is not poison, it's *insane!"*

Apologetically, Reynolds spoke after another pause, "Well, at least I suppose I finally see how this gets into the homosexual business—"

The interruption was sharp, "I'm afraid I have to say you do not see that at all!" Dr. Kohn deflated Reynolds for the ten-thousandth time.

In session after session, the doctor held Reynolds to the painful grindstone, especially the shameful "acting out" incident, and the long-delayed confession about Ted Watson that Reynolds had finally poured out. Sometimes Kohn interposed open sarcasm: "And you thought you were ready to leave!"

It turned out that Reynolds' wish to kill/castrate Kohn/Father was a separate problem, hardly if at all involved in whatever latent homosexuality still had to be explored.

Uncovering this new tangle, Reynolds discovered a very different pattern taking shape. By now, he knew better than to be surprised by the unreckoned. What he came to see was that he had used his rage at his

father as a way of avoiding an even deeper and prior rage at his mother—
his infant fury at being weaned.

Reynolds cast light on this unexpectedly in one session when his
associations led back to the Ohio farm and another forgotten episode of
his life. He had been resting in his barn-stained overalls behind his
grandmother's creaking rocker on the porch. His mother and father had
arrived to return him to Chicago. He was six and had to start school. He
was sad. The Ohio night was cool at the end of August. The rising moon
was beginning to be tinged with harvest-time orange. The odor of the
ripening wheat fields filled the earth and sky. The sounds of cattle and
nickering horses came from the high barn beyond the buckeye trees he
loved to climb. (He had rubbed the buckeyes against stones to make
rings to take back to Chicago and the envy of the kids, who might then
stop calling him Ikey-Kikey if he made presents.)

Bats looped lariats of blind flight against the moon. Their chittering
was accompanied by the occasional whistle of a bird settling into its nest
and the rusty thrumping of his bullfrog friends down the cow pond
bordering the pasture. His father and grandfather were inside the house,
in man-talk, the way his mother was having woman-talk with his
grandmother on the porch. Neither of them knew he was there,
scrunched as small as possible so his shadow wouldn't spill and tell. He
kept swallowing with a secret excitement over listening to grown-up
talk not meant for his ears. He had not intended to hide, it had just
happened that they had come out and not seen him in the dark and then
it was too late and now he wanted to listen.

His mother was talking so softly he could make out only some of her
words. "So worried, born so puny . . . And trouble with my . . . You
know, I had never heard of that . . . your . . . cracked that way and—"

"Oh, yes," his grandmother had said knowingly. "Happens to a lot of
us."

Reynolds, boy, wondered what had cracked.

"So painful, you know, I . . . And sometimes . . . just couldn't help
it . . . Poor little fellow used to scream and kick . . ."

Reynolds, boy, wondered if they were talking about him. He remembered nothing of screaming and kicking, except when his father
whopped him.

"Hungry, hungry all the time . . . I didn't believe in bottles . . . until
doctor said so . . . yes."

His grandmother had chuckled. "He's eaten like a Poland China hog
all summer. Made up for lost time, I can tell you. Reminds me, Tillie,
there's some of my preserves to take back. He likes them real well."

In Dr. Kohn's office Reynolds remembered too his grandmother's cooking—her potatoes fried in country butter, he'd pay a ransom for that taste today, but where was it to.be had, and at what cost in guilt over cholesterol and calories? The pies—he had demolished whole pies at a sitting with goblets of milk warm from the cow. (Sometimes, he told Dr. Kohn, his grandfather had squirted from the teat to his mouth, with both of them howling when he got the stream in his hair, his eyes. Unpasteurized, unsanitary, pure delight!)

His mother's warm milk in the cracked nipple the poor woman had to pull away in pain from the criminal, biting, starving infant boy!

So that, remembered finally, was another of the ways it had been!

Oh, Lord, Reynolds called up again from the couch, the ways You find to cripple people!

It did not escape Reynolds, he explained to the doctor, how closely the clinical pattern in the casebooks fit that feeding experience. For one thing, it explained the lure of whiskey. Its warmth was the illusion of the full infant-pup belly, Reynolds told Dr. Kohn. But he could never get enough because it never satisfied. Being a substitute, whiskey never hit the hunger spot, no matter how desperately the infant within sought satiation!

Mulling it over, Reynolds saw another shaft. His traumatic weaning experience would support the books too in the etiology of an abiding rage at his mother even though he loved her at the same time. It didn't matter that her withholding of her milk was no fault of hers. Reynolds had read of cases where the child was deprived because the mother had *died,* surely not her fault. Yet, to the infant it was a personal injury, and the forming psyche blamed the mother for its loss. That early conflict between hate and love could also lead to the heavy drinking, Reynolds theorized, because the narcotic effects eased the inner confusion and frustration.

To Reynolds' amazement, he heard Dr. Kohn yawn deeply. He sat up, affronted. It was another case of discovering deep causes which did not seem to impress the doctor at all.

Dr. Kohn answered Reynolds' unspoken challenge. "Yes, that is all very important, but you have seen it all before, if not so dramatically. What I am waiting for is the new aspects you are taking considerable pains to sidestep."

Reynolds no longer argued back. Dr. Kohn was a son of a bitch; he always turned out right.

Back on the pillow, Reynolds invited his unconscious to respond. It came quickly to the bidding, with an image of a velvet theatre rope leading into a stuffy auditorium. On the screen there was a film of himself. He was wearing a surgeon's outfit, and apparently lecturing to medical students in an amphitheatre. In his mind's eye he saw the textbooks he had pored over on homosexuality. Rage at being weaned could lead to vindictiveness aimed at all women, surrogates of the mother. The logic of the unconscious was then clear. In the sexual area, the rejection of women led to men. Not only that, but revenge could be satisfied as well. If it seemed to the ravening infant that the mother was withholding her milk, the vengeful son could, as an adult, withhold *his* milk from women by turning to men. Also, in the homosexual act, he could himself become the woman/mother giving his milk, through his penis, but giving it to a man, not to a woman!

At this point, Reynolds sat up on the couch, his eyes puzzled, his palms lightly tapping the sides of his head. "I just don't understand! I *never* had any homosexual impulse, not the slightest. Not when I was a kid, not in college—"

Dr. Kohn came in with, "What about the hard-on Hal Basser gave you? What about the crazy episode you had in here?"

"Listen," Reynolds hammered across the room, "the one thing we both know is that I'm a cuntsman if there ever was one! Okay, Hal Basser got to me for a minute in some crazy way, like the way I blew my lid with you. But I'm sure there are other explanations!"

Reynolds was surprised and gratified when Dr. Kohn agreed at once. "There very well may be." Then, as usual, came a zinger. "But we can't just let this go by without leading it to water and seeing if it drinks, can we?"

When he dreamed that night, Reynolds' fantasy was direct and forthright, with little of the usual dream rhetoric of obfuscation, ambiguity, contradictions, charades of the unconscious. He was back in the theatre, this time sitting among the students, as all watched a hard porno film rated "K" (for Kohn, obviously). A handsome young man, in tight-fitting pants and T-shirt, is a clerk in a paint store. As the owner leaves for lunch, a husky fellow enters and asks roughly, "Can you match this color?" He takes out his sex as his sample. The two men go back to the storage room. "Just get down and see if your tongue matches this pink, eh?"

The movie then shows the husky man jamming his sex into the clerk's mouth. The clerk tries to pull away, but the man yells "The customer is always right!" In the audience, a student cheers "Right on!" Reynolds sees that the clerk's eyes are crossed with revulsion, and he has trouble breathing.

In the next scene the big man pulls the clerk down and wraps his legs around him as he would a woman. He maneuvers so that the clerk's cock slides up his ass. "Oh, Tiny Alice!" a student whispers to Reynolds. "A'llbee that!" Another student applauds, "Ream it out! Take it all the way, baby!" The clerk is steaming now, ramming and shoving up the big man, whose penis is photographed in a close-up hard against the clerk's stomach. They kiss passionately, then the camera pans down to show the big one shooting and shooting and shooting. It seems like a spray gun shooting paint as the clerk also comes, with his face twisted in passion.

The students start pulling each other off, but Reynolds hides in a corner, thinking how the clerk must now shit-stink, and how disgusting it was to see two men kissing. How must a man's lips taste? How kiss a hard, rough face feeling of stubble instead of the smooth inviting flesh of a woman?

When a student, who looks like Hal Basser, passes by and grabs for Reynolds' pants, Reynolds strikes him a blow that knocks his head clear off. As it rolls on the floor it becomes the head of a penis, jetting blood to spell the name of the movie's producer: Fred Gisumund.

Reynolds steps over it gingerly as Helena appears. She is wearing a see-through veil, and exudes a perfume that stirs him up immediately. Taking his hand, she says, "Remember, dear, the customer is always right, but your poor mother couldn't help it, could she?"

As they leave, a truck vending birth pills passes by, with a large sign: THROWSWORD INDUSTRIES. Reynolds stops it, and urbanely buys a package of pills for his mother.

28

In the weeks that followed, no matter what subject came up on the couch, Dr. Kohn firmly steered back to the homosexual connection. Reynolds kept balking, repeating that it was as irrelevant as it was odious to him. Until a dream brought him up short. It was a cartoon fantasy of two erect penises dancing together, and kissing.

What disturbed him, Reynolds reported on the couch, was that when he woke up he found himself consciously wondering how it *would* feel to touch another man's sex, have another man touch him.

Reynolds sweated as he confessed the insistent thought, wrestling again for the honesty the doctor's office demanded.

Dr. Kohn encouraged, "Stay with it, Phil."

The two penises kissing, yes. Two fat cocks in Reynolds' mind, rich with gism. Reynolds was consumed with a curiosity that overrode his loathing. There was a stirring in him he could not deny—there could be excitement in being with another man.

He asked slowly of Dr. Kohn: It would be like doing it yourself in front of a mirror? "An *amplifier!*" he called out. By feeling the pleasure building up in another man's cock, a man's own joy could be increased! With a cough of triumph, Reynolds sat up on the couch. His fantasy had not led to homosexuality when you truly analyzed it—rather, it had circled him back to his old *narcissism!* The shriving words poured out to the doctor. It wasn't anyone else's cock he wanted, Reynolds gloated, it was his own, multiplied and multiplied. In short, old King Shit wanted to feel *every*one's orgasm! To his own greater glory!

Reynolds got to his feet. Dr. Kohn's impassivity did not derail his enthusiasm this time. It was great to be able to ride down these foxes of the unconscious, not let them burrow away. Reynolds thought how confusing it must be to people without his experience. Surely any man having the fantasy of the two pricks would be terribly upset, would doubt himself. But Reynolds had not been fooled. He had followed the devious trail to the lair, where lurked not homosexuality but his old self-love!

A clearing of the throat from the desk brought a touch of disquiet to Reynolds as he paced and recited. He was beginning to recall something in the books he would just as soon not confront. *Narcissism and homosexuality were closely linked and related.* Both rested on the same underlying disturbance, frustrated orality, self-hate, feelings of rejection and inferiority, self-effacement, assuagement of a feared father.

Reynolds, still pacing, objected to Dr. Kohn that, while some of these clinical aspects might seem to apply, his case was signally different. With a show of reason and logic, he argued with the inscrutable face behind the desk: "I mean, if I can confront my obscene phoning—which, God knows, was as vile as anything—why wouldn't I be able to face homosexuality, which everybody accepts these days anyway?"

Dr. Kohn refused comment as Reynolds assiduously argued his circling ideas, and then it was time for another patient.

That evening an emergency telephone call took Helena to Georgia. Gordon Weslie had had a heart attack, might be dying. Blood was thicker than grudges, Helena's sister had wept. There had been no question in Helena's mind about going.

It was the first time Reynolds was alone in the house with his daughters. They got along easily, played Monopoly, drank hot chocolate together. Reynolds went to bed missing Helena, but happy in his home. Father and husband. Good again.

A week passed pleasantly. Helena phoned to say she had to stay on; it was touch and go with her brother. Selma, Dorothy, and Midge came to the phone and assured Helena they were getting along fine.

Reynolds thought during the week that Selma was looking peaked again, but put it down to the condition Duncan Talbott had described. He had no hesitation giving her permission to stay out late on Saturday night for the final meeting of the Junior Prom Committee; and no hesitation approving when Dorothy and Midge were invited to sleep-over dates. He found the house too quiet. He had become used to the pounding of feet up and down the stairs, the squalls of rock 'n' roll as one door or another opened, and the little arguments and quick laughter that wrapped them together as a family.

On Saturday night, although he felt lonely, Reynolds fell into a deep, undreaming sleep, free of misgivings.

When the phone rang at three in the morning, Reynolds was certain it was Helena with news of his brother-in-law's death. While reaching for the phone, he ticked off what needed to be done. Round up the girls, get them packed, call for plane tickets . . .

When the receiver reached his ear, Reynolds could not believe the voice. Incredibly, he heard, "Phil, it's Penny."

"Penny?"

It had to be a dream. Impossible. Why would Penny, out of the gone past, be calling him, and at this hour? It flashed into his mind that she might be in trouble. He sat on the edge of the bed, alert. Of course he would help her!

He heard her having difficulty speaking, she seemed to be crying. Had Ted Watson hurt her? But Penny was saying, finally, unbelievably, "It's Selma, Phil. You'd better get down to my place as fast as possible!" There was a crashing sound, the phone clicked off.

Bewildered, Reynolds dressed at once. What in Christ's name was Selma doing in New York? He sped down the Merritt Parkway as fast as he could push the car, hoping for a police escort. But there wasn't a cop in sight as he went screeching around curves at ninety and more, leaving the few other night drivers flabbergasted. There was no poor old lady on his tail this time, only a sense of his own apocalyptic doom he did not understand but feared with his life.

Penny's eyes were dry but her face was torn. "There's no sense beating around the bush, Phil. Selma's on some kind of drug."

The words, impossible to accept in any case, simply could not penetrate Reynolds' brain in Penny's bedroom. From a window nearly like this one he had stood so many happy times in Penny's first apartment. Now his daughter lay stupefied, sprawled grotesquely on Penny's bed. Her young face was a torpid mask of horror. Her long blonde hair was tangled and dirty on the pillow. Her caved-in cheeks were streaked with grime. Her eyelids were bilious with a garish green makeup. He could not grasp it.

Nothing Reynolds had imagined in his hectic trip down had been as devastating as this. A sob tore at his throat. Where was the fresh-faced, laughing high-school junior he had teased at dinner? Where was the tennis champ, chess whiz, fish in the club pool? Queen of the sophomore dance last year, cornily heart-catching in her golden crown and tinseled scepter—everything, everything, everything in the world to look forward to! Beloved daughter.

Who had been fleeing the Eumenides?

Penny stole out of the room. Reynolds was weeping beside the bed as he kneeled down to take Selma's limp hand. This had to be his private grief.

Coming later from the kitchen with coffee, Penny told Reynolds, "Selma rang my bell just before she collapsed. I couldn't get a doctor, so I phoned you. I don't know what she's on or how much she took. I don't see any needle marks, but she's spaced out for sure. It could be LSD or God knows what. I'm no expert on this scene." She led Reynolds away from the bed gently, and gave him the coffee. "I'm sorry I couldn't even get her cleaned up. She's sure been around somewhere." She held up a torn mini-gown by two fingers. The rag smelled sour.

Reynolds protested. "Selma never had a dress like that!" She certainly hadn't been wearing it when she left home.

"The kids swap clothes all the time."

They moved into the living room, and it shook Reynolds to see "the new Penny." Gone was the lack of confidence of her first furnishings.

Instead of the timid step upward in her first Van Gogh and Modigliani reproductions, her walls now held contemporary hard-edge, a signed Picasso lithograph, a strong Calder of her own. His taste was reflected also in the leather and steel furniture, as well as the general lack of clutter. New too was a drawing table very like the one he had in the Connecticut studio, with a professional taboret like his, and a large corkboard as crowded as his with layout tissues. Penny's roughs were striking, Reynolds saw at a glance. And they too were basically his approach, Reynolds noted with both a pang of loss and a teacher's pleasure in a successful protégée.

The first-rate work was more evidence of how far Penny had moved. It was clear in her face that she had answers now, given and taken, not just the questions she had flooded him with through their time together.

Penny brought Reynolds back to his crisis. "Do you have a doctor in the city?" she asked.

"I'd rather get Duncan Talbott."

"I'll help any way I can," Penny offered as he went to the phone.

"I appreciate it."

"I'm glad she came here. I've always loved Selma." It was said simply and genuinely.

Talbott's answering service came on, said they would deliver the message.

Reynolds returned to Selma's bedside. Being alone with Penny in the living room stirred too many memories he had thought were finished. He could not deal with her attractiveness now. It was the face of disaster he had to look at as he stood above Selma. "Glib," Helena had said. His wife was wise, he had been a fool taking in his own washing of hope. But what could they have done? What in the name of God had happened to their daughter?

Something made him call out to Penny. *"Has Selly been seeing Ted Watson?"*

Penny came into the room, plainly surprised. Reynolds spoke accusingly. "Come on, Penny! She has a damn picture of the three of you!"

Penny was looking at Reynolds uncertainly. "Selma saw Ted Watson here a couple of times before he left New York, yes."

"Where is he now?"

"We've been out of touch. I hear he's with black militants somewhere."

"I should have killed that bastard!"

Penny went stiff. "You're the one who loused *him* up, remember?"

"And he took it out on Selma!" It was a suppressed, half-crazy cry that made Penny O'Hara catch her breath. For the first time she realized what Reynolds was implying.

"Phil, that's insane!"

The word rankled. Reynolds wanted Penny to know that not only was he not insane, he wasn't neurotic any longer! But he recognized that he was off-balance. He remained silent, staring down at Selma bitterly.

Penny said, "Drugs are all over the place. You know that."

Reynolds couldn't stop himself; Ted Watson's threat echoed again in his ears. "He turned her on, didn't he?"

Penny's reply astonished him. Instead of another quick denial she said gravely, "I suppose in a way you're right. Everything that's happening to *all* the kids is part of it. The way blacks have been treated, now they're swinging their frustration around like a chain, and part of it is drugs, though they're certainly not the only ones. Somebody's bound to get hit. This time Selma."

Reynolds looked squarely at Penny. What she said seemed only too true. This secure woman before him was radiating the old magnetism she had held for him. The pull he felt was in the way she stood, moved, spoke. She had flowered—no longer cinnamon, or any spice or metaphor. She was an alluring woman. Beneath her dress Reynolds saw the curves of her fuller breasts, her hips broader than he remembered, her legs shapely and strong as his body had known so well.

A soft moan from Selma brought Reynolds' head around, but the girl remained asleep. Penny was going on, "Anyway, I'm sure Ted wouldn't harm Selma. No matter what, he isn't that kind of person."

Hearing Penny on the side of Ted Watson evoked all of Reynolds' vexation. It had taken the catastrophe of Selma to bring him to Penny again, but now Reynolds had to face the fact that old emotions were churning. Despite the new plateau of contentment he had reached with Helena, he felt his response to Penny was not so much embers springing to new flame as it was a flame that had never fallen to ember.

Reynolds could not accept it. The distance between himself and Penny was too great.

Also, nothing had really changed. Penny knew his sickness, out of her own horror. What could he do? Mawkishly ask her to forgive and forget, plead his analysis? He had been all through that, and was sick of it. No, you don't ask for love; it is there or not. Besides, what had been true before was truer now; he had no right to interfere in Penny's life again. (How right the Bible was to use the word "interfere" for rape!) Nor was he ready to give the lie to everything he had been feeling for Helena.

Selma made a thin, protesting noise just as the telephone rang.

Talbott was shocked, and ordered, "Get her up here right away!" He would meet Reynolds at his office.

"Can we manage her into my car?" Reynolds asked Penny.

Penny was doubtful. "She seems to be coming out. If it's a bad trip, they can be pretty wild."

Selma shrilled, "John!" The girl half leaped out of bed, and crashed to the floor. Penny hurried to help her as Reynolds finished at the phone, but Selma flung her off with amazing strength. She grabbed her pouchlike bag and scurried into the bathroom, screaming mindlessly at the top of her voice.

Penny called anxiously to Reynolds, "You'd better get the police!"

As he hurried to the phone again, it crossed Reynolds' mind that Penny knew more about the drug scene than she had opted to tell him.

A crash inside brought them both scrambling. Fortunately, Selma had been unable to lock the door. She was splayed on the green tile, surrounded by pink pills and broken glass. "She took speed!" Penny cried, turning off the splashing water.

Selma was a pathetic rag doll in Reynolds' arms as he put her back in bed. "Is there anything we can give her?" he asked, feeling stupid. "Coffee? Tea?" Educated, competent man! he flayed himself. Any "ignorant" street kid would know what to do, while he stood helpless, inadequate.

Penny frowned in her own doubtfulness. "I don't know. If she swallowed a lot of pills, there can be hell to pay."

In his bitterness, Reynolds created an aphorism: Ask not whose ox is gored, it is yours!

Selma's moaning ceased abruptly. Her eyes opened, dilated. They were lenses seeking focus beyond the horizons of this world, Reynolds thought with fresh dread. Without warning Selma bolted from the bed, uttering another mindless shriek. She was in terror of something pursuing her, it was clear to Reynolds and Penny. The girl was plainly out of her mind. Almost naked, she hooted, "Let me out of here!"

Reynolds grabbed to hold her. "Selly! It's me! Dad!"

The girl smashed at his face with her bag, tigerish. "Don't you touch me, you shit-eating bastard!"

With Penny's quick help, Reynolds managed to pin Selma's arms from behind. Penny tried: "Selma, it's Penny, honey. It's your father and me—"

"Fucking again?" Selma laughed derisively. With a tremendous heave, she escaped them, and went careening around the room, howling with glee. She swept the coffee cups crashing off the table, slammed a lamp to the floor, flung a heavy ashtray at the mirror on Penny's dressing table. Tormented, Reynolds remembered too well the example he had set the night he had wrecked their den. As he lunged to stop her, Selma whipped around and made for the window. Penny screamed. The glass shattered, and Selma was partway out hanging over Riverside Drive before Reynolds' flying tackle held her.

Petrified, Reynolds and Penny managed to wrestle Selma to the floor where they held her down only by sitting on her. Her strength remained unbelievable. She kept dislodging one or the other with her rolling and pitching. All the while she kept up a blood-chilling caterwauling. Reynolds despaired. How could this mindless animal be his daughter Selly? He could see the horror in Penny's face matching his own.

When the two policemen entered they took in the scene with experienced casualness. At the sight of the uniforms, Selma went still. "Ambulance will be here soon," one of the policemen told Reynolds as the other dialed the phone.

Selma stood quietly while Penny put a robe around her. Her pinched face stared insolently at the policeman. He asked Penny, opening his notebook, "Do you know what she took?" Penny shook her head. Selma giggled suddenly. "Bad shit, man!"

The policeman addressed Reynolds. "From the looks of it, she's into more than grass."

To Penny, Selma said in a surprisingly normal tone that even held a note of regret, "I'm sorry I wrecked your joint." To Reynolds she added, "You'll pay Penny for it, won't you, Daddy?"

Reynolds was dumbfounded at the transformation of the madwoman to the cajoling girl. Her eyes were still vacant, and he could see her body taut and wary like an animal about to spring. She was stalking them, sniffing them to see who might be the weak one. To the policeman who had moved from the phone to the door, she gave a vulpine smile. "Lemme go, fuzz, and I'll blow you."

Reynolds' stomach heaved. Where was bottom, Dr. Kohn?

Penny called sharply, "You cut that out, Selma!" Reynolds was grateful, he could not speak. He choked again when Selma gave a barking laugh: "Oh, you Penny! You think I didn't know when you and Daddy were screwing each other blind?"

The furious shout now was Reynolds'. "Shut up!"

The policeman looked up from his notebook. "You're wasting your breath, mister. They say anything when they're stoned. She'll never remember this."

Selma was cackling. "Fucking right! He wasted his breath whenever he talked to any of us. *We* weren't clients or big shots!"

Despite himself, Reynolds protested, "Selly, that's not true!" Whatever else he had loused up, he had never dreamed that was the way his daughters saw him.

Penny's hand was on his arm. "Don't pay her any mind, Phil," she said softly, understanding his desolation.

Outside, a siren was coming closer. Minutes later, a man in a white jacket was in the crowded room. He nodded knowingly as the policeman whispered to him. Selma gave the newcomer a bold look. "Fuck you, you mother! I'm not going into any ambulance for you to ream!"

Reynolds tried not to hear his daughter's vulgarity but it hit at his head like a hatchet.

As the man in white grasped her arm, Selma turned with a venomous look at Reynolds. "That was sure a neat fuck you gave Ted Watson, Daddy, wasn't it?"

"Come on, now," the policeman said.

As they approached the door, Selma cried to Penny, "Help! They're gonna do me, Penny. Up my back and up my front at the same time!"

Reynolds had to turn away. Was Selma raving, or did she know what she was saying?

Penny tried to embrace the girl. "Please, baby. *Don't!*" She was weeping too.

Reynolds hurried to follow Selma as the attendant drew her outside. At the door, he turned to Penny and said across the room, "Thanks for your help. I'll call you and let you know."

With a cry, Penny was at his side, tears running unchecked down her cheeks. "I'm coming with you! Did you think I wasn't coming with you?"

The waiting ambulance had attracted a crowd. As Selma was brought along, the people ogled the procession avidly.

"What happened?"

"Man tried to rape the girl!"

"Yeah, I heard her screaming for help."

"Ought to cut yer balls off!" a man fumed at Reynolds.

"Motherfucker!" a woman yelled at him.

Passing them, Reynolds thought how people love disasters. It's not curiosity in their burning eyes, it's victory. They are *gloating* that it isn't happening to *them*. They are looking not at TV or a movie, but at reality, into the piercing eyes of Fate, and it is passing them by. So they can enjoy their *Schadenfreude,* their plastic eyes straining like vulture beaks for blood. At least, thought Reynolds, vultures had the decency to wait until death. God, he sometimes loathed the celebrated Pee-uple!

But the only thing that mattered to Reynolds was Selma in the siren-speeding ambulance ahead of the police car in which he and Penny were riding. His head began to race. As soon as he spoke to a doctor, he would have to call Helena in Georgia. And check Dr. Kohn, and Duncan, about the next step after the ambulance got to—ROOSEVELT HOSPITAL, the lettering said. The policeman informed him that cases like Selma's were usually transferred to Bellevue. It would be up to the doctor in the emergency room.

Reynolds recoiled. *Bellevue!* It conjured a fearsome image of dismal green halls, griminess and unspeakable madness behind shadowed bars. This didn't happen to people like them! That could not possibly be his daughter, Selma Weslie Reynolds, on the way to Bellevue! But it was.

The wailing siren sounded like Reynolds' own guilt flaring. He berated himself that what was happening was his fault, part of a punishment he deserved. His contriteness was a physical agony. His veins felt on fire, his bones were cooking in his flesh, he could hardly breathe. He was a blind man in an earthquake with buildings crashing all around. He suffocated in a tidal wave sweeping him to oblivion. Reynolds moaned to himself. If this was guilt and remorse, no wonder he had spent his life trying to flee his conscience.

He realized that something inside was fumbling for his Off-Switch, and he knocked it aside with a spurt of self-hatred. Let this *hurt,* dammit! For once let him face real pain, let this be his baptism of fire. Maybe something good would yet be born out of the convulsions and turmoil of his life. The siren wailed. *Welcome, welcome, this hard-won, precious torment!* Reynolds did not even want the comfort Penny was offering with the pressure of her fingers twined in his. Only let Selma be all right, he pleaded with God.

Reynolds was grateful that Penny was with him while Selma was being examined. It was true that just the presence of another human being helped you bear up.

The doctor's report was that Selma was severely disoriented. Diagnosis was acute drug psychosis, at the least. She would have to go to Bellevue. No, it wasn't possible for Reynolds to have custody with a private physician, not at this stage. He might be able to arrange that at Bellevue later.

The brisk woman doctor, glancing over her shoulder at the line waiting outside her office, said impatiently that this was the best procedure for both the patient and the parents.

"Parents." Reynolds glanced at Penny. She turned away from his eyes.

By now it was past six in the morning. Outside, in the fresh light and gentle breeze of early June, Penny looked with sympathy at Reynolds, worn and unshaven. "Let's get a cup of coffee."

Reynolds hardly heard Penny. His mind was still with Selma, seeing his daughter as she had walked crookedly down the long hospital corridor, leaning against a nurse, with Penny's robe dragging the floor. No prom-queen train, this. Selma broke his heart, looking like a papier-mâché moppet that could be crumpled like waste sheets. Down the hallway she seemed to grow smaller with each step, like a forlorn Alice in Wonderland until she might disappear entirely. His sunny daughter, Reynolds lamented. He straightened as the attendant took her around a corner and out of sight. His task and purpose now was to keep Selma from disappearing. He would do whatever it took to bring her back.

Reynolds heard himself saying to Penny on the sidewalk, "I've got to call Dr. Kohn. He'll know how to get Selly out."

"It's too early," Penny reminded him.

"I'll call his service," Reynolds said doggedly.

Penny's response came with strength. "Mightn't it be better to hold off your big guns, Phil? I mean, let Selma see what it means to be in a place like Bellevue without an influential father rushing to help her."

Reynolds gave her a wry smile. She sounded like Dr. Kohn. And, like him, she was right. He had slid back into his old bag—his ship was rolling, call out the Coast Guard!

Yes, the wind was howling; waves were washing over the decks, it was the worst of all the storms of his life, but these days he knew what he expected of himself. Up on the bridge, in control, not running like a child yelling for his father. *He* was the father.

They sat in a back booth in a just-opened luncheonette. Looking across the plastic table at Penny, all Reynolds could see was Selma's vacant stare. Guilt punched him again, and he had a hard need to drill to the core of it, get it clarified.

"I see how it happens," he said, more to himself than to Penny. "Kids of my generation were brought up with our wings clipped by our parents, school, religion, rules, laws, obedience. We swore that when we had kids we wouldn't cripple them the same way. What did we do instead?"

Reynolds paused, thinking how to say it, and went on in a voice abrasive with self-accusation as Penny listened intently. "We knew better than to clip their wings. *We* took our little birds up to the highest cliffs, in the midst of the worst, lashing storms in human history, and we tossed them free!

" 'Fly!' we encouraged them. 'Fly, dear, free, unbound children!' And we felt so righteous and noble, so forward looking and Utopian! 'Make your own decisions!' we urged them, 'choose your own directions, be your own free spirits!'

"That's what we *enlightened* parents did to our babies when crazy hurricanes were knocking eagles out of the sky! When our children most needed our guidance, our protection, our boundaries, we left them naked and exposed to every danger in the name of 'Permissiveness!' I swear to you, Penny, that is the filthiest word I know! We sacrificed our kids in the infamous name of Permissiveness!"

Reynolds stopped, ashen at the searing truth he experienced. "Is it any wonder so many of them fall? Where should we expect to find them if not at the bottom of the cliff, battered and crushed?" He went on, almost in tears. "We didn't clip Selly's wings, ah, no. *We* made her risk breaking every bone in her young body!"

Penny had been listening with her old absorption, her eyes warm and caring on his face. She said now, "Selma's not broken, Phil. She went off the road, but she's not really hurt, I'm sure."

"I hope to God you're right," Reynolds said. "Thank God she had you to come to."

He did not have Penny to come to, Reynolds reminded himself. It did not matter what old feelings were fluttering inside.

It was a relief when the waitress came with their order.

As they ate, a resolve formed in Reynolds. There was one thing, at least, he wanted to try to set straight. He needed to complete it for peace of mind for the rest of his life. It had been another hovering shadow that, he realized now, had never let him rest. He did not know if or when he would ever see Penny again. There was no way to do it except to do it, no matter how difficult, how ripping, or how perilous.

Reynolds started slowly: "Penny, I must talk to you about the telephone call. I can't take it back, but—"

Penny slashed him silent across the table with a fury that appalled him. Her outrage had never lessened, it was plain in her twisted face.

She hissed, "How a man like you could do a thing like that!" Her never-forgotten disgust and bewilderment brought tears to her reddened eyes. "I nearly did go to the police that night, you ought to know!"

Mournfully, Reynolds remembered Dr. Kohn once saying that he would have been lucky if he had actually been arrested early on. He might have sought help sooner.

But he spoke to Penny matter-of-factly, not asking for sympathy. "I put *myself* in jail, Penny, and I've been serving my sentence." He was not going to add that he was being tougher on himself than a judge might have been.

"You always did have an answer for everything." Penny's heart had gone out to Reynolds in his sorrow over Selma, but that was a different man from the one he was talking about now.

"I understand how you feel," Reynolds went on, "but even worse criminals get parole after a while."

Penny kept her distance from the small smile he tried. "I still can't believe it was you!"

Reynolds said, in a final tone, "Penny, it's the human condition that's obscene, not me!" Dr. Kohn would understand; he did not expect Penny to. But it had to be said. Not as apology or excuse, but as his own acceptance of himself, his place in things—he, Philip Reynolds, good, bad, and indifferent, in a good, bad, and indifferent world he had not made. Penny would never know how long it had taken him to reach that answer, and he wasn't going to plead the harrowing pain of the effort.

Penny's fingers clenched into small fists on the table. "Saying you're not responsible, that's even more disgusting."

Reynolds was tempted to give up, but his self-knowledge was too secure now. He was able to say, still quiet and assured, "You said it—I was a different man then, literally someone else. That's what should count between the two of us."

Penny's attitude did not alter. She could not meet his eyes as he went on firmly, "I don't make obscene calls anymore, but I don't pretend I never made them. Some day you may understand what I said about the human condition."

Penny shook her head stubbornly. "Not that awful."

Reynolds tried once more. "People say what's done is done. That's not true. The past can be changed."

"Nobody can change the past."

Reynolds said, so softly Penny could hardly hear him, "By forgiveness."

There was a silence. Penny met his eyes finally. Her voice dropped. "It was so much worse *because* I loved you. I respected you more than anyone in the world. You knew that."

There was another pause. Reynolds said, "That's what we can both remember, then."

Her eyes stayed on his. "Is that what you meant by parole?"

"At this time I suppose it's all I can mean, isn't it?" he answered, the question addressed to himself as much as to Penny.

She rose at that, saying, "I'm sorry, Phil, I forgot you don't know that I'm engaged to be married."

Reynolds was beyond surprise. He was too bone-tired to get up as quickly as he would have liked. "Congratulations." He came to his feet finally and shook her hand, impersonally, as he might a client's. "Do I know him?"

Penny's eyes dropped again. "I don't know." This wasn't the time to say it was one of her agency's senior partners.

Reynolds let it go. He had no right to the jealousy that was stirring inside. Their lives were irrevocably on separate tracks, he told himself again. He tried to smile in a friend-of-the-family way, but his face was frozen.

It was clearer than ever to Reynolds that life provides its answers to its questions in its own time in its own way. He had done everything open to him to do. If there ever could have been or should have been more with Penny, the chance was gone. It is only when you look back that you learn your destiny.

They left the luncheonette. Penny said she would walk home to dress for the office, and Reynolds went to the curb for a cab. As he left her, Penny pretended she had a cinder in her eye. From the moment Selma had stumbled in the night before, Penny had been unstrung by the prospect of seeing Philip Reynolds again. Her boat was sailing a new course, and she didn't need old tides making waves. She felt she had been right to let him know her anger and disgust, as it would be wrong to let him see these tears of regret now. Anyway, Penny told herself as she watched Reynolds' broad back (broader and stronger-looking than she remembered?), she wasn't really sure what they had had. Maybe she had confused glamour with love originally, and was confusing sympathy with love now.

Maybe, Penny thought, it was too bad she wasn't just a naïve Brooklyn kid anymore. Maybe she had grown callous. She didn't believe so, she viewed herself as realistic. Philip Reynolds was too much for her to tackle. She would be forever grateful to him—for their time together, for his generous teaching, for the career he had helped her start, for helping her become the kind of woman who could attract her prominent husband-to-be. Maybe in her heart she would always feel the new, unbidden sting of loss she knew as Reynolds waved their final good-bye from his taxi.

Penny took her handkerchief quickly from her eye, and told herself sternly that you are grown up when you realize that your compromises are all you have to live with.

On Monday morning, Reynolds would tell Dr. Kohn that his experience with Penny was a lesson in how a relationship could be stretched too far. Like a rubber band, it then breaks or loses its resilience. There had been no way to resume; there could not be any new, suddenly flowering world. Hope should never have sent its flat stone skipping across the too-wide river between them.

Meantime, all that counted was to get Selma back on the track. That would take Helena and him working together. And Midge and Dorothy would need them both more now, together.

Reynolds told the taxi driver his destination. The words were cactus thorns in his mouth: "Bellevue, please—the psychiatric ward." He supposed the man knew where that Stygian entrance was.

The driver touched his cap and said respectfully, "Yes, doctor."

29

Helena Reynolds spent no time on recriminations or lamentations. Nor did she recoil from the grim scene at Bellevue. Calamity had struck their family, they would do everything possible to remedy it. Along with Reynolds, she was glad no new complications of their own stood in the way. No Georgia complications, either; Gordon was better.

Dr. Kohn spent time with Selma at Bellevue. He knew and recommended a sanitarium for her, not far from their town. Helena and Reynolds could visit easily, and Dr. Kohn would be able to check Selma's progress with doctors he knew there. It was a fortunate setup all around.

At the end of a week, Dr. Kohn told Reynolds that the prognosis was promising. The girl's psychotic behavior was transitory, drug-induced. In a way, the experience had been salutory. Selma had been experimenting with heavy stuff for the first time that night, and had seen for herself how dope could shatter her. In her stay at Bellevue, sobering up, she was learning what no admonitions could teach. All around her she saw that dope wasn't smart-ass and euphoria—it was horror, and panic, and self-destruction. Selma told Dr. Kohn her head felt three feet off her shoulders, felt split apart and stuffed with cotton—later she told Reynolds and Helena that she hadn't been able to think. Her brain had been filled with black bubbles that burst into poison gas. If that's what blowing your mind was, the cool cats could have it; her mind hadn't been expanded, it had been raped, she wept to her parents, and she was God-thank happy to have a mother and father who understood and were trying to help her get her pieces together again.

To herself, Selma vowed that she would never forget the sights and sounds and smells of the wreckage she had lived with during the nightmare week before Dr. Kohn approved her transfer out of Bellevue.

Reynolds remained wary of a con job, but it was Helena now who believed their daughter's sincerity. Dr. Kohn was on Helena's side. Selma, he said, had been profoundly shaken. He doubted they would have anything of this kind to worry about from her again.

Helena Reynolds liked Dr. Kohn immediately, and was impressed by him. At Bellevue, he was a pillar of strength and encouragement. She saw how the hospital staff greeted him with deference, even awe. Clearly, Dr. Kohn was one of the greats of his profession, as Duncan Talbott had promised her.

When Helena visited Dr. Kohn at his suggestion, she found it easier than she had thought to answer the personal questions he asked about herself and Selma. She sat in a chair, but was extremely conscious of the gray leather couch. There was a real couch, she almost gasped to herself. That was where Phil lay down when he came to his sessions. There was sudden new meaning for her in Talbott's saying that Phil was in a kind of surgical procedure. There before her was the "operating table" on which her husband went under the scalpel several times a week. Phil had been too proud to bid for her sympathy, but it was movingly clear to her now that these walls had heard him cry out as she had not. That towel on that couch had been wet with tears she had never seen.

Above all, from Dr. Kohn himself, Helena received a powerful, concentrated sense of purpose. This doctor with the grave, chiseled countenance—and the disconcertingly merry eyes when he smiled at her—could not be fooled or trifled with. He would not spend a minute with anyone, she saw, unless honest, genuine work was being done, work that Duncan Talbott said required an "inward heroism" they should all respect. The words had stayed in her mind. The phrase, she realized in this office, might not be an exaggeration.

Until now, for Helena, Philip Reynolds' psychoanalysis had been basically a vague and distant undertone of their lives. All at once, it was concrete and immediate, and she was stirred in a new way. They had turned to Dr. Kohn to salvage their daughter, Helena thought; it might turn out to cement their new marriage as well.

By mid-July, all the physicians agreed there was no reason why Selma should not resume her normal life at home. Dr. Kohn wanted one last interview, and Helena brought Selma down to the city from the sanitarium. They were to meet Reynolds at his new office for a celebration dinner in town.

When the phone rang, Reynolds picked it up on the first ring, thinking it would be Helena from Dr. Kohn's office. But the receptionist said, puzzlingly, "A Mr. Soloveitchik to see you. He has no appointment, says it's personal."

"I don't know anybody by that name."

"He says, *Barney* Soloveitchik—"

When the door opened, Reynolds was amazed. A smiling young man stood clean-shaven, in a dark suit with a buttondown blue shirt and a modestly striped tie. He could be an applicant for a male model—good-looking, athletic, an appealing mouth. All had been hidden under the scruffy beard at the Center.

The young man smiled at Reynolds' open astonishment. "Hell," Barney said self-consciously, "this costume is just as quirky as the other one, so what?"

"I didn't know your name was Soloveitchik."

"We never got that intimate."

Reynolds laughed. He had liked this person from the start. He came on strong, but it was less an offensive impudence than an attractive chutzpa.

Barney was explaining, "I was in the city and thought you might like a visit, fill you in on our mutual friends."

For a moment, Reynolds tensed. This could be the not-unanticipated blackmail.

But the young man was talking about something quite different. "Mary's fine. So is Terry. They've split to a commune in Oregon somewhere. Those two cunts haven't got their shit together yet."

The clothes had changed, Reynolds observed, but not the vocabulary.

"Actually, Mary split because her father was trying to lay a college trip on her." (So she had a father, alive and fatherly!) "I don't blame her, you know. What's the big deal about college?"

Reynolds asked, "How far did you go?"

"You know who are the real drop-puts?" Barney challenged. "All those infants taking their endless masters' and doctors' sucking on Universititty!"

Reynolds gave an appreciative smile.

"Actually, that's why I'm here. I thought you might be able to help me get a job."

Reynolds said honestly, "I'd like to help, but as you see, I'm working alone these days." He sensed that the visit had not been easy, and he could see defensiveness rise in Barney's face at once."

"I knew it was a crock of shit. Okay."

"Sit down and let's see if we can put anything together." This young man was obviously trying to develop a new agenda, as Dr. Frank would put it. If fellow voyagers didn't help each other, who could be expected to? "I know where you're coming from, Barney, and I may have some friends who can use you, if you're willing to—"

Before Reynolds could finish, the door opened. It was Helena with Selma. The girl seemed fresh as a summer flower. She ran to Reynolds at once and hugged him happily. "I'm sprung! I *love* your Dr. Kohn!"

Reynolds reached for Helena's hand. Her smile was careworn but contented. She said, "Congratulations to all of us."

Barney moved to the door politely, and asked brightly, "Somebody's birthday? Don't let me interrupt." He lifted a palm outward to them. "I'll try you again, Phil."

Nodding his assent, Reynolds caught Barney's admiring glance at Selma. He smiled to himself. More consequences? He knew by now in what devious ways Destiny unwound its inscrutable skein.

Selma smiled as she watched the door close behind the man. "You know," she said, "that fellow would be dynamite if he grew a beard."

In his dream that night, Reynolds was driving down the Las Vegas Strip. The neon signs, garish in every glaring color, began to melt. They drip onto his head, becoming Medusan snakes. He eyes himself terrified in the car mirror, and doesn't see the child run into the road. Sickeningly, he strikes the girl.

Reynolds runs to the bloody form in the road. It is a kid, about six. Her clothes are torn off by the accident. She has a deep, reaching wound from between her pips down to her hairless angel-hole. Reynolds tries to heal her by putting his spit on the wound. The girl is thankful. She unzips his pants and wants to kiss him there to show her gratitude. He shrieks that she mustn't—he doesn't have a penis, but a zillion-volt electric eel, powerful enough to electrocute a dinosaur, burn down a city.

The girl is too young to understand. She wants it, she weeps, and grabs him there. She fries immediately to a sputtering death.

Reynolds spurns a lawyer, he will plead his own case, he knows he is innocent. The prosecutor is relentless, "Did there come a time when did you or did you not lift your eyes from the road, where it was your duty!"

The jury as one man points fingerless stumps at Reynolds: "We find the defendant guilty as not charged. Sentenced to death and no parole forever!"

Jouncing to the guillotine in a crimson tumbrel, Reynolds waves to the festive crowd. "Yes, I deserve this! It is a far worse thing that I do today than I have ever done!" When his head rolls off, the dead girl comes over to kick it into a wicker basket his Jewish grandmother had used for her knitting. There is an inscription on the lid: "TITTLE LILIET, How Can You Rest in Peace After All the Harm You Have Done to Me?" The head inside answers in squeaking tones, "Ask not what you can do for your country, but what your cuntry can do for you!"

When he awoke, without understanding the dream, Reynolds somehow had a sense of comfort and healing, as if something had been resolved. He would have to figure that out with Dr. Kohn.

There was a real, overt healing at home. With Selma restored, Helena found she was ready to follow Talbott's advice about her scar. The shared ordeal over Selma had brought her closer to Reynolds than she had thought would ever be possible again. It was more than their rediscovery of each other in bed. It was a flowering of mature affection and respect that brought new understanding and tolerance. Helena no longer wanted the badge of righteousness. The simple cosmetic operation had been performed and, as Talbott promised, there was no mark or sign on her cheek.

Reynolds understood, and was grateful. It increased his determination never to backslide. It was a sign of support from which he drew fresh strength for his continuing work with Dr. Kohn.

At the end of July, Helena had another call from Georgia. Her brother had suffered a relapse after his recovery from the first heart attack. He wasn't bad, but one never knew, Helena's sister sobbed. Reynolds agreed with Helena that it would be right to take the girls.

They were family, after all, and they enjoyed their rare visits to "the ol' plantation."

Reynolds welcomed the chance to be by himself. Selma's crisis had knit him to Helena, but the meeting with Penny had unsettled him more than he had wanted to admit. In the last session before Dr. Kohn's August break, Reynolds said from the couch that he needed to deal with his "leftover emotions" or else his "remarriage" to Helena would be a cheating on both of them.

Dr. Kohn observed silently that Reynolds' reaction was predictable. In this phase of a deep analysis, a patient's pendulum often swung from license to overrighteousness.

Feeling new health, Reynolds decided to press Dr. Kohn again. "When you get back in September—I thought we might drop to one session a week. What do you think? It's over three years."

"I think it's premature."

Reynolds protested, "Even the homo business didn't amount to any-thing. I hardly drink now. Even the crisis with Selma didn't throw me."

"I never said you couldn't handle crises. Characteristically, you do that extraordinarily well. But I believe you still have a lot of material to work through, including your impatience to finish."

"That's a hell of a Catch-22! I feel good enough to get off the couch, so that means I mustn't!"

"Phil," Dr. Kohn sighed, "when you are ready to leave, I will be happier than you. Believe me."

With the family away and Dr. Kohn gone, Reynolds felt a heavy sense of responsibility rather than freedom. It was a test, almost as if the doctor had planned it. Well, he would show them that he was fit. His new acceptance of himself was working two ways, Reynolds observed. "B.A."—"Before Analysis," as he and Helena had come to talk of it—he had glorified himself to compensate for inferiority feelings. "A.A."—"After Analysis"—he could accept himself without either derogation or exaggeration, at least not worse than anyone else. Dr. Kohn had said it once: "Every human being sometimes faces temptations too powerful to resist. Any person who excepts himself is either lying or dead."

A hearty laugh from the desk surprised Reynolds as Dr. Kohn added: "The greatest assurance of temperance is declining hormones. It's a wisecrack I read somewhere, but it's God's truth."

A call from his new client in Chicago was a welcome change of pace for Reynolds. They wanted him to fly out for a meeting before they launched the campaign he had created for them. It had tested promisingly, and the brass were excited about it.

In the plane, Reynolds recognized Chicago two hundred miles away, hanging in the sky. Its map stretched above the earth, made of the city's spew and phlegm. Reynolds turned from the pollution. That should be his next step, he thought—get into more *pro bono publico* causes. He could do some good. Dr. Kohn had been urging him to start "looking away from his belly button" to larger goals. Good-o, as Mary Humphrey would have said.

The stewardess was reaching up to a nearby compartment. Her short skirt lifted high on her silken thighs. The curve of her buttocks was inviting to Reynolds. He had to resist his impulse to reach and touch the soft body. He a *homo?* Dr. Kohn could strike that off his fever chart once and for all! He was performing with Helena like a stud and, as this girl was proving right now, there wasn't anything wrong with his hormones yet either.

Reynolds saw that the girl had become aware of his staring, and did not seem to mind. He had never asked a stewardess ("flight attendant" this generation) for a date. Might he succeed with this charmer, or would he be rebuffed? Was the rumor true that you became an "Eagle" if you made out with one of them in the lavatory?

Okay to fantasy it, but no touch!

Reynolds hadn't discussed it with Dr. Kohn, but his new conviction was fully formed. It wasn't a question of being faithful to Helena. It was a matter of being faithful to himself, for the same reasons he was refusing the drink the girl was offering again.

New thoughts kept revolving in Reynolds' mind. It was clear to him that all forms of self-indulgence had to disappoint, because the body is finite. (No such thing as "unendurable pleasure indefinitely prolonged.") Making notes on the plane, Reynolds' logic ran: "There is only so much a man can eat, drink, screw, before *satiation.* And satiation is the ultimate frustration. So if a man's only bag is satisfying his body, there's nothing left but dying or going crazy."

Looking out at the Chicago sky again, Reynolds recalled a line of Diogenes. "The gods gave man an easy life to start with, but men spoiled it by seeking luxuries and pleasures."

Another window opened in Reynolds' head. For a man to live beyond his psychological means is to court emotional bankruptcy. Life's payout then is only a small share of what it could have been. The tragedy of neurotics like himself, Reynolds saw, was the ghastly waste of so many years! A healthy man is a rich river nourishing all around him to a green bountifulness. A neurotic's river goes underground, leaving a desert above. Psychoanalysis can help the river resurface, but what has been desolated is lost forever.

Reynolds wrote down: "It isn't true that 'all's well that ends well.' Too many people have to go through too much hell to get there! And for many there never is an end!"

A poem seemed to be forming out of these circling thoughts. Reynolds took his pencil out again. "It comes to this/ that man lives in his body the way a fish lives in water./ A fish/ can hide under a rock/ but it can't stop being a fish./ A man/ can't escape the sun/ by standing in his own shade."

Reynolds read it over and liked it. At the risk of bringing the Muses down on his head, he had come to suspect that advertising and poetry were less alien undertakings than might seem. One sold products, the other, feelings. One loosened purse strings, the other, hearts. They possessed in common the severe use of words to reach people. One celebrated ceremonies of commerce, the other ceremonies of spirit, but both required high priests trained in the rites of moving other minds.

The afternoon in the cloud-high offices on Michigan Boulevard was a triumph. The president of the company wanted him to take on all their new product launches. Astronomical sums were named. Reynolds put them off—too many commitments, for the present anyway. It would sound puerile to these go-getters to say that he preferred to save time for his poetry. There was a cocktail party at which they kept twisting his arm, and he finally took white wine. There was more drinking, and wine at dinner, and brandy after, with Reynolds growing a little foggy, wanting more to drink, but leaving for his hotel determined not to fall too far off the wagon.

But in his room, he was glad there was liquor on a table with their card. He needed a nightcap to simmer down.

Bladder pressure brought Reynolds awake. It was only eleven o'clock. He had forgotten how fuzzy alcohol made his head feel. It wasn't unpleasant. He swayed toward the bathroom half enjoying the sense of sleepwalking. As he relieved himself, he kept up a rambling private conversation. No need to chastise himself. Had a right to celebrate, a good job well done. (Loud laugh.) Those turkeys would piss if he told them why he was turning down all those bucks! Speak of celebrating, he ought to check when Penny's wedding, send telegram, gift. Didn't want her to think him hangdog, and she was Selly's good friend—and his! Why not? Had meant a lot to each other.

Coming out of the bathroom, Reynolds tried to get sober. Had to stop thinking about Penny. Finito! Wonderful while it lasted, gift of the gods and all that, life poorer without his having known her, but think about Helena. That's where it was at. Still lovely Helena.

Thing to do is get away. Distance. Perspective. Right. Go, say, to Greece. Good notion! The Peloponnese—Olympus, Delphi, the roots of it all. Not too late for them yet to taste together the waters of the Castalian spring, source of poetry, inspiration of the Muses. His stuff getting better every day, would write more.

Reynolds sat on the bed naked and reached for the phone. Call Helena pronto, start arrangements. It was a certainty to his alcohol-fevered mind that if he delayed now the trip would never take place, and suddenly it was the most important undertaking in his life.

In Greece he would court Helena again, woo her and really win her back. Reynolds reveled in his vision: Helena *was* Penelope—what better place to claim her fully than the Greece to which he, the victor, Ulysses, was returning from his arduous journey in search of himself after slaying all the cunning beasts that had imperiled the passages of his life? (Cunninglinguis beasts?!)

In a sweeping illumination it came to Reynolds that Homer's poem was a great allegory of psychoanalysis! It celebrated Every Man battling for his soul against unimaginably terrible enemies! *Every* man confronted lotus-eaters cajoling with false promises of eternal bliss. *Every* man contended with a murderous Cyclops, the blinded giant of his own unconscious. *Every* man's ears were pierced by Circe-song—she whose evil-sweet seduction of drugs, drink, sex, and self-love transformed men into swine. All, all the enemies in Every Man's mirror!

Wait until Dr. Kohn heard *this* insight! *How had Freud and the others never discerned this brilliant truth?*

Reynolds' drunken hand sought a pencil and paper to write down the revelation. His groping fingers touched the telephone. Great idea! Call Georgia, tell Helena! Right! It's what he had started to do in the first place.

The dial clicked quickly. When Reynolds heard the strange woman's voice, he dropped the instrument in a spurt of horror. He leaped off the bed and went to the table for a glass of soda. Dropping ice in the glass he asked himself what the *hell* had broken through his new armor. Impossible! Drunk or not, the telephone was a serpent he had slain!

Hadn't he? From what murky cavern was the stinking harpy stirring now?

What he needed was another nightcap to help him sleep, Reynolds decided. Sleep now, call Helena in the morning. He wouldn't want her to hear his slurring voice anyway. She would think he was more intoxicated than he was.

Reynolds swallowed the drink in one gulp. The old friend didn't disappoint, was seeping through him with the lulling satisfaction he hadn't felt for too long. The sensation was like being stroked inside the body.

Reynolds rested contentedly on his bed. Earlier it had bothered him to be by himself, now it was a blessing. He was alone not only in the hotel room but in the clouds outside, the sky over the Lake, the stretching world seen from the stratosphere, the planets, all space beyond all galaxies. Karma? He began to doze, and a fantasy formed. He accepted it idly as a dream in which he could indulge himself with innocence. Why not? Floating safely within his own space, drifting back to earth, his fantasy could hurt no one. With languid anticipation, Reynolds submitted to the gathering memory of how the lurid calls had once excited him.

In his imagination he was starting, in the subdued foreign accent he always had assumed, "Is Suzie there, please?"

"You must have the wrong number. I'm sorry."

He imagined his disarming laugh that so often kept them on the line. "Come along, Suzie, honey, don't try to kid me. I know your voice when I hear it."

"No, really, you have the wrong number." This one would not hang up; he was writing the scenario, he smiled to himself.

He made his voice low and winning, edging into it. "Oh, you sure were the right number last night, baby." Following quickly with the testing—"Remember when I opened my pants and took it out, honey? Oh, you got him so big and fat he was sticking out like a baseball bat . . ."

Time to wait a moment. Sometimes there was a shocked, "You degenerate pervert!" and a slammed receiver. But sometimes there was a low catching of breath at the other end. (The pure, innocent, angel-haloed ladies were not always unintrigued!)

Now Reynolds anticipated the woman's next reaction—fear. She would hang up swiftly if she believed he was someone who might know her. So he would say at once, "Listen, if you're not Suzie, I got a wrong number, honey, and I don't know who you are, but just the sound of your voice got me so hot, I got it in my hand now, honey, ah, I wish you could see what I got in my hand, how big you got it!" Work on their imagination . . .

The hook was in deep if she didn't hang up then, she was ready to accept that they were both cozy-safe in a soft bed of anonymity. "Ah, my dick is so big and smooth, he feels so good, I wish you could have your hand on him, honey." Sometimes this brought a deep sigh, and he would be sure the woman was imagining him with his pants open, his sex out large and flushed in its secret erection. Sometimes—and it was bliss!—he would hear the female voice say, "I know, honey—"

He invited her to merge her fantasy with his by pretending he still believed her to be someone else. "Ah, Suzie, remember when I put my hand up your skirt and you had nothing on?"

"Mmmm?" Curiosity now.

"How I put my finger on your spot, how good it felt? Oh, you were so wet and sweet I had to go down on you." (Curiously, some didn't know what that meant! He spelled it out. If they were listening this far, they wanted to know.) "Remember how you spread your legs and my tongue was kissing you up your thighs right up into your slit?"

Sometimes there would be a self-conscious titter and something like, "Hey, mister, you're nuts!"

He always took this as a sign she was reacting physically now, getting juicy between her legs, imagining his huge erection, feeling his tongue on her clitoris. He could see the faceless woman moist with hot desire. He went faster. "How I sucked your sweet pussy-pussy. Oh, how I love to suck your sweet pussy-pussy." His hand was pumping harder as he asked, "You touching your sweet spot, honey?" He importuned, "Touch it now, baby! Oh, I'm pullin' off so sweet. Oh, watch me jerkin' off and you do it too, baby!" He would bring the phone closer to his mouth so she could hear him panting more urgently as his climax approached. "Oh! Oh!" the gasping for life itself. "I'm starting, honey! Oh, pull me off, honey! Oh, *do* it, baby! You doin' it, baby?"

"Uh-*huh!* Yeah, sweetie!" In his fantasy, the sound of her panting would tell him she was with him.

"Oh, baby!"

"Pull that big cock, sweetie!" Sometimes they did say things like that, those spun-sugar, God-haloed females. "More! More!"

"Yeah!"

"*Jerk* him off for me!" one woman had cried into the phone, she a favorite of mothers and fathers, she-cherub made of angel smiles, sugar and spice and everything nice . . .

When their orgasms were close they could hardly speak.

"Oh, I wish I was in you, babe!"

"Ah, fuck me, honey! Gimme that baseball bat right up my throat!" One voice had choked with jungle heat, ripe and open for his vocal rape.

Without restraint, a shout: "Now, darling! Now, love! NOW!"

"Darling!"

"Love!"

How many strange things there truly are, Reynolds wondered, remembering. For the spontaneous cries *were* endearments. The telephone wires made a net not just of a strange lust, but a bond for unknowns reaching across an empty carnality to each other in a mockery of love, but a live, flowing current!

Degraded? Sick? Leave that to Dr. Kohn! The *feeling* was as pure as it was taboo! Reynolds had argued on the couch that something real did move between the two strangers, that the eruption of anonymous sex was accompanied by a genuine, if deranged, passion. It was not false, he emphasized to Dr. Kohn. He had felt—and heard back—affection, yes, love. It could not be love for *him*, who was unknown. It *could* be a desperate need for love held in a secret vessel that his call pierced. So, in the partnered fantasy, there was created a world of its own, self-contained, in which strangers could share hallucinated desire. Reynolds had told Dr. Kohn that, with the few women who stayed on the line, he always felt a desperate reaching that matched his own compulsion.

Dr. Kohn had responded sternly that it was all a distortion out of his own unbalanced psyche. Reynolds had not bothered to reply. In this, anyway, the doctor was unknowing. The telephone emotions were morbid, yes, but unreal, no!

Imagining the episode so vividly had engorged Reynolds. He lurched to the bathroom and splashed cold water over his face, beginning to sober. This kind of fantasy he didn't need, he rebuked himself as his head cleared a little.

What he did need, he lectured himself, was to remember that his telephoning was a cancer in his soul. Nothing mitigated the sordidness and the damage to himself and the others, especially if he chanced on a young girl unable to handle such a heavy sexual confrontation. He must remember that he could do lasting harm. Neither one was left unscathed.

Coming out of the bathroom, his erection still large, Reynolds could not take his eyes from the phone. It suddenly seemed to fill the room. It whispered audibly. "Why not? *One last time!* Safe here in Chicago!"

Reynolds tried to turn. He recognized that, despite himself, the temptress did not intend to let him pass without a struggle. The whiskey was on the cozener's side. It transformed the phone into a woman in a transparent black negligee, legs open, beckoning to him. Long, red-painted fingertips were playing over her Venus mound. She twisted and sighed with pleasure, inviting him to share.

Circe! Circe! Reynolds cursed to himself. He tried to stifle the blandishments of his lopsided brain, seducing him with the old irresponsible refrain: "Only live once, why not?" And, "They can hang up if they don't want it, can't they? If they want it, it's consent, isn't it?" The drunken logic was irresistible, did not appear specious at this distance from the couch.

Reynolds' eyes turned up in an ungovernable seizure. He grabbed at the phone. It was a boozy exultation to unleash himself after the long abstinence. With a grunt of abandon, Reynolds jettisoned the safety belts he and Dr. Kohn had buckled around Ikey. As he dialed randomly, Reynolds had an image of a barefoot goat boy reveling around the room. He always pictured his unconscious as barefoot. He let out a rasping laugh. There was his Id-Ikey hopping jubilantly like a horny goat unfettered, though he believed he had it chained away! The rank rut-stink was divine in his nose again, an arousing ordure that hardened the erection he carried.

Let Dr. Kohn's house of cards tumble! Freud should be spelled *Fraud!* The years on the couch were a brainwashing lie! Like all *honest* men, he, Reynolds, was a beast, putrid, untamed, unholy! Yes, Baal! No more pretense! He was not going to cheat himself of his pleasure for the hypocritical morality of a world whose headlines of terror, foulness, decay, rip-offs, venality, and inhumanity he could never begin to match!

If Dr. Aloysius Kohn were here watching him, he would invite him to listen! Let all the sanctimonious listen with their psychiatric stethoscopes to the sound of the human heart where it really beats—in the jungle beyond right and wrong, in the ceremonies of the slaughterhouse, beyond good and evil! *Heil,* Nietzsche!

A man lives where he *needs,* where his bones and teeth take him, where his belly and balls go first, dragging his soul after like the baggage it is! The human beast is its own truth, salacious, venereous, reveling in its stench—not slouching to any Bethlehem *or* Gethsemane to be born, but stalking the world in its (God-created, let us not forget!) iniquity!

Staring at the phone in his trembling hand, Reynolds laughed to himself. Compared to, say, the beasts in human form at Auschwitz (many of whom still walked free, respected, and comfortable), how innocent was this tiny eccentricity he was about to indulge!

Confounded with unaccustomed drink, Reynolds finally completed a telephone number. It might be a man, it might be an outraged old lady, it might be a— He swallowed in his anticipation. His left hand started downward in the compulsive pattern. The waiting itself was part of the infernal ravishment. Best if it was a girl, maybe baby-sitting, maybe 14-

15. (It did not occur to Reynolds to think of his daughters, they existed in another universe.)

"Hello?" Reynolds' head snapped up with joy. *Jackpot!* He had reached a fresh, young voice. After so long, it would be now!

The girl was formal. "Who is this, please?"

Perfect! Young enough to be curious and enticed, old enough to catch every nuance when she realized what was happening. Reynolds sensed that she was alone, it was a kind of ESP.

He began in his muffled voice. "Hello. Suzie?" Ah, Christ, how much he had wanted this! How right it was. Every nerve and cell in his body was inflamed. He didn't exist except for the phone under his salivating mouth, his hot fingers working below, and the pull of the fresh voice, still unsuspecting, saying, "This isn't Suzie. You must have the wrong number, sir." Polite. Decent. Nice little girl. Clean. Haloed.

The facile words came from him as if there had been no hiatus. Reynolds' face was distorted with the old desire as he went on.

But there was something new this time, never experienced before. Reynolds heard a crash of static in his head that interfered, made him cough and stutter. With it came a vivid memory of Selma's face, drug-buckled on Penny's bed, her unearthly screams. It carried with it echoes of his own voice, vibrant with his insights in Dr. Kohn's office. It became a turning wheel of faces: Helena, his daughters, Penny, Dr. Frank, Mary, Rod Graham, Lillian Schuster, Ted Watson, Duncan Talbott, Dr. Kohn. All were shaking their heads in dismay.

Above all, there was an image of himself, in funereal slow motion, trudging to Dr. Kohn's room morning after morning, winter snow, summer rain, briefcase full of work, sometimes half asleep but never missing an appointment. *What was that man doing with this telephone in his hand?* His lewd hunger might be voracious, but he was no longer defenseless against it. Reynolds started to lower the instrument, but the girl's giggle froze his arm. "Is that you, George? Stop kidding around."

Reynolds' voice was a hobgoblin's. He was sweating to stop his mouth, but the set words croaked past. "Remember last night when I—" He strangled with his effort to stop.

The girl's giggle was louder and more inviting. "George! *What* did you do?"

Reynolds was lost. It was the exquisite, always longed-for setup. He said, loud, "Last night when I opened my—"

His teeth clamped shut. Suddenly Dr. Kohn appeared across the room, an accusing phantom. *"Do you realize you are ruining everything?"*

It was Ikey who answered at once, infuriated at the interruption.

"Shut UP!" No conscience wanted here! Into the phone instead, huskily, "Like it was last night, baby—"

The girl was provocative, "Oh, you're bad, mister. Bad, bad."

She knew it wasn't any George, Reynolds thought triumphantly. She was teasing him, waiting and wanting. She loved and desired what she suspected was coming, and Ikey was going to give it to her no matter what it cost, no matter what head-shaking phantoms were trying to halt him. *"When I opened my pants and took out my—"*

The imagined doctor bounded headlong to the bed and grabbed the phone. "Stop it! Damn you!"

The girl's voice kept playing the game: "Why don't you tell me what happened last night?"

Reynolds moaned. Why didn't the damned Lorelei hang up!

Ikey grinned crookedly at the mouthpiece. "I'm talking about sc-sc-screwing—"

The words would not come. The choking was real. Reynolds strained to inch the receiver away from his ear. He would *not* go on! But the phone was as difficult to move as lifting a grand piano with one hand. Ikey was fighting with Cyclopean strength. The girl's provocative voice was Ikey's ally. "What did we do last night?"

Reynolds felt as if he were plummeting through the mouthpiece, a monstrous maw opening to blackness. He knew with dread certainty that if he did not control himself now, he would be doomed forever. This was not another skirmish, it was the decisive armageddon in his private war. If after all his progress he could still surrender, could not mobilize the power to drop this accursed phone, drunk or sober, he would be gone in hell beyond all hope, help, or redemption. It was not Ikey he was battling. He was wrestling with Death itself.

Reynolds managed to move the receiver from his ear, but could not press it all the way to the cradle and safety. In his despair he mocked himself, "Valiant Saint George facing the dragon!" He burned in the sulfurous flames of the girl's voice still coming loudly from the phone: "Did we do something nifty last night?"

Last night I sucked your pussy, pussy, pussy!

The words to Penny—but Reynolds did not say them again. Despite the cloven hooves clattering in his brain, he shouted into the phone, "I'm sorry! Wrong number!" His neck muscles swelled with the labor and discipline. He drew on his final energy to say, "No, really. Sorry. A mistake." Even then the deviant claws were grappling to hold back his hand. But he wrenched the phone free and slammed it down finally.

Reynolds collapsed on the bed, groaning feebly and sweating.

But he lay there only an instant. After the violence of the combat, his stomach was cartwheeling. As he vomited, he kept banging his fist on the rim of the toilet until it was bloody. *Oh, Christ, would the temptation and the agony never end?*

When Reynolds finally staggered to sit on the edge of the bathtub, feeling a little better, a new reflection washed over him like fresh air. He *had* been Saint George, and he had been victorious! He had mastered Ikey!—vanquished, annihilated him!

Reynolds stared at his hands, not able to credit what had happened. He had actually hung up on a girl, a teasing, divinely inviting girl who was all his old reveries come true! Revery? No, mongrel nightmare! The years were not a waste! The acorn was rooted! He had not demeaned himself again, had not surrendered to the dark dominion of temptation and degradation. He had found the power to stand against his former self-brutalization and the havoc it had played with his life.

Reynolds uttered a silent prayer of thanks.

Reynolds showered himself sober. When he returned to bed, he felt not beat but incandescent. It was remarkable to contemplate over and over this proof of his health, to savor this clear evidence of his real growth. All the ingredients of disaster had been upon him, but the dragon was met, and slain!

Reynolds tried to sleep, but his ebullition did not subside. He found his memory turning back to a day when he had visited a friend in an eye hospital. As he came off the elevator, a door opened and a father and mother led a little girl into the corridor. She was no more than six, in a white gown and pink slippers, with a true angel's face under a mop of blonde curls. Her enormous blue eyes became the whole of her being as the child stood taking in the miracle of the dingy, brown wainscoted hall. It was obvious that she had been blind and was seeing for the first time. She was too exalted to speak. Her gaze was life itself. Finally she whispered, unbelieving, "I can see! I *see!* Mommy, I *see* you! Daddy, *I can see!*"

Her parents were weeping unashamedly. Reynolds, along with nurses and other visitors, brushed welling tears from his face.

Until this moment, Reynolds had forgotten that child's eyes radiantly drinking in the world. For the girl, the dim hospital hall was Paradise Found. That was how he felt now. Soaring, Reynolds never wanted to sleep again. When you could feel this through-and-through sense of oneness with yourself, when you could look within and luminously like and admire what you saw instead of secretly despising it and having to rationalize your guilt, you wanted to stay awake forever to enjoy it!

Reynolds wanted to sing and dance. There was a fountain of happiness in him that could not stay bottled up. He got out of bed to do vigorous calisthenics, feeling fit, virtuous, young. He would nightmare no more of a psychopomp father, of scampering mice with piranha teeth tearing his flesh. With Dr. Kohn's help he had called himself, as Lazarus, forth from the tomb.

At that hospital of the child given sight, her surgeon had been spoken of with reverence: "He has the fingers of God." So, Reynolds was ready to proclaim, did Dr. Aloysius Kohn.

The Indian legend of the Skunk-Man came into Reynolds' dream that night. At the beginning of time, the two most powerful gods were Eagle-Man in heaven and Skunk-Man on earth. They were friendly until Skunk-Man coveted Eagle-Man's wife. Skunk-Man climbed the mountain where Eagle-Man lived. He carried on his back his bag of Powers. They were the greatest on earth, and matched only by Eagle-Man's in the sky.

An invisible loudpeaker hung in the sky was telling the tale.

Eagle-Man was not a god for nothing. No one knew where or how he had found his wife, but he had her. It was one of the Mysteries that humans asked about only at risk of their sanity, lives, and holy souls. The Shamans proclaimed it suffices that Eagle-Man enjoyed a consort, whence-wherever. She was his eternal property. None, least of all Skunk-Man, might presume to steal her from him.

In the dream, Reynolds interrupted from his glass-and-steel desk. "That is all high-energy stuff," he shouted, "but we space-buyers want to know where Abel and Cain's wives came from. Seems like Editorial slipped. If you don't want us to doubt your Circulation Figures, tell us one thing: Namely: If Eve was the only woman in the Garden of Eden, did the boys screw their mother?"

In the dream, Eagle-Man came out of heaven, put on Dr. Kohn's hat, and smiled, "Can't you learn not to be disruptive?"

Reynolds withdrew. "Okay, now you, Eagle-Man, are talking . . ."

Eagle-Man loosed an enormous boulder, which knocked Skunk-Man off the mountain and sent his bag tumbling to the raging river far below. Skunk-Man chased his Powers as fast as he could, but the rapid waters carried the bag away. He followed it everywhere, crying out in anguish when he could not catch it and watched it grow smaller and smaller as it was buffeted down raging rivers and over storm-wracked oceans.

Many, many eons later, Skunk-Man found his bag floating in a distant pond. He rejoiced, only to howl with loss when he opened it. All his Powers but one had vanished.

Stirring in his sleep, Reynolds smiled. He understood this dream without Dr. Kohn. Typically, the subconscious had played its reversal game. He, Reynolds, was Eagle-Man, and Ikey was Skunk-Man. *All the power Ikey had left was his stink!* And Reynolds was resolute even that would fade away as he kept alert from now on.

Part Eight

"Out of the night that covers me,
   Black as the Pit from pole to pole,
I thank whatever gods may be
   For my unconquerable soul."

   —William Ernest Henley

"Thou art punished no more: no torture except
thy own raving,
   would be proportioned to thy fury . . ."

   —Dante, *Inferno*

"A mighty flame followeth a tiny spark . . .
The lantern of the universe riseth unto mortals
through divers straits . . ."

   —Dante, *Paradiso*

══════ 30 ══════

Reynolds carried his sense of triumph and transfiguration to Dr. Kohn like a precious gift when they resumed in September. On this day, Reynolds eschewed the couch, wanting to face his doctor with his joy. He had known nothing like this sense of unburdened freedom since he was a boy bouncing awake on a Saturday morning with a sunny day to do with as he pleased. In Dr. Kohn's office he could almost feel the cement sidewalk under his pounding sneakers as he had once leaped to join waiting friends playing stickball between sewer covers.

Dr. Kohn probed to see whether it might be fool's gold Reynolds had mined once more, but the telephone victory did seem a genuine alteration at last.

With enthusiasm, Reynolds told Dr. Kohn of the trip to Greece he was planning with Helena. Returning from Georgia where her brother had again recovered, she had been delighted with the idea of a real vacation together. When they had kissed on it, Reynolds knew she was remembering the dark hours with him in Bellevue's green halls, when they shared their despair over Selma. It came to Reynolds that it is not enough to care for others, a person must care *with* others as—almost despite themselves sometimes—he and Helena had witnessed together in their years of marriage.

"That's what marriage is—a witnessing," Reynolds said to Dr. Kohn, trying to describe the new commitment he felt toward his family. He smiled. "The marriage vow should be 'I promise to love, honor, and *witness* you till death do us part . . .' And I mean 'witness' in the religious sense of testimony. Sometimes, traveling alone, when I saw something beautiful I would find myself turning to share it with Helena. That's what we really mean when we talk of love as sharing, isn't it?—by my witness I make your joys, your tears, more real, as you give substance to my life by your witness. And when you are not with me to witness, my own life is less. We amplify each other, and so life has more meaning." Reynolds nodded reflectively and repeated, "That's what marriage is!"

"A very good way of putting it," Dr. Kohn said.

When the flush of Reynolds' elation began to fade, the doctor suggested he move to the couch. But Reynolds remained seated at the desk, giving a cheerful laugh as he stayed in charge. "Not today, thanks." He saw Dr. Kohn tilt his head disapprovingly, and said confidently in answer, "I've wondered how it would happen. I suppose you can never tell in advance."

"How what would happen?"

As if the old fox didn't know! "Why, finishing up. Ending the analysis." Reynolds smiled. "Look, I know I don't 'graduate.' I'll always be a sort of cripple, and have to be on guard. But thanks to you I *know* it. And I've proved I can handle the challenge when it comes. I'm not on top of the mountain, but I'm high enough up to see where I've been and where I want to go. I remember your once saying something that got right to my belly. I remember your exact words: *'The difference between an animal and a man is that an animal's life is lived, a man lives his life.'* Well, I'm free now. *I* can choose. That's what makes the difference." Reynolds ended, "I know I'll never get everything perfectly sorted out, but I've got enough together to go on by myself."

In a neutral tone, Dr. Kohn said, "Take the couch and tell me about it."

Reynolds shrugged. He would oblige even though he was convinced it wasn't necessary. After all, concluding an analysis—three years and four months of relentless application in his case—was a solemn matter in its own way, and he certainly wasn't taking it any more lightly than Dr. Kohn. If Kohn felt there was a last session to rummage through, it was only to be expected.

Reynolds submitted to the couch. The flow came readily. Reynolds had anticipated that Dr. Kohn would be sticky, and had half consciously prepared the case he wanted to present. "I used to complain that I was a Job. How many plagues were visited on me! But that was a cop-out. I caused my own unhappiness. Oh, we both know that I did have some tough breaks as a kid but, as you said, *I* was the one who decided my reactions even then."

That was the first proof that he was ready to leave this room. He was honestly taking responsibility for his life, no longer blaming his mother and father or anyone else, no matter how legitimate that might seem to be.

Reynolds gave Dr. Kohn a chance to respond, but there was only the familiar pen-scratching. Well, it was his day in court; it was enough the judge was listening.

"Actually, I felt less like Job than—the Greek Eumenides pursuing me. When I drank I justified it as an escape from the Furies whom I blamed for hounding me from one disaster to another. But of course I was my own Fate. I made myself a loser."

Reynolds repeated softly, "a loser." He mulled it over. "I remember your saying that nobody ever voluntarily does anything that doesn't serve some purpose for him. That used to puzzle me. Then I saw how my temper binges and drinking and the obscene calls did bring me satisfaction even after I knew how destructive they were. Because I *wanted* to self-destruct!"

"Ah," Dr. Kohn sounded, and Reynolds took it for more approval.

"I see that I enjoyed bitching myself up. For one thing, I was a kid telling my mother I was going to eat worms and die and then she'd be sorry. Only I did start eating worms! On a second level, to be in pain, to be an outlaw because of my parents, was a wonderful excuse to indulge in the sauce and sex. And on a third level, I suppose I did have a real case of the Freudian death wish. I mean, I was trying to escape my conflicts by being an infant—that is, killing my adult self, or by literally erasing myself with alcohol. Or ruining myself by risking arrest for my calls!"

Reynolds waited again. He was pleased with his summation so far. Before going on he hoped for a sign that he was getting across to the judge.

Dr. Kohn said merely, "Yes, I know all that," and waited in his turn.

"At the same time as I made myself a loser," Reynolds resumed with renewed determination to rouse Dr. Kohn, "there was always the contradictory drive. I wasn't just going to spite my father by being Ikey-the-Jew-bastard. At the same time, I was going to be the most glorious winner they'd ever seen. And that contradiction built more fire in my gut—that needed more whiskey to put out.

"The real question underneath it all was, which one was *I* really? And I escaped answering that by pointing to my medals!—*But who was the man behind the man who wins the medals?* That's the master key! Who is the man *who* tries to write poetry, the man *who* is a husband and father?

"Asking that question is what analysis is all about! I'm finally in touch with the man *who* does all the things I do. I've finally come home to myself!"

A smile of certainty and self-assurance came on Reynolds' face.

Disappointingly, Dr. Kohn said, "So?"

Reynolds replied with a touch of asperity, "So I know I have to watch for my weaknesses; I've got Ikey in jail, not in a grave. But it doesn't scare me anymore. I guess I'm saying I have courage now, real courage." Reynolds cleared his throat. "Damn, I've said enough lousy things about myself in this room, it's time I laid on a good word or two!"

"I agree with that wholeheartedly," Dr. Kohn said.

Reynolds sat up on the couch, his face clouded. He was moving to a crucial discovery—one he had explained to Helena the night before. "Some of my biggest battles with you were about what sense it made to be 'cured.' I've truly doubted whether I wasn't better off in my 'unreal' world. But what I see now is that *the question is false!* I don't need to ask what life means, where I'm headed and why. All anyone has is the trip itself, and it doesn't really matter to where, or whether the track is smooth or bumpy, or whether there are wrecks along the way. The trip is all we can know."

Reynolds leaned on the doctor's desk. "Kohn," he said—supremely conscious that it was the first time he had spoken the man's name without his title—"do you believe in ESP?"

"I don't think I know what you mean."

"I'd like to share this with you." Reynolds gave the doctor a piece of paper. "I just happened to see this in an article on grave inscriptions just last night. It's from a German headstone of someone named Martius Biberach, dated 1498!"

The clipping read:

> I live, I don't know how long;
> I die, I don't know when;
> I go, I don't know where;
> I am amazed that I can be so cheerful.

Reynolds was delighted with it again, and remembered Helena's sharing laughter when he had shown it to her.

Dr. Kohn rewarded him with an unrestrained chuckle. "Beautiful, yes. I must have Mrs. Wheatley make a copy of that."

Reynolds laughed, "And they didn't even have psychoanalysts then. I told Helena I want it on my grave."

Dr. Kohn, still smiling, said, "Well, let's hope you have a long time before that."

Reynolds nodded. *"Now* I hope so." His fingers tightened on the rim of the desk. "Well?" he asked.

"Well what?"

Reynolds bridled. It was no time for evasion. He had earned the right to his convictions, and Dr. Kohn should honor them. After all, if it came to push and shove, there were experts who were questioning analytic therapy nowadays. They wouldn't put down a man of Dr. Kohn's stature, but even Kohn was not God Almighty. Reynolds' jaw tightened. He would make his own decision, as his own person, even if it meant an unpleasant confrontation with the man he respected more than anyone he had ever known, including Duncan Talbott.

It should be done with a smile: "I'm asking you to have that drink with me. And our mutual friend Martius Biberach."

Dr. Kohn's answer was measured, but without strain. "You may feel ready to extend the invitation, Phil, but I am not ready to accept it."

Reynolds threw his hands up. "How much better can I know myself?"

Dr. Kohn stood up so that his face was level with Reynolds'. "That's just it. You know! It's still largely in your head—"

"Not true!" Reynolds interrupted with vexation. "Everything I've said on that damned couch has gone down into my gut by now!"

Dr. Kohn allowed Reynolds a nod. "Maybe halfway."

"All the way," Reynolds insisted.

Dr. Kohn sat back heavily and looked up at Reynolds with sad eyes. "I think you want to quit at this point because you are heading into more painful material."

"Oh, come on! We've shoveled every *kind* of shit!"

"All I know is my feeling that you haven't faced everything as you should."

"Then that's my responsibility."

"Of course. It always has been."

"Then it's settled."

"I've told you from the beginning that nobody stays in analysis when he wants out."

Reynolds pressed, "I don't understand why you don't agree!"

It earned him a cheerless smile. "I can see why you're a super copywriter, Phil. You just delivered a great ad for selling the couch. But I don't buy it."

Reynolds was torn. He remained convinced that the analysis had brought him to the point of release, but he badly wanted Dr. Kohn's blessing.

He wasn't getting it. "I can't stop you from leaving, but I recommend against it. Strongly."

The familiar steel rod of obstinacy was up Reynolds' spine. "I've made up my mind, doctor. I appreciate everything you've done for me, and I don't have to tell you how grateful I am, but I want to be on my own now."

Kohn took Reynolds by surprise, thrusting his hand across the desk. "Then we should say good-bye."

Shaking Dr. Kohn's hand was unreal to Reynolds. This abrupt tableau was not the ending he had foreseen, and it unsettled him. What he had expected was a quiet talk, and a meeting in the evening in the bar downstairs where there would be an exchange of friendship. After all, this was a man who knew him even more intimately than he knew himself.

But Dr. Kohn was not his friend, he was a surgeon who had cut him open to drain poison out. The thought helped. It sterilized their relationship. As it should be, Reynolds nodded to himself. Imagining Dr. Kohn in a green operating gown made it easier to start walking to the door. His feet felt strange. This room had become as much a part of him as his body. Reynolds had a flashing image of the smashup at the bridge. His hand on the doorknob was suddenly a driver's on the wheel of a skidding car. The door he was opening was a curve so sharp it stopped his heart. Could he negotiate it? Would he crash?

He turned at the door. Was he really never to see this man again? It seemed impossible, but it was going to be true.

"Good luck," came from the doctor.

Reynolds stopped and turned. "I want to say good-bye to Mrs. Wheatley!" The words sounded strange, improbable. He crossed the room in the unfamiliar direction, acutely aware of the empty gray couch. He felt a pang akin to jealousy as he realized that someone else would be lying there talking to Dr. Kohn in "his" hour. He did not look again. For the first time in his years of visits, Reynolds left Dr. Kohn's office by the front door.

Mrs. Wheatley looked up from her desk, astonished. His beaming face bore the message. "I want to thank you for all your kindnesses,"

Reynolds said genuinely—her morning smile, the hot coffee she brewed, the intercepted messages from his office.

The woman studied Reynolds steadily. "You mean you're 'graduated'? Doctor didn't say anything—"

"We just decided."

"Well, I'm very happy for you, Mr. Reynolds." Mrs. Wheatley half rose to extend her hand. "Doctor doesn't let anyone go unless they've done extremely well."

Unaccountably, Reynolds felt like a schoolboy on promotion day expecting an embarrassing kiss from a fond teacher. He shook hands crisply, and left the analyst's office directly.

It was over, finally! No ceremony and no Roman candles, but over!

Behind him was the best education he had ever had, the solid preparation for the new life he was now to enjoy, without crutches.

On his way, Reynolds wished the elevator faster, the train speedier out of Grand Central. He couldn't wait to tell Helena of the giant step he had taken, and how wonderful it made him feel, though it still grieved him that there was no way he could undo the hurt he had done in the years of his affliction.

Watching the familiar landscape go by, Reynolds regretted that instead of "lighting a candle in the darkness," he had blown candles out. It would be an abiding sorrow. But his passage through the Cimmerian labyrinth of the analysis would make amends possible. There was one merit in regret; it would temper his character to resist the old enemies, and help him help others with understanding and tolerance. His family was still vulnerable—Selma had surely not learned all her lessons, and who knew what maelstroms Dorothy and Midge must yet encounter in their own swimming toward their adult shores?

But, Reynolds ruminatively recalled someone's aphorism, "Large defeats can be borne if there are small hopes." And, indeed, his new hopes were large.

If he, freed, himself, at last, could now help the acorns around him with healthy soil and atmosphere, safeguarding them from pollutions, it might not be too late. The young trees might yet flourish and be as fruitful as they had it in them to be. It was all the redemption there was to hope on. It had to be enough.

For himself, Reynolds' thought flowed on, he was humble as well as happy that, with Dr. Kohn, he had found the strength to overcome the foe within and forgive the enemy without. There was a separate reward, he discerned, more important than all the others: What he had done in his psychoanalysis was nothing less than break the grisly chain of neurosis that stretched, so miserably backward and forward, "even unto the seventh generation."

In this there was, finally he might pray, expiation.

In this he had delivered his Prometheus and would still, with his newfound understanding and self-discipline, live the rest of his life well.

Helena, smiling, was waiting at the station to drive her husband home.

31

Mrs. Wheatley knocked on Dr. Kohn's door without waiting for his buzz. The doctor was just shutting the notebook labeled PHILIP MARCUS REYNOLDS.

"Mr. Reynolds said good-bye." The woman's tone made it a question.

"Yes." Dr. Kohn got out of his chair stretching and yawning.

Mrs. Wheatley nodded sagely, "He's the kind has to spit out the bit about this time. I'd have predicted it."

The doctor laughed. "I'd take away your license to practice analysis if you hadn't."

"What's the prognosis?"

"Oh, excellent, I'd say. Excellent in the long run."

"He'll be coming back then," Mrs. Wheatley said knowledgeably as she reached for the notebook.

"Hell, yes, Agnes," Dr. Kohn said with a tired smile. "Even Mr. Reynolds knows that."